SUDDENLY A GREAT WALL
OF FLAME

seemed to rise out of the earth. The heat drove me back along the forest path. I whirled about and started to run. Before I'd taken a hundred steps the fire was to the left of me. The wind carried firebrands high and dropped them at the foot of a full grown pine. Small flames licked at the lower branches, there was a brief pause, and then the entire tree seemed to explode.

I cupped my hands to my mouth and shouted, but there was no answer. The heat of the fire was beginning to sear my skin now and I knew I couldn't stop running. A stream ran through the forest. If only I could reach it! Then I saw a yellow and crimson glow directly ahead. I was surrounded by fire!

I began screaming. Suddenly I saw a dim form lurch out of the heavy smoke. A soaked blanket descended over my head. I was saved.

It was only later that I began to ponder the strange, unnatural, *encircling* course of the fire, and the suspiciously *prepared* circumstances of my rescue . . .

Was I being threatened? Was I being alerted to the fact that it would be very easy for my death to be arranged?

Warner Books
By Dorothy Daniels

A Mirror of Shadows

Dorothy Daniels

WARNER BOOKS

A Warner Communications Company

WARNER BOOKS EDITION

Copyright © 1977 by Dorothy Daniels
All rights reserved

ISBN 0-446-89327-7

Cover art by Ben F. Stahl

Warner Books, Inc., 75 Rockefeller Plaza, New York, N.Y. 10019

 A Warner Communications Company

Printed in the United States of America

Not associated with Warner Press, Inc. of Anderson, Indiana

First Printing: May, 1977

10   9   8   7   6   5   4   3   2   1

A MIRROR
OF SHADOWS

BOOK ONE:

Maeve O'Hanlon

ONE

A crescent of white sand, with the sea brilliantly blue on the far side; the air full of the flash of gulls and the fragrance of wild thyme growing on the hill where I stood, nineteen years old in the year 1895, trying to still the restless urging of my heart with the beauty of the day and of the Irish countryside.

The mountains behind me, which I'd loved all my life, were the Blue Mountains of Achill and the waters were those of Clew Bay. I was, I believed, in the most beautiful part of the most beautiful country God ever created, and into my mind there drifted a daydream of being here on the arm of a handsome young man who was saying, " 'Tis grand, surely, Maeve, but how can I look at the scenery when you're here beside me?" And then his arm moved tighter around my waist and I turned my face up to his . . .

But the wind touched my face and the daydream stopped abruptly. The late afternoon sunlight was no longer comfortingly warm. Suddenly I felt cold, and the sea was a menace. It had been foretold that sorrow would one day come to me in a stormy sea. Trying to shrug off the feeling of desolation, I started home.

It was a brisk ten-minute walk back to Kilcrea, the village where I lived with my father, in the house where I had been born and where my mother had died in the spring of 1876, giving me life. It was no thatched-roof cottage, but a genuine two-story house of stone and brick and mortar. My father was Brian O'Hanlon, a medical doctor whose patients came to him for miles around and for whom, to my dismay, he traveled the same miles when they were too sick to come to him. Many's the day and night I spent alone, often caring for the minor troubles of those who came to claim his professional care when he was not there. For he had taught me well how to handle routine business.

I turned away from the hill and sought the worn path so familiar to me and to Jim, my older brother now studying medicine in Edinburgh. Although I thought of him as a surgeon with a great future, and was happy for him, life in Kilcrea was the lonelier without him.

I walked swiftly, in the chill of the oncoming evening, and I planned in my mind the supper I would make for my father—colcannon, mutton chops, brown bread and butter. What for a sweet? Stewed gooseberries, I decided, with heavy cream.

Kilcrea, as I saw it now, was not a village to be painted for gaudy postcards like those depicting the best of Dublin and our other fair cities. It was just a gathering of a hundred and fifty or so cottages, mainly occupied by older people. The young ones, like myself, were inclined to abandon the village for work in the cities. The boys became butler-housemen, carriage drivers, or hostlers. The sturdier and less-mannered went to the harder work of driving drays and manhandling the cargo they carried, or they went into the mines. The girls almost universally entered domestic service—the prettier and luckier as ladies' maids—and worked for a pittance and their keep. All held their chins up when they came home to visit, however, and many of my old friends urged me rather patronizingly to follow their example. They were in a great city. They were learning about the world, and fashion. There were many young men about, and their chances of marriage all the rosier for that. I had often been sorely tempted, and only my father kept me from experimenting with what a great city could do for me.

I remained in Kilcrea because my father wished me to and also because I could not bear to leave him. Since my birth he'd been a lonely man and, with me gone, it would be all the worse for him. So I stayed on. Surely I owed him that.

Oh, there were still boys in the village. Brawny ones who liked the soil and the long hours that farming requires. Cathal Dolan was one of these, and before me I saw him sitting on a stone wall waiting for me. It was not like Cathal to come to meet me, but to let me come to him as he sat there like a king on his throne. Except that the throne was a rough stone fence and Cathal didn't look much like a king in an old cap, a faded green sweater that had seen better days, and rough pants, the cuffs of which were still crusted with the earth he'd plowed through this day.

I'd known Cathal since we were children. I liked him, but I certainly had no intentions of settling down with the man, as he was beginning to urge.

He was a rugged man if not a handsome one. He worked hard and he had never been in any trouble. A few of the girls gave him the eye often enough, but he gave them no heed in return, and I knew it was because of me. Which made it all the harder for me, because Cathal was not a man I could ever love.

His ambition was to own a dozen acres of barley, some pastureland and a flock of sheep, and a barn six times as large as the shanty he'd provide for a home. I would have, as his wife, the chickens, the potato patch, and the Church as my whole life.

Besides, Cathal smoked a clay pipe stuffed with shag that smelled worse than wet peat afire. If I

11

scolded him for smoking this terrible stuff in the presence of a lady, he blew the smoke my way and regarded it all as a lark. Not thinking I meant it because every man smoked that kind of pipe and there was little else to be smoked here except the rough-cut shag.

"Your father's been home this hour or more, and you not there to make the man his tea," Cathal said. "Ye'll not get away with that married to me, my lovely Maeve."

"I am not your Maeve," I said crisply.

"Ah—but you did not deny that you are lovely," he said with that wide grin of his.

"And I shall not be married to you, Cathal Dolan. Not this year nor any of the following hundred years of my life. I ask you most kindly not to tell others that we will be, for it is only embarrassing to me and it is a lie you're telling."

" 'Tis not, Maeve. You know very well you will one day marry me. It was foreordained that we should be husband and wife, else why were we brought together as children and why have we always been so close? I have been in love with you all of my life, and you well know it, but never did you say you did not love me until you were well grown."

"Until then I knew no better," I said. "If you came here to walk me back, then walk me, Cathal Dolan, with less of your blathering talk."

He slid down off the stone fence and joined me. As always, his rough hand sought mine to hold it, and I didn't draw away. We had held hands walking ever since we were children. There was, I thought, no harm in it.

"I will let you teach me those things your father taught you," he said. "Arithmetic and language, even Gaelic. I will read good books, and I will study hard."

"Why not start now?" I asked.

"Time enough after we're married."

12

"If I marry you," I said, looking up at him for he was six feet one to my five feet five. "And a dark day that'll be, to be sure."

"You will marry me. I have said it."

"Aye, that you have, but not once have you heard me say it, Cathal Dolan. Besides, my husband must know more than I."

"Excepting your father, there's no man in this village who does."

"He will not be of the village."

"Oh, you are sure of this, are you?"

"As I walk with you."

"Then pray that he is stronger and a better fighting man than me, Maeve O'Hanlon, because I'll knock his block clean off."

"Oh, Cathal, learn to think with more than your fists."

We were making our way down the middle of the dirt road now, between the rows of small cottages. There were eyes peering out of windows, as usual, and there'd be busy tongues speculating on when Cathal and I would post our banns and face Father Burke before the marriage altar.

"Tell me, now," Cathal said, "how you will know this great man when he comes along."

"I have seen him, Cathal. I know what he looks like. When he comes, I will know."

"You talk like addled Padraic Flynn before they came and took him away. Where do you get your information and your second sight, Maeve? From the little green men in green tunics?"

"You are growing impertinent, Cathal," I said sharply, stopping short. I pulled him to a halt, as well, for he didn't let go of my hand. "Cathal, you wish to wed with me mostly because you wish to bed with me, and for little other reason. I have read this in your eyes and in your silly grin every time we're together. I will have none of it. And none of you.

As you well know, my mother was a descendant of the High Kings. . . ."

"Ah, Maeve," he said with a wrinkling of his nose and half turning his face from me in disbelief, "every Irishman claims to have descended from the High Kings. Even I could lay claim to it if I chose, for all of the claims are without foundation."

"Mine is not, for with the gift of this inheritance came the heaven-given privilege to see into the future. Darkly perhaps at times, dimly at others, but sometimes clearly and the man I will marry I saw well. Believe me, he was not you."

"You're daft," Cathal said promptly. "If there is a medicine for your troubles, see that your father provides it. Yet, darlin' Maeve, I am not angry or insulted by what you say. This man you think will come your way is like a wisp of fog that will go off with a touch of sunlight. And when it does, I will be here. You are forgiven, Maeve O'Hanlon, for I am by nature a forgiving man."

I looked up at him in a blaze of anger. He forgave me, the pig-headed dolt! And yet, even in that flare of rage, of wanting to pummel him as I had when we were children, I knew that part of me didn't want to lose his friendship. He was a good man, even though his ways at times annoyed me. One does not simply abandon a man known since childhood, who has been such an important part of a girl's life. And yet I would be doing him a favor by cutting him loose from me so he might seek another girl to become his wife. He was not one meant to live alone, but so long as I remained available, a single girl of marriageable age, with no one else seeking my hand, Cathal would be there. Often enough to sometimes become a nuisance.

I took a deep breath and said, "Thank you, Cathal Dolan. I am grateful for your forgiveness, and now I ask that you either take me home or let me go there by myself. There is no need for you to escort me."

"You are wrong, Maeve," he said. "No queen should ever walk home alone. One day you must show me your crown."

"One day," I said sharply, "I will show you the door and slam it on your back, and we will both be sorry for it."

Cathal knew he had gone too far, and he was quickly contrite. "I do beg your pardon, Maeve, and I will beg it again on my knees if that is what you wish."

I softened my tone. "Stop your silly blathering. You're not for me, Cathal Dolan. Find yourself another lass. I have known for some time that Maureen McLinden has an eye for you and you could do far worse."

"Any girl excepting the likes of you would be far worse," he said. "I will not give up. This has gone on too long. You are still young, with a soft brain that looks into the past and sees visions and then looks into the future to see if they come true. When you learn they do not, my lovely Maeve, then you will know I am right and you will be happy that I am here. I will not walk you the rest of the way. After what you have been telling me, the devil take you for the rest of this day. Good day to you, Maeve O'Hanlon."

He stalked away in high anger, and I was sorry for that, but I was glad he no longer walked with me and in his mind held me in his possession as his wife. I had tried to discourage him long ago, at least two years now, but it had never worked. He was always there, underfoot sometimes. The village talked of it, waited to see what would happen. Father made no issue of it. I wasn't quite sure what he expected of me, but I was now bound to find out before this day was over. If he was on my side, well and good. If not, then I would keep silent from that moment on and never mention either Cathal or the man I had glimpsed in the ancient mirror of Queen Maeve, from whom I am descended and for whom I was named.

Father's stone-and-brick house, glowing in the late afternoon sun, looked impressive in comparison to its surroundings, for the thatched and whitewashed cottages of the village were small indeed. There was one central room, where a turf fire provided heat and a place to cook, and one or two tiny bedrooms. They were not uncomfortable, though, and they were not hovels. Few of their owners would trade them for a palace—at least, not the older people.

It often amazed me—and Father—to see how the elders reacted when their children returned from the great cities for a visit. They came in splendid clothing, bearing wonderful gifts, and yet it was plain to see their elders were sorry for them—for the foolish fancy that caused them to desire to live elsewhere. Father didn't know if this was good or bad, and neither did I.

Before I could turn in to the brief path leading to my front door, I was hailed to a stop by Mrs. Mooney, prematurely wrinkled and stooped, with a gray shawl over her head and the woebegone expression of a woman who had birthed eleven children.

"It has come to me, darlin' Maeve, that I do not wish to disturb your sainted father, but can you give me somethin' strong for the rheumy pains that run up and down me back like the divil's hot pitchfork was torturin' me?"

"I will bring you some medicine after supper, Mrs. Mooney," I said, and I added the magic words she was dying to hear. "Of course, since you did not consult with the doctor, there will be no charge."

"Heaven bless you for that, me a dyin' woman. Don't be too late with the stuff, else I'll not get me night's sleep."

"I will not, Mrs. Mooney," I said. "Depend on me."

She'd been depending on me for quite some time now. When I walked through the waiting room before Father's private office and treatment room, I was gratified to find it empty. Sometimes I had to delay supper for hours. It had been a good day in the village. Not many people were ill.

Father was in his office, his feet propped up on the rolltop desk while he read a medical journal that had come in the mail from London yesterday. He was a tall, sturdy man who could row a *currach* with the best of them even now, in his forty-fourth year. His hair was beginning to gray, especially at the temples, and this gave him a distinguished, wise-man kind of look which I liked and he hated. He had the clear blue eyes of the O'Hanlon family, as I did. Like mine, his nose was straight—longer than mine, but truly a fine one, set above a generous mouth meant for smiling and gay laughter. Our faces were round, but where he had a square kind of jaw, mine was softer of line and my lips were not as full. Father often said I had much of my mother's beauty, but when I looked at the old pictures and paintings of her, I didn't believe it. She was far more beautiful than I could ever hope to be.

Yet I was reasonably satisfied. I would have termed myself as comely. Enough to attract a male eye which, after all, is most important to a girl of nineteen.

"I cheated you out of a bag of potatoes, Father," I said. "Mrs. Mooney caught me fair and square before I could get by her, and I promised to deliver some medicine."

"I'm tired of potatoes, anyway," he said with a gay laugh. Nothing in the world characterized this man as much as his laughter. It rang true and clear and was never sardonic or cruel. When there was something to laugh at, he laughed. It was a grand sound to hear.

17

"You'll be having them with more of that mutton you earned by setting the Mullaney boy's busted arm. Are you that hungry I should put on supper now, or can we talk?"

"Talk, by all means," he said. "It's as good as meat and potatoes when it's interesting."

"Maybe this is not. I would believe that it is not, but I think it should be said. Cathal Dolan asked again to marry me this day and I turned him down as I have done fifty times before, and I am tired of it. I tried to discourage him this time. I told him of the man I will one day marry."

Father nodded slowly. "You do have more faith in the old mirror than I, but then your mother's family always did have."

"I saw but a glimpse in the mirror. I told you that."

"It is enough if you believe in it."

"Don't you, Father?" I asked.

"Well, let's say I don't have that much faith, though I will admit it can be uncanny at times." He closed his eyes as if he'd suddenly grown very tired. "Your sainted mother saw in it the prophecy that robbed me of her. She saw that a new life would be traded for an old life, but I paid no heed when she spoke of it."

"Father, had you heeded the warning, you could have done nothing about it. The mirror tells what is to happen and whatever it is, will happen despite the warning."

"I know that to be true. I often wish a man could see his future in that mirror, but it was decreed that only the women would have that privilege."

I retained my composure with all the effort I could summon, for once I had looked in the mirror, wondering about him, and I had seen an angry sea, boiling and contorting itself into an awful wildness. That was all. And it was Father whose future I had been thinking of when I consulted the mirror.

18

"I cannot see anything of my own, either," I said. "Perhaps it is not always possible for one to see one's own fate, but only that of others who are close."

"You saw this young man you say you are going to marry," he reminded me.

"Oh, aye, I saw him well and good. But that is another thing. It is not my fate—my life—that was shown to me, but only a segment of it. An important one, yes, but not the ultimate finish of me. And knowing you as I do, I am sure that is what you would be seeking."

He laughed again. "You read my mind as your mother used to do. This vision in the mirror—what was the young man like? You never did tell me."

"Handsome, of course."

"Naturally," he chuckled.

"Tall and very thin he was. Which gives me cause for worry, for he did not look strong."

"Why should that worry you? Men who are thin are usually quite healthy."

"Oh, aye, that they are, but this one did not look to be rugged, and Cathal, who is so strong, has promised to knock his block off."

"You told Cathal about the mirror?" Father was serious now, his tone anxious.

"No, Father. I only said that there was a prophecy as to whom I would marry. I did not tell of the mirror, though I did inform the lout that I am descended from Queen Maeve."

"Everyone knows that. No harm done, then. You did not speak of the torc?"

"No, no, Father. You warned me never to mention it, and never will I."

"It is best that way. I have it secure, mind that now, but still it would be a target for any man who coveted such things. Your mother's family kept it secure for who knows how long, and it will remain forever with you and yours, God willing. Your mother

19

used to tell me that some of her ancestors starved from poverty, even died of it, but the torc was not bartered for even a life. Better to die than allow it to leave the family hands. Something dire and dreadful would happen if it did."

"Is it worth a great deal of money?"

"Maeve, it is priceless. Not for its gold, but for its linking us to our proud Celtic past, before we became the poor apes of England. Still, in terms of cash it would bring a fortune. It's finer than any in the National Museum. You have not seen it since you were a little girl. On the day you marry, I will bring it from the bank vault where it is kept, and it will then be delivered into your hands, for it will from that day on be up to you to carry the family into the future. You and your brother are the last of the O'Hanlons now, and your brother is much too prosaic a man, too firm a scientist, to believe in luck brought by a torc. I would not trust it to him. Only to you—and this handsome man you will marry. The mirror of Queen Maeve, of course, is passed on only to the women in the family."

"Thank you, Father," I said sincerely. I arose and went to him. I drew my arms around his dear neck and I kissed his cheek and I loved him above all men on earth.

"Now start acting like the lady of the house and get my supper, woman," he said in mock severity, but I knew he wanted to be rid of me so I'd not notice the tears that threatened to well out of the corners of his eyes. I wasn't ashamed of mine, but I did flee to the kitchen and I began preparing his supper and mine.

We were never lonely, Father and me. At mealtimes we chattered like magpies and broke in on one another's sentences shamelessly.

"The mutton is good," Father said. "It wasn't bad pay for setting a broken arm."

20

"I like chicken better," I said. "Next time ask for a fat hen."

He wagged his head as he speared another chop. "They do manage to slip me the tough old birds as payment of my fee," he said. "It's almost worth it to hear them tell of what a glorious bird the poor thing was, and how it is going to be missed around the barnyard, while I suspect the poor old thing died a natural death of old age, and often my teeth and jawbone know it."

"Jimmy says he'll have none of this," I said, speaking of my brother.

"Jimmy is a clever lad, Maeve. Medicine is beginning to grow up, as well it might and must. Jimmy will grow with it. He has his heart set on becoming a surgeon. That is, do only cutting and not treat some foolish runny nose or bellyache. From what I have been told by his teachers, he is exceptional. I believe he will do very well."

"I know he will not be coming back home," I said.

"For what? To set broken arms for a tough old hen or half a ham? No, my girl, he will remove such things as tumors and sew up wounds and rid people of ulcers. And he will be well paid—in cash. Lots of it."

"You could have done the same," I reminded him.

"Aye, but that was twenty-five and more years ago. Things were different. People in Mayo were dying for want of doctor care, and I could not stand by to see that happen. I was a lad when the potato famine hit and a million good men and women—and children—died for want of food. There was no one to help us. No one seemed to care enough, and we died by the thousands. That was when I made up my mind to become a doctor and to return here and do what I could without heed to what I got out of it. Except to see a man, dying one day, be walking the streets later on because I didn't let him die. There's

21

more to life than money, though I will admit it comes in handy now and then."

"You have done well," I said. "Despite all else, we are not poor."

"No, we are not, thank God. I can support Jimmy well indeed so he can devote all his attention to study, which is a great help. Now, getting back to this young man. Was there any indication in this prophecy as to when he would appear in your life?"

"No, Father. The mirror gives only faint glimpses; more often than not they aren't even clear, though this one was."

"I am only concerned that you will not become an old maid waiting for him to appear."

"Never that. I saw him as a young man. If years were to go by before he came to me, then he would have looked older."

"Aye, you're probably right about that. Maybe the first thing we ought to do is teach him how to fight, so he can stand up to Cathal Dolan."

"Father," I chided him, "if Cathal so much as looks cross-eyed at him, I'll beat up Cathal myself, I will. Now, fix Mrs. Mooney's medicine or she'll come tapping on the window. First making sure you're not in the room."

I delivered the bottle of medicine and for thanks I was reminded that I'd taken my own good time about it while a dozen divils were poking her with their pitchforks. I returned to our house and did the dishes. I turned down Father's bed and cleaned the waiting room and the office. Father went to bed at nine. At ten-thirty Mike Hennessy nearly tore down the front door banging on the knocker.

"It's me Grania," he explained, "she is sore ill, she is that. It's come to me she may be dyin', and I have spent these two hours and more fetchin' the priest. . . ."

"You listen to me, Mike Hennessy," I said. "Next

time you find the doctor first. Do you hear me? Go home now. Father will be starting out soon as he's dressed. Go! Go along now."

Father grumbled a bit, but he got dressed while I went out to the barn and hitched up the buggy. I wore a flannel robe over my nightgown, but I was chilled. Yet I waited for him, keeping the horse quiet, for she was a frisky mare.

"Get back in the house," Father said crossly. "You'll get your death and have me waking up in the middle of the night to care for you. Mind you, I won't be able to collect any more of a fee from my own daughter than I'll get from Grania Hennessy, herself that's dying. For the sixth, or is it the seventh, time this year? I'll be home as quick as I can."

I fled back to the house as he drove away. I closed the door and basked in the warmth from the fireplace, down to hot coals but giving off great heat. I knew I'd not sleep until he got back, so I made a pot of tea and drew a cozy over it, hoping it might stay warm in case he wished some after his drive through the chilly night.

I sat at the fireplace, sipping the tea and thinking about the image I had seen in the mirror. It had been both intriguing and frightening. I had asked that I see the face of the man I would marry. Only the middle part of the mirror was still shiny enough to reflect or show anything, and that was where the face had appeared. For an instant only, but clear as a bell, and it had shocked me so that I dropped the mirror as if it had become red-hot.

I was unable to sit still. I gulped the rest of the tea instead of sipping it, poured another cup, and promptly forgot about it. I arose to pace the floor and to look about me and wonder what it all meant and where it would lead.

My home, as homes go in Mayo, was virtually a

palace. My dear mother had exquisite taste, and she had brought most of the furnishings overland from Dublin and from London by sea. Mother had come of a family situated as Father and I were now, able to afford some few luxuries at least, and she had provided well.

We had a dining room, for instance, with a fine mahogany table that could be pulled out to seat a dozen, with chairs to match and a china cabinet and a sideboard, now graced with pure silver service that tested my patience because it needed polishing so often.

Our parlor had a sofa and four large chairs, their cushions stuffed with down. They were dark green velvet, no less, with more mahogany tables. Our lamps were shaded by green glass to reflect the lamplight the better. There were genuine oil paintings on the walls and a thick rug on the floor. It was heavy and big and took two men to carry it outside for a beating every six months.

My kitchen was as modern as any in Dublin. There was running water, an iron sink, cabinets in sufficient number, and fine china and silver. Our good glassware was from Waterford, where some enterprising men had begun a factory which turned out superior products bound to take an important place in the world of commerce one of these days.

Upstairs were two bedrooms, ample in size. A double bed in Father's room and a single bed in mine. Our linens were of Irish manufacture, of which none are better. I had inherited my mother's instinct for color, so our house was bright and cheerful.

Even the stairs were carpeted, and we had shades on the windows and draperies in the parlor and the dining room. Oh, we lived in style and comfort. If any envied us, they made no fuss about it, for Father was a well-liked man and thought to deserve everything he had. Of course, if we'd been snobbish, Father and me, things might have been different. But we were a part of these people. We belonged and they knew it.

I grew tired of pacing and sat down, picked up the cup of tea, and found it had grown cold. I emptied it into the sink, but poured another which was suitably warm. I sipped this slowly, again thinking, torturing my brain with problems not yet in being, and therefore useless to try and solve, but I tried anyway. Such was the nature of me.

First of all, where and when would I meet this stranger? And would it come to pass that he would recognize me somehow, as the girl he was destined to meet and fall in love with? For my part, I had no doubts. I knew I would love him well, even with only the fleeting image of his face to guide me in this decision.

More importantly, would he ever consent to remain here with Father and me? I would not leave Father for anyone, or for any reason. He was lonely enough without my mother all these years. I had taken her place, and I would continue to do so for the rest of his life. Then I remembered the stormy sea the mirror had shown me, and I shuddered, wishing him safely at home.

I had to do something, and the first thing that came to mind was the mirror. I set my cup down and before I changed my mind, I went upstairs to my room. There, buried under my best finery, I kept the mirror wrapped in a layer of silk, enclosed in an envelope of felt. This, in turn, was in a thick muslin pouch I'd sewed especially for this purpose.

The mirror was oblong. Father had measured it once, out of curiosity, and discovered it to be ten inches in height and eight inches wide. It was made entirely of metal for, of course, there'd been no glass in those days when Queen Maeve lived. It was slightly concave, too, and the centuries had taken their toll, for only the center of it still retained enough metallic luster to reflect and be called a mirror. It was on this surface that the images appeared so mysteriously when a female descendant of Queen Maeve addressed it in her name and asked that she be shown whatever she wished to know.

At times the image that appeared was so fleeting it was difficult to recognize. Other times it was clear and existed long enough that the eye could appreciate and remember it well.

When Father first told me its history and showed it to me, I believed him somewhat daft. For how could a piece of metal, hundreds of years old, reflect anything? And how could it ever have been able to let anyone see into the future? I soon learned to believe in it, though, for the mirror foretold, at my prayer, several things that later happened in the village, exactly as they had been depicted. I was convinced of its powers by the time I was fifteen.

It frightened me sometimes, though on the whole I found it more of a comfort than an object to fear—until the incident of seeing what I construed as the prophecy and manner of my father's death.

I wasn't thinking of that at the moment, but of the image of the man it had already told me I would marry. I wanted to see his face again, impress it upon my memory so when I did meet him, there'd be no doubt or error.

I arranged the lamps on the bureau for the most light. I carefully dusted the surface of the mirror with the silk and I held it before me and looked into it to see my own dim reflection. I then held the mirror close to me, pressing it hard against my breast.

Aloud, I said, "Good Queen Maeve, whose name I bear and from whom I am descended through countless generations, bear with me again and let me see in this mirror, which you blessed by looking into it, once more the face of the man I will marry."

Nothing happened, but it sometimes didn't—at

least, not immediately. I was content to wait, being patient in such matters, as well I should be because of their importance. Then, in the center of the mirror, I began to see the face take shape. It was the same face, in profile. A sensitive face of a man I judged to be about twenty-three or twenty-four. Certainly no more than that. He was handsome, delicately so, with a rather long nose and a high forehead, but a firm chin, strongly outlined. The tilt of his head seemed to give him a patrician air.

But something else was there, too. This was the same man I'd seen before, no mistaking that, but behind him, also in profile, there seemed to be another. This, too, was the side view of a man, his face partly jutting out beyond that of the one I would marry. The face of an older man, by three or four years. A handsome man, he looked stronger than the first. As his face, too, became clear, I stood there staring at the images of two men in that magic mirror and not knowing what to make of it. Slowly the images faded until there was nothing. I brought the mirror to my lips and kissed it gently before I touched it once more with the silk and carefully put it away. Then I went downstairs again to sit before the fire, more confused than ever.

Two men! What did it mean? Except that both would be in my life. But the one I would marry came first, so he was of major importance. Then I began to think that if I was to marry the one, it must be that I would also marry the other and that meant . . . the first one would die or he would leave me. We would somehow be parted, and then the second man would come into my life.

"Be damned to you," I said aloud. "Whoever you are. My love came first, and to him I will give my love and spare none for you who came later."

I had to compose myself when I heard Father's buggy pull by on its way to the barn. I put on fresh water for tea and had it hot and ready when he came in, blowing on his hands, for it had turned colder. He hung up his hat, shook off his heavy coat and then his jacket before he settled himself in a chair to one side of the fireplace.

"How was she?" I asked.

"I brought her back from the brink of death with my magic potion. It's a wonder what an ounce of Irish whiskey will do for a woman who refuses to keep a drop of the stuff within the walls of her home. Not knowing of course what she was taking. But she did smack her lips, and she looked a deal brighter. Especially when I informed her that heaven was not ready for the likes of her yet, and she would have to stick around awhile longer."

"That makes six night calls in the last seven or eight months," I said. "If this keeps on, she will become addicted to whiskey, Father."

"Aye, that she will, and no worse for it."

The frown he wore since he returned belied the lightness of his talk and it bothered me. "There is something wrong, Father?" I asked.

"Well, not exactly wrong, but upsetting, I might say. It will get your blood to boilin', I'm thinking. Cathal Dolan is going about telling one and all that you and he will soon be wed. When I first spoke to her, Grania, using her last breath as she told me, mentioned that she hoped to live long enough to attend the wedding."

"Blast his miserable soul," I said. "I will tear out his hair in great chunks tomorrow. I told him only this afternoon there would be no wedding."

"Aye, that I know, but Cathal is not one to take no for an answer. You have never encouraged the man?"

"Never! In no way! Father, I will tomorrow visit the priest and inform him that there will be no banns

28

said no matter what Cathal tells him. Oh, that man! That miserable great ape of a man."

Father nodded slowly. "There is something else, my dear child."

"What in heaven's name could there be worse than what you have just told me?"

"I didn't say it was worse. Tell me again about this man you saw in the mirror. What was he like?"

"Father. . . ."

"Tell me what he looked like, that's all I ask." Father spoke sharply.

I settled down with an effort, not knowing what he had in mind, but suspecting what he kept back.

"I would say he was about twenty-two or -three years old. Just right for me, of course."

"Of course. Now I have his age. Was he unbearably ugly?"

"Father, he is handsome. He has a rather long face, I would say, but a fine one. I think his hair is light in color and that would make his eyes blue or gray, now, wouldn't it?"

"Likely. Go on."

"What else can I say? Mind you, I saw only the side of his face. Why do you ask?"

"A man such as this came into the village yesterday and is boarding with Mrs. Halloran."

I brought both hands to my face and, despite the fact I was seated on a stool at Father's feet and getting great heat from the fire, I shivered. "Father, help me. What must I do? He is here and I don't know what to do."

Father smiled at my discomfiture. "The prediction of the mirror means that you two will meet and there is nothing for you to do. Except wait."

"Will he come to me? Or shall I go to him?"

"Who knows? What will happen, will happen."

I regarded him between my fingers still covering my face. "I'm fearful."

"There is no reason to be. The young man has no knowledge of this. He doesn't know that his destiny will also be yours. Or that he will somehow be drawn to you."

"I shall not sleep this night. I am even inclined to dress and go over to Mrs. Halloran's to either peek in the window or borrow a cup of sugar."

"It's two o'clock in the morning, my dear girl. That will be no way to start off a romance. The young man will think you're mad. Bide your time. He may not even be the man of the mirror."

I shook my head. "I have a feeling he is."

"Ah, you have looked in that cursed mirror again, have you?"

"This night, while you were gone."

"The face came back?"

"Aye. Clearly so. The same face, just as before."

"It is possible, then, the prediction is about to come true."

"There was something else. Behind the face of this man appeared that of another. It never happened before. I don't know what it means."

"Another face in the mirror? You're certain?"

"It was as clear as that of the man who will be my love. It was there, the face of a stronger man, a good man, I'm sure. But what are two men doing in my life? I cannot help but wonder if the one I shall soon meet will somehow give way to this other."

Father nodded gravely. He believed in the power of that mirror. I suspected at one time he had not, but when it accurately predicted my mother's death and my birth, he changed his mind.

"Does it mean my love will die?" I gave voice to the dark thought within me.

"Not necessarily. The second man came without your asking, so he may only be someone who will come into your life, and that of your young man, and be a friend to both of you."

30

"I have a feeling he does not represent anything evil, but I also have the feeling he will be waiting and if he waits and there is to be fulfillment, then my love has to die or leave me. I could not bear either, Father."

"Now you are doing the predicting, not the mirror. It is no more than a wild guess and not something to worry about."

"What will I do then?" I asked.

"As I said—wait! You cannot make the prophecy come true. It must come true of its own accord. Go to bed now. Try to sleep. If you are to meet this young man soon, you must look your best, not like some harried woman with blue circles under her eyes. Go to bed, girl. Give a man some peace."

I managed a smile as I kissed him good night, but I was sure I'd never sleep a wink, though I did, finally. And I slept later than usual, to be awakened by a banging on the front door, for Father had also overslept. It was a patient demanding immediate care. I sat him down in the waiting room, then awakened Father. I went about getting breakfast mechanically, thinking all the while that not a quarter of a mile away a young man was up and about. A young man who didn't know that his image had appeared in a magic mirror and that he was destined to meet me and there was nothing in this world he could do about it.

I decided it was quite nice to have been descended from Queen Maeve.

TWO

That day nothing happened. I strolled about the village streets until my feet ached, but I saw no sign of the stranger. I heard no mention of him, and any visitor in our village became a topic of conversation five minutes after he arrived. I began to feel that Father had been wrong and the young man had either not been here at all or he'd come and gone before anyone knew of it.

Usually, we chatted and gossiped while eating supper, but that night Father seemed unusually quiet and, from time to time, he looked at me gravely as if he had something on his mind. I held my tongue, for if I demanded an answer, I'd get a rough one. He'd tell me when he was ready.

"Maeve," he said finally, "lock the waiting room door and hang up the sign saying I'm out."

"A call?" I asked.

"Aye. To Mrs. Halloran's. She sent me word she has a boarder who is not feeling well. I am going to see him. You had better come with me, for it may be that I shall require your assistance."

I ran around the table and hugged and kissed him. "You have kept this from me all day, but I forgive you, though may the devil belabor your bones, you old fraud."

"Now, my girl, had I told you about this, would I have sat down to a nice hot supper? No—it would have been cold cabbage and cold potatoes and weak

32

tea and anything else you could throw upon a plate without devoting a single moment of thought to what you were doing."

"All right, Father. But I refuse to do the dishes until we get back. Come now, for all you know, this man may be very ill. We dare not delay, since I am to marry him. He is the most important patient you will ever have."

"He suffers a slight chill and fever, probably from a cold. He came here from Scotland by way of Dublin where the climate is a mite warmer. This change may have brought on this condition, which I can cure readily enough, as you well know. We shall leave at once."

"Half an hour," I said.

"I thought you were in a blasted hurry."

"That I am, but not so much I don't want to look my best. If you grow bored waiting for me, you may do the dishes. I will not mind at all."

He settled back in his chair. "I will not be bored," he assured me.

I hurried to my room. There, I spent five precious minutes trying to decide what to wear: I dared not appear overdressed, but of course I wanted to look my best. I finally selected a dark blue skirt, full and flounced, with a pale blue blouse. I belted it with a wide band of velvet ribbon. I was grateful for my trim waist.

I forced my feet into matching shoes and attended to my hair, arranging it high on the back of my head. A few short wisps touched my brow. It was a hairdo I'd copied from a painting of my mother, and it looked almost as well on me. I drew on gloves—then removed them. Who would expect a doctor's assistant to be wearing gloves? I touched my nose with rice powder. Excitement had colored my cheeks and brought a sparkle to my eyes. I regarded my reflection in the bureau mirror. Satisfied, I heeded, at last,

Father's bellowing command to come at once. He'd tarry no longer.

"The poor man may have already gone into pneumonia," he shouted. "Be done with it, Maeve. He will not expect the Queen herself to come calling."

"Shush," I told him, at last on the way down the stairs. "And mind your manners when you're with him and . . . oh, Father, be sure he is not too sick. Make him well quickly."

"I will be grand and my examination will be thorough and my cure complete with no mistakes," he said. "Ah, who am I fooling? Here I am, about to lead my daughter to a man who will likely take her from me. I should be weeping, not laughing."

I stopped him before we reached the door, and I drew my arms around his neck. "Father, he may be the handsomest man on the face of this earth. He may be the richest and the most powerful, with more to offer me than a girl could dream of. But if he says we should leave you and this village, I shall have no part of him, prophecy or not. Do you understand that?"

He kissed me lightly and his eyes regarded me with tenderness. "I understand, Maeve. Let it happen first, but I appreciate what you have just said."

"I mean it, Father."

"That I know. As I know you. Now stop acting daft. Let us see if there is anything to this."

"Let us see, be damned," I said loudly. "It is a fact! It is an omen that will not be changed under any circumstance. Now I feel better. I have told you off. Next I shall inform this young man, whoever he may be, that we shall soon be wed."

"Wait until he is well," Father warned blithely. "Sometimes a sick man who receives such a shock grows much worse promptly. Give the man a chance —and me as well, to cure him without complications."

"So I'm a complication now, am I?" My voice

wavered. "Take my arm and steer me away from the potholes full of dust, Father, I'm scared to death."

He took the paisley shawl I held and placed it over my shoulders as he spoke. "Seeing you put it that way, so am I, but I'll watch the potholes."

We made our way down the street, returning greetings from passersby, but I scarcely knew who they were. I felt a bit like a bride starting down the aisle with her brand-new husband leading her—and a bit like I was being led to my execution. I tried to quell a growing sense of panic. I, who at fourteen could stand by and help my father amputate a leg or an arm and not faint dead away, except for the first time. I had always prided myself on keeping my feelings under control, but at this moment they were certainly not.

The Halloran cottage, one of our larger and better ones, seemed ten miles away. I wondered why good Queen Maeve could not have arranged for this young man to have requested a room at Father's house. It would have been much easier.

"How do you feel, darling?" Father asked.

I glanced at him. "Your necktie is frayed a bit. You should be more careful of your appearance. You are a doctor. An important man."

"And about to meet my son-in-law-to-be, eh? The tie has been frayed for weeks, and this is the first time you ever noticed it. Besides, it's only a very small fraying of the material and not likely to be seen by any but eyes as critical as yours are at this moment."

"Still," I said, "you know it doesn't—"

"Be quiet," he broke in, "or I'll tell this young man the moment I lay eyes on him that he is doomed to marry you. You're scolding me to take your mind off yourself. Calm down, or I'll send you home."

I closed my eyes for a moment and held onto his arm. "I will be good, Father dear. I will be very good and your tie is hardly frayed at all, though when we get home—if we ever do—I shall throw it into the fireplace."

We finally reached our destination. The cottage door opened to Father's knock, and Mrs. Halloran greeted us respectfully, though she seemed a bit surprised to see me. We were led at once to the bedroom at the back of the cottage. I was holding my breath until I thought I must have turned blue, and I let the air out of my lungs slowly. I'd expected the bed would hold a pale, sickly young man. Instead he was fully—and very well—dressed and sitting in an armchair. He arose at sight of me, and I had my first good look at the man I would marry.

He was tall enough, but not so tall as Cathal, and he was thin, almost too thin, but ah, he was handsome. As I had believed all along, his hair was light in color, almost blond, and he had clear blue eyes. Bluer than mine—or Father's. His generous mouth was that of a man who enjoyed smiling and to whom turned-down corners were all but unknown. As the mirror had shown me, his nose was thin and long, but still a good nose.

When he spoke, my heart stopped, for his voice was deep and resonant. Father addressed him by name, shook hands with him, then introduced me. I automatically extended my hand. When he took it, I gathered he was stronger than he appeared to be, for his handshake was firm.

"A pleasure, Miss O'Hanlon," he said. "Do all Irish doctors come accompanied by such attractive assistants?"

If a young man from hereabouts had said that, I'd have chided him for his blarney. I was almost tongue-tied, though I managed to mumble something. I never did know what it was, and I stupidly didn't withdraw my hand until he released his grip.

Father said, "You're American, aren't you, Mr. Cameron?"

So that would be my name. Cameron. I liked it, despite the fact that it did seem more Scotch than Irish, but I could put up with that. I could have endured any name, including that of an Eskimo.

"Yes, sir," Mr. Cameron said. "I'm American."

"What seems to be the trouble?" Father asked professionally. I thought he could have maintained this unprofessional line a little longer. We soon discovered that all Mr. Cameron had was a deep cold brought on by the sudden and drastic change of climate. Father's bag contained fine medicines for that, because the malady was a common one in county Mayo.

Father said, "If you take this as I have directed, you'll be yourself in no time."

"Thank you, Doctor. What is your fee? I'll pay you now."

"Oh, there's no fee," Father said. "We don't charge strangers who grace our little village by their presence. May I ask how you happened to come here?"

I knew why. Mr. Cameron didn't, but I did. The mirror had brought him.

"I set out to see as much of Ireland as possible," Mr. Cameron explained. "I purchased a horse and buggy and set out. I took any road that looked good enough to travel and to my pleasant surprise, I found myself here. Actually, I hadn't planned it. But I'm glad it happened that way."

He was looking at me as he said that, and I felt the blood slowly making its way up my throat and cheeks. I knew I was behaving like a foolish schoolgirl. I'd never before been at such a loss for words.

"I am pleased you like our village," I said inanely.

"I hope you mean that, Miss O'Hanlon. I'd like someone to show me the village and the beautiful coastline. I'm sort of an expert on coastlines, coming from one of the worst in the world."

"And where would that be?" Father asked, before I could get a word in.

"Maine. The State of Maine. The section near where I live has the rockiest coastline I've ever seen, and yours seems to be a gentle slope ending in sandy beach. Would your daughter help me explore it?"

"I guess I can spare my daughter long enough to see that you learn all about our coastline," Father said graciously. His eyes met mine briefly, and I caught the twinkle. "You will be well enough to go about tomorrow, but it might be wise to visit my office first. You can meet my daughter there for your first trip of exploration. I guarantee that you will learn much from her."

Mr. Cameron took my hand again and held it briefly. All of half a minute. His eyes searched my face, and I grew so bold as to raise mine and return his gaze as frankly. And then we both smiled, and I knew it was all right. I knew it from the bottom of my heart, and I felt giddy with delight, hoping mightily it didn't show.

Mrs. Halloran accompanied us outside the cottage, respectful of Father but frowning her disapproval at me for what she probably considered my boldness.

"He's a fine young man, though I know nothing about him except that he paid me room and board, twice over what I asked, and right then and there before he moved in. I would hope he'd stay a long time. It was my hope as well that you would decide he should not be allowed to travel for a time, Doctor. He is that frail looking."

"Mrs. Halloran," Father said, "I have a feeling he'll be with us for some time now."

Her plump face widened in a smile. "I'll be glad of that. His baggage is very expensive stuff. He must have wealth."

"No doubt," Father said.

She sobered and regarded me sternly. "I have heard

it said the banns for you and Cathal Dolan will soon be read, Maeve."

"You have heard idle gossip, Mrs. Halloran," I retorted, in high anger, for she spoke loud enough that Mr. Cameron might have heard, as she very well meant he should. "There never was an agreement between us, and there never will be. He speaks for himself, not for me, and I would like that clearly understood. I would be pleased if you passed the word about, Mrs. Halloran, as word has passed about concerning what Cathal said. Good afternoon."

I marched away, ahead of Father, who had to widen his step to catch up. I was muttering something about giving the busybody a tongue-lashing as he caught up with me.

"I liked him," he said.

"That gabby, loud-mouthed woman was doing what she could to spoil it."

"Now, Maeve, there is no reason to worry about that. Whatever happens, is the will of the good Queen. Mrs. Halloran can gossip all she likes, and it will have no effect. And the poor man in there can't do a thing about it, either."

I looked at him quickly. "Do you think he might wish to?"

"Speaking frankly, I do not. There was a warmth in his eyes when he looked at you before we departed. It was his own suggestion about you taking him around. To see the coastline, he says. Coastline, my eye. It's the lines of you the man is interested in, or I'm losing both my eyesight and my instinct. Yet I do like him."

"It will not be hard to love him, Father," I said.

"He comes from far off. There will be a day when he will wish to go home." Father's voice was gently chiding.

"He will be free to do so if he does not mind

39

traveling alone. Or in the fine company of his father-in-law as well as his wife."

"Now since when can't I take care of myself?" he asked irately.

"Since I said so. You're not a man to endure loneliness."

"I could marry again," he said with a grin. "I'm not that old or ugly, and there are widows. . . ."

I wrinkled my nose at him. "That will be the day!"

He nodded. "Aye, that will be the day." And I knew he was thinking of my mother. I slipped my hand around his arm and grasped it gently, and I looked at him with warmth and love. A look he returned, for we understood one another and we were happy, as we had always been. For a second or two, I forgot Mr. Cameron.

He didn't forget. Next morning, much earlier than I had expected, he came to the office. Father was out on a call, but I brought him into the private office. I occupied Father's chair and he took the one facing me.

"Mr. Cameron," I said primly, "have you had any more coughing spells?"

"Not one. The medicine worked wonders. Your father is a good doctor."

"You do not feel any congestion?"

"Slight, perhaps, but nothing serious. I think some fresh air would do me good. If you have the time. And, of course, the inclination to show a stranger about."

"I will be glad to, Mr. Cameron."

"If we're to walk about and be friendly, I think we should use our first names, don't you? Mine is Joel."

"Joel," I repeated slowly. "It's not a usual name in Ireland, I must say. I am Maeve."

He laughed. "In Maine, they'd not even regard that as a name."

"Wouldn't they now?" Tartness touched my voice.

"I didn't mean anything by that, Miss O'Hanlon," he said quickly.

"Maeve," I reminded him.

"I think the name is beautiful, Maeve."

"It's the name of a queen who once ruled Ireland."

"And you were named after her. I'm sure she'd be pleased. I wasn't named after anyone. Probably just a name my mother fancied."

"I like it. My brother's name is Jimmy."

"Does he live here?"

"He is studying to become a surgeon at the University of Edinburgh. It's been two years since he set foot in this house, more's the pity . . . May I ask what you do, Joel?"

His smile was sheepish. "I wish you hadn't asked. I'm an expert in doing nothing. If anyone wishes concrete facts about doing nothing, I have all the answers. I get bored to death, so I travel, and I still get bored to death. Until I came here."

His last sentence gave me hope. "Do you have a home and family?"

"Oh, yes. A home and family I have plenty of. They are the reason I travel. One day I'll tell you about them, but just now, I'll not bore you."

"I wouldn't know about a family one does not care for, Joel. I assume that's what you're saying. I manage the house and help my father. I've never known boredom."

"You are fortunate. Will you help me forget there is such a thing?"

I nodded, a bit impishly. "I could take you down to the sea and throw you in. The water in Clew Bay is cold. You'd not be bored getting out of the sea."

"I'd even agree to that," he said. "Let's go down and have a look at Clew Bay."

I knew, as we moved along the street, that we were being watched from every house. Just to make it more

41

interesting for them—and because I secretly wanted to—I took Joel's hand in mine and we broke into a half-walk, half-dance. Gossip would have it I'd completely lost my head over a stranger before the day was done.

I brought him to my favorite hill and explained that the sweet smell he commented on was wild thyme that grew in bushes leading up the green slope to the mountains. I took him along the path down to the beach and the sea.

"Why, Maeve," he said, "you're shivering—and it's warm today."

I nodded without looking up. "It's the sea. This bay, when there's a storm, has claimed many a life and there's some say that it must take a life now and then to satisfy its hunger or lust."

"That's a fairy tale," Joel said. "You can't believe in it."

"I don't know anything about where you live, Joel. Or how folks think there. But here in Mayo we believe in many things that seem uncanny, and we chide ourselves for believing in them, and we say out loud that we do not and never will, but inside us we do. It's hard to explain. One day I will try to make you understand because . . . because in one of these myths, you are now involved, and if you ask me to explain that, I *will* throw you into the sea."

We found a likely place to sit down on the soft grass well above the beach and the calm water. He was right. The day was warm, the air perfumed with thyme. Nearby, a songbird added to the magic. I'd known from the start that I loved this man because I was destined to, but I never realized what a glorious feeling being in love actually could be. It required all of my willpower not to tell him how I felt about him, for that would have been unseemly. Besides, it could well be I'd scare him away.

He broke the silence. "May I ask you a personal question?"

"You may." I remained serious, but my heart gloried in his interest.

"What did Mrs. Halloran mean when she spoke about banns said for you and someone called Cathal?" he asked. "I know what the word means, being of the same faith."

"So you heard that? As she wished you to. I will tell you about Cathal. We grew up together. He was a good friend of my brother's, and he became my friend as well. I liked him, until I grew up and realized what he really was, a man without ambition. Ah, Cathal was never meant for me. Yet he took it upon himself to think we were to be married one day, though I never so much as said a word to that effect and never would. It was only a few days ago I told him to stop this nonsense, but he is that conceited he will not believe that I mean it."

"I see."

I turned on my side to look at him. He lay on his back, a bit of tall grass between his teeth. His eyes were closed, and I was sorely tempted to brush his cheek with my lips.

"You see what, may I ask?"

"I wondered if you were betrothed."

"And what would that mean to you, Joel Cameron?"

"I would leave here today."

I sat up quickly. "You'd leave because I was spoken for?"

He turned on his side and his eyes were open now. "Yes, I'd leave."

"I think you're a bit daft," I said.

"It may be. I feel that way for some reason. I'd go because I don't think I could stand it if you were going to marry someone else."

"Now what business would that be of yours?" Oh, I was carrying on a wonderful act and hurting myself

43

doing it. Taking a risk, too. Perhaps depending too much on that mirror.

"They do say, Maeve, that if a man meets a girl and falls in love with her on sight, the attraction is only physical. That such a love will soon wane. Do you believe that?"

"I might, if I knew what you were talking about," I said, and the effort to keep this game going was growing harder.

"Well—I fell in love with you the moment our eyes met. That's supposed to be silly. Even impossible! Everybody says it can't happen and last. I used to believe it. Then I came to a strange village in Ireland, half sick, bored beyond description, not giving a damn what happened to me, and I looked into a pair of eyes . . . sparkling blue eyes . . . or are they a pale lavender. . . ."

"Blue," I said, holding my breath.

"Yes—blue. Though in some light. . . ."

"Get on with it, man," I urged.

"What else is there to say? Now you can sit back and laugh at me. Or tell me to get up and leave town. You can feel sorry for me and maybe put up with me, but I had to tell you this."

He began to get up and was kneeling when I dropped to my knees before him. "Will you stop this wiggling around?" I said. "And for heaven's sake, man, kiss me before I bust every maidenly rule and regulation and kiss you first. I've been in love with you for weeks. For months . . . all my life. Like one of those princesses in a fairy tale, I've been waiting for you. What kept you, Joel Cameron, that you made me wait this long?"

He didn't move. He simply stared. I bent toward him. I placed my hands against his cheeks and I pressed my lips against his mouth, and suddenly his arms were around me.

"This," he said, "isn't true. Day before yesterday

44

I sat in a village inn ten miles from here and tossed a coin to see what direction I'd take in the morning. I cursed the cold I'd picked up somewhere, but it was heaven-sent because it brought me to you. Has a miracle happened to me, Maeve? Are you real? Is it you beside me? Have I really held you in my arms and kissed you? Tell me I didn't imagine any of it."

"It's all very real, and I knew it would happen."

"What nonsense are you talking?"

"Be patient," I said. "And it isn't nonsense. It was foreordained. Don't ask me any questions now. I'll tell you before we marry." I gasped and slipped free of his arms, having the grace to feel embarrassed by my daring.

He laughed and drew me close again. "Will you marry me, Maeve O'Hanlon?"

"That I will, Joel Cameron."

"Even though you know nothing about me?"

"What do you know of me, may I ask?"

"You're lovely. Also, spirited and mischievous. You kiss like an angel, yet you're woman enough to state your love. And I know you have much to give. You're what I need to complete myself. You're Maeve O'Hanlon. That's sufficient."

"Aye, and for me you are Joel Cameron, also enough."

"What will your father think?"

"He will be delighted."

"And what of this man Cathal?"

"He has sworn to meet the man who marries me and knock his block off."

"Is he big?"

"Twice as big as you, my love."

"Well, we shall see."

"I will break something over his hard head if he so much as raises a fist to you, Joel."

"You'll do nothing of the sort. I fight my own battles."

And I had my first worry about the man I loved.

For long minutes we lay back, letting the warmth of the sun make us comfortably lazy so we could fully enjoy this miracle which had happened to us. We talked, a million words of conversation, all of it of little consequence. It was not a time for serious considerations or brave plans. Our love was too new for that.

Late in the afternoon we walked slowly back to the village, not speaking at all. Joel's arm was around my waist and we marched in step, with me looking up at him every few paces, and if there were eyes watching, which I knew well there were, our love for one another was by now a well-known fact through the village. Or would be in the next half hour.

Father was treating his last patient of the afternoon, and he was soon free. I had installed Joel in the big easy chair in our parlor and when Father walked in, he came to a stop, legs apart, hands on his hips looking formidable as he bent forward a trifle and regarded this interloper into his family life.

"So you've come to tell me you two are going to be married," he said.

Joel's look of consternation made me laugh aloud, and Father joined in until Joel was laughing too and Father was shaking his hand as if it was the handle of a well pump.

"I can see you haven't been told the truth of the matter as yet," Father said. "But you will be, and I trust it will make no difference. Even if it does, there's precious little you can do about it, you poor mortal man. Seriously, I'm happy for both of you. That's not easy for me to say, because except for taking your pulse and temperature I know nothing about you, Joel Cameron."

"There seems to be mystery on both sides," Joel said. "I ask that you excuse me, for the time being,

46

of talking further about myself. Believe me, I hold no secret that I'm ashamed of, but before I give you the facts that concern the bleakness of my life—up to now—I wish to obtain the reaction of others."

"Your family, of course," I said.

He nodded. "I use the word loosely, darling Maeve."

"Would it be a religious objection perhaps?" Father asked. I knew why. If he thought Joel was not of my religion and we were not married in the Church, we might as well plan to go away and live elsewhere, such was the devotion of our people to the Church.

"No," Joel said. "I was raised in your Church. I have the baptismal papers with me to prove it. You know, it's a strange thing. I left home suddenly, as if something got under my skin and made me go. Not that I didn't want to, but it seemed urgent that I should, and for no reason that I can think of, I packed my baptismal papers. Now why did I do a thing like that?"

"I know," I said softly. "Aye, Father and I both know."

Joel wagged his head. "Mystery upon mystery. But I don't care how it happened or why. When will we marry, Maeve?"

"There will be the banns first, of course. I would say in a month."

"That will be perfect. I will have to go away for a few days. To Dublin. It is necessary. I swear to you that I will come back and I will leave with you all of my possessions as insurance of that promise."

"No need," I said. "You leave your love and take with you mine. That's enough. When will you leave?"

"Would you mind if I left tomorrow? I want to get this over with. It's not a pleasant thing I have to do, but now it is more necessary than ever."

"That is for you to decide," I said.

"Then that's settled. When I return, I promise I'll

tell you all about myself. Why I have to make this journey and what the results of it are. Maeve, thank you for the trust you have in me."

"As you have in me, for surely you must know that what has happened to you is not something your own will has directed."

"Was it witchcraft?" he asked with a smile.

"No, something akin to it, perhaps, but not witchcraft. Nothing of an evil nature. Is that not so, Father?"

Father sighed deeply. "Not this time, Maeve. Surely not this time." And I knew he was thinking of Mother and the prophecy of her death that she had seen in the ancient mirror.

Joel quickly changed the subject, realizing he had somehow unwittingly entered upon touchy ground. "Will you arrange for the banns, then, Maeve?" he asked.

"Aye, in plenty of time."

"Good. I'll leave you now, because Mrs. Halloran will have supper waiting and, seeing I paid for it, will insist I eat it, hungry or not. Early in the morning, I'll be on my way and back before you know it."

Father said, "Excuse me, you may not be hungry and my daughter's not in any mood to fix me my supper, so I'll fix it myself and at least be certain of what I'm eating, for I don't think she'd be aware of what she was fixing. A good journey to you, Joel Cameron, and once again I am happy for you and for Maeve. And for myself, because now I no longer have to worry about the brat that she is."

They shook hands, and then Father left. Not to prepare his supper. He didn't know how to make tea, but to be certain that Joel and I had time alone before he would leave.

"A remarkable man," Joel said. "A fine doctor, and a remarkable man."

"Aye, Joel. And I worry about him."

48

"Your father? He looks to be healthy as a man can be."

"His health will have nothing to do with it. These are matters that require explanation, and this is not the time for it. When you return, then everything will be in the open. Is that not so, Joel?"

"Yes, in the open. And I'll be sorry for it. Mind you —it has nothing to do with me as an individual."

"Hush, man, I know that. Kiss me just once, hold me a moment or two, and then begone with you before I start blubbering like I swear I never do. Ah, Joel, I love you so. These days you are gone will be black ones, worthless ones, except that as each passes, you will be that much closer to coming back."

"I still can't believe what has happened to me, Maeve, but I bless whatever force is responsible."

I led him to the door and he kissed me once again and then he left me, with great strides, never looking back like a man who believed if he did, he'd not leave. And me standing there wishing to heaven he wouldn't.

I prepared our supper, and Father sat down with me to enjoy it. I ate, but without appetite, and my mind was elsewhere until Father called me back.

"You told him nothing of the mirror or the torc?"

"Not a word, Father. But I will tell him when he returns."

"It would be well. The poor man must be half addled trying to figure out how all this came about."

"He will know, Father. There is one thing I wish you would do for us. Will you talk to Cathal Dolan and warn him if he raises a hand to Joel, it will be like striking out at me? If he cares, as he says, he will respect my wishes."

"Yes, I thought of doing that. Cathal has a violent temper, and he's quick to anger."

"You know Joel would be no match for his strength

49

or his cruelty, but Joel will stand up to him, even if he knows he will be beaten."

"I'll do what I can."

"Thank you."

"On your wedding day, I shall show Joel the torc, Maeve. Because from that day on, it is yours—and his. You will remember that it has passed through many generations and it must pass through many more.

"Aye, I'm aware of that."

"And you will also remember—and warn Joel—that having possession of this treasure is against the law, so we do not display it, nor do we talk of it to others. And it is to be kept safely in a bank vault, no matter where you may be."

"I will remember."

"Good. Then we have concluded our serious talk for the day and I will now say that I have tasted better beef pie than this and your tea is that weak it can hardly stand up straight in the cup."

"I'm sorry, Father," I said.

"You are forgiven. Once . . . ah, yes, once I was in love, too. It does strange things to a man, as well, and I hope that your Joel winds up in Dublin and not Kilkenny, because he doesn't know what he's doing."

"He's a man of considerable intelligence," I said firmly. "Father, I will go to see Grania Keohane in the morning."

"Now what would you want from her?"

"You yourself call her the Wise Woman."

"You will ask her advice of matters your own father cannot give?" he demanded indignantly.

"Father, there are things best asked of a woman by a woman. What manner of medical man are you not to realize that?"

"Ask her, then. But if you doubt what she says—the wisdom of it—come to me."

"Have I not always done that?"

"Aye," he said, mollified as I knew he would be. "Bring her a basket."

"I have two kinds of jam and I will roast a chicken in the morning and bake her a fine loaf. We have a tin of tea, if I may have it. If not, I'll steal it."

"Take it. You'll not be a thief on my account. And there are two tins of biscuits she dotes on. High pay for the words of wisdom she can give you that your own father can't."

I slept well even with the ten million thoughts that raced through my mind. Perhaps it was because they concerned but one subject—Joel Cameron. At any rate I wakened refreshed, and I put a chicken in to roast and made the bread. I fed Father hurriedly, because he had a call a good distance beyond the village and had no time to spend on eating.

I ate my own breakfast leisurely and thought about what I would say to Grania Keohane. She was a strange woman who lived alone in a small cottage made comfortable by her neighbors and friends. She was very old, some said near one hundred, but Father didn't believe it. He gave her ninety years at the most. I'd known her since I was able to recognize anyone. She used to come to care for me when I was a baby, and it was she who taught me many things not ordinarily taught to young girls. Before Father came to the village, she was the only doctor the people knew, and she had functioned well. She knew the value and the curative powers of herbs for one thing, and this she had taught me. I used the knowledge often in helping Father treat his patients, for there were those who would refuse to take his medicines but would accept the herb treatment, and then it would be up to me.

Grania taught me also to respect my heritage, for she alone, in this village, knew about it. She was that familiar with the days of Queen Maeve that I often wondered if she'd actually lived then and by some miracle been transported to these modern days of 1895. She often predicted matters that did come to pass, and once she sent Father to see a man who she said would fall off the roof of his barn half an hour later and he would be "bad hurt," but if Father left immediately, he would be there in time to help him. Father went as if the man had already fallen— and Father didn't have his tongue in his cheek, either. The man who did fall was dumbfounded but nonetheless grateful that Father arrived so promptly.

I packed the basket, tidied the house, and drew a shawl over my head because the morning was a bit foggy. We were coming into fall weather now, and mornings and evenings could be chilly. I walked down the street, acknowledging the greetings of those who passed me by, or stood in their doorways, appearing by magic just before I reached them. They were aching to have me stop, as I often did, and tell them about Joel, but I was in no mood to tell them something that was still too new and too sacred to discuss with anyone.

I walked into Grania Keohane's cottage and found her sitting before her fireplace where the turf had burned down to white ash and gave off great heat which she favored and needed.

"Come in, Maeve darlin'," she called out before I entered the parlor. "I been expectin' you."

"Have you now?" I asked. "I've brought you jam and a chicken, bread and tea, and Father asked me to give you tins of biscuits that are very sweet and will be bad for your teeth."

She raised her wrinkled face with her turned-in lips over toothless gums and cackled with glee and pleasure at the joke. I unloaded the basket and put the food away, except for one tin of biscuits. I made tea, brought the pot into the parlor, and served her a cup, having one myself. She dipped the biscuits into the tea and ate them with a relish that was a joy to behold.

"When will you marry the young man?" she asked.

"Who's been talking?"

"Do the good women miss anything of importance here, Maeve?"

"How could they know of marriage plans?"

"They don't. I have guessed this. Or perhaps I knew it somehow. Like I know many things I cannot account for. Like the reason you came here, because you are troubled. What is it, child?"

"Grania, there are matters which trouble me, and they are not easy to explain. The mirror . . ."

"I thought as much. A blessing and a curse on it. Whatever or whoever gave that thing the power to reveal a woman's future should have made certain only the good would be revealed and never the bad."

"First of all, the young man who came to me I saw in the mirror long ago. I knew he would come. I knew I would love him and he would love me. That is the good thing, Grania. Ah, it is a blessed thing. But I looked again at that mirror much later and while his face appeared once more, that of another man also appeared behind his profile. I cannot know what it means except that I fear it is not good."

"A second man to come into your life?"

"Except as a friend, that cannot be while Joel Cameron is my husband, my love."

"Aye. It is not a good omen. But whatever is to happen may not happen for many years."

"The second man is also young, Grania."

"Ah, me. I do not like the look of it, Maeve, yet you must endure it. The first young man came to you, and this you could not prevent. If he leaves, you cannot stop that, either."

"I know. It is the manner of his leaving that worries me. Then there is Father."

"He was also in the mirror?"

53

"Not himself, no. But when I look into the thing and ask that I see what is in store for him, I see water—the sea, and it boils and churns as if there is a great storm."

She glanced away. "Maeve, take comfort in the fact that your father is not a lover of the water. He owns no craft, not even a *currach*. I have never known him to put out to sea, have you?"

"No," I said, swiftly searching my memory. "Yet the sea rages in the mirror. . . ."

She patted my hand, then said, "How will all this go with Cathal Dolan, may I ask?"

"I don't know. He has threatened to harm any man I go to, and I think he means it."

"Aye. You should see the priest and have him warn Cathal. Your father should talk to him, and there is one other who may influence him. See Banker Finn, for he holds a considerable mortgage on Cathal's farm."

"At once, Grania."

"And I would not let your young man know of this. He'd be that prideful and it would hurt him to know that you took steps to keep him from harm. And harm it would be from that big, ignorant hulk of a man."

"I will also talk to Cathal," I said.

"He has a small but cunning mind, Maeve. Beware of that man. I feel he will one day do you no good, so be prepared for it."

"I'll remember that, Grania. And I am grateful for your advice."

"You are like me own, Maeve. For you, great things are in store. But great things come slowly and often with pain and sorrow. You must prepare for that, as well. You are strong and you are wise. . . ."

"As you have made me, Grania," I said.

"Aye, I have helped. It gratifies me to know this. And keep in mind that you come from a line of Kings and Queens of which the world has never seen the like since. And never will again, worse luck. Now tell me the gossip, for there is aplenty of it in this village and hereabouts."

She settled back to listen while I informed her of the latest goings-on, mostly trivia, sometimes breaking the confidence between a patient and a doctor where it would do no harm and knowing what I said would go no further. Grania did enjoy gossip and she munched her tea-soaked biscuits and listened with cackles of glee and sometimes sighs of concern.

The fieldstone church we attended was a modest building, erected by the men of the village. It was a tribute to their faith and ability, for not a drop of water squeezed through the roof, despite the heavy rainfalls. The interior was spartan, having only benches and kneeling rails. But we managed two statues, one on either side of the altar, plus the Stations of the Cross, which had been carved from wood by a man dead before I was even born.

I knew Father Burke tended his small garden at the rear of the church at this hour. He must have heard me approach, for without even a glance over his shoulder, he spoke my name.

I said, "Father, I have to talk with you."

"Have to or want to?"

"Both. So will you please give me your attention?"

"That I will." He dusted the dirt from his hands, rubbed them lightly over the grass to remove any remaining grains of earth, then arose to face me. He was a handsome man, tall, sturdily built, with iron-gray hair, strong features, and piercing blue eyes, deep-set beneath jet-black eyebrows. He was respected by all and feared by a few, but he was a fair man and devoted to his calling. He was tolerant also, realizing humanity had its weaknesses as well as its strengths. He knew life was not easy in these parts

55

and it was all a man could do to provide for his family.

"Well, Maeve," he said patiently, "say what is on your mind, as if I didn't know."

"How could you?"

"Don't look so surprised. Since when are there secrets in the village? Even if there were, it's written all over your face. I don't suppose it concerns Cathal."

"If you know what's on my mind, you know it does," I countered.

He studied me intently. "It concerns the banns of marriage."

"Not so far as Cathal is concerned," I replied quietly.

He nodded. "The stranger."

"He's no stranger to me. His name is Joel Cameron."

"Is it to be a church wedding? You know what I mean."

"You mean is he one of us."

Father Burke nodded slowly.

"Yes. He has baptismal papers with him."

"Then what is the problem, my child?"

"It is Cathal Dolan, Father."

"Oh, and how is that?"

"I'm depending on you to talk with him. He's sworn no other man shall have me. I do not love Cathal. I fear him."

"With your spirit?" Father Burke smiled.

"Not for myself, but for my Joel."

"So it's 'my Joel,' is it?"

"It always will be, Father. Will you speak to Cathal? He has threatened to harm anyone I marry."

"Yes. Though he doesn't always listen to me. Now about Joel Cameron."

"You will marry us, won't you, Father?" I couldn't keep the worry out of my voice.

"More for Joel's sake than for yours. He makes more sense."

"What do you mean?"

"He's already been to see me. There will be no obstacle."

Blessed relief flooded through me. "I didn't know he came to see you."

"He loves you. He discussed it with your father. Or perhaps it was the other way around. In any case, I met him, and I approve. I'll speak to Cathal. He is a stubborn man, but I'll do my best."

"God bless you, Father."

"God bless you, Maeve. And your Joel. I will announce the banns of marriage beginning this Sunday. Make a visit before you leave."

"I will, Father. Thank you."

"Well, be off with you. Can't you see I have my garden to tend?"

I remained in the little church a good while, for I had many prayers of thanks to say. I even prayed that Cathal would put behind him any bitterness he might feel toward Joel.

Banker Finn, portly and amiable, escorted me into his office, seated me beside his desk, then eased himself into his tall, leather-padded chair. I wasted no time stating the reason for my being here.

"You no doubt have heard of Joel Cameron," I said.

Banker Finn nodded. "He has captured your heart, Maeve."

"True. And we are to be married."

"You seem more worried than happy."

"I am, and for a good reason. I refer to Cathal Dolan." Quickly I explained, concluding, "I need your help, Banker Finn. If Cathal harms Joel, Cathal will be arrested and he will go to jail. He will also find himself sued with surely a judgment against him which can be satisfied only by the taking of his farm. Now, the bank holds the mortgage, and there would be great trouble for the bank should such a thing happen."

"I shall call in Cathal and tell him if he harms this

57

man there will be no renewal of the mortgage," Banker Finn said promptly. "I am grateful that you have warned me. Not that the bank couldn't face the trouble, and more, but I would not wish harm to come to this young man. I trust he will open an account with us."

"Aye, I trust so as well," I said. "Thank you and good day to you, sir."

I returned home, for it was dinnertime, and I prepared the noonday meal of boiled potatoes and a piece of tender ham. There was fresh bread from the morning's baking, and while we ate, I told Father what I had done.

"It's well," he said. "I'll also give him a talking to."

"And so will I. This very afternoon. While you are taking care of your office visits, I shall drive down to his farm. He must know that he has to behave himself before Joel returns."

When I pulled up the buggy at the edge of Cathal's barley fields, I brought my hands to my mouth and called out to him. He came loping in from the fields, a sweaty and dirty man, though I surely did not hold that against him. He didn't climb into the buggy, and I didn't get down.

"So you've come to tell me you will marry another," he said bitterly.

"You have heard, then?"

"Aye. Father Burke was here, and so was the banker. I expect the rest of the village at any time."

"Very well, Cathal. You know then what it is I ask of you. This man I shall marry is a fine man, but physically he cannot stand up to you, though I know he will if you challenge him. So that you must not do. You and I have been friends for a long time. Now I hope you and my husband can be friends, for there is little to gain by being enemies."

"And I say there is little to be gained by being friends, Maeve." Cathal's broad face was dark with

58

anger. "You have tied my fists so I cannot strike out at him as I swore to do, but if there are other ways, I will find them. You have not heard the last of me, Maeve O'Hanlon. You and your fine husband. You, or he, have naught to fear from my fists, but as I said . . . other ways . . . aye, other ways. . . ."

He turned and walked off, and I exhaled in cold anger at the stupidity of the man before I whipped the reins down on the back of the poor horse unnecessarily hard.

THREE

Ten long days passed before Joel returned. I'd heard not a word from him, and I was beginning to worry, though Father did his best to reassure me, pointing out that he himself was a poor letter writer. It did nothing to ease my concern. I thought too often of the mirror with a stranger's face behind his.

And so when I heard the sound of a buggy driven hard and pulling up fast, I ran from the house so swiftly I almost lost my footing on a loose cobblestone. But my startled cry quickly changed to one of delight when Joel's arm caught me and held me fast. He kissed my brow, my cheeks, and my chin, and then his lips touched mine. My arms closed tightly around his neck. If there were inquiring eyes, we neither knew nor cared. It was evident his loneliness had been as great as mine, for when he released me, he pressed my head against his shoulder and whispered my name over and over. There was both longing and desire in his voice.

"Let's go inside. I have something for you," he said.

His arm enclosed my waist, and we practically ran into the house and closed the door. His hand reached into his coat pocket and he withdrew a velvet box. It had a hinged lid, which he opened. I gasped aloud at the lovely diamond in a gold setting. Alongside it was a wide yellow band. A wedding ring.

He withdrew the engagement ring and asked me to hold out my finger. The ring slipped on easily. A perfect fit!

"How did you know my size?" My voice rose with excitement.

He raised my hand and pressed it to his cheek as he spoke. "I'd like to say it was intuition, but your father made a circle on paper of one he gave you. The jeweler used that. I hope you like it."

I slipped my hand free and held my arm at full length, letting the sun's rays, slipping through the window, catch the facets and cover the walls and ceiling with shimmering shafts of light.

"It's beautiful," I whispered. I'd never seen anything so magnificent.

He snapped the box closed. "I'll keep the wedding ring until I place it on your finger. Which I hope will be soon."

I brushed his cheek lightly with my lovely diamond. "You were gone longer than I expected."

"I'm sorry. As usual, my family proved difficult. The cables that went back and forth were endless."

"Did any concern me?"

"Some. However, I told them I was marrying you, not they. There was nothing they could do about it. Besides, it doesn't matter. They'll never come here, and I'll never bring you back, for I would not go back myself."

"Would that be because you're ashamed of me?" I asked. "Or are you afraid of them?"

"Darling, no one could possibly be ashamed of you. No one! The truth is, I cannot tolerate this family of mine, and their ways. I'll tell you why later. I'm not afraid of them, be assured of that. But these days in Dublin, waiting while cables were being exchanged, I grew lonely again, away from you. The same awful loneliness I endured before I met you. The kind that sent me traipsing over the world looking for something that waited for me here in Kilcrea. Now, holding you in my arms, everything is right again, and the loneliness is gone."

"Then I'm glad," I said. "All is right with me, too, when I can raise my eyes and once again look into yours. I've been lonely, too, my love."

His arms tightened about me. "Darling Maeve, there will never again be a reason for us to be lonely."

I wished I was as sure, for I thought of the mirror and the image of the second man. I had to dismiss such morbid ideas so I freed myself of his embrace and linked my hand under his arm. "You must be starving after such a long journey. I'll have food on the table by the time you bring your things over to Mrs. Halloran's, put away the horse, and come back here."

"I'll be quick about it, too," he said.

He spent an hour at it, part of the time taken up by Mrs. Halloran, who insisted on asking him countless questions, the answers to which she could pass on to the village women and increase her stature as a well-informed gossip. Father was still out making his rounds, so Joel ate a late midday meal with me. I plied him with endless questions about his journey and about Dublin. In his luggage he had brought two beautiful silk scarves for me and a prayer book in white leather to be carried when we were standing before the altar.

61

"It's beautiful," I said. "It must have been terribly expensive."

He looked across the table at me. "I'm not boasting, Maeve, when I say you will want for nothing."

"I want for nothing now, Joel. With you, I have everything."

His kiss drove everything from my mind, and such a heat rose in my body that he must have felt it through my heavy gown. Still, until we were married . . . Head swimming, I broke away and changed the subject. "Have you made any plans as to where we shall live?"

He seemed surprised at the question. "Well, I could build you a mansion, even a castle, if you like. But it has always been in my mind that we would live here with your father. He needs you—and maybe I can help him, too."

I said, "There may be a million reasons why I fell in love with you, and what you have just said must be one of the most important of them. God bless you for being so thoughtful."

"Well," Joel said gravely, "there is the question of this fellow who threatened to knock the block off any other man who married you. If we live with your father he'll be there to give me what first aid I require." He laughed, so I did, too.

"Cathal is big and he is powerful and can be mean," I said, "but he's promised me not to hurt you."

Joel's hands were around my waist again. "When, then, is the date?" he asked.

"Two weeks, come next Saturday, if that suits you."

"It does not," he said promptly.

"But Joel . . . there is a required wait. . . ."

"I'm aware of that, but I still don't like it."

"Joel, you will abide by the rules. I am firm about this."

62

"As you would say," he remarked with a smile, "aye."

"That's settled, then," I said. "Now there is something else you should know. And it must be told while Father is not present, for it concerns him and his future. It will be best if we do our talking in the parlor so if he returns, we will be warned in time to stop talking."

"You sound so serious, Maeve."

"And with good reason. It's a very serious thing we will go into—after I explain how you were trapped into coming here and marrying me."

He seemed amused. "What game are you playing, Maeve? There was no trap."

"Ah, but there was, without your knowing it. You could not have avoided it if you had wanted to."

"Are you a witch, then, to be telling me I was under some spell?"

"No, darling. It was not witchcraft, and it was not I who set the trap, for it was meant for me as well. All this was done by another woman. A great Queen who died two thousand years ago."

"I admit I'm puzzled," he said, "but it doesn't matter how it happened. I'm grateful that it did. Even if it was done by a Queen . . . two thousand years old?"

"Aye, and I will prove it. There is something I must fetch from upstairs. I'll be but a moment."

I closed the bedroom door behind me and pulled open the bureau drawer to take out the mirror. I removed the wrappings and the silk, and I carried the mirror to the window for the best light. I held it pressed to my chest, and I implored good Queen Maeve to let me see once again this image of the man who was now part of my very existence.

I held the mirror before my eyes, tilted it slightly, and Joel's profile appeared, but so faintly. It was there, recognizable, but not as clear as before.

Then, as I watched, the second image appeared. This one was darker, far clearer. I gasped and had an urge to hurl the mirror from me. As the thought entered my head, the images vanished and I saw only the dim reflection of my own tortured face.

Joel was no longer part of a prophecy, I reminded myself. He was here, a part of my future. The prophecy had been fulfilled. What the other man meant I didn't know and I didn't care. I breathed deeply a few times, rewrapped the mirror, and carried it downstairs.

"Sit with me," I said, and motioned toward the sofa. There I held the mirror in my lap and I told him about Queen Maeve and the High Kings.

"Two thousand years ago, my love, there were glorious days for all of Ireland. In county Meath, near Navan, there was the Hill of Tara and until the sixth century, this was the seat of Ireland's High Kings. It was there they were crowned on the *Lia Fail,* the coronation stone. And there were six *raths* —these were hill forts surrounded by earthworks for retreat in time of danger. There were brave warriors in those days. They feared naught, and the most valorous of all was the High King."

"And you are descended from the Queen of one of those High Kings?" Joel asked.

"Well, not the High Kings, no. We do not claim this to be so, though almost everybody in Ireland today does make such a boast. Well, to get to my story, there was a most important Queen named Maeve of Connacht and she ruled with her consort Ailill. She ruled well, and she was a dear woman from what was passed down over these generations."

"Is it she you were named after?"

"Aye, and the same blood flows in my veins. At least, I have been led to believe this, and I trust it is true."

"No doubt it is," Joel said loyally.

"You are a man after my own heart," I said with a smile. "And come to think of it, you have it already. Well, now, Ailill fought a deadly battle with a warrior named Cuchullain. It lasted for days and poor Ailill was defeated and he died fighting in the river that ran red with their blood. Cuchullain took his place, and it was he to whom Queen Maeve gave the torc."

"Torc?" Joel asked; the word was no doubt new to him.

"It is a heavy piece of jewelry worn about the neck. For proof that we come straight down the line from those ancient people, Father has this same torc now in his possession. It has passed from one generation to another for centuries."

"Really? It must be quite valuable."

"Father says it is priceless. Joel, I am telling you this in confidence because you will soon be one of the family and you have to know about the torc— and other things. Let me say now that keeping the torc in our possession is against the law, for all such ancient relics have been made the sole property of the National Archives and we have no legal right to it. However, Father will not let go of it, and neither will I. As for value, its worth can hardly be counted in pounds or in your dollars. So you know one of our family secrets and except for the three of us, no other soul knows of the torc. Father says it has brought good fortune and fine health to our families. This I can scarcely believe, though maybe I should, because there is something else that came from Queen Maeve which is even more strange and which I do believe in. And it does concern you."

"The object wrapped in that cloth?" Joel asked, eyeing the wrapped mirror which rested on my lap.

"Aye. I shall show you what it is." I freed it of the cloth bindings with the greatest care, as always, and when I placed the concave piece of dull-edged metal before him, Joel looked at me wonderingly.

"What in the world is it?" he asked.

"As you know, long before glass was invented, pieces of shiny metal were used to reflect a woman's face. This is a mirror, Joel. Queen Maeve owned it originally. It passes in each generation to the first girl in the family and is hers until she must pass it on to another generation."

He reached for it, and I promptly moved it out of his reach. "Please, Joel, it is too precious to be touched by anyone but me."

"But you can't even see yourself in that. The shine is all off it. There's nothing left that will reflect."

"Ah, but there is. Not much, but enough. In the middle part, it shines. When I hold it and I ask the good Queen to show me what I wish to know, the mirror brings me an image."

"Oh, Maeve, do you really believe this?" A hint of worry touched Joel's voice.

"I believe it. The mirror brought me the image of you—weeks ago. I recognized you the moment I saw you. I had described you to Father, and he, too, recognized you."

"Did he see the image, as well?"

"No man can see in this mirror. The gift is granted only to women."

"And you saw me . . . in there . . .?" He peered into the concave piece of metal and shook his head.

"You don't believe it, and I cannot say I blame you, but how else could I have described you perfectly to Father those weeks before I even laid eyes on you?"

"I can't explain that," he admitted.

"And even if you think it was naught but my foolish fancy, let me put it to you this way, Joel Cameron."

"I might believe more readily if I were Irish," Joel admitted.

"Aye, that is so, but consider this, my fine disbeliever. You came to Ireland with no reason for doing so, except to get away. Why did you not go to Spain —or Italy, or France, or even England, for that matter? Why did you choose Ireland?"

"I . . . just did."

"And did you journey to my village on the mere strength of 'you don't know why'? Or 'you just did'?"

"I got here. What need is there for a reason?"

"You said yourself you tossed a coin to decide you and the toss brought you here. Isn't it possible some power you did not recognize caused the coin to fall in that manner so you would come here? Where I was waiting?"

He drew an arm around my shoulder. "Darling Maeve, I don't care how I got here. If your Queen Maeve was responsible, all hail to her. I'm here, I'm in love with you. Come to think of it, we fell in love at first glimpse of one another, didn't we?"

"Now you're beginning to think like someone ready to believe," I said.

He nodded slowly. "It's possible. Strange things do happen. One can't be too hard-headed about them."

"Not in Ireland," I said promptly.

"No, surely not in Ireland."

"Joel, the mirror has told me something else I do not care for, and it worries me sorely."

"Something in the future? Like a prediction?"

"Aye." I had made up my mind not to mention his own fading image and the growing clarity of the stranger. I wasn't going to refer to that, for it made no sense to me.

"An evil prediction?"

"Because I was curious, I asked the mirror to tell me what was in store for my father. All I saw was the violent sea. A great storm."

"You think your father is foreordained to be lost at sea?"

"It has to be something like that."

"Does he go out to sea often?"

"Never does he go out. He hates the water. Yet the predictions come true, my love. The mirror does not fail. Of course I haven't told him of this, and I never will. If the prophecy is true, it's not well for a man to know how he is going to die."

"Have you looked there for my future?" Joel asked.

"That I have, with no answer yet. Perhaps it is needful that we marry first. I don't know. Perhaps I should put the mirror safely away and never look at it again. I'm frightened of it."

"It brought me to you, darling," he said.

"I know, therefore I could never destroy it even if I'd a mind to. Which I have not. Now you know how you were trapped. You couldn't help yourself. It was fated that we meet and fall in love."

"I don't object to it. I have no fault to find. I would place the mirror in a shrine and bow to it daily for what it has done for me."

"Thank you, dearest Joel." I arose with the re-wrapped mirror in my hands. "As a reward, you may peel the potatoes. I'll put the mirror away and join you in the kitchen. It's time to start supper."

"We are not yet married," he objected in mock dignity and dismay.

"Aye, consider yourself in training, then. You peel potatoes with the sharp side of the knife."

Father returned and administered to two patients who waited in the office. Then he joined us for supper, and a good one it turned out to be if I say so myself. Old Grania, before she became quite so ancient, told me how to cook lamb to its best advantage, and I had a fine leg of it with a minted crust, potatoes, and leeks; there was a good sponge cake laced with fine brandy for dessert.

"I have told Joel of the mirror and the torc," I

informed Father when we sat down to dine. "I told him of his image that I saw. I don't think he is quite ready to believe it yet, but he will."

"She described you exactly," Father told Joel. "That must have been six or seven weeks ago. I don't blame you for finding this hard to accept. I used to doubt it. When I married, Maeve's mother had to convince me, too. At first I thought little of it as perhaps no more than some token of the past with a strange history attached to it. But before Maeve was even conceived, the mirror told my wife what she would be like and even brought forth the name she should be christened by. It also predicted that my wife would not live. I only regret that it will reveal things to the female sex and never to a male. Perhaps there is a reason for this. If so, I've never been able to fathom it."

"There have been a few times when it also predicted accidents to people who became Father's patients," I said. "Twice it predicted a recovery of people we were sure would not live and yet they did."

"Does the torc have any such meaning or power?" Joel asked.

"Oh, no, not at all," Father said. "But it serves to remind us of what sort of people we sprang from."

"I feel I must now tell you about my own family," Joel said with a sigh. "Perhaps we should be more comfortable in the parlor. It's going to take a while."

"Maeve, bring more coffee and a tray. I'll have my pipe. Joel, there are new pipes, and I have some choice cigars. . . ."

"Thank you. I prefer not to smoke. I don't object to it, of course, but I was never allowed to begin, and I feel it would be a trifle foolish to start now."

"It's not the cleanest habit in the world," Father said, to which I fervently agreed. We finally settled ourselves in the parlor with the coffee service on the table before us along with a decanter of fine brandy

69

and glasses I'd polished until they gleamed. Joel began his story.

"First of all, let me say that my family consists of my father Gabriel. He is an austere man, a great lover of wealth, and while no miser, he is not a man to waste money or material. My mother is Evelyn. She will wear a diamond choker and a diamond tiara on occasion, and every day will load her fingers with rings, her arms with bracelets, and her throat with necklaces and lavalieres. Father indulges her. She entertains often and lavishly, and they are accepted in fine social circles where they encounter people who do business with my father. Which is the reason why he goes. My older brother Abner spends his days fishing, hunting, and otherwise doing nothing."

I sat mute while Joel paused to sip his brandy and coffee. Father leaned back, puffing on his pipe. Joel resumed speaking as if he hated every word, but knowing they were necessary.

"I have an older sister named Helen who wears my mother's jewelry on occasion and associates with the same class of people my mother dotes on. She is married to Ashley Easterly. He is an important business man in the office of the factory my father owns. And finally, my mother's sister, Marcy Tabor, lives with us. She is a pillar of the church, in her opinion, and holds me in contempt because I won't conform to the rest of them."

"May I inquire what you mean by conforming?" I asked.

"I don't want to devote my life to the making of more money than I know what to do with. Especially when it is bled out of the hides of men and women who have to work too many hours each day to provide it for us. Slavery was abolished thirty years ago, but my family refuses to recognize it. Let me explain. They own and operate a very large cotton mill. It is good fabric, I will say that for them. The factory employs upwards of three hundred men, many women, and a number of children in light work. These people are paid as little as possible for as many hours as they will consent to work."

"Why do they keep working for that mill, then?" Father asked.

"They have nowhere else to go. The work is specialized, and they know nothing else. Two generations of them have worked at the mill. Father owns all of the houses, save a very few. He rents them to his employees. He owns the stores, the saloons, the stables. He owns everything. The people are always in debt to him, and they spend their lives working out the indebtedness. Father's not the only one to do this. It's common all through the States. That doesn't lessen my disapproval, and when I was ordered into the office to supervise these people, I refused. Father was furious. He threatened me with all sorts of dire things, but I happen to be invulnerable to anything he proposes as punishment. Because when my grandfather died, his will stated that my father inherited one-third of the mill and property, my sister one-third, and I the remaining third. This arrangement could never be disturbed. So I receive large sums every month. The money is sent to Dublin while I'm in Ireland; otherwise it is sent to the largest city nearest to wherever I happen to be."

"Your older brother did not share?" Father asked bluntly.

"Grandfather had little use for my brother. Even before Abner reached his sixteenth birthday, Grandfather had decided he was hopelessly lazy."

"Your father, then, runs the factory?" I asked.

"Father is at the helm," Joel said. "But the man who handles most of the corporation affairs is his brother. My uncle, Loran Cameron. Grandfather was no saint, and he didn't shy away from exploiting the village people, or the factory employees, but even he

71

could not put up with the way his oldest son handled matters. He left Loran absolutely nothing and stated his reasons for cutting him off in the will."

"How terrible that must have been for him," I said.

"An ordinary man would have been shocked and mortified, but Loran laughed. He thought it extremely funny. He knew my father could not run the business without him and his methods and, therefore, Loran was perfectly safe. Father knew it, too."

"I don't quite understand this," Father said with a frown.

"It's not easy to understand, sir. Whatever my father is, there still runs in him a spark of decency. It's not deep, and it's well hidden by his greed and avarice, but it's there. He would not, for instance, order some employee fired, hold his wages because he is in debt to the company, and then have him dispossessed from the company house with nowhere to go. Uncle Loran not only has issued such orders, he enjoys doing it, and he often makes a point of being present when the eviction takes place. I sometimes think he takes nourishment from women's tears and men's curses."

"Then you'll not be going back to them," I said impulsively.

"I have refused to do so. That's what kept me so long in Dublin. I was in communication with the family by cable. I told them of our coming marriage, and they were against it. In fact, they ordered me home, and I refused. They threatened me, but if it is possible to laugh at them by cable, that is what I did, so they disowned me. Or I disowned them. However —this did not change my status as an heir. I still get one-third of all profits and I can retain a one-third vote in any company proceedings if I choose."

I moved to the side of his chair and bent over him to place my cheek against his. "I would not have had it said that I came between a man and his family, darling Joel, but in this case I have no regrets. If you do not."

"Regrets?" He burst into a mighty laugh. "I've been trying to find a reason to make the break clean for the last two or three years. Now it's done, and I'm free."

"A sad thing, no matter how it came about," Father said. "Family ties are stronger here, I suppose. It's done, however, and you should be the better for it. They can make no trouble?"

"None. Grandfather's will was specific and legally airtight. They tried to break it before, and their own lawyers told them it was impossible. So we will make up our minds, at this moment, not to speak of this again. I want to forget all about it, or at least keep it so far back in my mind that it grows more and more unimportant to me with each passing day."

"I agree," I said.

"And I," Father added.

"Only one thing more before we drop the subject. There is a lawyer in New York who represents me, and he will look after my interests. His name is Paul Arnold. He is well known there and a fine attorney."

"My wedding gown is already in the making," I said, pretending I'd not heard a word.

Joel's features softened, and he broke into sudden laughter as he jumped up and seized me in an embrace.

"Now that," he said happily, "is what I call changing the subject. You will be the most beautiful bride Ireland has ever known."

"Only among the most beautiful," Father put in. "We do not claim championships. Aye, she will be beautiful as her mother was. But I'll not shed a tear in losing her. She's been a trial to a man, and she'll worry you as she did me."

"Indeed," I said, "the pleasure will be all mine with two men to worry over me. Father, you know very well there will be few changes here. In fact, you'll have a man to drive you on calls and to perhaps hold the lanterns while you help some woman give birth or treat some child's sore throat."

"I have been wondering," Joel said, "if I shouldn't take up the study of medicine after I've worked with you for a year or two. I'm only twenty-three years old. There's time enough."

"Splendid," Father said. "You would take over from me, and the village would never be without medical help. I say it is a wonderful idea."

"I do not approve," I said. "Perhaps later on, but not now. The studies would take you away from me. Or, if I went along with you, take me away from Father, and we both know he cannot possibly do without me. The poor man would starve to death in a week."

"It's all in the future," Joel said, "and only an idea. I've wasted enough time. Traveled all over, seeking my destiny. I found it here. I want to serve. To do something worthwhile."

"For the moment," I said, "think only of the next two weeks and our wedding. It is going to be a grand affair. Father is seeing to that."

"I wish to pay all expenses," Joel said.

"You cannot," Father said promptly. "It is the responsibility of the bride's father. However, I knew you were going to make this offer, and I have been giving it some thought. Not a great deal, for I didn't know just what your financial condition might be. Now that I do know, I have a suggestion. You are not bound to it, understand; it is your decision after all. But I will point out that you are a stranger in our village, and we are a tightly knit band of people. You will live here from now on, and it should not be as a stranger. It happens that the church is in sad need of repairs and fresh decoration. We have the help— every man in the village will pitch in—but the paint and everything else is very expensive. Now if you could see fit . . ."

"Whatever the church needs, I will pay for gladly," Joel said. "Tomorrow I will talk to the priest and make the arrangements. The work must be done before the wedding so my bride may be married in the splendor that befits her."

We talked into the night, exchanging confidences, learning our likes and dislikes, arguing gently about trivial matters. Father had no further calls and went to bed early. It was late when I finally sent Joel to his room at Mrs. Halloran's and I went to my room.

Just before I blew out the last lamp I stood before the bureau and felt the temptation to unwrap the mirror and look into it once more. To see if I could have been wrong, or something had happened that Joel's image would appear and not be shadowy and weak but plain to see and strong as that of the second man. I couldn't bring myself to do so because I was afraid. For the second time since I'd seen the omen concerning Father in the mirror, I was afraid of it.

With morning, all fears left me. Joel and I visited the church to inspect it and decide what must be done. Looking at it through a stranger's eyes, I was appalled at its condition. Joel gave no thought to what this was going to cost. We visited with Father Burke and got the benefit of his advice plus his approval, then we drove to the largest nearby town to make arrangements about paint, lumber, a new rope for the bell and, by sheer coincidence, we learned of another church that was being dismantled about a day's drive away. The next day Joel drove there alone because he would have to remain overnight. When he returned, he refused to say what he'd done, but I knew there was a great amount of activity at the church and, at Sunday Mass I could see that much of the work had been started. He still refused to give me a hint of what was really to come about.

We spent our days in long talks, in planning, in

giving voice to our hopes and ambitions. We often went down to the beach, and I thought Joel was doing his best to take me there often so that I might lose some of the fear I had within me since I saw the prophecy in the mirror.

It was too cold for swimming or even boating, but we did dare to wade into the water a bit and retreat with shouts of pretended agony at the cold and the dread of getting our clothes soaked. Otherwise we were content to walk about, enjoying the warmth of the afternoon sun, to lie on the sand or on the grassy slope. Twice I filled food baskets to be enjoyed, and twice we brought baskets to Grania Keohane so she might get to know him.

They got along splendidly. Joel was, by nature, a warm and loving man with a great deal of charm, which enthralled the old woman and put her at ease immediately. Later, I learned Joel visited her alone several times to tell her stories of life in America and to bring her small gifts and listen respectfully to her sage advice.

I, too, visited her alone one afternoon when Joel was busy at the church. It came to me that I wanted to see her and in the midst of cleaning my room, I suddenly stopped and changed my dress to pack a basket and hurry down to her cabin.

"Sit down beside me, Maeve," she said. "Why were you so slow in coming?"

"Grania, what do you mean? If you sent for me, no messenger came."

"Since when did I have need of a messenger?" she asked.

"So that was it! Somehow you made me understand you wished to see me."

"I can reach those who love me well, as you do. I have the wish to talk to you about your young man."

"I know you like him, Grania."

"Aye, that I do. Too much, for there hangs over

76

him a cloud. Not yet black, but deep enough that it means trouble for him. Trouble and danger. There are those who hate him because he has defied them."

"You have second sight," I said, thinking of what he'd revealed about his family.

"He will not heed a warning coming from an old woman like me. But he will heed you because he loves you truly and well. So make him understand that he must be on guard. That he must not trust anyone, especially those close to him. The danger is not far off. Warn him, Maeve. Be on guard yourself. For his sake and the love he bears you."

I could feel the cold chill of fear. "I will that, Grania. Do you foresee the final outcome?"

"Not even a small part of it. But I have a feeling that if he overcomes this danger that now is nearby, then the danger will be over. That is the feeling I get."

"Could it be Cathal Dolan, Grania?"

"I cannot say, only that it is close."

"Thank you, Grania. I'll leave you now and find Joel, to stay with him as much as possible. After we are married, I will not leave his side again until you tell me the danger is past."

"Ask your sainted father to come for me so that I may attend your wedding. These months I have found little reason to leave my cottage, but I would not miss that."

I kissed her wrinkled cheek. "You will have the front pew, and I will favor you above all others save my husband and my father."

I left her and walked straight down to the end of the street and the church, where several men were at work on the roof and the steeple. I hadn't quite reached it when Joel came out to greet me. He turned me around in the direction I'd come.

"You'll see the results on the day of your wedding," he said. "It's one of my ways to insure your not

77

backing out. Come on, it's a fine afternoon. Let's go down to the beach."

His carefree joy infected me to the extent that I forgot Grania's warning and my decision to all but keep him under lock and key until our wedding. It was a fine day, no harm could come to him on the beach, and I needed something to buoy my spirits after my talk with Grania. Hand in hand we walked briskly to the path which led us to the hill and down its slope to the shore and the sandy beach. There was no one about. A more peaceful spot I could not imagine, nor a safer one. Nobody could come close to us without revealing himself.

"You looked upset when we met," he said. "Was something bothering you, Maeve?"

"Only that you keep me away from the church. How do you know I approve of what's being done? And you have just about every man in the village working there."

"That reminds me. After the wedding we shall arrange the biggest and best banquet the village has ever seen. I shall want all kinds of roasted meat, vegetables, fruits, puddings, whatever you can get. Whatever is difficult to get, leave to me—and the procuring of the liquid refreshments. It may be that we shall not be well-remembered, nor kindly, the morning after, but we shall be remembered. At least, until the hangovers subside."

I had removed my shoes and stockings and carried them while I kicked up the sand with my bare feet. I did venture into the edges of the water, but only once. It seemed deathly cold and made me shiver. I quickly ran back to the warmth of the sun-drenched sand and took Joel's arm as we moved along, blithely occupied with our own thoughts, our minds busy and our tongues quiet.

Two things happened simultaneously and without warning. We heard the crack of a gunshot, and we saw the sand give a spurt about two feet in front of us. Joel seized my hand and tugged at it until we were both running a zigzag course across the sand toward the hill where there was brush. When we reached it, he pulled me down beside him, and we crawled a few yards before we came to a breathless stop.

"That was a shot," Joel managed at last. "It wasn't meant to miss, and it didn't by very much."

I lay in his arms shivering again, this time not from the chill of the ocean, but with a spine-tingling terror.

"Whoever fired it must have been well up on the hillside and hidden by the same kind of brush that hides us now," Joel said. "It was a rifle, for a revolver wouldn't carry that far. What of this man Cathal? Does he have such a weapon?"

"All the men have guns," I whispered. "I know very little about them, but they hunt much of the time. Some of them all of the time. Joel, could it have been a shot fired at some animal and came close to us by accident?"

"That's what you're hoping, and I don't blame you. But look about you, Maeve. The hillside is mostly cleared space except for these few bushes. Wild animals would hardly graze on open land so close to the village. If they have been hunted, they'd stay well clear of people and houses and they'd trust more to deep brush and the forests than to open hillside like this. I doubt it was an accident, though I hope it might be, just as you do. If it was, whoever fired it may come forward and admit it. But that's the only way I'll believe it was not intentional."

"Joel, why would someone wish to kill us?"

"Cathal might. I have heard of his ungovernable temper and his thick-headedness which might make him incapable of forgiveness. I want you to stay here. Don't show yourself. If there is any more shooting, don't move. Promise, Maeve?"

"Aye—so long as you are not hurt."

"Even that—stay here where you cannot be seen. I don't think the man with the gun would dare remain close by. The shot might have been heard by someone in the village. Remember—don't move from this spot."

Before I could reply, Joel crawled out from behind the bush and stood up. He faced the hillside, scanning it intently. Nothing happened. He glanced my way and gave a nod of assurance to indicate all was well, but that I was still not to move. Then he went loping down the hillside to the beach. I turned cautiously to watch him. He reached the spot where we'd been when the shot was fired at us. I could see a gouge in the damp sand where we'd turned to run, and it seemed to me that Joel had dug his heels deeply to mark the spot. He bent double now, looking at the beach. After each step he would pause, reach down, and let sand sift through his fingers.

He also kept a careful watch on the hillside, but it was evident now that the person with the gun had not remained long after firing the shot. I disobeyed orders because I could no longer endure just sitting there. Besides, like Joel, I believed the danger had passed.

When I appeared, he raised one hand in signal that it was safe for me to join him, so I broke into a run. The dry grass and frequent stones hurt my feet, and I suddenly realized I was still barefoot and I'd left my shoes and stockings beneath the bush which had been our hiding place.

Joel had found what he was looking for. In the palm of his hand he held a bullet. It was still originally shaped for it had struck nothing too solid and had not been distorted by the impact with only sand.

"It's probably from a Winchester," Joel said. "I know about guns. A modern weapon, I would say. The bullet was fired from far up the slope, and it had lost so much velocity by the time it hit the sand that it wasn't flattened or greatly damaged."

"Would it have been too far to have harmed us?"

"No. It could have killed one of us. Where does Cathal live?"

"Close by his farm. In a shanty. Not much more than that."

"I want you to lead me there. At once. If he fired at us, we may find the gun and I can tell if it was used recently. So we won't stand here and try to guess who tried to kill us, but do our best to find out who, without wasting any time about it."

"My shoes and stockings . . ." I said. "I must get them. . . ."

"Get them. Be quick about it, for we've little time to lose. If Cathal was responsible for this, I want to know it so I can take steps to see it never happens again. If he did not fire the shot, then at least we'll know it came from someone outside the village, and I can go on from there."

I returned to the spot and managed to get my shoes and stockings on before he caught up with me. We hastened to the path and walked along it until we reached the dirt road that led to Cathal's farm.

"He raises barley, mostly," I explained, "and he keeps a few sheep. I'll not say he isn't a hard worker, but his ambitions do not rise above a few acres."

We reached the summit of a slope at the bottom of which Cathal's farm spread before our view. Close to us was his shanty, and we could see Cathal far out in the fields, raising dust as his plow cut the earth where he was preparing land for winter planting.

We came to the shanty, and Joel pushed open the door to walk in. I remained just outside, keeping an eye on Cathal in case he saw us, but he kept on with his plowing, unaware that anyone was watching him or had invaded his home.

Joel appeared with a gun. A huge sort of thing

which he examined briefly. "This is the only weapon in the place, and it didn't fire the bullet I have in my pocket. This is an old gun, and the cartridge wouldn't have fitted. So unless Cathal has another weapon hidden somewhere, we can be quite sure he was not responsible for what happened."

"Shall we call him and talk to him, Joel?"

"I don't think so. If he does have another gun, he'd deny it. This way we'll give him a little more rope. Let's go home. And listen to me—referring to your house as if it's already my home."

"It is, darling. It has been from the first time we met. Oh, Joel, I wish everything could have been peaceful. I'll worry about you now."

"No need for that. I'm warned, and I'll be careful. You might ask if any strangers appeared in the village, even for a very brief time. I'll see if anyone else saw Cathal in the fields. I want to eliminate him if I can, because he'd be the most dangerous, for he can move openly. A stranger, less familiar with the area, would be handicapped."

In the village we parted. I visited a few friends and stopped at the market, and I asked about strangers, but no one had seen a new face. I felt satisfied that if a stranger had arrived, he'd not shown himself, but circled the village and probably escaped without anyone seeing him come or go.

Joel learned nothing except that all doubted Cathal had any other gun than the ancient one left him by his father. So far as they knew, there were no new Winchesters in the village. They were a very expensive weapon, and no one had the money to spend on one.

The proof of Cathal's innocence came later when Father returned from a call outside the village. He listened to our story in amazement and horror, but he absolved Cathal. "I passed his farm going and coming, about half an hour apart. He was there both times. The way you tell it, to have fired the shot he would have had to be absent from the fields when I went by. Besides, he has no such gun. He wouldn't know how to use it if he had. And there is one more thing."

"What could that be?" I asked. "There are already too many things."

"That old gun you inspected, Joel, It's been in Cathal's family for many years. If he fired that thing at you—you'd be dead. Cathal never misses with that gun. I would say he had nothing to do with it, and I have no idea who could have been responsible, or why such a thing would happen."

"It was an accident, then," I said. "A hunter from some nearby city perhaps. He saw what he had done and fled. By chance no one saw him, and he was not about to reveal himself as an idiot who didn't look in the direction where he was shooting."

"I guess you're right," Joel admitted. "It has to be something like that. So let's stop talking about it and worrying about it. We've other things to occupy our minds. Like getting married day after tomorrow."

"You will kindly not call on me tomorrow, then, nor on the day of the wedding. I'll be busy with my gown and veil, and our best village seamstresses are coming to help. It is not good for a man to see his bride in her wedding gown until he stands waiting for her in the church. But Joel, darling, be careful and take good care of yourself. I am inclined to forget the rules about not letting you see me before the wedding. After what happened—"

"We agreed it was accidental," Joel said. "We agreed to forget it, and we should. I'll not come near you until you come to me before the altar. So this will be your final kiss as a single woman, and see that it lasts you."

He held me a long time and I clung to him, not wishing to let him go. But finally he shook hands with Father and went his way down the street to Mrs.

83

Halloran's where he would spend this night and one more before he came here to live.

"Tell me," Father asked, "do you think it was an accident, Maeve?"

"No, Father. I do not, but I have no idea who was responsible or the why of it."

FOUR

I could not rid myself of the dreadful feeling that Joel was in mortal danger. Not until the seamstresses arrived and matters grew so hectic did my worry abate. Their chatter and gossip served to calm me, and my thoughts turned to my wedding.

The gown had been my mother's, and little adjustment was needed, but a new veil had to be made, for hers had yellowed and given way to the ravages of time. And, of course, the women had to fuss with every detail, no matter how minor, until they were almost satisfied, an hour before the wedding, that they could be proud of their work.

Father, seeing me for the first time in the gown which brought back so many endearing memories, restrained his tears with an effort as he took me in his arms.

"You're as beautiful as she was, darling. It makes me young again to look upon you. Joel will have a right to be proud and happy."

"Have you seen him? Is he all right?" I asked.

"He's fine. The boys gave him a party last night. Wisely, he took it easy, so he'll stand without swaying this morning, which is more than some of the others will. And by lot, his best man was chosen, for Joel wasn't here long enough to establish any special friends. It turned out to be Mike Cullane, who said he didn't think the honor was worth it because they refused him drink last night so he, too, would stand straight. Of course he didn't mean it; the man is proud as a peacock. But as far as I know, you have not chosen a bridesmaid, darling."

"I chose her long ago, Father. Even she doesn't know it yet. You will please me to fetch Grania to the church, and she will stand by my side. Can you think of anyone better fit to stand with me?"

"It will be different, at least, and Grania will be overcome with happiness. Yes, it's a grand idea you have come upon. I'm all for it."

Father had a fine carriage for me, and we rode the brief distance to the church. When I entered, I came to a halt in sheer surprise. It was almost a different church. Everything looked new, it was that freshly painted and decorated. There were stained glass windows above and on each side of the altar. They were second-hand, but nevertheless new to us and very fine. The notes of a new organ resounded for the first time in my honor, for the wheezy one had been retired. It would take some visits to the church to see all the renovations, but those I noted now certainly lent an unexpected splendor to my wedding.

Joel came to me, straight and tall and wonderful to behold. I made my responses and I accepted his kiss eagerly and with all of the warmth within me. My happiness was marred only by the sight of tears in my father's eyes, but then, what Irishman isn't that sentimental? They were tears of happiness, and I could accept them along with his warm embrace.

The rest of the day was chaotic, what with everyone in the village congratulating us over and over again while the feasting and the dancing went on.

85

Finally, Joel and I managed to slip away. Father had the carriage waiting, and we were off for the long ride to Galway.

It was a goodly distance and not so close we could reach it without stopping for the night at a lovely little inn where, without my knowledge, Joel had arranged our stay.

He saw to the care of the horse while the buxom, smiling woman who kept the inn escorted me to our room. By the time Joel returned, a table had been set up and plain, country food was brought in so we might dine in private.

Joel dragged the table out of the room and into the corridor after we had eaten, though neither of us boasted a great appetite. Finally Joel held me in his arms, and we regarded one another with something akin to awe at the wonder of it all until his kiss put an end to our silence.

"It's beyond me," he said, "a man who had never had a thought of marriage, and now I have the loveliest and most wonderful wife in the world."

"What of me?" I asked. My arms were still clasped around his neck. "I have a man I can love dearly for the rest of my life, and while I never did believe in what the old ones say—that something of this nature must be the luck of the Irish—I am now coming to believe it."

"But I have so little to offer, Maeve. I'm a bitter man, once a lonely man, for I had only a family I am close to despising because of their greed and thoughtlessness. I was consigned to roam the earth looking for something I couldn't describe, and suddenly you were there and everything changed."

"Aye, my love," I said softly. "It changed for me as well."

"I've no job, no training for one."

"What does it matter? You'll find yourself."

He drew me closer. "I've found you, Maeve. That

was the beginning of a new life for me. I want to stay here with you the rest of my days. I'll find something."

"You do ramble," I said with a smile. "Must we consider the future when the present is so sweet and lovely?"

"I was but trying to explain—"

"I am married to a man I adore, and there is nothing to explain. At this moment we have one another, and what is more important than that, Joel, my love?"

"You will be happy," he said. "I'll see to that."

"But I am happy. This is the greatest day of my life."

"I will love you always," he said. "But you will have to teach me, Maeve, for I grew up in a house without love."

I brushed his lips with mine. "There will be love in your family from here on," I vowed. "Your new family."

He kissed me then with a passion I'd been waiting for, and we remained in one another's arms for a long, long time. He was gentle and kind, as I knew he would be. I slept in the comfort of his arms that night, and I knew my life was now complete.

We finished the drive to Galway next day and stayed there for four delightful days. Galway was big enough, and rich enough, to have a few good stores where I learned what it was like to be able to spend whatever I wished and buy anything my fancy desired. At Joel's insistence I bought presents for Father and Grania and Father Burke. And yet, with all the excitement, I was glad when we began the journey home. I missed the village and my old friends, and I missed Father most of all.

We discovered that he had changed the house somewhat, giving up the large bedroom he'd shared with my mother and taking my smaller room for himself. As there was no arguing the matter, we gratefully accepted the change.

So Joel and I settled down for what we hoped would be a long and happy life. The first night we were home, Father made a ceremony of showing Joel the Celtic torc for the first time.

"I keep it in a bank vault," he explained, "for it is too valuable and too precious to me to keep in the house. It will be Maeve's now, and then her children's."

Joel examined the heavy twist of gold, turning it over in his hands.

"Whatever happens," Joel said solemnly, "I promise that the torc will receive as good care as you and all your ancestors have provided it."

"That's good enough for me." Father reverently put the torc back in its case. "Tomorrow it goes to the bank. I have already made arrangements that you and Maeve have access to the vault. And now, what may your plans be?"

"I thought I'd ride with you and discover for myself whether I would like to follow in your steps," Joel said. "That way I can learn much even before I begin my formal studies, if I decide to do so."

"And you, Maeve, do you approve of this?" Father asked.

"I do," I said. "It is a grand idea."

"Then it shall be done," Father promised. "And a proud man I'll be if my son-in-law does finally take over my practice. And I may add, the village gratefully speaks of the magnificent banquet you gave the day of your wedding and your generosity in renovating the church. There will be no problem of your acceptance in this village, man."

"I'm gratified to hear that," Joel said. "Though it was not my intention to buy this acceptance."

"And what of you, Maeve?" Father asked.

"What of me? With two men now to do for! And a family to raise! What of me? Oh, I shall be the grand lady of the manor house. I shall give lawn parties and high teas and have royalty here now and then when I am in the mood to put up with them. Perhaps I shall raise fine horses to enter in the Grand National. Oh, I shall manage to keep busy. What of me? What a question!"

But as the winter weeks went by, there was no beginning of a family, and Father, I knew, was growing worried. He and Joel had become familiar figures riding the countryside, and Joel had taken to the study of medicine in a great way. He planned to ride one more year until he had the fundamentals well learned and then he would enter medical school, perhaps in Edinburgh where Jimmy was still studying that hard he never even came for the wedding. It wouldn't be easy for me, separated from Joel, but I could see the wisdom of his move. A man couldn't go through life idling his time away.

It was a wonderful time, that winter. We were snug against the cold. I gave suppers for a few people, we had Grania over a few times, and I visited her every three or four days. She was beginning to fail, but Father believed she'd see a hundred before she left us, and I was beginning to agree with him.

Most nights Joel studied medical books. On nice days we roamed the beach, fighting the biting wind and romping about as we'd done before we married.

In all this time I'd not looked in the mirror once. Joel never mentioned it. I had an idea that while it mystified him, he couldn't bring himself to thoroughly believe in it and he had likely lost interest. I took care not to bring it up.

Joel had become quite expert in setting broken bones, removing casts, and setting new ones so that Father allowed him to handle some of this tedious work. It came about that Father was called very early this late winter morning, to attend a small boy who had symptoms of a bad appendix, which meant

89

he would have to operate then and there, on the kitchen table. And, at the same time, a call came from old Mike Shanahan that the broken leg which had been in a cast for many days now was beginning to ache severely, which meant there could be an infection. Not an impossible thing, for Mike, broken leg or not, hobbled about on crutches, doing stable and henhouse work where infection was easily able to reach him.

"Joel, take Maeve along with you," Father said, as he packed his bag with surgical instruments. "My patient can't wait, and it may take some time with him. Neither can old Mike wait, especially if there is an infection. Maeve knows how to clear it up if there is one, and you know how to handle the cast. So off with you, and we'll meet back here later in the day and compare notes. This is one time I'm glad you decided to study medicine, Joel, and that I taught Maeve how to care for wounds and infections."

We had a carriage besides the buggy now, and Joel and I used it. We drove the four miles out of the village and found old Mike badly off. His leg was swollen and growing red above the cast, which now fit too snugly because the leg had ballooned from the infection. Joel cut off the cast to expose the wound Father had created to get at the slivered bones and the bad break.

I bathed the wound with an antiseptic fluid and snipped away dead flesh, paying no attention to Mike's howls of pain. When I was satisfied the wound was clean, I bandaged it, but we decided it could not be placed in a cast until we were sure all the infection had been cleared up.

"We'll come back in two days," Joel told Mike. "Meantime, you stay off the leg."

"And stay in the house," I ordered. "You could die of this, Michael Shanahan. If it becomes red and swollen again, there will be little we can do for you."

"Aye, but who takes care of things, eh? You go

tell me cows I can't milk them, and tell me chickens they can't be fed."

"Last I saw," I said tartly, "was your wife at work in the stable. And as I recall, those chores you been telling us about were done by her anyway. If we have to come back before two days are up, we'll charge you double."

We left him and climbed into the carriage. The wind had come up and the sky turned black. We were too far inland from the sea at this point to hear the waves, but I knew they'd be running high.

"That'll get him to behave," I said. "Telling him we'll charge double."

Joel laughed softly. "How much is double of nothing, Maeve? But I suspect he'll obey orders. Do you think we should drive over to the house of the lad your father is tending?"

"He'll have gone by now if it was an operation," I said. "We were longer than you think with Mike. That was a dreadful infection he had. The poor man. But he'll feel better now. We'd best go straight home, I'm thinking."

We reached the house in early afternoon. Before we came to the village, the road skirted a hill overlooking the bay, and we could see the wildness of the water.

"It's a late winter storm," I explained. "I've always thought they were the worst of all. I hope nobody's out there. Those waves can swamp almost anything."

"They're high, all right," Joel admitted. "We have storms on the Maine coast, too, but not usually as severe as this."

I didn't answer him. I didn't speak for a long time. My mind was on the mirror and the roaring water I'd seen in it when I thought of Father. When we reached the house, I got down off the carriage before it fully stopped and I hurried into the house, calling him as the door closed behind me.

There was no answer. I ran upstairs, but there was no sign of him. I looked in his office. His instrument and medicine satchels were not there. True, he'd taken them when he left early in the morning, but he should have finished that case by now.

I heard the door open and close, and I ran to the hallway, but it was only Joel. "Father's not here," I said. "He's nowhere about."

"Maeve, you're worrying without reason. If he operated on that boy, something could have gone wrong—"

"Take me to the boy's house. I have to know."

"Maeve, what's gotten into you? We've come home a hundred times and he's not been here."

"It's the storm . . . and the mirror. Don't you remember? Quickly, Joel! Oh, don't fail me now. Take me to the boy's home. I'll show you how to get there."

"Come, then," Joel said, and we fled to where he'd left the carriage. He used the whip, something he never did, and we reached the house in fifteen minutes. I ran to the door and pounded on it.

A tired-looking woman opened the door. "Oh, it's you, Maeve. Well, if your father sent you, my son is doing all right. Sleeping like a babe he is, and himself is sittin' by the side of the bed watchin' him as he was ordered to do. Your father cut the lad open, but he's all of one piece again, thank God."

"When did my father leave?" I asked. "How long ago?"

"Oh, that was not long after he finished here. He wasn't intendin' to leave, but they came and told him there was a ship in the bay and a man bad hurt. . . ."

"Were they going to bring the injured man ashore?"

"He was that bad hurt they couldn't take him in a boat through this awful storm, so your father was being rowed out to the big craft. That he was."

I closed my eyes and turned away.

"You'll be wantin' to see the lad, Maeve?"

I said, "Oh, yes. Yes, I'd best look at him."

Hardly knowing what I was doing, I went into the house. The boy was sleeping quietly. The house smelled of ether and antiseptics, but the boy breathed well, and when I felt his pulse, it was steady and good. His forehead was cool.

"He is doing well," I told his father.

"Aye, lass, and it is thanks to your father that he is."

"Watch him now," I said. "Feel his face, and if it gets hot and sweaty, send someone to me. And don't let him get up for at least three days. Give him only liquid food, and not much of that."

"Aye, your father also told me these things. He's gone out to sea, and I don't like the look of it from what I saw an hour ago. It's gettin' worse instead of better, that it is, and I'll be prayin' he comes back safe and sound."

"Thank you," I said.

I hurried to the carriage where Joel was waiting. I climbed onto the seat beside him and pressed my face against his shoulder. "He's out there, in the storm. A seaman was hurt and couldn't be moved, so they asked Father to go out, and they rowed him. Likely in a *currach*, which will pitch like a cork in such a storm. Oh, Joel, my heart is heavy with fear. If the mirror is right—and it always is—Father will not come back to us. I have this premonition."

"Maeve, until you know differently, your father is safe and sound. If he was taken out to a ship, it was by men who know the sea."

"You will see. Aye, you will see. Drive down to the hillside overlooking the dock, and we will sit there and wait. I know for what. I know what is going to happen. I have known it for months and feared it. Now it is here, and my fear is that great I am numb. When we are waiting, hold me very tight, but do not put off my thoughts by telling me encouraging

93

ones, because it is too late for that. Too late, Joel. The mirror has never failed. It is Father's time."

"Did he know of the prophecy?" Joel asked. "Did you finally warn him?"

"I had no heart to tell him. Would you care to hear the prophecy of your own death?"

"He might not have gone. . . ."

"He would have gone, and laughed at the prophecy because he was needed out there. Aye, he'd have gone if he'd seen what the mirror portended himself."

We reached the hill above the little dock, and Joel pulled up. The waves were lashing the dock and the shore, sweeping across the sand where we used to romp and play, reaching up for the hillside grasses as if to slake its appetite with them. The roaring and crashing was a frightful din and made talking difficult unless we shouted

A full hour went by. I was freezing with chill even though Joel had wrapped his own coat about me and held me tightly against him. I never took my eyes off the little dock. If they came back, that's where the *currach* would head. A fragile thing to venture into a storm like this and yet, when a man's life was at stake, Father and anyone in the village would have risked it.

It was dark as early evening set in, and the storm was howling as if in triumph when we first caught sight of the little craft, rising and falling with the waves. It was tossed like a small cork and yet it was fighting its way toward the shore.

I leaped from the carriage and ran down toward the dock. The craft came alongside finally. A man leaped to the dock and saw me coming his way. He advanced toward me and took my arm, forcibly turning me back. Joel, who had stopped to tie the horse, reached us.

"Maeve, darlin'," the man from the boat said. "It is not for you to see as they take him off. Joel, it would be well if you took Maeve home. We will bring your father there, never fear."

"He is gone, then?" I asked.

"Aye. He saved a man's life, but as we were on our way back, he slipped out of the *currach*. We tried to get a hold on him, but it was done so fast we could not reach him and he disappeared under those waves so he could not be found until . . . there was nothing to be done. We found him. Heaven's the richer this day, we the poorer."

Joel took my arm firmly. "Come, Maeve. Let them do what has to be done."

I said, "I will wait at the carriage until they bring him past me. I will have it that way, Joel."

"If that is your wish."

Joel led me to the carriage and helped me onto the seat where I sat huddled, shivering and quietly sobbing until he told me, hoarsely, that they were coming.

Men from the village had been sent for, and there were more than a score of them. Someone had found a wide plank and, as was the custom, Father's body had been placed on it and the plank raised to the shoulders of all the men who could fit beneath it. They began their slow march to the house.

More and more villagers braved the storm. Women were weeping, and there was a keening that broke my heart. I got down off the carriage and stood beside Joel as Father was carried by me. No one looked my way.

I said, plainly and loudly, *"Beidh a cuid fein ag an fharraig."*

"What did you say?" Joel asked.

"It's Gaelic," I said. " 'The sea will claim its own.' The words have been said for a thousand years, and for a thousand years men have died in the sea. Take me home now."

They carried him into the house and laid him on

his own bed. They prepared him that night while Joel sent for a suitable coffin, and next morning we held his wake. The house was filled until morning, and the wails of the keening women became nerve-wracking until I was compelled, by Joel, to rest and finally managed to sleep.

At the funeral, the church was filled and the street outside lined with mourners. Then Father was carried to the cemetery where he was no doubt welcomed by my mother's spirit and laid to rest beside her. Staring over the raw earth of his grave, I could look down the slope at the sea, which had finally grown calm.

Joel and I went home. The house where I'd been born, and which had given me so much joy, seemed empty and forlorn. Someone had laid a fresh fire and lighted it so the parlor was warm. I removed my coat, hat, and veil. Joel left me for a few minutes and made a pot of tea.

We sat before the fireplace, not speaking, sipping the tea, and my thoughts were with Father and the years I'd been that lucky to have him. I finally gave a great sigh and turned to Joel with my head raised once more.

"We have plans to make, my love. And the first one is to find a doctor to take Father's place. The village is in need of one."

"I know, but it won't be easy," Joel said. "Doctors don't like to work for nothing. If I can persuade someone to come here, I'll promise him a certain sum, but even so . . . it's going to be hard."

"Between us, we can do what we can for them, until someone does come."

"Of course we'll do that. What of us, then? After one arrives. Will you wish to remain here?"

"It's my home," I said, surprised that he'd even ask.

"True enough, but if I enter medical school, will you come to the city with me?"

"Yes, Joel, for we'll be coming back one day, and then Father's place will be well filled and he'll be at rest. Oh, yes, I'll go with you."

"I'll look into it on my next trip to Dublin."

"I will not go there with you," I said. "You have never asked me, and it is personal business, I know. I have no wish to interfere."

"It is not more than sending and receiving a great many cables. Going to a bank, sometimes arguing a few points that do not satisfy me. I do not intend to be cheated, and it is not above my uncle to cheat."

"He comes there?"

"Oh, no. I don't think he'd spend the money. He sends cables, and when I go to my hotel, I always find a batch of letters that tell me what a fool I am. I have never answered one of them."

"We will have to explain to everyone that we are not doctors and only hope to do the best we can. Grave illnesses must be treated elsewhere. The nearest town with a doctor is forty miles to the north. I don't like that, Joel. Sick people could die during such a trip."

"We'll do what we can to find another doctor," Joel promised. "I'll be going to Dublin in four days and I'll arrange to have advertisements placed in all the newspapers and in any medical papers I can discover. Perhaps by the time I come back I'll have someone."

"It will be a miracle," I said. "But you must try, anyway. Joel, would you gather up Father's things and see that they go to those who are in need? I'll pack a basket and go see Grania. She will be grieving terribly."

I had this strange feeling that I must go to her, as if some message was reaching me and I must obey it. I filled a large basket, and when I left, I could

97

hear Joel up in Father's bedroom emptying the clothes closet. I had dreaded that task.

I walked swiftly down the street, my shawl over my head, masking my face against the chill. The basket was heavy on my arm, and I walked fast.

Grania, looking thinner and older than I had ever seen her, sat huddled before the turf fire, looking as if she couldn't get enough heat. She lowered the black shawl over her thinning hair and swayed slightly from side to side as she spoke.

"It is done with, the damned prophecy," she said. "Have you looked in that cursed mirror these last days, Maeve darling?"

"I have not had the heart or the courage, Grania." I set about heating a pan of chicken-barley soup. I had the thought this poor soul had not eaten in some time.

"Look then, child, for I have an evil feeling that the end is not yet come to us."

I looked up from the soup kettle over the fireplace flames. "Grania, do you have an omen that Joel will also be taken from me?"

"It has come to me that there will be trouble. I cannot say what, but it might be the mirror will tell the rest of it."

I shook my head. "I will not look, Grania. I will, instead, guard Joel as the most precious thing in my life, for that he is."

"Aye, that he is." She stared into the fire for a long moment. "Once I could foretell things and in my mind see them clearly, but everything grows dim these last days of my life. I have little time left."

"Father said you would reach a hundred, Grania," I said. I dished up the soup in a large bowl and placed it before her.

"Were he alive, perhaps that might be, but now with him gone from us—rest his soul—I think my time is short. That is why I called you to me."

I sat down beside her while she ate. "What is it you wish to tell me, Grania? Old you may be, but the years have not weakened your wisdom, only made it all the better. And I will have no more of this foolish talk that you haven't much longer."

"Travail, it's that you will have. Great travail. I have known this since you were a wee girl. You must have the strength to face it, child. When you think you can no longer bear it, that is when you must remember what I say now. Face it and grow angry. Defy those who try to destroy you and have patience with those who love you, and those who should love you, yet who do not. For sorrow and anger and travail will all pass, because love is stronger than all of them combined. You will not believe this. Many times you will not believe in it, but in the end you will find it is true."

"I'll remember, Grania," I said. "I have never been weak by nature, and I am not now. Whatever is in store for me I can face, and I can fight those who defy me. And fight I will. Have you no inkling who it may be that will try to destroy me?"

"My powers grow weaker and weaker. What I have told you came to me when my powers were stronger. Now there is little left, and I can no longer help you. It is time to go back now. Pour me the rest of the soup and be on your way."

I refilled her bowl. "Tomorrow I'll be back with more, Grania."

"Aye," she said. Her thin arms reached up to embrace me, and I kissed her cheek. She seemed to hold me in that weak embrace for a longer time than usual, though I thought nothing of it then.

I banked the fire and brought in a basket of turf for the night. Then I started for home, but on an impulse I detoured to the hillside where Father rested.

I knelt in prayer until a certain peace came to me,

then rose and walked slowly away. Joel awaited me, and Joel was my love. I began walking faster.

Joel and I settled down then to reorganize our lives without Father. Villagers and those from outlying farms came as usual for medicines and treatment just as if Father was still alive. And we were that needed we did what we could for them, until finally Joel knew something had to be done. He had advertised in Dublin papers and in Galway without getting a single reply. It was now time for him to make one of his regular trips to Dublin, and he asked me to go with him.

I didn't like Dublin. It was too English for me. The hotel was too fancy and the stores so big I found it hard to make up my mind about my purchases, though Joel insisted I make an unholy number of them, spending money in sums unheard-of for me.

Joel's business required considerable time on his part, and he received a number of letters and cables when we arrived. After he answered by cable, more came. There seemed to be legal matters that required settling, and Joel was arguing certain points which made little sense to me when he tried to explain.

We ate our meals in opulent restaurants where, in my finest, I attracted approving male eyes and not so friendly female stares, all of which delighted Joel and gave me a certain amount of pleasure once I grew used to it. I knew also that in the dresses I wore at home, I would not have been allowed past the velvet rope blocking the restaurant entrance.

In our two-room hotel suite, Joel told me some of the trouble he had with the business, one-third of which he controlled.

"There's been a presidential election," he said, "and a man named Grover Cleveland was elected. My father and my uncle think he's against business and may take some kind of action to increase wages paid

100

to employees. That scared Papa to death and he wants to start a lobby to influence Congress. . . ."

"I cannot follow you, my love," I said. "Your kind of government is beyond me. Why shouldn't a man be paid fair wages if he earns them?"

"I would like to be close by when you said that to my family." Joel's smile was cynical. "They would disown you on the spot."

"I have a feeling they have already disowned me. Never one letter or even postcard did we receive at our wedding, nor even the smallest gift or remembrance."

"I'm sorry, darling Maeve. They are like that. Thank heaven, somewhere in our family there was a man who had a warm heart and the trait passed on to me. I will now compose a long cable, an expensive one, and send it collect to the factory. I will object to any attempt on our part to influence our lawmakers one way or the other. Then we'll begin packing, and in the morning we'll go home before the answer comes. I don't want to read it."

"Ah," I said with closed eyes, "those are the words blessed by heaven and which I have been aching to hear. I will not come again when you must visit Dublin. Unless I am sorely needed."

"Well, at least you know what it's like and what I have to do here. The business of banking and dealing in business by letter and cable is boring. I fancy Dublin no more than you do."

Nothing looked so beautiful as Kilcrea sprawled out by the sea. We came within sight of the little village, and even Joel gave a great sigh of pleasure.

"After we bring the luggage into the house, I will visit Father," I said. "And then bring Grania her gifts."

"Be sure not to spend too much time, my girl," he said in mock seriousness. "A man's starved after a journey like that, and I long for ham and potatoes

101

and cabbage. Mayo is no poor county when it can provide food like that."

I made my way to the cemetery without changing clothes. So I was still dressed for the city and for traveling in a plain, tailor-made skirt and a blouse of white muslin, warm and serviceable.

As I came into view of the grave, I saw a man kneeling at the foot of it. Sudden fear struck at me. This man was a stranger. The cut of his clothes proved that. He must have heard me gasp, for he arose quickly and turned around. He was a broth of a man, broad and tall, with fiery red hair and lots of it. His face was covered by an equally red beard, and slowly his arms arose toward me.

"Jimmy!" I cried out. "Oh, it's really you, Jimmy!"

I ran to him to be hugged in a great embrace that took the wind out of me, but it didn't matter. This was my brother. Except for Joel, he was all I had now.

"I came this morning," he said. "I found nobody home so I tramped the countryside, though I intended to stay at the house this night whether you and your Joel were there or not."

"We just came back from Dublin," I explained. "It was Joel's business sent us there."

"Dublin's a foul place to me. I'm sorry I could not be here for Father's funeral. But of course he was buried before I got word. You say you just came back. You have not talked to anyone in the village?"

"Not yet, Jimmy. You look so serious suddenly."

"To your left, behind the big tree. You can see part of the new grave. Grania is there."

I wept for her then. I held onto my brother and wept for an old lady I'd dearly loved. We went to her grave, and I knelt and prayed and berated myself for going away when she needed me most.

"The poor soul died in her sleep," Jimmy explained. "It was a fine way for her to go. You should not

102

grieve long. She would not have it, as I remember her."

"Oh, Jim, you're right. These things happen so fast. I'll be all right now. Come—and meet Joel. He's my beloved husband and a grand man. Without him I would now be lost."

"A good thing he came to you, Maeve. Father's letters said he was a rich American."

"He is that. We have more money than we know what to do with, but he uses it wisely and well. He will study to be a doctor, Jimmy. Like you. But then, not quite like you, for he only wishes to return to the village and take Father's place."

"That is more than I would ever do," Jimmy confessed. "I shall become an expensive surgeon and gain as much wealth as your Joel has. I will use it well, too, though perhaps not as wisely."

They met, these two men of mine. They were so different. My brother, bearded, shaggy-haired, muscular and huge. Joel, fair-haired, slight of build, and beside Jimmy looking almost boyish. But they became fast friends upon the shaking of hands.

"Aye," Jimmy said to me, "he's all you claim for him and more. I can see why Father approved. I welcome you, Joel Cameron."

"Thank you, Jimmy." Joel glanced at me. "I heard about Grania. I'm very sorry."

"Jimmy pointed out that she died quietly and that was a heaven-sent gift for her," I said. "I only regret that I was not here."

Jimmy said, "Unless you have an appetite for good burnished Irish whiskey and have drained the supply of it, I know where Father used to keep a goodly quantity of bottles, and it is time we should have a drink together, Joel, my lad. While my sister gets busy and makes our supper. I'm that starved I could eat it raw."

So while I might have grieved far more for Grania, Jimmy's homecoming kept me too busy for that. He ate with his usual enormous appetite. Then we discussed Father's legacy. There was no need of a will. What he left should have been shared between us, but Joel insisted that Jimmy accept it all, for he would need it to finish his schooling and set up in practice.

"I have more than enough for Maeve and me," Joel explained.

"I will have the house, however," I said.

"It is yours," Jimmy agreed. "I am that greedy enough already. You have my thanks, and if there comes a time when you require surgery, Joel, I shall perform it for half price. My sister, of course, pays full. Now for more of that whiskey."

"Take a supply back with you, Jimmy," I suggested. "There's enough down there for ten of us. Many of Father's fees will be going down your throat, but it's all good whiskey."

We stayed up half the night, for there was much to talk about. I finally went to bed, so tired I couldn't even think of missing Grania beyond a prayer shared between her and Father. Jimmy and Joel still stayed by the fire, talking and sipping their whiskey.

I was sorry when Jimmy went back to Scotland, but there was no help for it. While he was with us for two weeks, the sick people of the village never had better care, for Jimmy was a fine doctor even now, before he graduated. It was he who saved old Mike's leg, which had again become infected while Joel and I were gone. And he gave old Mike the tongue-lashing he deserved, though old Mike was inclined to blame Joel and me for the spread of the infection.

"You got out of bed, as they told you not to," Jim railed at him. "You went out into the fields and the barns, and you got the wound infected again. Mike, the third time this happens, Joel and Maeve will have to take your leg off. It's the only way they'll be able to save your life. So if you don't want to stand on a

104

wooden leg, then you do as I tell you and no mistake about it."

"I must see to me animals," Mike insisted.

"Then see to them and lose the leg," Jimmy said, and his red beard bristled with anger. "I have to tell you that neither Joel nor Maeve is a doctor and they cannot give you ether to put you to sleep while they cut off the leg. All they can do is give you a hard rap on the head so your screams won't disturb people all the way to Killarney. It's up to you."

Mike stayed in bed for almost a month, we learned later, and he never had any more trouble with the leg.

So we saw Jimmy off and we settled down again. Before long, Joel would have to make the journey to Dublin, and this time I would stay home. So far, there'd been no replies to our advertisements. Nobody wanted to take Father's place, and Joel and I struggled along doing our best, which was good enough to serve the purpose until some real emergency came along. We stood in dread of that day.

Joel left for Dublin in May, this time convinced that, one way or another, he would force the company and his relatives to handle their business with him closer to his home. He was tired of the trips to Dublin. Galway would have been far better, and much closer, and he had his heart set on it.

The first days of his absence were hard to endure. After Father's death, Joel had made it a point to remain with me as much as possible. We were rarely apart, and then for only an hour or two. So it required four whole days before I became accustomed to this big, empty house. I didn't even have Grania to visit. Her cottage stood shuttered and abandoned.

I received a letter from Joel on the sixth day, which helped, although it was more solemn than I liked and seemed to indicate that things were not going his way. There was no joy in the writing. He did say he'd be home on the usual day, and as that was only forty-eight hours away, I looked forward to it.

In preparation for his return, I did some routine shopping at the village store, buying vegetables and a supply of flour and meat. On my way home, I saw Cathal coming along the street. I was half tempted to avoid him, but I decided that would be childish. Cathal was an old friend, even if my marriage had angered him. He should be over it by now.

"Good afternoon to you, Cathal," I said.

" 'Tis never a good afternoon for me, nor a good morning or evening, and you well know it, Maeve." He glowered at me.

"Oh, come now, Cathal, it's over and done with. You could wish me happiness. I have been married a long time."

"May I remind you that I have not? There is no forgiveness in me, Maeve O'Hanlon. I am a stubborn man, and I spent half my life expecting you and me would wed. You betrayed the love I had for you, and one day you will pay for it. You and that lily-waisted man of yours who would have a hard time swatting a fly."

"Good day to you, Cathal Dolan," I said. "I will even make that a goodbye to you. Such a man as you are, I do not care to know."

I marched off, not looking back, and I seethed with anger at the stubbornness and stupidity of him. I went home and put away my purchases, but afterwards I had no heart for the cleaning and washing I had to do.

In my new-found worry, I thought of the mirror. It had been months since I'd looked in it, and while I dreaded what it might show me, I began to feel I must consult it. If it showed that harm might come to Joel, it would be safe to assume the harm would come from Cathal and we could take precautions against the man's anger.

I went upstairs and brought out the mirror in its

106

wrappings. I carried it to the front window and sat down beside it. I slowly unwrapped the mirror, but I placed it face down on my lap. I was torn between the desire to peer into it and the wish to put it back without looking. I recalled the last time, when the mirror showed me Joel's profile, which had been so plain before, as a faded image.

I turned the mirror around and held it up. I spoke aloud. "The prediction of my father's death has come true, like everything else this mirror has predicted. I ask it now, by the memory of Queen Maeve, whose ancestry I may claim, what is in store for my love? My beloved husband?"

I tilted the mirror toward the light. Nothing remained long as a reflection. There had been times when I wasn't even sure there had been an image, it was that fleeting, so I had to be ready to absorb what I saw quickly.

The profile of the man who had appeared behind that of Joel had taken firm shape. But of Joel there was no sign. So far as the mirror was concerned, he had vanished.

I turned the mirror face down again and wrapped it, angry at my weakness for looking, fearful of what I had seen, mainly because I didn't understand it. Joel had been there before, and now he was gone.

I returned the wrapped mirror to its place deep within the bureau drawer and resumed my chair near the window. Joel was no longer in the mirror because there was no need for him to be. He had come to me and fulfilled the prophecy which concerned him; therefore, the mirror had cast him out. That was the answer, logical and likely true. I felt a little better. Some of the uneasiness left me.

Yet I didn't sleep well that night nor the next, and I rode our carriage horse far down the road to meet Joel's buggy on its way home. While I waited, standing beside the horse, my worries began to return, and then I saw him. I mounted in a hurry and rode to greet him.

"You will have an escort back," I shouted to him when I was alongside.

"Thank you," he called back. "I am not accustomed to having beautiful girls meet me."

"You'd better not have it happen when I'm not around," I warned him. "How are you?"

"Tired," he said. "I'll explain when we get home. It's good to see you."

I nodded, waved, and rode on ahead so I might reach the house in time to have a drink of good whiskey to greet him. At least, I knew he was safe.

He came in to envelop me in his embrace and to kiss me with a hunger that left me both breathless and proud that I was a woman he longed to return home to.

We always made a little ceremony of his return with the dram of whiskey, and we raised the glasses now.

"*Slainte*," I said.

"In English, it's good to be home," he added his own toast. We drank, and then he brought the horse and buggy to the barn. Half an hour later, he was with me again, having put his luggage away, watered and fed the horse and cooled it. In the kitchen, supper was over the flames.

I eyed him critically. "You look a bit pale, Joel."

"I wouldn't be surprised. I had a bad time of it. So many arguments and such hard-headedness on their part. I had a strong desire to throw the whole thing away and never mind the money, but that would please them too much."

He went into no further detail about the trouble, and I didn't ask him, for it was all too complicated for me to fully understand, anyway. Joel's face was etched with fatigue, so I insisted he go to bed early. After the full dinner such as I gave him, he grew sleepy and consented readily to retire.

108

I joined him in bed some hours later, relieved that he was in deep sleep. I awoke to daylight and a sound that brought me immediate concern. Joel was vomiting severely. When the attack was over, he went back to bed. He was as pale as the sheets on which he lay.

"What is it, Joel?" I asked him. "Do you have pain?"

"It's that foul food they served me in Dublin. It felt heavy on my stomach all the way home. I'll be all right. I need rest mostly."

His forehead felt slightly feverish, but not enough to be concerned about. He assured me he felt better, so I stayed by his side until he fell asleep and then I tiptoed out of the room and went downstairs to put on the kettle and made myself a bit of toast. I'd let him sleep as long as he could, I decided.

Two hours later, I looked in on him for about the tenth time, and he still slept, but his face was drenched with perspiration this time. His fever was very high. I went for medicine, knowing what Father used to give for a condition like this that came from bad food.

He got the medicine down and insisted on sitting up against propped pillows. I drew up a chair. He reached for my hand. His were icy cold, though sweat still glistened on his forehead and upper lip.

"Don't be alarmed," he said. "I've nothing more than a queasy stomach. A bad one, maybe, but no more than that. Still, being ill has reminded me that if anything should happen to me, you don't even know what to do."

"Some other time, darling, when you feel better," I said.

"No, Maeve, now is the time for it. Otherwise, we'll never get around to talking about it, and this is important. I want you to listen to what I have to say and to remember it well."

"Aye, my love. I promise."

"My own family regards me as an enemy. It sounds stupid. It is. But it's the truth. And now, since you're married to me, you are an enemy, too. So one day you may have to fight them. Maybe we'll both decide to take them on. Between us, we might get the best of them, though that would be a miracle."

"Between us," I said, with a gaiety I didn't feel, "we could defeat anyone."

"You don't know them, my love. Well, that's little to do with what I want to say. Mind you now, I'm not being morbid. I'm only using common sense. A married man has to peer into the future the best he can. We don't all have a magic mirror."

"Now you're making fun of it," I chided him.

"No, really, I'm not. The fact is, my darling wife, while I was in Dublin this time, I got to thinking about matters and I went to see a barrister and had him draw up a will. It names you as sole benefactor and it's airtight. It will have to be, because if you ever had to use that will, my folks would start a battle where no holds would be barred."

"By the time I use that will," I said, "your folks will all be dead of old age. Now you slide down in this bed and try to get some rest."

"Not yet. I want to talk this out now so you'll understand. Maeve, you should know about matters. I sent copies of the will to our lawyer in New York. His name—I think I told you before—is Paul Arnold. He's a man you can trust with your life. Go to him first."

"You're telling me to leave my home and go to the United States?" I asked. "The fever's made you mad, Joel. Tell me, what does this Lawyer Arnold look like? Is he young? One who might be interested in a widow?"

"Now you're making fun of this whole thing," Joel accused me good-naturedly.

I wasn't, really. It had crossed my mind that Paul

Arnold might be the man whose image I had glimpsed in the mirror.

"I'm sorry, darling," I said. "I shouldn't be teasing you like this. It is important that I know about these things."

"Paul is nearly sixty, I think. A none-too-handsome man with a great shock of white hair, but what he lacks in manly beauty he makes up for in brains. As I said, go to him and trust him."

"Fine," I said, trying to terminate this talk. "Now I'll leave you alone so you can rest."

"A few more minutes," he insisted. "Likely you would have to go to the United States to handle legal matters. If that ever happens, don't let my family dominate you. Not for one instant. If they gain an inch, you'll be lost. Stand up to them. They understand that, though it took me most of my adult years to find it out. You will be wealthy; you will have a great deal to say about running a successful business and in the management of an entire town."

"How could I do that?" I asked. "I have lived my life here with people who are my friends. I can manage this household and nothing else. Besides, there'll be no need for it. You can handle whatever this business calls for."

"All right," he said, giving in to my dislike of the subject. "Just let me say a little more about the town so if you ever do wind up there, you'll understand a few things. Mind you, the conditions there are little different from what they are in most mill towns. The people are set to long hours and paid as little as possible. Even their children are set to work far too early in life so they can bring in a few extra pennies. It's a cruel and unfair life for them, but it's also a free country and they can quit whenever they like. Of course, to do that they need a bit of money, and there's the hitch. Working for the wages they get, it's

111

impossible to lay away enough to buy a rail ticket to the next town."

"But, Joel," I said, "can they not help one another? We of Mayo are poor. Glory be, there could be none much poorer these days, but no one is in dire need. We all see to that."

"I know. It's different there. Now you are married to a United States citizen. That gives you a priority over the regular quota of immigrants. Paul Arnold can help you if need be."

"If you do not get down in that bed and rid yourself of the fever, I'll be calling on Mr. Arnold personally in the next few days. I will not listen to this talk any longer if I have to go to the United States to avoid it, Joel Cameron. Will you rest now?"

"Yes," he said with a smile. "I had to get that off my chest. I feel better. In a couple of days, I'll be as good as new. Don't let me sleep all day."

I tucked him in, and I kissed him tenderly and went my way, but when the door closed behind him, I hurried downstairs so he wouldn't hear the sob I'd been restraining all that time. He was talking like a man who expected to die. I had a terrible feeling of doom, and there wasn't a thing I could do about it.

I kept busy doing household chores. I made him broth, and a pudding which I knew he liked and might eat. I read more of papa's medical books. I was tempted to send a messenger for the old doctor several miles away, but decided against it. It would take him hours to get here, and when he did, he'd not know any more about what should be done than I did.

I looked in on Joel several times, and he seemed to be in a deep sleep so I took pains not to disturb him, but kept myself busy doing work I'd already done. I tried knitting, but to no avail. I found myself unable to sit. I was too worried. I had to keep busy.

He was still asleep at suppertime. Carrying a cup

of the broth, I went to his bedside and touched his face. It was hot and dry. I spoke his name, but he didn't respond. His pulse was galloping, and he seemed to be taking short, quick breaths. I didn't like his pallor, and I ran out of the house to find a neighbor who had the fastest horse. I begged him to ride to the next village and bring back the old doctor. It was a gesture of desperation, for I'd not changed my mind about that doctor's ability. But if he had even a glimmer of an idea about what to do—and got here in time. . . .

When I returned to Joel, I discovered he'd vomited again, without any awareness of having done so. He was moaning softly, but he hadn't awakened, and he acted to me like a man drugged, though I knew that was impossible. I changed the bed linen and cleaned the floor on his side. I bathed Joel and convinced myself he seemed to be a little better. I sat beside the bed, holding his hand, blotting his face with a cloth wrung out in cool water.

Neighbors, who had learned of his illness by now, came in and I had to leave the bedside to assure them Joel was not able to have visitors. I was resentful of every minute I spent away from him.

By three in the morning, when the village and the house were as still as death itself, I felt myself slipping into a doze brought on by sheer exhaustion and lack of sleep. I felt his brow and found it reasonably cool. His pulse was fairly good, and he appeared to be breathing better. If I remained seated beside him, I'd be of no value if he needed me, for I was in danger of falling fast asleep myself. It would be better if I went to Papa's room and slept an hour or two so I'd lose this awful feeling. It came to me that I should have asked one of my neighbors to relieve my vigil by the bedside, but since I hadn't done so, I could hardly waken someone at this hour to take over.

I made certain again that Joel was comfortable,

and then I went to Papa's room. There I literally fell into a deep sleep halfway through my prayer for poor Joel.

When I awakened, the sun was full in my face, and I was covered with a quilt. I stared at the ceiling a moment, trying to figure out how I got here, in Papa's room, and why I was fully dressed. Then I remembered, and with a cry of horror at my failure to see to Joel, I ran out of the room.

Two neighbors were in the hallway, and so was the old doctor from the next village. He came to me, and his grave expression told the story I dreaded.

"He's gone, Maeve," he said. "He passed away this hour ago without ever waking up."

I stood in stunned silence for a few moments, and then I went into the arms of the kindly old man. I was far too long a doctor's daughter to go rushing into the room to throw myself upon a dead man. I waited until there were no more tears and then I went to Joel. He hadn't suffered. I could console myself on that.

"I can't well say what killed him," the old doctor said. "He was sick to his stomach once after I got here, but when he went, it was very fast. I think I might state that he died of a severe inflammation of the bowels."

The chronic illness of Mayo and the chronic cause of death when they didn't know the real cause. It was over. The cause was now of minor importance so far as I was concerned. I was alone now, and never in my life had I felt so lonely.

Somehow, everything got done. Once again there was the wake, the procession to the church, and then the cemetery. Joel would lie next to my mother, and on her other side my father's grave had not yet grown green over the raw earth.

I wrote out a cable to Joel's family. The old doctor would see that it reached Galway for dispatching. I could do no more, and I waited in vain to hear one solitary word from them. Of sympathy or instruction. Nothing came. Gradually, anger began to mount within me.

Jimmy couldn't be reached in time, and when I sent him a letter telling of Joel's death, I also told him that I might be in Edinburgh before too long. I wasn't exactly sure why I said that, but I'd not made up my mind what to do. And I was so lonely.

A week alone in that large house was the undoing of me. A woman can weep so much and have too much to weep for, and then she must get away from it all or go mad. That's how I felt. I had Papa, Grania, and now darling Joel to weep for. My tears were spent, and a numbness replaced my grief.

I made up my mind one evening as I ate a solitary cold supper in front of the fireplace. I'd been thinking of what Joel had told me, those last few hours he'd been conscious. I'd surely not suspected he was going to die then, and I was positive he didn't realize it, either. He didn't seem ill. He was only giving me instructions which any husband should give his wife. Especially if there would be complications after his death, and after Joel's, I feared there'd be many of them.

I thought Joel realized that in the event of his death, I'd be compelled to go to the United States. If not to live, at least to claim my inheritance and adjust matters with his family. I dreaded the very idea of it, but I didn't feel that I could allow them to simply take over, perhaps disregard me and be secretly glad that Joel was dead and no longer able to interfere with their scheming and their greed. Certainly they were taking no steps to reach me.

I was never one for dawdling at decisions. Once made up, my mind centered on the quickest possible way to carry out my decisions. I didn't know if I'd ever return to Mayo. If I had to remain in the United States to protect the interests Joel had left, then I would do so. But if I could settle them, then I would return, for this was my home. Modest, no doubt, compared to what Joel had been used to, but he had loved it and so did I. Besides, on the sloping green hill overlooking the sea lay those I had loved so well.

I wrote Jimmy a letter telling him what I had decided to do and asking him to make arrangements for my passage to the United States. I had no idea of what this entailed, or I might not have asked his help, but handled it all myself. Then I prepared the house for a long departure. I arranged with the old doctor to visit the office twice a week. I guaranteed him his fees and gave him full use of Father's equipment and pharmacy supplies.

I then had the sad experience of giving away all of Joel's clothing to the villagers, though their gratitude made the ordeal less oppressive. I arranged with neighbors to keep the house up and the furniture covered. I knew that if I returned twenty years from now, everything would be in its place exactly as I'd left it. Next, I packed Joel's bags and trunks for the long journey. When it came time for me to go, I climbed onto the carriage, driven by young Tim Fennelly, to whom I'd given the carriage and the horses. In return, he would drive me all the way to the railroad and there I would get transportation to Dublin and then to Scotland where I would join Jimmy.

I didn't look back as the carriage rolled down the dusty street. No one came out. Goodbyes had already been said, and none wished to see me leave for they knew full well how I felt and how close to tears I must be.

I had brought with me a small leather carrying case of Joel's papers, and on the way I studied these, trying to understand them. Most I did, some were

116

vague, but the New York lawyer would clear these up for me. I quickly knew that I was a wealthy widow. Not only by way of Joel's interest in the textile mills and the town in Maine, but in actual cash and investments. I hadn't, prior to now, known there was that much money in the world.

When we reached Dublin, I discovered I'd not have to go to Scotland, for Jimmy had traveled to Dublin to meet me. I scarcely left the hotel during my stay there, but I still disliked that city and I didn't make any excursions through it. Besides, Jimmy had to go over all those documents with my help, and he was considerably impressed with my lot.

"From now on," he said, "I shall have to doff me cap whenever the lady passes me by because you've more wealth than some of the earls and dukes and maybe a genuine royalty possesses. Whatever this business Joel's family is in, it is a profitable one."

I said, "Jimmy, I shall establish an account for you to draw upon as you see fit. If I am wealthy, my brother is not going to scrimp."

"Scrimp, is it? Don't you know our father left a good estate and you took not a farthing out of it? I don't need your help, darlin' Maeve. But if I do, I'll let you know without being bashful about it. Now, tell me about Joel. It seems strange to me, this manner of his death."

"It seems strange to me, as well. He came home from Dublin a very tired man. He said it had been an exhausting trip and there had been much to do there. I don't know what he meant by that, but he seemed angry at his family. He had stomach pains soon after he returned, and finally he had to go to bed. He developed a fever quickly, but it came and it went. I didn't know what to do. Joel must have had some premonition because he told me in great detail what must be done if he . . . died."

"He was a wise and thoughtful man. If he had not

117

given you these instructions, what with the manner of his estate, I don't think we'd have been able to settle it properly."

"He worried lest his family take advantage of me, thinking me some backward Irish country girl who didn't know a sixpence from a diamond tiara."

"Remember, then, he knew his people well. He prepared you, and don't let them frighten you."

"I'm ready for them, Jimmy."

"And don't forget, I'm here, too. If you need help, send a cable and I'll be on the next boat. You sail tomorrow, and I'll see you aboard the ship. It's a fine one and you have the best cabin, as befits a woman as rich as you."

"I'm grateful for your help, Jimmy."

"What's a brother for? Now, what of the mirror? This magic mirror you put such store by."

"Jimmy, it foretold Father's death at sea. It foretold the coming of Joel, and it foretold his death, too."

Jimmy shook his massive head. "Now darling, I'm a man of science and I can't make myself believe in these things. I would have to see them for myself."

"No man can look in the mirror and see anything," I said. "You know that."

"Do you think you should keep the cursed thing?"

"Aye. It has already shown me another man's image."

"In the name of all the saints, you are going to look for this other man you've never met and likely marry him because you think you saw a reflection of him in a two-thousand-year-old bit of rusty metal?"

"Bit of metal or not, it has always worked for O'Hanlon women, Jimmy. Though I'm not thinking of marriage. Now the torc is another thing. Would you care for it?"

"I would not. I don't believe in the mirror, and I

118

think the torc belongs in the National Museum. I told Father so many a time."

"The torc is family property," I said sternly. "If you do not wish to guard it, then it must go with me, and when I reach wherever I'm going, I shall put it in some safe place, as Father did."

"What do you intend? To pass it on to your children?"

"Jimmy!" I said angrily.

"Now wait, darling, you're young. Not much more than a slip of a girl. And you're as pretty a colleen as I've laid eyes on. Besides that, you're afloat in money. If Joel could give you no children, someone else might. You're not a girl to live alone, satisfied by only the memory of Joel, however wonderful a man he was."

"I have not given that any thought, and I do not intend to," I said.

"Oh, but what then of this man you say you saw in the mirror? You saw Joel and you married him. Will that not happen again with this other man you've not yet found?"

"Ask me that in a year or two," I said. "Of course, you're right. Joel wouldn't want me to worship his memory in that way. Above all, he was not a selfish man. It's true, we did not have a child. I have often wondered why."

"Ask the mirror. If it can show you a husband you've not even seen in the flesh, it certainly can tell you if you will have a child."

"We'll not speak again of the mirror," I said severely. "Now, if you will excuse me, I wish to do some shopping. I have dresses enough, but I shall look for one in the very latest fashion that I may wear when I first go to visit Joel's family. Perhaps I can stun them into silence while I take stock of them. As if I have to. They will be skinny, and pinched, and mean. Their mouths will be thin with no lips and

119

their eyes filled with greed and their voices shrill except when they speak of money. For them I do not need a magic mirror."

"Not with your imagination," Jimmy chuckled. "I'll go along with you to make sure the dress you buy will capture the fancy of a mere male. Besides, I have heard that there are some very pretty girls who will model."

"Come along, then," I agreed. "You may also escort me to supper. In the fanciest of restaurants, that I may begin to grow used to my wealth."

Suddenly I fled to him and put my arms around his neck and held back the tears with an effort. "Oh, Jimmy, I'm not fooling you or myself. I hate leaving Mayo, our home. And you. Yes, even you. I grieve to leave behind me the graves of those I loved so well. I care little for this wealth that has been thrust upon me. I would rather give it all to the people in our village. But I know such things are not possible and I must learn how to adapt myself to a new life. Perhaps Father knew one day I might have to face some situation like this and he taught me well so I have the education for it."

"And the poise, and the beauty, and the native intelligence," Jimmy said. "Along with two more important things. You're rich and you're Irish. You can't beat that combination."

We spent the rest of the day exploring stores. I bought Jimmy whatever his whim fancied until he protested. I bought for myself some new luggage, more feminine than that which Joel had left me, and I gave Jimmy all of Joel's. We had our supper amidst the trappings of wealth, and I must confess I didn't dislike it. Jimmy stated bluntly that it was all to his taste and he was coming to it when he was established as a surgeon. When we returned to the hotel, there was the ordeal of transferring all of my possessions from the old luggage to the new, and that took half the night even with Jimmy's help.

He knew I was keeping myself busy and making myself so fatigued I'd not think too deeply about leaving in the morning, which came all too soon. We were driven to the waterfront and we stood by while my luggage was carried aboard the great ship, already bustling with the activity of near sailing time.

Jimmy had seen to it that I had a luxurious cabin, and obviously he had explained to ship's officers and the purser that I was a girl with considerable wealth, which would make a great difference in the way I was treated and guarded during the voyage.

The enormity of what I was doing struck me as I kissed Jimmy goodbye and then watched him hurry down the gangplank which, obviously, was being held for him. He turned and waved, raising his hat to reveal that crop of fiery red hair glowing in the midday sunlight. I walked slowly away, smiling in answer to greetings from fellow passengers, but I went straight to my cabin and closed and locked the door.

I sat down in the large, soft, overstuffed armchair. I could feel the motion of the ship. Ordinarily on such a journey I would at least have been watching the land fade from the porthole, but I couldn't face that today.

What I finally did do was to begin unpacking. I answered a knock on the/ cabin door, and a maid asked if I wished help.

"Thank you," I said. "Perhaps later. I'm tired now, and I wish to rest a bit."

"Ring when you want me, ma'am. I'll turn down your bed while you're at dinner."

I almost expressed surprise because dinner to me meant the noonday meal, but I realized she spoke of the evening meal, which wasn't even served until eight o'clock. I closed the door and went back to my suitcases and trunks. I found the mirror, unwrapped it, and went over to stand beside the porthole for maximum light.

"If ever," I said aloud, "I needed help, it is now. Let me see what is in store for me."

I turned the mirror around and looked into its remaining shiny surface. The image was there. The same one. The profile of the man who had first appeared behind the image of Joel and gradually took precedence over him until Joel disappeared. It was a fleeting glimpse I had, for the image did not hold. None of them did, and sometimes I wondered if Jimmy could be right and my imagination was a bit too strong. But that couldn't be. How could I imagine, at least three times, the outlines of the face of a man I'd never seen? Just as I'd seen the face of Joel and watched it fade as the prophecy turned from one of joy to sadness and death.

I wrapped the mirror again, put it away, and proceeded to change from my traveling dress to something more comfortable. I would wear a fashionable gown at dinner, and I hoped I would be seated with companions who would be friendly, but not too friendly.

I couldn't have respected Joel's memory any more than I did, but I couldn't spend the days of the long voyage locked away in a cabin. As Jimmy had said, I was young and before me was a full life. I meant to live it.

BOOK TWO:

Maeve Cameron

FIVE

I was on deck when the silhouette of New York City came into view. Never had I beheld any sight so awesome. As a privileged passenger, thanks to the efforts and, possibly, some fairy tales composed by my brother, I was given excellent treatment. However, I was extremely worried about the torc, which was packed in one of my smaller bags. There were a dozen more, of regular size, augmented by several large steamer trunks. I had learned that baggage was subjected to inspection by some agency called customs.

Prior to docking, I had changed to a sedate traveling dress which was a drab, mousy color, but that proved to be the luckiest move I could have made. I was hurried through the passport division with no trouble, for I was the widow of an American citizen, but then I had to go through customs. Baggage handlers behind me were lined up, but as they stood politely to one side, there was nothing to show that they were actually handling my baggage.

My porter placed a suitcase and the smaller bag on the long table before the customs man, both impressive and terrifying to me in his blue uniform, brass buttons, and shiny peaked hat. He glanced up at me, and I looked at the broad face of a man who couldn't possibly be anything but Irish. Which was no consolation, for he'd recognize the meaning and the historic value of the torc if he laid eyes on it, which now lay directly under his nose.

"Mornin' to you, ma'am." He touched his cap. "You be from Killarney, perhaps?"

"No," I said. "Though it's a fine place to be from."

"To be sure. It's where I'm from, and I like to get reports now and then, direct from people coming from there."

"I'm county Mayo myself, sir," I said.

"Ah, so that's it." He reached for an official stamp, and my heart fluttered. "Now, there'll be no need to open your bags for inspection, ma'am. No indeed. Anyone from county Mayo wouldn't have so much as a fake earring to declare. Good luck to you."

I gestured to my porter, who moved quickly to pick up my bags and whisk me out of customs. I didn't look back. I wondered what the customs agent was thinking as a procession of luggage handlers streamed after me, all getting his official stamp.

By cable, Jimmy had reserved rooms for me at a fashionable hotel called the Waldorf-Astoria, and there I went, in a hack, followed by a lorry bearing my luggage. We no sooner left the dock area than I felt that I'd suddenly been dropped into the middle of a whirlwind.

Horse trams with clanging bells made their noisy way up and down the avenue. Heavy lorries, hansoms, buggies, great beer vans, and every kind of vehicle jammed the streets, and the sidewalks were thick with hurrying and scurrying people. Everyone seemed in a frantic rush to go somewhere. When we reached Fifth Avenue, things were not quite as frenzied, and I had my first glimpse of the great stores, the fabulous homes of the wealthy, and the stylishly dressed women, some walking and others in ornate carriages.

I was quickly installed in a two-room suite of this opulent hotel which made those of Dublin seem tawdry by comparison. I remembered to hold my head high and my shoulders back and to meet firmly the eyes of those who addressed me. I signed the register, my signature giving no hint of the nervous excitement within me. Polite hotel officials had me escorted to an elevator which rose ten times faster than the only other one I'd ever ridden during my visit to Dublin.

Before I could object, a pair of efficient maids were at work unpacking my things and exclaiming over them. I wasn't quite sure whether the gowns were, in their opinions, truly beautiful or they were merely trying to make me feel comfortable. After seeing those women along Fifth Avenue, I realized Dublin had a great deal of room for improvement in the way of women's fashions.

Once left alone, I bathed and rested awhile before venturing out. I made my first visit to one of the fashionable stores where, I discovered, they had ready-made dresses which could be altered to fit in a brief time. I ordered six in varied styles and colors to be delivered the next day. One, which fitted me perfectly without alterations, I wore when I left the store, sending my old one back to the hotel. The dress was simple in style, worn under a rose-colored waistcoat.

I consulted a small notebook I carried in my handbag, then requested the doorman at the department store to summon me a hansom. I gave the driver the address of Paul Arnold, who had been Joel's barrister and was now mine.

His office was a considerable distance away, and the hansom fare was a dollar, which I thought extravagant, but it was a pleasant and interesting ride. I added a gratuity and then walked into a red-brick, four-story office building. I found Mr. Arnold's name, located his office by its number, and went in to be faced by a gray-haired woman who left her desk to come forward to greet me. I identified myself, and she studied my face, nodding as she did so.

"Of course, you are Joel's widow," she said. "He described you well in his letters."

"Thank you." I was touched by her friendly greeting.

It seemed ages since I'd been spoken to so informally.

"Mr. Arnold will see you at once. Did you have a smooth voyage?"

"That I did, thank you. And this is an amazing city, though a bit confusing to a country lass. Why is everyone in such a hurry?"

Her laughter was soft and pleasant to hear. "They really don't know. It's a habit. Be glad you won't have to adapt to it. You'll be going to a small town far from here. Things move at a leisurely pace there, I'm sure. My name is Gloria Travis, and I'm Mr. Arnold's secretary. If you need anything, telegraph me at once and I'll take care of it. Now, please follow me."

Mr. Arnold, behind a large desk in a paneled, book-lined office, stood up as I entered and came around the desk to welcome me, both hands extended. I touched my cheek to his. It was an impulsive gesture, but Joel had often told me what a friend and ally he was. I judged him to be about fifty, graying, partially bald, his craggy features still giving evidence of his good looks. His pale blue eyes sparkled in good humor, and his smile was warm and wide.

"Welcome to the United States," he said. "Maeve, you're lovely. Gloria, have you ever seen such fresh-ness? Look at her complexion!"

"I have already, and been beside myself with jealousy," Gloria replied. "I'll leave you two so Maeve can learn all about her new family. Heaven help her."

"Is it as bad as that, Mr. Arnold?" I asked.

"I'm afraid it is, Maeve. Please sit down. This will take some time. I'm not going to hold back anything. From what Joel wrote me, you're not a shy, frightened little girl who can easily be cowed. And believe me, that's good. First of all, let me tell you about the textile business, one-third of which is now your property. About a hundred years ago, perhaps more, Joel's ancestors cleared a space to farm and hunt and prosper in what was then a rugged part of this country. It still

128

is to a certain extent. During the years that followed, they and their children and grandchildren developed a town. They began making textiles, cotton goods of exceptionally fine quality. No matter what you say about the Camerons, the product they produce is the very best. They've enough business sense to know it's the only way to success."

"Aye," I nodded. "In Mayo we have women who weave tweed in their kitchens and they are not satisfied with but the best."

"I'm sure of that. Now they have a mill up there that employs more than three hundred people, has modern machinery, and working conditions are not bad. Not the best, mind you, for that would cost too much money, but sufficient so production isn't affected. You know what I mean. Also, while giving the appearance of being benevolent to their employees, they are not."

I was fast losing heart with these new-found, never-met relatives of mine. "Aye, sir. Penny-pinching can go just so far before it becomes repugnant."

"Exactly, and they know where to stop. As they developed this town, they built all the houses on land they own. They built the stores, the town hall, every last building, and they all belong to the Cameron family. Every structure is rented out save one or two—and the mansion in which they live and which rests upon a knoll that overlooks the whole town. As if they keep watch there with telescopes. Every worker in that town is employed by the mill, except the few who have to keep the stores and maybe serve the public as town officials. These are appointed, mind you, not elected. There is no mayor, no council. The Cameron family runs the town politically, too. So every employee pays rent to the Camerons, buys clothes from their stores, groceries from their markets. Even their taxes pay for the town hall. And, of course, the town is named Cameron."

"The town bears the name of the family. Which is now also my name," I said. "I will confess I do not like all this, sir. Though I came prepared, having been told much by Joel."

"You'll like it less when you meet these people and when I tell you what they've been up to."

"I sent them a cable about Joel's death. They never acknowledged it."

"Of that I have no doubt. They did approach me. Loran Cameron, Joel's uncle, came here and said Joel's affairs would be taken out of my hands at once and that you would be sent a sum of money in full settlement of his estate."

"Good heavens!" I cried out in surprise. "Joel led me to believe that what was his would now be mine."

"It is. But the Cameron family wasn't going to accept that if they could get away with it. Joel foresaw this, and even if he was young and in apparent good health, he was wise enough to know that unfortunate things could happen, and he prepared for them. I have the power to administer his share of the family property in your name. We will make absolutely no compromise whatsoever. At least, I will advise you not to give in."

"You have my word I do not intend to, Mr. Arnold. Joel warned me they would make trouble. I'm prepared to face it."

"Good. I hoped you'd have backbone enough to stand up to them. It won't be easy, especially since you're in a land strange to you, with customs you won't always understand. But you have me to rely on. I'm being paid for it, so don't hesitate, Maeve. And it's not the fee I charge that induces me to say this. It's my friendship for Joel, a young man I loved and respected. Tell me, what happened to him? I know he wasn't the most rugged of men, but I thought his health sound enough."

"I don't know, Mr. Arnold. He came home from Dublin that sick he couldn't eat. He went to bed and fast grew worse. My father was a doctor, and I know

130

something of treating common ailments, but I never saw anything like this before. There was a high fever and then no fever. There were chills; his heart grew weak; he began to sleep heavily. I called an old doctor from a nearby town, but he arrived too late to do anything. I entertained little hope he could, but I was desperate. He said poor Joel died of an inflammation of the bowels. That's what they say about the death of anyone when they can't pin it down."

"They do the same thing here, but they give it a fancier name. Did you get sick?"

"Oh, no. Whatever caused it was something he picked up in Dublin. If not there, then he got it on the way back. It was a long journey."

"I see. Well, now let's go into the financial side of this matter. As I said, every month profits are distributed. Joel's grandfather arranged that he get one-third of the profits and he controlled one-third of the business. This part of the old man's will is irrevocable. Nobody can change it for any reason. It also plainly stated that upon his death, Joel's share would go to his widow, or his children, or both. So legally you're safe. They can't deprive you of a penny. They may try to cheat you out of it, but they cannot deny what you are entitled to. Is that plain, my dear?"

"Aye, quite plain, Mr. Arnold, and I'm that grateful to have you to tell me these things."

"Now—as for the family, you say Joel has told you about them."

"Well, now that I think of it, not to any great extent. He didn't like to talk about them. I think it pained him to do so. As you know, he was warm and compassionate. It troubled him that his family lacked those qualities."

Mr. Arnold nodded. "I'll prepare you further. His father and mother were lacking as parents. That may sound like a terrible thing to say, but it's true. At least, I believe so. He concentrates on making money, she on

131

becoming a socialite. Joel's sister is like her mother. And who can blame her, being raised in such an atmosphere? She married a man named Easterly. Ashley Easterly, not because she loved him, but because he had social position in Boston and elsewhere, and he and his family are accepted at Newport and Saratoga. Those are the watering places, resorts where the wealthy go to show off. Joel's older brother Abner is a rebel like Joel but, sadly, in a different way. Joel sought to get clear of them, but Abner meekly accepts, spends his time doing nothing, and isn't taken seriously by anyone."

"I do think Joel liked him," I said. "He rarely mentioned his sister."

"No doubt of that. Then there's Marcy Tabor, the sister of Joel's mother. She is elegant, precise, mean as sin. She'll hate the very sight of you because you're attractive and she never has been. She lives off the family fortune. So does Loran, Joel's uncle, but in a different way. He's the man who does the dirty work. If there's a family to be dispossessed, he handles it. If a man is to be fired, he does the firing. He earns his way, though no one with an ounce of self-respect would take the job."

"It sounds dismal. I understand why Joel traveled. How can I hope to stand up to them?"

"That will be up to you, Maeve. You'll have to face up to them. Perhaps you're what they need. Just remember—you belong there. Now a few words about Cameron—"

"Excuse me, Mr. Arnold, but it still seems strange to have the same name as the town."

"It doesn't to a born Cameron, since they named the town. As I was saying, I went there to look about, and what I saw sickened me. However, you will likely have little to do with the business part of it. They can still outvote you and have their way. What I wish to say is that there's an inn there. It's owned by the Cameron family. Oh, yes, of course it is. And its used mainly

132

by drummers who come through and by buyers who arrive to inspect the output of the mills. Therefore, it's a very good inn with fine rooms and good country food. I suggest you check in there."

"Do you think they'll have me now?" I asked.

"If they wish to argue the point, remind them that you—yes, you—own one-third of the establishment. You'll probably have to keep reminding them."

"I would dislike doing that, but I will if it comes to it. I intend to see this big city for a few days before I leave for . . . what can I call it? Home? I don't think so. A way station, perhaps. That's more like it. And after I arrive, I'll write and tell you how I was received. At least, I hope I will be."

"If there's any trouble, use the telegraph."

"Aye, I will that. But after hearing you tell me what Joel already told me, I wonder if I'm strong enough to stand up to them."

"You seem sensible and strong to me. Anyway, remember that I'm prepared to adopt whatever legal action is necessary to protect you and your interests—which are secure, I assure you."

We talked for another few minutes, Mr. Arnold mentioning various points of interest I should see. The hansom awaited me, and I asked the driver to take a slow drive about the city and explain to me everything that required explaining. I drank in the sights and reveled in them, but the more I saw, the more awesome this city became. And I thought of the whole United States, so new, so vital and alive. Everything moved so fast and in so many directions at the same time.

I dreaded going to Joel's town to meet his family. While I wouldn't have admitted it to Mr. Arnold, I was very frightened of them, for I knew money was power, and they had a great deal of both. While I was a stranger—an interloper—who had no business sense. That alone put me at a disadvantage. They would hate me because Joel had married me and because he had

133

left me an important part of a business they wished to own entirely. I would be costly to them, and they would resent that.

I was exhausted by the time dinner was served, and I ordered a tray sent to my room. It came as a table, with a complete meal on it. I ate in solitary splendor, thinking of the steps I would have to take from here on.

Actually, making plans was impossible. I didn't know what the outcome of my meeting with the family would be, so I planned no further ahead than my arrival in Cameron. I would register at the inn and explore the town, at least familiarizing myself slightly with it. Perhaps that would help me understand them better. Not until then would I approach the Camerons. If they discovered I was at the inn, well and good. They could come to me if they wished, though I imagined that would be quite beneath their dignity.

There was one important task I took care of the next morning. I went to the largest bank near the hotel and there I arranged, after a verifying call over an instrument called a telephone, to Mr. Arnold, to rent a safe box in the vaults of this bank. There I put the torc. The mirror I planned to keep with me at all times. I felt better once this all-too-precious heirloom was safe.

Mr. Arnold had made arrangements for Pullman travel to Boston and from there by a smoky, sooty train to Cameron. It was an interesting ride to Boston, through busy cities and sleepy little towns. The speed of the train was frightening, but I soon guessed that it was perfectly safe. I even slept in the train, in a private little room where a seat turned into a bed and there was running hot water in the little cubicle of a bathroom which was completely private. I was quickly learning the advantages of being wealthy.

I saw little of Boston, being whisked from one railroad station to another. My luggage, except that which I took with me, would be sent on later by the New

134

York hotel. I traveled lightly because I didn't know whether I'd stay a day or a lifetime.

The two-car train that wended its noisy and smoky way through farmland and forest took almost all day to reach Cameron, and I felt encrusted with soot by the time I stepped down off the car.

The depot was at the south end of the town which spread out before me on the beginning of a flat plain that slowly climbed to a low hillside until it turned higher in a sharper ascent and at the top of this hill stood the mansion. From the depot I could barely make it out, but I knew that was where Joel had been born and had lived during his growing years. The house he had fled.

In the late afternoon sun, scattered through the maple and elm trees that lined every street, the town at first looked like a pleasant place. Only when I drew closer did I see that the houses were drab, set too close together with only small yards separated by rickety-looking fences of pointed wooden stakes. At least, that's what they looked like to me, who was accustomed to fences of fieldstone built to last for hundreds of years.

From the perfectly straight main street, side streets grew off it at measured intervals as if the whole thing had been laid out on a massive board, previously scaled by a ruler. Only in the very center was there any deviation.

I carried my two bags, which were not light in weight, and I slowly approached this area in the center. There I found a freshly painted, two-story building with a steeple just like that of the church across the street. A sign over the door stated this was the Town Hall. On either side of the street were the stores. One grocery, one meat market, a clothing store for men, another for women, a millinery, a seamstress shop, a smithy, a stable, a pharmacy that brought back sad memories of

135

Father. And the inn. The sign over it had burned-in letters spelling out CAMERON INN. What else would it be called, I asked myself.

I was still a distance away when I saw a boy of about twelve, barefoot, shyly watching me from a doorway. I beckoned to him, and he approached somewhat reluctantly.

"I'll gladly pay you if you will carry my bags to the inn," I said.

"Yes'm," he said. He promptly relieved one of the heavy luggage, much to my relief.

"What's your name, lad?" I asked.

"Eddie. You talk funny, ma'am."

"Aye, that I do, but to me you talk funny, too, so we can laugh at one another, eh?"

He tried not to smile, but when I burst into laughter, he followed. He was much more at ease now, and I felt I'd made a friend.

"You don't have to pay me," he said. "Papa told me I must always help ladies."

"That's thoughtful of him, I will say, Eddie, but I pay my way. When you set down those bags in the inn, you will have earned . . . what do you call it?" I opened my handbag and took out a coin. "I mean this."

"That's half a dollar," he exclaimed, his eyes growing wider with every step.

"So it is. In my country we call our coins by different names, but I suspect they buy the same things. If you have enough of them. So it's yours for helping me."

"First half-dollar I ever had," he said.

"Oh? Then perhaps there'll be another if I have need for you. And I do thank you."

I paid him before the desk in the lobby, and he went running off, clutching the coin as if he still didn't believe it. A middle-aged man eyed me with both interest and suspicion.

"You intending to register, miss?" he asked.

"What would a lady be doing here if she didn't intend

136

to stay, sir? I want the best rooms you have to offer. Two of them with a door between."

"You . . . have business here?"

"Aye. Important business."

"A buyer! You're a buyer, and I'd guess you're from abroad. First time the mills ever had a buyer from Europe. And the first lady buyer! Am I guessing right?"

"Partly so." I hedged the answer. "I may stay some time if I approve of the rooms and the food."

"They're very good, especially for buyers. We hold them as important folks. Mr. Cameron says nobody is more important than a buyer, so you get the best. I'd appreciate if you'd mention this to Mr. Cameron when you see him."

I nodded, making no verbal promise.

He carried my bags, leading the way to a suite on the second, which was also the top floor, of the inn. The rooms were surprisingly large and beautifully furnished. They could not meet the standards of the Waldorf, but that was hardly to be expected, for the cost was a fraction of what I paid in New York.

He went off, happily contemplating that I'd pass on the fact that he was a fine hotel-keeper. I removed my hat and gloves and sat down in a rocker set before a window that overlooked the street.

I'd barely settled into it when I half arose at the blast of a whistle that shrieked through the former silence. It blew three times and then was silent. I turned my lapel watch around. It was six o'clock. I looked out into the street, and from the far end of it, where the long, low structure that must be the mill was located, came what looked like a parade of men, all in work clothes.

Somewhat behind the men came a group I had difficulty in identifying at first, for they moved in a slower fashion as if they were at a point of near exhaustion, but as they came closer to the hotel, I saw that they were children, both boys and girls; some appeared no more than ten or eleven years of age.

Gradually, the procession thinned out as members of it left to go to their individual homes, and it was all over in a matter of ten minutes or so. I remembered that Joel had told me how the mill hired children for light work, but the way those youngsters moved, I doubted the work was light and certainly the hours must have been very long.

True, in my village back home, children went to work early, but they also received an education, and work in the fields was done after school hours. Besides, no child was worked to a point where vitality was as far gone as it appeared to be with these children. I also recalled that Joel had said it was common throughout the States.

The sound of a bell could be plainly heard through the closed door. I assumed it was announcing the supper hour. I changed to a simple dress, not wishing to call attention to myself.

A terrible loneliness assailed me as I made my descent to the dining room. I'd always had a man by my side. First my father, who had taught me how to care for the sick and ailing; then my beloved Joel, who had captured my heart and whose rapturous love I had known so briefly. I blinked the tears away. I could not afford the luxury of indulging in self-pity. I had to learn to live with my loneliness. The journey had been helpful, but now that I was in the town where Joel was born and raised, the pain and anguish which had engulfed me when he died returned.

I was given a table by myself. There were only about a dozen people being served, and I guessed that some of them belonged in the town. Probably as town officials, or important people at the mill. The rest would be drummers passing through, stopping to sell their wares to storekeepers and, perhaps, to the mill itself.

I seemed to be an object of interest. I pretended not to notice the diners observe me as I entered the room.

I could imagine the conjectures that were being bandied about as to what I was and, if a buyer, what kind of business establishment would be so foolhardy as to send a woman to handle this kind of work.

The food was excellent. Plain, the kind I was accustomed to, and of fine quality. The beef was tender, the vegetables crisp and fresh. There was apple pie for dessert, better than that at the Waldorf-Astoria. If it became necessary that I live at this inn for a considerable period of time, I could endure it very well indeed.

I was enjoying my coffee when I happened to look up as a man moved rapidly past the wide entrance to the dining room. I had little more than a glimpse of him, but it sent such a shock through me. I stood up without realizing what I was doing. The man, in profile, which was all I saw of him, was the one whose face had appeared in the mirror. The one whose image had replaced Joel's.

I hurried to the lobby. The elderly night clerk was behind the desk busy with bookwork. There was no one else about. I approached him.

"Excuse me, sir, but a moment ago a man passed this desk. I think perhaps he went upstairs. He resembled someone I used to know. Did you see him?"

"Nobody came through here, ma'am. Nobody. I'd know it if they did. Didn't see a soul."

I said, "I'm sorry. My eyes must be playing tricks with me. Thank you."

I didn't return to the dining room. Instead I went upstairs. The corridor was empty. I listened as I walked slowly along the hall, but no voice reached my ears. Could I really have been imagining things?

In my rooms I removed the mirror from one of my suitcases, which I had kept locked. I unwrapped it and turned up both lamps on the bureau for maximum light. Then I tilted the mirror to obtain the best reflection.

"I am in a country so new to me," I said in a whisper, "I cannot know if the magic of the mirror has followed

139

me here. I saw in it one man I later met and wed. I know now when the vision faded, it was a prophecy of his death. Just as the boiling sea I observed in the mirror predicted my father's death. The mirror also brought forth the image of another man who is still a stranger to me. It has been a long time since I saw that image. I remember it well. A few minutes ago, I was sure I saw a man who resembled the image. He disappeared as if by the kind of magic the mirror has shown. I ask now to see that face again so I can be sure it is the same as that of the man of whom I had a bare glimpse."

Speaking these words, I refrained from looking into the mirror until after I'd spoken. Then I moved the mirror slightly for the best light, and I saw the same profile. That of the image I'd seen in Ireland and aboard the boat. That of the man who I thought had passed the entrance to the dining room.

It was there and then it was gone, hardly more than a flash, but enough to tell me the charm of the mirror was not confined to Ireland and that I had not been mistaken in my memory of the profile I'd seen before.

I rewrapped the precious thing and put it back in the suitcase, locking it up, though I felt that there was likely no more need for that here than in Mayo. Still, the mirror was priceless to me, and I could afford to take no risks with it.

I was tired, for it had been a long day and a long journey. By nine I was in bed and ten minutes later fast asleep. And a good thing, too, for at six the next morning the blast of that factory whistle wakened me out of a deep sleep. I sat up quickly, wondering where I was and what banshee wail had awakened me.

I went over to the window and through the lace curtain watched the parade reversing itself on its way to the mill this time. It came to me then that these people worked from six to six. They could have time for little else.

I returned to bed and tried to go back to sleep, because I wanted to be fully rested. Today I would meet Joel's people for the first time, and I wished to be alert and well prepared to face them. I found further sleep impossible, so I got up, bathed, and spent time on my appearance, choosing a simple black dress. I was the last one to be served in the dining room, and breakfast was the full equal of supper in quantity and quality. Since I had overeaten, I decided to take a walk before I set out to make my presence known to the Cameron family.

I made my way down a quiet, shaded street. Some paint and repairs would have freshened the place to a remarkable degree. Despite that, the yards were neat, grass was well-tended, and the fences were kept up. Small gardens were visible behind the houses, a mixture of flowers and vegetables growing there. Washing waved gently in the easy morning breeze, and the clotheslines behind each house were full. Work of every kind began early in this town.

No one was on the street yet. I continued my stroll until I came to the mill. I judged it to be at least half a mile long, located on the bank of a river which, at the far end of the mill, made a sharp turn so that the town was avoided and explained why I'd not even seen this stream before. I wondered if this diversion of the flow was man-made.

I could hear the sound of the machines, but no voices. It was an eerie sensation. Like being in a town inhabited by unseen beings busily and noisily at work.

As I retraced my walk, I began to grow more and more apprehensive about my visit to the Camerons. Well above the mill, on that hilltop, the mansion looked grim and forbidding. The people inside, I already knew, were not about to welcome a girl from Mayo who had married their son and, at his death, inherited a sizable part of the family interests. There was bound to be trouble, and there was fear within me because of my youth and ignorance regarding everything in this country. There'd been no time to familiarize myself with the customs here. I felt like a child about to face a family of giants.

I kept my eyes open for the chance appearance of that man I thought resembled the image in the mirror. That was another complication I felt unequal to cope with. What did this man mean? Where did he fit into my life? Was it even possible that he was real? I reminded myself the clerk at the inn had denied seeing anyone pass the desk. Yet I couldn't believe my eyes had deceived me.

I stopped at the combination harness shop, smithy, and stable where I was waited on by an elderly, soft-spoken gentleman, eager to rent me a carriage, in good condition, and a gentle horse. He made no inquiries as to who I was or where I lived. I suspected everybody knew a strange woman had arrived and was staying at the inn, and in all probability was somehow connected with the mill and its owners.

I drove the carriage back to the inn and left it in front long enough to go to my room and freshen up. Then I returned to the carriage and braced myself for the meeting that would soon take place. I wondered whether the Camerons knew I was in town—and if so, what was their reaction. I'd soon know.

I didn't touch the whip in its socket. If the horse cared to move at a snail's pace, I was content. I'd never been less in a hurry to somewhere than now, The closer I came to the mansion, the bigger it seemed to be. Had I not observed the granite and marble mansions of the very wealthy in New York, this would have been the largest and most opulent dwelling I had ever seen in my life. Even so, I was considerably impressed by it.

At the very top of the hill, a drive sloped gently

downward toward a garden area dominated by the mansion. There were several smaller structures, too, all but one on the other side of the drive. I learned later that these were called dependencies and it was there that the servants lived. The other building, separated from the mansion, was a square, glassed-in structure with a miniature steeple atop it. This, I came to know, was the summer house. I vaguely recalled Joel speaking of a smaller, independent house where the children played.

The mansion itself startled me by its size and by its fanciful structure. There was, first of all, a large two-story shingled dwelling with a wide, sweeping, fan-like marble stairway to a marble open porch. One corner of the mansion was perfectly round, partially ivy-covered and mostly glass. I'd never seen anything like it before, and its purpose escaped me at the time. There were towers and cupolas, small curved verandas, large, wide windows. Somehow this part of the building seemed older than the rest of it, as if another section had been added to it at a later date, for the newer portion was built of limestone and timber, but with just as many decorations and useless-looking verandas. Chimneys dotted the peaked rooftops of both sections of the mansion.

If the entrance was meant to impose, it did. My heart started to pound in fear as I left the carriage and walked slowly toward the marble stairs. No one came out. I'd hoped someone would.

I was sorely tempted to turn, go back to the carriage, drive to the hotel, gather my things, and leave this town, the name of which was the same as mine. I think now it was the memory of Joel that gave me the backbone to keep walking up the stairs. My heels made little clicking noises on the marble which further served to set my nerves on edge. I approached the massive door with its huge knocker, big brass sconces on either side of it, and the tall, narrow windows through which,

143

no doubt, I was being carefully and critically observed.

I lifted the knocker, paused, then calling upon my courage, let it fall. The resulting clatter made me wince. The door opened almost instantly, and an austere woman in a gray uniform with dark hair pulled severely back peered at me through small, steel-rimmed glasses.

"Yes?" she asked, regarding me as if I were an interloper.

"I am Maeve O'Hanlon Cameron," I said. My voice didn't falter, though I almost did.

She made no reply, but stepped aside, allowing me entry. I walked into a wide, long reception hall where two large Waterford chandeliers hung. I knew they were worth a fortune. There were four high-backed chairs upholstered in dark red velvet and a little sofa for two in the same wood and upholstery alongside the walls. The floor was richly carpeted in a thick rug of burgundy.

The woman closed the door, passed me by, and signaled curtly that I was to follow her. She led me into a room as spacious as six or eight county Mayo cottages combined.

There was furniture enough for all of those cottages, too, but most of it was so large and opulent that the pieces would never have fitted. A great fireplace with a mantel of white marble had a row of life-size oil paintings hung on either side of it. If these were the past and present Camerons, there were certainly a great many of them and they were formidable-looking. A portrait of Joel was not among them.

I realized after a moment that I was alone. The woman who had admitted me was obviously a servant of some sort. I sat down decorously, in case there were eyes watching me from some hidden observation point. I felt very much ill at ease, and I realized my feet were firmly planted against the carpet so that I could rise quickly and depart at a dead run if need be. I was ashamed of my cowardice and turned my thoughts to Joel.

I knew now what he meant when once he'd said he disliked the mansion. It was certainly representative of wealth. Everything in it was meant for comfort and beauty, but the atmosphere was cold. I felt as if the walls would enjoy closing up and crushing me.

Two people marched into the room. If there'd been martial music, I wouldn't have been surprised. The man was of slight build, as Joel had been. He was growing bald, though the remaining hair still had its original dark brown color. He had a thin face, but his wife's was thinner. Here was a woman who, one could tell at a mere glance, would be uncompromising in all things, a woman who would insist on having her own way and heaven help those who opposed her, including the man at her side.

The man spoke first. "I am Gabriel Cameron, and this is my wife Evelyn. We are Joel's parents. Please remain seated."

I had started to rise to greet them, but I settled back in the chair, my curiosity now overcoming my fear.

The woman said, "We have arranged to grant you five thousand British pounds, and a draft will be placed in your hands within twenty-four hours. This is on condition that you clear out of here and return to Ireland where you belong. I hope I have made myself well understood."

"Aye," I said slowly. "Understanding the English language as I do, you've made yourself quite clear."

"In return, you will be required to sign certain documents which my brother-in-law will bring in a few moments."

"May I ask what these documents are?" I asked.

"A surrender of all claims to my son's estate. You're not entitled to anything. We grant you this large sum

145

out of the goodness of our hearts and to avoid further complications."

"I have in my possession the last will and testament made by Joel," I said. "It grants me full right to whatever he left with no exceptions. I am told it is a strong will."

"May I see it, please?" Joel's mother asked.

I opened my handbag and took out the folded document. She accepted it, but didn't glance at the paper. Instead, she clutched it with both hands as if she expected me to snatch it from her.

"There is a writing desk to your left," she said. "You may use it to sign the release papers."

"I will not," I said. My voice may have quavered, even cracked, I wasn't sure, but horses wouldn't have dragged me to that writing desk. I was frightened half out of my wits, but I wasn't giving way to them.

"You mean you won't sign?" Joel's father asked.

"Yes, sir, that's exactly what I mean."

I could scarcely believe it was I talking. Actually standing up to them, as Mr. Arnold had stated I must.

"How much do you want?" he asked.

"I want what is already mine, not a farthing less or more."

"So you're going to be difficult. We can also be difficult," Mrs. Cameron said. "I won't argue with you. Loran, my husband's brother, handles anything disagreeable to us."

"Mrs. Cameron," I said, determined to give motherly instinct one chance, "do you not even wish to know about the manner of your son's death? How he and I met? Of our marriage?"

"My son is dead," she replied coldly. "Discussing him will not bring him back. Neither my husband nor I, nor any member of our family, is interested in you. A fortune hunter."

She applied some pressure on her husband's arm and

they left the room as they'd entered. Cold, belligerent, and haughty.

I was too stunned to be angry. That would come, and when it did, I felt I could be a match for them. As they left, a tall, thin man who seemed to resemble Joel more than Joel's father had, came briskly into the room carrying several documents. He was less formal, bowing slightly as he approached. He sat down opposite me.

"I am Loran Cameron, Joel's uncle," he said. "I understand you have refused a very generous offer."

"I have, sir," I said. "It was an inhuman offer, if I may say so."

"You have also indicated you intend to hold us to the will Joel made in your favor."

"Indeed, I intend that, and no more than right it is."

"Ah, yes. So you say." He had the will among the documents, and he began to scan it.

"I think you know the terms of the will," I said. "As you likely know everything else that's taken place in this room."

He tore the will into shreds, and let them fall onto the carpet. I stared down at them as he said, "Let me tell you what will happen if you fight us. We'll drive you out of this town. We'll hold up any money due you, we'll see to it that you learn nothing of what goes on in connection with the business. We'll contact the immigration authorities with the idea of having you deported as an undesirable. We'll see to it that you will be quite unable to support yourself, and unless you sign these documents now, we will never again offer you a single dollar."

I arose slowly, adjusted my gloves, and spoke calmly. "These are matters you will take up with Mr. Paul Arnold, who is a barrister in New York. He is handling my affairs."

"Paul Arnold is a New York attorney not licensed to

practice law in Maine," Loran said. "He can't help you here. Not one little bit."

"We shall see, Mr. Cameron."

I walked past him, left the room, and headed for the door. He followed me—somewhat grimly, I thought. No servant loitered in the hall to open the door, so I did.

Then I turned back and faced Loran Cameron. "The will you destroyed, sir, was merely a copy. Mr. Arnold has the original. Did you think me so stupid as to allow you to get possession of the original?"

I went out to where the carriage waited, climbed onto the seat, and drove away. As I rode up the slope of the drive, I kept my head high, but when I started down the hillside toward the town, I pulled over, got out my handkerchief, and wept. Not tears of frustration or of fear, but of sadness for Joel to have had to live with such people. I marveled he'd been given the gift of love and compassion.

I had yet to meet Joel's sister, his brother, and his aunt, but certainly, if they lived in that house ruled by those people, I had little desire to meet them. I didn't know what I'd do. I would have to wait and see what happened next. My first step would be to write Mr. Arnold a letter concerning the offer they'd made and informing him of their threats. The idea of being deported worried me, for I wasn't familiar with the immigration laws. People of such importance and influence could wield power. Money could perform miracles here, in Ireland, anywhere. Those people could create enough mischief, intimidate enough people, to get their own way. I would have to rely on Mr. Arnold for protection, but I felt sure he would provide it. Meanwhile, I intended to remain in Cameron. It might be a lonely existence, but the death of my father and then Joel had already helped me to endure loneliness.

What I wondered was whether I could handle Gabriel and Evelyn Cameron.

I drove the carriage back to the stables and prepared to pay the stableman a week's rental.

"That'll be fifty cents," he said, somewhat sheepishly, I thought.

"Why, that's reasonable," I said. "I'll pay a week. . . ."

"Only the day," he said. "Tomorrow I won't have a carriage, ma'am."

"Well, the next day then, and I'll arrange now to have it reserved—"

"We don't do business that way, ma'am. I'm awful sorry."

"Do you mean I won't be able to rent a carriage again?"

"If everything I got is busy. . . ."

I walked away, puzzled, but granting the fact that if the stable had only two or three horses, perhaps I'd have to wait my chances. Or buy a horse and carriage. I could certainly afford to.

I had crossed the lobby of the inn when the clerk at the desk called me back. He placed before me a bill for my stay.

"I intend to pay by the week," I replied with quiet assurance.

"Ma'am, everything in the hotel is reserved for the next two weeks."

The truth dawned on me then. "I see. I notice you have charged me for today, so I take it for granted that I may stay the night."

"Oh, yes, ma'am."

"Because there is no train out of here until tomorrow?"

"Well, there ain't a train, that's true, but you're welcome to stay. . . ."

"Thank you," I said. "I'm that obliged for your kindness."

He turned away from me. I wondered how the Camerons had reached these people so quickly. I walked out

of the inn and hurried up the street to the depot. There
I wrote a telegram to Mr. Arnold, informing him that
I was being denied facilities for remaining in Cameron
and that they had threatened me. I passed the message
to the operator, who scanned it, pushed his green visor
further back on his forehead, and looked at me.

"That'll be two dollars and seventy cents. It's a long
telegram."

I gave him the money. As he turned away, I said,
"I shall remain at this window while you send the
message, sir. If you fail to do so, I shall take it up with
the railroad at once. I do believe they might be a trifle
more powerful than the Camerons. Do you understand
me, sir?"

"Yes, ma'am," he said. "I'll send it."

"There will be an answer. I shall sit down and wait
for it."

He muttered something, but he moved to the table
where his wireless key rested and began to tap out the
message. I listened as though I understood what he was
sending. He sighed deeply after a look at me and continued to send.

It was an hour and a half later that Mr. Arnold's
reply came through.

HAVE RETAINED ELIAS BLAKELY,
ATTY IN PORTLAND, TO HANDLE
STOP MESSAGES FOLLOW TO CAMER-
ONS AND OTHERS STOP STICK BY
YOUR GUNS.

The operator was receiving more messages and
writing them down rapidly. There were several. I
didn't wait, but walked briskly back to the inn. I went
to my room and sat there, fuming silently and trembling
with anger and frustration.

A tap on the door startled me. I opened it to face
the hotel clerk. He stood there, his manner as meek

as his tone. "I've discovered the reservation for this room has been canceled and you may have it for as long as you wish, ma'am. I'm sorry I inconvenienced you before."

"Thank you," I said.

So Mr. Arnold's influence was beginning to be felt. I made up my mind at that moment not to budge from this town until everything had been settled.

At suppertime I changed my attire. A deep purple dress, simple in line. I took down my hair and arranged it with a coil at the nape of the neck. I had a slight headache, due to nerves, but I'd regained my calmness, so I made my way to the dining room. There were a few people about, and I gave each one a casual glance. I was searching for the face of the man in the mirror, but I saw no one who even remotely resembled him.

There was a marked change in the attitude of the desk clerk and the dining room employees, however. I was now being favored above the other guests and diners. I believed also, that good as the food had been, it was being especially prepared for me, and to my palate it seemed exceptional. Apparently these good people were making up for their former rudeness.

I noticed a man who seemed strangely familiar to me. He was somewhat heavyset, like a man who lacked exercise but not the bottle, nor an idle existence. He was watching me somewhat intently, and when he arose and came to my table, I wasn't surprised.

"Mrs. Cameron." He bowed slightly as he addressed me. Even his voice seemed familiar. "I beg permission to intrude."

"Who might you be?" I asked.

"I am Abner Cameron."

I extended my hand and managed a courteous smile. "Joel's older brother! Of course! I was trying to decide why you looked so familiar. You do resemble Joel. Please sit down."

"Thank you. After what happened this morning, I'm surprised you didn't crown me with the water carafe when I identified myself. I wouldn't have blamed you."

"Joel was fond of you, Abner. I think, of the entire family, you were the only one."

"I guess I was the only one who understood him. And I think he knew why I didn't want to go through life struggling to make more money when I had all I needed. Still, Joel and I were different. He was a dreamer, looking for something. He didn't know what it was, but he went searching, while I stayed on, content to be plain lazy."

"I'd like to think Joel found what he was looking for."

"He found you, Maeve. He wrote me about you, and his plan to become a doctor. Yes, he found what he was looking for."

"It's good of you to say that."

"At least, he had happiness for a while. But . . . there are matters you have to know. Frankly, the family sent me here to do some explaining. Nobody up there wanted that task. They're all too proud to apologize. Even if they did, they wouldn't mean it, so they sent me. I do the dirty work, which, in this case, is delightful."

"You're like him," I said gratefully. "It's wonderful to hear a kind word. I was beside myself after my visit with your parents and their rejection of me. I didn't know which way to turn."

He summoned a waiter, ordered brandy for himself, then gave me a smile. "Oh, yes, you did. You turned to that New York lawyer, and he turned to probably the most influential and powerful lawyer in the State of Maine. Telegrams began coming, the family learned a few facts. In short, they're stuck with you, and there's not a thing they can do about it. Not a nice way of putting it, but that's the way they feel. You'll have to learn to deal with them."

152

"I did not come to make trouble," I said "Joel told me, not long before he died, that I must not let the family intimidate me and that I should claim what was rightfully mine. That is all I am doing, Abner."

"Ah, Maeve, I know," he said. "Now here's the situation. Whatever threats they may have made—and I know they made some, because they always do when they can't get their own way—forget them. But they suggest that you go back to Ireland and Joel's share will be sent to you automatically."

"In other words, they do not wish me here, nor am I welcome at the mansion."

"That's about it. Mind you, they can't compel you to do anything. Though, of course, they don't have to welcome you into the family—and they won't."

I laughed at the very idea of it. "I do not go where I do not wish to go, welcome or not, sir. But I do wish to know more about this business and this town."

"Why?" he asked bluntly.

"Because Joel did not approve of it. I think whatever goes on here gave him pain and a hurt that stayed with him. He left because he couldn't live with it and was powerless to do anything about it. He spoke very little of the town and the factory."

"Joel left because he couldn't abide it. I have a different way."

"And what might that be?" I asked.

"I refuse to have anything to do with the business, and I get roaring drunk when it gets me down too far."

"They tolerate you in the face of that?"

"They have to. They don't dare throw me out or make things so difficult I'll leave. Because if that happened, I'd stay drunk and ruin the reputation of the family. As it is now, they can control me to a certain extent."

He was served his brandy, a rather large amount of it, I thought. He took to it as if it were tea.

153

"Then, of course," I said, "I will not press you to answer my questions."

"On the contrary, I want to answer them. Joel must have told you the history of the family up to the present time."

"Aye. Enough that I know the first of them fought and worked hard to gain what they did, but those who came afterward found the going easier and easier."

"And more and more profitable, because they have exploited all the people here. Maeve, the family owns almost every piece of property and the buildings on it in this town. Every family pays us rent save two or three. Every storekeeper works for a salary. He does not own the business. Everyone able to work is employed by the factory. Those who say a harsh word against us, or who shirk, are fired. They are set adrift, because it's impossible for them to find any other work here. If they leave, all they own is taken from them. Oh, it's legal. Everybody is in debt to the family. We see to that."

"Joel ran away because he could not bear it," I said. "Now I know why."

"As I told you, I get drunk."

"Couldn't you fight them?"

"Fight the family? It would take more guts than I've got. Joel wasn't a fighting man, either. He tried to make them understand, and they thought him addled. It would have done no good if he did put up a fight. Others have tried. Nobody ever came even close to winning."

"A little while ago I defied them, and though they threatened, they could do nothing about it."

"Not so far as you being Joel's widow and his heir. But if you stay, they'll find ways to make it unpleasant."

"I can see that. What would you have me do, Abner?"

"I know I sound like a coward, a man with no stomach to face them. I am. But I would advise you to go back to Ireland. You've no friends or kin here. You've money enough, and no doubt you'd make friends easily. But, from what Joel wrote, things are different in county Mayo. You'd miss it too much."

"And I wouldn't upset what's going on here. I can see I will have to make my own decision, Abner, but to make things more pleasant for yourself, you may inform the family that, in all likelihood, I will go back to Ireland. My heart will be forever there, but I will not be rushed."

He finished the brandy in one swallow. "Whatever you do, Maeve, I'm with you. I may not have the guts to show it, but morally, I'm on your side."

"I do thank you for that, and I believe you have the courage, if it came to the point where you had to use it."

He moved restlessly. "One more thing. How did Joel die? What was the illness?"

"I don't know, but it was puzzling. He came back from Dublin feeling poorly and that night he grew very sick. It was his stomach—he could keep nothing down. He had a high fever, and there were chills as well. As you know, my father was a doctor and I know something of medicine, but I had seen nothing like Joel's sickness before."

Abner's brow furrowed. "Joel wasn't rugged, and I remember he was sickly as a boy. But his death came so quickly."

"You're the only one here who has expressed the slightest interest in it."

Abner nodded. "He wouldn't go along with their plans. Well, it's over for poor Joel now. As for you, I'll go back with the news that you're not going to make trouble and you are about certain you will return to Ireland."

"Aye, tell them that. Though I retain the right to change my mind, and you will be kind enough to remember that, too."

"I'll not mention that part of it. If there's anything further, I'll be the one to come, no doubt."

"It's good to know I have one friend here. I thank heaven for that."

He gave a reassuring smile, got up, and left the room. I followed.

Once in bed I fell asleep promptly. I awoke once, feeling vaguely uneasy. I sat up, swung my legs off the bed, and shivered a little at the cold air coming in from the open window. I almost fell off the bed. It was then that I realized I felt ill and dizzy. I had a terrible urge to throw up. I tried to control this, but it was no use. I ran to the bathroom, where my stomach emptied itself.

I finally went back to bed feeling miserable. I covered myself with all the blankets because I was cold. My stomach was still queasy, and I still felt weak and giddy.

I tried to account for this sudden illness, but there was no reason for it. The food I'd eaten had been wholesome. I knew that. And yet, this feeling of nausea wouldn't leave me.

Then I gasped, and a terror came over me, for this was how Joel had been. The symptoms he'd shown I now had. Was the same thing happening to me? Would I be dead within a matter of hours? Or was it merely a matter of tension and nerves? What had happened to me since my visit to the Camerons was enough to make one's stomach turn.

SIX

From time to time I dozed, but for the most part the remainder of this night was sleepless. Just before dawn I was again sick at my stomach, getting nothing up, but retching as Joel had done. I realized that if there was a doctor in this town, I'd have difficulty reaching him at this unseemly hour, and I wasn't even sure I needed his services.

My illness was not the same as Joel's. I came to know that when common sense overwhelmed the fear that first came to me. I had no fever or chills. I suffered from a simple malaise caused by excitement, my visit to the Camerons, and, likely, fatigue brought on by the long journey.

Back in bed, I began to feel better, and I was gratified I'd not given way to panic. If the Camerons heard of that, they'd have been pleased and, perhaps, considered me weak in body and spirit both.

I was not too steady as I went down the stairs to breakfast. I had a tendency to feel giddy, but I managed to reach my table and I ordered a rather light breakfast. I barely touched it before I knew I was going to be sick again. I left the dining room as inconspicuously as possible and once in my own rooms I promptly threw up again.

There was no longer any question of my seeing a doctor. There was definitely something wrong with me, and whatever it was was not caused by emotion or fatigue. I waited until I felt less faint and somewhat stronger before I went downstairs and asked the desk clerk if there was a doctor in town.

"Yes, ma'am. You turn left when you leave the inn. Walk straight along Main Street. You'll come to a white fence. There's a sign nailed to it with the name of Glen Kinnery on it. He's the doctor, like his father was. You feeling poorly, ma'am?"

"I have a headache," I explained. "I need only a headache powder. Thank you."

I followed his simple directions and found the doctor's house and office promptly. I opened the white gate and walked down a path lined with clumps of yellow daisies in full bloom. Two giant oak trees framed the house, covering it with the shelter of their branches. It was a two-story frame house with green shutters and, unlike the other houses in this town, it was freshly painted and in a fine state of repair. It was also much larger, with a spacious yard.

I entered the waiting room and sat down. A little brass bell, set into motion by the opening of the door, had announced my arrival. I looked about. It was a pleasant waiting room with rows of chairs and a comfortable-looking sofa against one wall.

The door to the private office opened, and a man came out to stand and regard me with a warm smile of greeting. I could scarcely breathe at the sight of him. I couldn't even move, or speak, and I marveled that I didn't faint.

I was staring at the man whose image had appeared in the magic mirror!

He moved toward me, the smile gone, a look of concern taking its place.

"You are ill . . . so pale. . . ." he said.

I managed to regain some of my composure. "It's my stomach, Doctor. I can't seem to keep anything down, but I don't think it's anything serious."

"You let me be the judge of that, Mrs. Cameron."

"So you know who I am?"

"Everyone in town does. Let me help you. . . ."

He assisted me out of the chair and brought me into his office. He closed the door after helping me into a chair before his desk. It was an office Father would have gloried in. A white table, a white cabinet in which instruments were displayed behind glass doors. A small pharmacy was off the examination room; it was stocked with bottles of medicine and not herbs gathered in the fields.

"Now," he said, "what exactly seems to be the trouble?"

"It's my stomach, Doctor. I've been throwing up."

"From anything you can account for?"

I hesitated. How could I tell this man about my suspicions concerning Joel's death? He would think me daft.

"No," I said. "I can't account for it. I've been blessed with good health. And rarely have I had a stomach upset."

"Then I shall have to make an examination, Mrs. Cameron."

"Aye, I realize that."

I was studying him without seeming to, and I knew for a certainty he was the man in the mirror.

"I'll call someone to help," he said. He opened another door leading into the house. "Jennie!" he shouted. "I've need of you at once."

He came back and sat down again. "Joel was a patient of mine—also a friend. When he left, there wasn't anything wrong with him. May I ask what caused his death?"

"We don't know, Doctor. My father was a physician. He died shortly before Joel. I did what I could for Joel, knowing a little about medicine, but he only grew worse."

"Didn't you send for a regular doctor?"

"Aye, but too late, and the man who came was not competent. An old man long out of touch with modern

159

medicine. You see, sir, in county Mayo there are very few medical men because there's no money to pay them. So they never settle there."

He nodded. "I see. There's not much money in this town, either, but . . . well, that's another story. So, in what manner was Joel ill?"

"His stomach. He came home from Dublin feeling poorly. His stomach was very upset, and he grew worse. There was fever and chills. I don't know what it was. Perhaps he ate something that was poisonous. Like the wrong sort of mushrooms . . . something of that nature."

"That's possible. I don't suppose an autopsy was done?"

"Who was to do it, sir?" I asked. "Joel was laid out, waked, and buried. That's the way it is done there."

He looked as puzzled as I had been and still was. The window light was on him, revealing his strong, masculine features, making him seem handsome when he really wasn't. He was tall and sturdily built. His hair was dark brown and he was clean-shaven which, to me, had appeal. Most of the gentlemen in this country wore beards or full mustaches. His quiet gray eyes were appraising me in a professional manner, and I got the feeling he was an excellent doctor. He was serious, as was befitting one in his profession, yet on the few times he had smiled, it revealed a warmth and compassion which had been so evident in Joel.

Was I staring at the man I would one day marry? Or had his reflection appeared because he had known Joel and would be as good a friend to me as he had been to him? But of one thing I was certain—his was the face which had appeared in the mirror.

I shuddered a bit, wondering if the mirror would go further, as it had done with Joel, and predict this man's death. I came out of that reverie when the woman he had called to assist him in his examination entered the room. She was young and regarded me with interest and friendly warmth. I gathered she was the doctor's

160

wife. I felt no disappointment. I was of the firm belief no one could take Joel's place in my heart.

"This is my sister Jennie," the doctor said. "Jennie, this is Joel's widow."

Jennie smiled and extended her hand to me. "Welcome to Cameron, Maeve. We're sorry about Joel, but pleased you came here."

I could have wept with joy at her friendliness. I even forgot what had brought me here until Dr. Kinnery suggested I prepare myself for an examination. He retired from the room while his sister helped me.

"Will you be here long?" she asked. "I've heard what happened at the mansion, of course. Everybody in town has. The servants gossip."

"I'm not sure," I said. "I like it here, even though my welcome was less than friendly."

"Like it here? This town? A girl with your looks? I find it hard to believe."

"Now, on the same subject, Miss Kinnery," I said, "you're not a sight to offend the eye by any means. So what keeps you here?"

"My brother—and memories. I'll tell you about it one day. Well, climb on the table. This won't take long. And call me Jennie. My brother and I like informality."

It required but fifteen minutes, and the examination was done with tact and brisk efficiency. The doctor left the room again while I dressed.

"Other than paleness, you don't appear ill." Jennie spoke reassuringly.

"I'm sure it's nothing serious," I said. "At this moment, I feel quite well. A good stomach remedy will put me back in shape, I'm sure."

"Be kind enough to call on me when you can," Jennie said. "I'm starved for good company, and I can tell you a great deal about this town. If you're interested."

"I am. And I'm starved for company, too, Jennie. I would like for us to be friends."

161

"And we shall be. Good luck."

She left once Dr. Kinnery entered and began a further examination. He studied my eyes and my throat, and he took my temperature. Then he sat down opposite me and asked a score of questions. I was beginning to feel concern until he smiled.

"I'm that relieved," I said. "A doctor wouldn't be smiling as you are if he had bad news."

"When did Joel die?" he asked, once again serious.

I thought back swiftly. "Why, it's eight weeks to next—" I stopped talking and gaped.

He nodded slowly. "You guessed right. You're going to have a baby."

I brought my hand to my mouth and gasped aloud. I didn't know whether to burst into tears or shout in happiness, so I did both.

"It's a miracle," I exclaimed. "I . . . lost track of things over these weeks, I've been that upset. I should have guessed, but it never occurred to me. What will they say up there on the hill? What will they think now? Of me and the child?"

"I can't answer that, but I wouldn't worry about it. Are you going to remain in Cameron?"

"I don't know. I've thought about it. This changes everything. I'm not sure what I'll do."

"I'll want to see you in two weeks, if you're still here," he said.

"Aye, Doctor, I'll be here. A bit of personal advice I'm asking now. Would you think it wise of me to let them know—'on the Hill,' as you refer to the Cameron residence?"

"They will be the grandparents, Mrs. Cameron."

"Aye, and since that is so, they have a right to be told. It'll be worth it, just to see their faces. It's a blessed day for me because of many things, not the least of which is the fact that Joel will live on."

He nodded agreement. "You have the right attitude. The more cheerful you feel, the easier it will be. By

162

all means tell them and . . . please come back and tell me how they reacted. I'll waive any and all fees just for that information."

"I'll not allow that, Doctor, but I'll be back. Thank you—for more than you know. I hope we are good friends."

He held out his hand. "As you'd say, Mrs. Cameron, aye, that we are."

I thought my meeting him a rather good beginning, but I wished to be certain I'd not been mistaken about seeing him before.

"Night before last I thought I saw you at the inn," I said. "Or was it my imagination?"

"No indeed. I have a bedridden patient there. I call on him two or three times a week."

"I was bold enough to ask the desk clerk who you were," I said. "In the brief glimpse I had you looked like someone I used to know."

"Henry can't see two feet before him and won't admit it because he's afraid of losing his job."

"At least I know it wasn't my imagination," I said as I arose. "About the Camerons, I'll decide soon, and if I visit them with the news, I'll come back and give you a full report."

"I'll be obliged," he said, with a smile, "and interested."

He followed me through the reception room into the open front yard. "It's a lovely place you have, Doctor," I said. "Far better than most in this town."

"That's because I own it and the Camerons don't. My father built it. He was the doctor here, too, for about fifty years. That's why I came back. I was needed, and it seemed more important to me than making more money than the town will provide."

"I know all about that. It's the way my father felt, and him a good doctor with a fine education, who could have gone far. My brother Jimmy, now, he's not of that stripe. He's in his final year at Edinburgh where

163

he studies to be a surgeon, and a great one he'll likely be, but not in Mayo."

"Don't fault him, Mrs. Cameron. He has a point, and I admit there are times when I'm sorely tempted."

I saw my chance at that moment, and I took advantage of it. "Not being as yet a married man, you can accept the risk of not making much money. At least I assume you are not married."

He smiled and shook his head. "There's been no time for that. Learning how to become a good doctor consumes every minute, and since I came here I've been busy."

"Aye, I have been well aware of that for a long time with my father a doctor and my brother about to become one."

"One of these days, Mrs. Cameron, things will change. For all of us."

"Good day, Doctor," I said. "I'll be back."

I walked slowly to the hotel, not with Dr. Glen Kinnery on my mind, but with the child of Joel Cameron taking precedence over all else. It seemed a beneficent heaven had given me this child now. What better way to keep the memory of Joel alive? I felt like breaking into song. Even before I reached the inn I made up my mind that before this day was done, I'd tell the Camerons what was in store for them. The sad note was that my father wasn't alive to share my joy, for he'd have been that proud. And if Joel had lived, he'd have walked tall among men and there could have been a happy future for all of us. And yet, with all this sadness, who was I to deny the beauty of this miracle?

The first thing I did, in the privacy of my rooms, was to bring out the mirror and carry it close to the window for the most light. I gently rubbed its surface with a linen kerchief, then tilted it for the best reflection.

"Once again I ask that the image of one in my future be shown to me that I may be certain. I ask this in the memory of good Queen Maeve for whom I have been named, and to whom this mirror once reflected her own beautiful image."

The inner surface glowed briefly, or so it seemed to me, and the profile of Glen Kinnery appeared for an instant of time. Long enough that I could now be positive that there was no mistake. I sat down slowly, still holding the mirror.

"I ask one more favor. Within me is my first child. Will it be a boy or a girl? Will it be a healthy, strong child?"

I tilted the mirror several times at different angles. Nothing flashed into view, and I grew apprehensive and frightened. Then, when I was about to give up, I saw a shadow, but I was unable to tell if it was a boy or girl, so fast did it appear and fade. But even so, it did revive my spirits, and I was grateful for that much of a prophecy. Had there been nothing, I would have had to conclude that there would be no living child. It seemed to me that the mirror gave me this fragmentary glimpse only to assure me that my baby would live. I put the mirror away with the realization that it could not only be a beautiful thing to foretell the wonderful events that were to happen, but a deadly one as well. As it had proven with Father and with Joel.

At the noonday meal my appetite was ravenous. Now that I knew the truth, I found myself eager for food. Afterward, I went to the stable, where the owner promptly provided me with his best carriage and a sedate horse.

I wore a tan skirt with a dark brown shirtwaist and pinned a small, modestly decorated hat in brown straw to my hair. I wished to make a suitable appearance without being ostentatious in any way.

I drove up to the hill and as I began to pass the large glassed-in house entirely separate from the mansion, a young woman stepped out and held up her hand in an imperious fashion. It was a command for me to pull up the carriage, and I did. I had no idea who this was until she approached me, and then I saw the resemblance to Joel. This had to be Helen Easterly, his sister.

She was a slim girl, about Joel's height. Her complexion was fair, her face narrow, a characteristic of the Camerons. Her eyes were like her mother's, clear, but cold and shrewd-looking, and she possessed the same rigid cut to her chin, giving her that indomitable family appearance of arrogance.

"What do you want here?" she demanded with an uncivil curtness.

I couldn't be hurt now, or distressed. "May I ask who wishes to know? Seeing that I've never before laid eyes on you."

"I'm Helen Cameron, and you very well know it."

"But then," I said complacently, "I did believe Joel's sister to be a married woman. I must have been deceived in that thought. . . ."

"I am Helen Cameron Easterly."

"Why didn't you say so in the first place?"

"I asked you a question. You are not welcome here, and you know that, too."

"Aye, I well know it, and were it not for some fresh news I bring with me, I'd not be here at all. What I have to say affects the family of Joel Cameron."

"What do you know that can possibly interest us?"

"I'll be glad to tell you when the rest of the family is there to hear me as well," I said. Then I softened my voice because I did wish to be accepted by these people. Especially now that I knew I was bearing Joel's child. "Helen, what is the sense of bickering? I have done nothing to offend you or yours. I married Joel because I loved him and he loved me."

"Joel was a fool!"

"Then I was a fool, too, but we were glorious fools. Those days we shared were precious and happy. To Joel, being happy was a strange feeling, but he had those weeks and nobody can take that away."

"You're insolent as well as greedy," she said.

166

I sighed deeply. "If you believe those things of me, I can do little to change your mind, nor will I try. But you are Joel's sister. He bore you no malice, even though your ways were not his. I'm sorry for you, Helen Cameron Easterly, but don't let that fool you. I'll stand up for the rights your brother left to me— and neither you nor yours can change that."

I slapped the reins smartly and sent the carriage on toward the entrance to the mansion. There, the same austere woman in the same severe uniform greeted me without uttering a sound or betraying the slightest facial expression. Evidently she had already received orders to let me in.

In the drawing room both Joel's parents sat in large, gilded high-backed chairs. They resembled royalty in the act of receiving a supplicating peasant. More and more I understood Joel's abandonment of his family.

"You were asked not to return," Mrs. Cameron said. "I take it that since you did, this must be a matter of some importance."

"It is that," I said. "Of such importance that I would like the rest of the family present."

"If you are about to announce that you have acceded to our request that you go back to Ireland, the rest of the family can be told later."

"I am not going back, and that is not what I have to announce. Will you call the others? Or shall I leave and let you wonder what it was that I came here to say?"

"Martha," Mr. Cameron raised his voice, addressing, I presumed, the austere housekeeper who was likely in the reception hall listening. Evidently he had no need to deliver orders. In a few moments Loran Cameron sauntered in, greeting me with a cool nod. Then Abner arrived and came directly to me. He took the hand I offered him and bowed over it quite formally, but he said nothing. It hurt me to see how fearful he

167

was of these people, for Joel must often have felt the same way.

A slender man with a thin mustache walked briskly into the room and gave me a long, appraising look with more than casual interest in it. I hadn't seen him before, but I assumed he was Ashley Easterly, Helen's husband.

He was followed by the more stately entrance of a woman in her mid-sixties with an abundance of gray hair styled high on her head. She was heavyset and, as Father used to say, broad of beam. She presented a formidable appearance with lips tightly compressed and small eyes regarding me with open hostility. Joel had described her well. This was his aunt Marcy Tabor. She spoke no word of greeting.

I looked about the room. "Helen is not here, but then it really doesn't matter with her, for she doesn't approve of me, either."

Mrs. Cameron said, "Will you tell us what earth-shaking reason caused you to come back? Or shall we call this interview at an end? You are trying my patience."

"I will call it at an end," I said, "after I announce that I now bear Joel's child and in approximately seven months you will be a grandmother, Mrs. Cameron. I have no intention of returning to Ireland. I may even remain in Cameron. As Joel's people you had a right to be informed of this, and I have now completed that duty, so there is no further reason for me to remain. I shall never again impose upon you, nor will I allow you to impose upon me."

I got up and walked quickly to the door. No one had said a word. Not one blessed word, and not one of them had shown the slightest emotion. They were like a family of wooden people.

I had reached the marble veranda when someone caught my arm and turned me about. It was Abner, his face aglow in a great and wonderful smile.

"Maeve," he said, "that's the most delightful news I have ever heard."

I kissed his cheek. "Thank you, Abner. I'm grateful for your kindness."

"In there," he angled his head toward the drawing room, "they just don't understand. . . ."

"Yes, Abner, that's why it's so wonderful that you do."

I left him standing there and returned to my carriage. I drove straight back to the stable and turned it over to the hostler. I walked to the inn, went directly to my room, and sat down in the rocker beside the window. I hadn't removed hat or gloves, and I sat there in a state of bewilderment about people so cold they didn't even comment when they learned a child would be born into the family.

How different it would have been if I'd entered my home to tell my father and Joel that I was going to have a child. Their shouts of joy would have rung rafters and the entire village would promptly have been called in to enjoy Father's best grog.

I wished I'd not put myself out to go to the Hill and tell them. It wasn't worth the effort. The experience left me with a vast sense of loneliness. I had to be with someone, talk to someone. I left the inn and went to Dr. Kinnery's office. There were two people in the waiting room. I sat down to await my turn, praying no one would come in after me.

One patient was an elderly man who held a cane between his knees, clutching at the curve of it with arthritic fingers. If he saw me he gave no hint of it. The other was a buxom homebody type of woman who greeted me with a smile that lifted my spirits somewhat.

"Good afternoon," I said.

"You're Joel Cameron's widow, aren't you?"

"Yes, I am. It's good to talk to someone who lives here. There are so few people about."

"We've not dared talk to you, ma'am."

"And why not, may I ask?"

"You're a Cameron."

"Ah, yes," I said. "I am that. But I'm also an O'Hanlon, and we O'Hanlons are friendly folk. We don't keep our noses in the air, and we have never considered ourselves better than the next person. So think of me as Maeve O'Hanlon, and not Cameron, if that helps."

"I said you weren't stuck up. I knew it. Somehow I could tell, but . . . still. . . ."

"There will be no buts about it," I said. "I'm that lonely I need friends, and if you offer me friendship I'll be delighted. I would consider it an honor to call on you."

"My name is Mamie Dexter. I live in the second house to the left of the third street off Main Street. The houses ain't numbered because the old . . . that is, the landlord says numbers ain't necessary because everybody knows everybody else."

"I'll be pleased to call," I said.

The door opened, and Glen Kinnery looked out, not in the least surprised to see me. He helped the elderly man into his office and ten minutes later helped him out again. Mrs. Dexter spent ten minutes with him, and then Dr. Kinnery held out his hand to me. I took it, and he led me into the office.

"Jennie and I have wondered how it went up on the Hill. Now, I'm not asking you to betray any confidences. It's really none of our business. . . ."

"Then I shall make it your business, Doctor, because if I don't confide in somebody, I'll bust. You can't imagine what went on."

"What did they say?"

"Nothing. Not a single, blessed word. They were as cold as the Little Folk of Ireland when you've found their pot of gold. When I told them I was bearing Joel's child, they acted as if I'd informed them it might

170

rain next Tuesday. All but Abner. He was happy for me."

Glen said, "It really puzzles me, because I thought they'd be all for it."

"Oh? And may I ask why that would be?"

"There are no heirs. Nobody to carry on the Cameron name or the mill. Or hold the town intact when the others are gone."

"What of Joel's sister, Helen?"

"She's barren. I can tell you that in confidence because, after all, you are a family member, even though they won't accept you. Abner will never marry. They'd come to the end of the line—until you came along. That's why I thought they'd be overjoyed."

"Well, they were not. They care for naught but their own narrow interests, and not even the future means much to them. I've had my fill of them, except for Abner. I will not again pay that mansion a visit."

"I can't say I blame you. What will you do?"

"I could go back to Ireland, but that would suit them too well, so I will not. I could make a home somewhere else, perhaps a great city like New York or Boston, but that, too, would take me away from them so they could easily forget that I exist. Joel fled because he could not bear them. I owe it to his memory to remain here, with his child. They didn't mourn Joel, but the child will serve to remind them of him. I shall build me a house here, and I shall do what I can to relieve the misery I believe afflicts the people of this town. Thanks to the miserliness of that family to which I unfortunately now belong."

"Those are big plans, Mrs. Cameron."

"I'm not even liking the name," I said. "It's mine and I will use it, but I want my friends to call me Maeve. My friends," I said with a sigh. "You, your sister, and Abner. A small circle to be sure, but I'm grateful. And hopeful."

"They may be able to keep you from carrying out

such plans, Maeve. They're powerful, and they don't hesitate to use that power."

"I'm no longer afraid of them. I will defy them, and I'll fight them if necessary. Ah, what makes them be that way? I cannot understand such people. And Joel was so different. So kind and understanding and sympathetic in all things."

"It was born in him. As for the others, put them out of your mind if you can. My sister and I will be your friends."

"You are already that, Doctor. I'll not keep you longer, busy man that you are. I'll go back and think about what I will do, and when I make up my mind you'll be the first to know."

"Good. I'll do all I can to help. Remember that."

"Indeed I'll not forget it."

I was almost happy as I left Dr. Glen Kinnery's office.

When I approached the inn, a carriage was drawn up before the door and a driver in a gray uniform sat on the high seat, rigid as the post to which the horse was tied. Inside, the lobby seemed to be muted, as if it was expected everyone would walk on tiptoe. The desk clerk came to me and spoke in an undertone.

"Ma'am, she's in your rooms. She made me let her in."

"In heaven's name, whom are you talking about, man?"

"Mrs. Cameron! *The* Mrs. Cameron."

"I see. It's all right. I don't mind her being there."

I climbed the stairs wondering what was going to happen now and what new threat was going to be made. I paused momentarily and took a deep breath. Then I opened the door and entered the room. I held the upper hand now, and she was the intruder.

She was sitting at the window. No doubt she'd been watching for me. I crossed the room slowly. To my astonishment, a smile of welcome touched her lips. She

172

arose, slowly raised her arms, and started toward me. I paused in utter astonishment, unable to believe my eyes at the change in her.

"Maeve, please forgive me. Forgive all of us."

She attempted to embrace me, but I stepped back, beyond her reach. Her arms slowly lowered to her sides, and her features sobered. "I don't blame you, my dear. I deserve the rebuff. Please—can't you find it in your heart to forgive me?"

"I'm a great believer in forgiveness," I replied coolly. "My feeling—if I can manage any at this moment—is one of deep suspicion."

She nodded and momentarily lowered her eyes. A weary sigh escaped her. "We did you a grave wrong when you came. We were rude and made you feel unwelcome. I suppose we felt you guilty of Joel's death."

"How could I be?" I exclaimed in high indignation. "I gave him love, Mrs. Cameron. Happiness, companionship, joy, and I will give him a child. What did you give him?"

She covered her eyes with her hand. "I . . . I . . ." She paused, and I had the feeling she wanted me to come to her. I did not, for my suspicions were no less.

She looked at me again, her eyes begging for understanding. I made no attempt to speak.

"Maeve, regardless of what you may think, Joel was my favorite. A mother does have a favorite, you know. She will never let that child know, but there's always one she loves above the others. Joel was that one."

"A pity you never let him know it."

"I am not an outgoing person. I find it so hard to . . . make people understand. I . . ." She closed her eyes tightly and clenched her fists. "You've no idea what agony it is for me to stand here and apologize. To try to make you understand. I'm Joel's mother. I loved him. I wanted to shelter him, but the others . . . my husband, Loran . . . Helen . . . please, Maeve . . ."

"You seemed so . . . cold when I told you about the child."

"I was stunned. We all were. Oh, my dear, everyone makes mistakes. Ours seems to have been a blunder beyond forgiveness, but we did consider you to be an adventuress. The world is full of them, looking for someone like Joel. We were wrong. So terribly and cruelly wrong, my dear. And now you have brought me the most wonderful news a mother can hear, that her dear son may be dead, but a part of him lives on. I . . . cannot go on. I've said all I can say. I cannot blame you for turning away. . . ."

"I'm sorry," I said.

She released a long breath. "I'll go now."

"Why didn't you acknowledge our marriage? Joel was terribly hurt when you sent no word. Perhaps he expected nothing from the others, but you . . . his mother . . ."

"My dear, we sent a long cable . . . I swear we did. Oh . . . oh, you didn't receive it. How can I blame you for feeling as you do? Maeve, there must be a copy on file. . . ."

"And when I cabled you that Joel had died?"

She bent her head. "I was overcome with sorrow. The others . . . were angry. We did nothing and I'm ashamed of it." She looked up at me. "Well, I can say no more, I have no excuses. I hold no hatred. . . ."

"I think, deep in his heart, Joel loved you," I said. "As I will."

She came to me then, and we wept, as women will in moments of joy. I felt that I'd misunderstood her, though I could find no liking for the others on the Hill. Not yet.

"Maeve," she said, "we beg of you, come live with us. At least until the baby is born. Then you may wish to have a home of your own, and we can see to that as well. We will make no demands on you. What we have is also yours. We hope you will remain with us always, although we realize you are very young and most attractive, so . . . there will likely be another man one day. All that is in the future. For now we wish only to be certain you'll be happy and comfortable. We want you to have every opportunity to have a healthy and wonderful baby. Let us share in your joy. Let us help you forget your loneliness."

"I'll come in the morning," I said, "and be happy to. Joel's child will be born among his people. I have no family."

"Yes, you have, Maeve. You're a Cameron. We'll prepare a suite of rooms. You'll see . . . it will all be very pleasant. We'll take fine care of you and make up for this horrible way we treated you."

"I'm glad you came," I said. "Up until now, the time I've spent here has seemed like a nightmare."

She embraced me again and shed a few tears before she left, leaving behind a mild aroma of lavender, which I liked. I felt better. At last I was going to be accepted and perhaps even loved. People could change. The Camerons had been disciplined to be cold and austere, domineering and conscious of wealth and power, but inwardly they'd had a trace of decency. It took the news of my baby to bring them to their senses, to make them human. Joel would have been shocked by the change in his mother, but happy they had accepted me.

I would pack now, then I'd return to tell Dr. Kinnery about this sudden turn of events. In the morning I'd go to my new home where my child would be born. As it was meant to be. As I wanted it to be.

Glen Kinnery was on a call when I arrived at his office, but Jennie brought me into the house proper and made me feel quite at home. Especially when she told me how much her life had been like mine. Her father, a widower and a doctor, his son studying medicine, living in a small town, that knew little happiness. It brought back memories, some of them fond, many sad.

"We grew up here," Jennie said when I'd been installed in the small parlor and supplied with tea and dainty cucumber and watercress sandwiches. "With the domination of the Camerons all around us, but without really touching us. Papa tended the sick, including the Camerons, and gave little heed to what went on because it was none of his business, he said. Now, Glen, he's a trifle different, being born so much later when men are beginning to realize these owners, like the Camerons, are just as dependent on them as they are on the Camerons."

"Thank heaven we had none of the like in my village," I said. "The men worked as farmers and fishermen, mostly on their own, but I will say there'd be none of them that wouldn't put up with much for homes such as these in this town."

"But Maeve, your people worked mainly for themselves. There's a great difference."

"I suppose there must be, though I wouldn't know too much about that, I'm afraid, not having been here long enough to really know what goes on. Though I have heard a few things I do not like. Tell me about your brother."

"Glen? Oh, there's little to tell. I adore him, of course. He's a fine doctor. In Boston we'd be living in luxury and giving fine dinners and balls, but these are our people in Cameron and they're in need of him, so we stay. We've often talked about leaving, yet we never do. There's always someone who is ill and can't be left."

"It's surprising to me that he's not married. I know he's not old by any means, and most men his age . . ."

"I know. I'm four years younger. I'm not that attractive I'm pursued by suitors. Frankly, there's not many in this town I'm attracted to. Perhaps it's selfish of me, but I feel that if I married any of the men here,

176

then I'd really be trapped. I'd never get out, and all hope of it would be gone. So I wait."

"And Glen waits for the same reason?"

"Glen waits because . . . I have a feeling he waits for someone. Some particular person he doesn't know yet, but who he feels sure will come along. Can you understand that?"

I nodded slowly, for surely I understood it. "Aye, Jennie, it's understandable. And likely well that he does wait, lest he make a serious mistake by not taking his time. They do say there's a right one for all of us."

"Was Joel the right one for you?" she asked candidly.

I had a hard time answering that one, and it gave me pause for thought because I wanted to give her an honest answer.

"Well, now, I must say yes, he was the right one. While he lived. Now that he's gone, perhaps . . . I don't know for certain . . . there may be a second time for me. Who can be sure of that?"

Glen came bounding into the house, having seen my carriage tied up outside, and his arrival saved me from the embarrassment of trying to explain further to his sister without revealing the fact that my fate, and Glen's, was already established.

"What's going on?" he asked. "I visited my patient at the inn and they told me Mrs. Cameron was there and left only an hour ago after spending a long time with you, Maeve."

"Aye, she did that. She came to make peace with me. I'm to come to the Hill and live in the mansion like a proper Cameron."

"Maeve, don't trust them. When they become kindly and apologetic, that's when they're the most dangerous."

"Doctor, I have to go somewhere. You have yourself said it would be hard to fight them."

"I think Maeve is doing the right thing," Jennie said. "She'll have the best care, and the surroundings

177

will be marvelous for her during the weeks before the child is born. And what can they do? I think they've changed toward her because they realize they can't merely dispose of the mother of their grandchild as if she were nothing. The family line has to go on."

"Maybe I'm too suspicious," Glen conceded, though reluctantly, I could sense. "It's just that I don't want Maeve to suffer any further at their hands."

"I thank you for that kind statement," I said. "I give you my word that if I even grow to suspect they have some selfish motive for asking me there, I will come to you at once and take whatever advice you may give, however drastic it may be."

He nodded. "All right, then, under those terms."

"Listen to the man," Jennie said with a tolerant smile. "You'd think he was married to you, giving orders that way."

"Well . . . I don't want Maeve to think badly of us here in Cameron. As I said, I don't want her hurt any more."

"I appreciate it, Glen," I said softly.

"Oh . . . it's because I'm your doctor and you're going to have a baby and . . . and . . . you've lost your husband a short time ago. Your father just before that. Enough is enough. I want you to have a healthy baby and to come out of it well and strong. That's what a doctor is for. To see that his patients not only stay well but happy, too."

Jennie covered her mouth to hide the smile, and I poured his tea so he could cover his confusion, too. The poor man, he had no idea what was in store for him.

He changed the conversation, and we talked about the mill and the Camerons until a patient announced his arrival by an impatient shout from the waiting room. We'd not heard the tinkle of the bell.

"Be sure to come see me once a week, Maeve," he warned, as he set down the teacup. "I want to be certain everything is progressing well."

"Aye, you can depend on that," I said.

After he had fled the room, Jennie burst out laughing. "Glen usually does not fluster so easily."

"Ah well, he does mean to help me and he is concerned."

"He sees mothers-to-be about once every two months until it nears their time. Now what would be unusual in your case to see you once a week?"

"I think he wishes only to know more about the Cameron family," I said with a laugh. "He does not want us to think he enjoys gossip, so this is his way of getting around it."

"I'm glad he wants to see you that often, because I do, too. And not for the gossip, though I won't forgive you if you fail to tell me what is going on."

I left on that happy note and set out for the inn to finish my packing and after a good night's rest, take myself to the Hill and my new life which seemed to give promise of many things, both good and bad.

I was prepared to face both.

SEVEN

What a different reception I received when I pulled up to the mansion next day. They were all waiting outside to receive me. Joel's mother and father, his Aunt Marcy Tabor, his sister Helen, and her husband Ashley Easterly. His uncle Loran Cameron was there and so was his warm-hearted brother Abner. Even the housekeeper, who broke her reserve enough to smile somewhat thinly and imperiously direct the other servants to remove my luggage and take it to my rooms.

Joel's mother drew her arm about my waist as we all entered the mansion. "We're so happy that you agreed to come and live here, Maeve. Except for Helen and Ashley, we're all getting on a bit, and it's nice to have a young face about once more."

Helen unbent, too. "Do you enjoy riding, Maeve? If you do, we can ride each morning. We've a wonderful stable, and I love to ride."

"I'd like that," I told her. "The countryside is so beautiful."

"It will be up to me," Loran said, "to instruct you about the business end of the Cameron family, though we don't have to go into that for a long time yet. Enjoy yourself first, before you begin to shoulder any of the responsibilities."

"I shall be ready to do what I can at any time, sir." I said.

Aunt Marcy kept smiling, as if the smile was frozen and she didn't dare let it warm up for fear of losing it entirely. She had nothing to say. Abner, of course, took advantage of the situation not only to embrace me but to deliver a lusty kiss as well, all in good friendship and in the spirit of a warm welcome.

So I settled down at the Hill. For a week I wandered about, getting used to the place. I investigated the glass-enclosed summer house with its pretty little steeple. Helen showed me the rare plants and the rather ordinary ones they grew there. I met the servants, all of whom proved to be too shy, or too frightened of the family, to do more than bow or curtsy and smile a little. Everything was done for me. My room was cared for, the bed turned down at night. My trunks had been brought from New York, and my closets were full of gowns and coats, hats and shoes. I'd supplied myself well, and even Helen was impressed.

I was due to visit Glen as his patient, and the morning of that day Mrs. Cameron informed me that a formal dinner and ball was going to be held in my honor in one week.

"I know it's somewhat soon after your arrival," she explained, "but we thought it best—before you begin to show, that is—you'd be more comfortable now."

"I would," I agreed. "Thank you for thinking so. And it'll be a grand ball, I'm sure. I'll do my best to behave like a lady."

She touched her cheek to mine. "Above all, my dear, you are a lady. We're no argument on that score."

A carriage with a uniformed coachman brought me to Glen's office, and I waited, with the people in his office, until it was my turn. I made sure I'd be last.

He led me into his private office, drew back a few steps, and surveyed me critically. "You haven't begun to look like a Cameron yet," he said. "Please sit down and tell me how you've been feeling."

"Quite well. I'm not even aware that I'm to have a baby. I've had no more sickness, though I do seem to have a remarkably good appetite."

"Don't get fat," he warned. He proceeded to give me a brief examination, quite superficial, which was all that was necessary, I knew. "How is life among the rich?"

"It's pleasant. How can I say otherwise? I think I would go soft if I lived that way too long, but of course I'm thinking of the baby and not doing too much. There's to be a formal dinner and ball next week. It is my wish that you and Jennie come as my guests."

"Did Mrs. Cameron ask you to invite us?"

"No, she did not, but as the ball is in my honor, I'm thinking I've the right to invite the only two friends I have in this town."

He shook his head. "Even if she had invited us, Maeve, we'd not come. The folk here wouldn't understand. They'd say we were finally selling out and joining them. We don't want that. I'd give my right arm to see you dressed for the occasion and to lead you onto a dance floor, but it cannot be. I hope you understand."

"Oh, aye, I understand all right, and I don't blame you. But it would not have been friendly of me not to ask you, Glen."

"Thank you, anyway. How do you feel up there? I mean, what is your attitude?"

"I'm ill at ease, if you must know. As if I don't belong and they know it and so do I. It's only a feeling, but it stays with me. I suppose it's caused by the way they treated me when I first came, and the way Joel felt about them."

"Yes, perhaps. Remember, if you grow too uneasy, if you think they're up to something, get out quickly. If you can't get out, send for me. Pretend to be ill—anything—but see that I reach you."

He seemed overly anxious about me. I liked that, but it disturbed me as well.

"Do you expect there will be trouble?" I asked.

"From that family I'd expect anything. Get them to show you the mill. Find out what it's like there."

"Loran has already invited me to inspect the mill," I said. "I will do that soon. But, Glen, I'm not afraid of them. They are very kind to me. My baby will be born under the best possible conditions, and I wish that above all else. I think they do, too."

"No doubt of it. None whatsoever."

"Helen has asked me to go riding. Will that be all right?"

"For now, yes. Later, I forbid it. I'll tell you when to put a stop to it."

"I'll be back in a week, then."

"Be sure of that, please."

"I will see Jennie, if it's not too much trouble."

"Jennie is caring for one of my patients. She acts as a nurse at times, and she's a good one. She'll be sorry she missed you. Perhaps next week."

"I hope so. I'll miss her."

I was driven directly back, the carriage traveling

182

quite fast through the Main Street as if the coachman had little desire to be seen behind the reins of that fancy contraption.

I felt that Glen was too worried about me. While I did appreciate his concern, I thought it overdone, but it was not for me to contradict him. He did know the Camerons better than I.

The days grew longer and longer with me having nothing to do. I began to feel restless. I'd inspected the mansion a dozen times. I'd walked the gardens until I knew every turn, and I was growing embarrassed at the frequency with which I caused the gardeners to jump to their feet, doff their caps, and bow as I passed. Had it been in my power to do so, I'd have put a stop to that.

It was on Monday that Helen reminded me I promised to ride with her. I had no riding habit, not having had the slightest hint that I'd be living in this style when I bought my first American clothes. But Helen had a habit which fitted me well. We were about the same size, though the skirt was a bit tight. Still I managed, and I set myself in a side-saddle on a pure white mare which, I was given to understand, would be my riding horse alone.

Helen and I rode out across the fields to a covered wooden bridge through which we clattered noisily. Beyond it was pasture land and quite large farms. Behind us we heard someone else riding across the bridge, and Helen uttered a mild imprecation.

"It's Ashley. I didn't ask him along."

"What does it matter, Helen? There's room for three of us. You ride well."

"Not as well as you, Maeve. I didn't know you did much riding in Ireland."

"That's how most of us get around. But we don't sit saddles such as these. More likely it's bareback with our legs astride the animal to keep from falling off."

"I'd like to try that sometime," she said with a light

laugh. "It must be nice over there. Did Joel ride much?"

"Only a little. He wasn't there long enough. Tell me, did he ever suffer from trouble with his stomach?"

"Why, no. Not that I was ever aware of."

"I don't like the way he died. It was almost mysterious. He was that sick several days, and then all of a sudden . . . he grew worse and it was over. I have often wondered if there was some long-lasting illness I knew naught of."

"Joel never was strong. Not like Abner, for instance, but he wasn't sickly."

Ashley joined us before we could continue this line of talk. He wore a fashionable riding habit topped off with a red felt hat and held a braided quirt which he raised above his head in a salute.

"Race you two," he challenged us.

He was off. Helen urged her horse into a fast run. Mine seemed to automatically accept the challenge and joined in the race. We gained on Ashley rapidly, and he kept looking over his shoulder as if he was chagrined at the fact he was going to be beaten.

I was alongside him when my horse suddenly broke into a wild run which I could not control. I didn't know what had happened, but all I could do was hang on for dear life. The horse was now a runaway, and I'd not the strength to pull her up. She cleared a low fence which I hadn't even seen, and when she came down I wasn't prepared. I flew off the saddle, partly because I wasn't used to a side-saddle and there seemed nothing to hang onto. I hit the ground hard and rolled over several times with the wind knocked out of me, and I wound up looking at the sky, trying to figure out what had happened.

Then Helen was kneeling beside me. "Maeve, are you hurt? Can you move?"

I raised my arms. "I'm thinking I'm all right, but I'm not sure." I tested my legs, and then I sat up. Helen helped me. Finally I managed to stand. I was sore and bruised. Ashley, pulling up, dismounted and came toward us. Helen, holding her quirt, suddenly lashed at him, and the whip cut across his face, drawing a thin line of blood. He cried out in pain and backed away.

"Damn you!" she shouted in anger. "Damn you for being so stupid."

"It was an accident," he said. "An accident, Helen."

"What was an accident?" I asked. "What happened?"

"I was using my quirt to get my slowpoke of a horse going faster because you two were passing me," Ashley explained. "You were close, and by accident the quirt landed on the flank of your horse. She went off like a shot."

"What horse wouldn't?" Helen asked. "Don't you realize Maeve is carrying a child?"

"Oh, my sainted mother," I cried out. "I'd forgotten that, too."

"Maeve, I want you to get on my horse. Yours may still be skittish. I'll handle her. Ride back to the house slowly. Ashley, if you want to make up for this stupid blunder, ride on ahead of us fast. By the time we get there, have Dr. Kinnery waiting."

Ashley, staring at blood staining his hand from the ooozing cut on his cheek, nodded bleakly and rode off. Helen helped me onto her horse, and we rode back in a most sedate fashion. I felt all right, but I wasn't sure whether that was a good sign or not. Helen's sudden rage puzzled me. For a moment I thought she'd been about to cut her husband's face to pieces.

"My husband," she said, "is a lazy, thoughtless man. There are times when I hate him, and this is one of them. He should have been more careful."

I was beginning to ache all over from my tumble and I quite agreed with her, but I thought her high anger uncalled for.

"I was riding close," I said. "And I must admit that if I'd been riding county Mayo style I'd not have been

185

thrown. I just slid off that slippery saddle as if it had been greased. Don't be too hard on the man."

"If you weren't carrying a child . . ."

"I'm all right, Helen. I'm sure of it."

Ashley wasn't back with Dr. Kinnery by the time we arrived, and nobody at the house knew what had happened. When the story of the mishap was told by Helen, I was instantly ordered into bed, and Mrs. Cameron hovered over me while the others gathered outside the door as if I wasn't expected to survive.

Glen arrived soon afterward, a sadly worried man. He ordered the room cleared before he sat down and asked me questions while he examined my arms and legs, made me sit up and bend over to make sure there were no back injuries.

"You've got a few nice black-and-blue marks beginning to form," he said. "Ashley told me he accidentally struck your horse with his quirt and it threw you. Is that right?"

"Aye, it's the truth, Doctor."

"Never in my life and experience around horses and horsemen have I ever heard of a rider striking the wrong horse with his quirt. Are you sure it was an accident?"

"What else could it be?"

"What cut his face that way? It's almost bad enough to need stitches."

"His wife did it with her quirt. She was that angry."

"You don't feel dizzy? Your stomach isn't sore? No pain?"

"Only where I fell. I'm sure I'm all right. I didn't send for you. Helen did."

"Such concern is strange coming from a Cameron," he said. "Well, come see me day after tomorrow. Unless you begin to feel ill, or there is any abdominal pain."

"Aye, Doctor."

"You're beginning to worry me, Maeve."

"Aye—and I'm glad of it."

186

"Oh, you are? Well, let me tell you—"

He stopped abruptly and began to look sheepish.

"Yes, Doctor," I said. "You were going to say . . ."

"Nothing. Nothing at all. I'll be going now. Don't be gallivanting about too much, and maybe you'd best not ride anymore."

"Whatever you say, Doctor."

"Thank you, Mrs. Cameron," he said formally. "Thank you very much."

He stalked out as if I'd offended him, the poor man. All he wanted to do was kiss me, and he'd not dared to. Had it not been for the dear memory of Joel I'd have kissed him. And that would have led to something, no doubt.

I insisted on getting out of bed, but three hours later I was that stiff and sore I was happy to have my supper sent up on a tray. When I'd finished eating, I decided to put on a robe and go downstairs for a little while. Atop the landing that overlooked the reception hall, I heard Joel's mother shrilly scolding Ashley.

"One more stupid mistake like that and I'll see to it that you not only get out of this house, but not another cent will you get from this family. You may be a handsome man, Ashley, and a value to the family for that reason, but a brainless man is a hazard and no asset. You have one more chance."

"I tell you it was an accident," he insisted.

The voice of Joel's mother grew harsher than ever as her anger increased. "Don't be ridiculous. The birth of Joel's child means that you do not take over the business when the rest of us go. That's what you married Helen for, but Joel fooled you, didn't he? There will be an heir."

I heard all this with cold horror. Was she right? Had Ashley deliberately caused the accident so I'd lose my baby? I turned away, not wishing to hear any more. As I did so, I saw Martha, the housekeeper, step back into one of the bedrooms where she'd apparently been at work. No doubt she'd not only seen me but heard enough of the tirade downstairs to realize I'd heard it as well. Martha was bound to tell Mrs. Cameron that I'd been listening.

I walked down the stairs. The angry conversation had stopped, and when I entered the drawing room only Joel's mother was there, everlastingly busy with needlework which seemed to occupy much of her spare time. She laid it down and invited me to join her.

"I do hope you were not painfully injured," she said. "Dr. Kinnery assured me there was no danger to the child, for which we can all be grateful."

"Aye, thanks be to the saints. But I'm afraid I have a confession to make, Mrs. Cameron. On my way down I heard you scolding Ashley. I'm sorry. But I find it difficult to believe that Ashley set my horse off with the intention that I'd be thrown."

"I am sorry you heard it, Maeve. It was not meant for your ears. It is my intention to keep you from all care and worry so that you will have every chance to give birth to a healthy child."

"Do you really believe he meant to harm my baby?"

"Well, no, I suppose not, but making him think that's what I believe will cause the man to be more careful in the future. He has lived in the hope that being the youngest of us he would some day take over everything. Now that idea has been wrecked by Joel—and you. Do you think you will have a son, my dear?"

"I do hope so, but it doesn't really matter. I'll love the child, boy or girl. Because in the child Joel will live again. I ask for no more."

"Were there more boys than girls in your family?"

"I cannot say I know the answer to that. I think, perhaps, there were more girls."

"Oh? I thought perhaps in . . . well . . . families who lived off the land as yours did . . . boys predominated. Just why, I don't know, except that boys were more needed."

188

"Mrs. Cameron, my ancestors go all the way back to Queen Maeve, after whom I was named. The family history goes back two thousand years, and over that much time some generations were rich, some poor, but all were healthy and strong, as I have heard it. And none were ever in need, nor did they ever shirk work or Christian duties."

"How interesting. I'm delighted to hear that. In the morning, my dear, Loran will take you on a tour of the mill. You should know all about it. One day this child of yours will control it. The operation of the mill has never, in any part, left the family, and we pray that it never will. That is why we welcome you so warmly, my dear."

"It was not the case when I first arrived," I reminded her, because I thought she should be reminded. I was not about to surrender meekly to this woman.

She reached over to grasp my hand. "Maeve, dear, we who are wealthy have to be always on the alert against fortune hunters. I confess that Ashley did deceive us, but we can control him and make the best of that bad situation. With you, we regarded you as some country girl who schemed to marry Joel for his money."

"When I agreed to marry Joel I didn't know whether he had a farthing or a fortune," I said. "I didn't care. I never schemed to marry your son. I dearly loved him, and nothing can give me greater pleasure or pride than to bring his child into this world, so I may love and cherish him—or her—as well."

"I agree fully. Accept us as we are and you will learn to love us, Maeve. As we have already learned to love you. We shall all be proud to introduce you to society, such as it is around here."

"Then I'd best get as much rest as I can and pray all my black-and-blue marks will vanish by the time I wear a ballgown. So if you'll excuse me I'll get myself to bed and be up early in time to go with Uncle Loran to the mill. I dearly wish to know all about it."

She kissed me. Her embrace was warm, her cheek against mine was a gesture of trust and love, but to me it was all cold. Like something calculated, tested, and now put to use. I was never going to feel completely at home in this house, but here I would stay until Joel's child was born. Then I would make up my mind what I would do. Whatever was best for the child would determine the moves I'd make. One thing I was sure about, I'd not permit the child to grow up and become as these people were. The people Joel fled from. If he found himself unable to stand them, his child was not going to be forced to endure it.

I was intrigued with Mrs. Cameron's desire that my child be a son. I could understand why. A boy would carry the name ever onward and perhaps be able to handle this family fortune and business better than a girl, but when I told her it mattered not to me what sex the child would be, I meant it. Yet I was curious so in the privacy of my rooms I brought out the mirror of Queen Maeve, and I lit both lamps on the bureau for all the light I could get. Then I sat down, tilted the mirror, and asked the memory of the good Queen if I would give birth to a boy or girl child.

The image flashed before my eyes so quickly that it almost seemed like an illusion. That had never happened before. It was the image of a girl. That much was clear, but it didn't remain long enough that I could even obtain an impression of what she would look like.

Then I was struck by the awful thought that there would be a girl born to me but she might not live. Perhaps that's the message the mirror was trying to imply by the quickness with which the image appeared and then vanished. The horror of the idea would plague me and torture me.

"Will my child live?" I asked the mirror. "Will my daughter grow into womanhood? I implore you, answer that. All you have ever given me has turned evil. My father died; my husband died. Now will my daughter also die? Answer me! Will she grow up?"

The image formed slowly this time. At first there seemed to be more than a deeper shadow in the depths of the concave bit of metal, but it took shape and became the profile of a grown woman. And then it vanished.

I gently wrapped the mirror, still confused by what it really meant but satisfied that my daughter would grow into womanhood. That much was assured me, and I was thankful for it. I locked the mirror away in one of my suitcases and got ready for bed. My mind was that relieved I went to sleep quickly and I slept well.

In the morning I breakfasted with Loran, the only member of the family who seemed to have awakened.

"I'm to take you to the mill this morning," he said, "and instruct you in some of the fundamentals of the family business. I trust you have a mind for this sort of thing."

"That remains to be seen, sir," I told him frankly, "never having handled many business affairs in my life, but I think I can follow you and know what you're talking about."

His gaze was cold and frankly appraisive. "I rather believe you can, too. Have you been in communication with your New York lawyer lately?"

"There's been no need for it, though I'm prepared to do so if anything should develop that calls for his advice."

He granted me a chilly little smile. "That sounds like a threat told pleasantly enough. Would you care for another biscuit, my dear? More coffee?"

"Yes, thank you," I said. "I don't believe in this silly business of having to eat for two, but I am hungry."

"You be sure to give us a healthy son, Maeve," he said.

191

"I have come to the conclusion that it will be a girl, Uncle Loran."

"Don't say that! It might influence the . . . the . . . the gender of the child, which can't be formed yet. I'm sure. Think only of your baby as a son. Someone once told me that often works."

"It is a foolish superstition," I said. "But if it is a girl, perhaps if I marry again I shall have a boy."

"Marry again?" He was aghast at the very idea. "You can't mean that. You married Joel. He may be dead, but you . . . married him. . . ."

"Do you think it likely I'll go through life as an eternal widow, Uncle Loran? I'm but twenty-one."

"You can't bring a stranger into this family. Damn it, that can't be done. We'll have to take steps. . . ."

I laughed gaily at his combined anger and discomfiture. "There's no need to be concerned right now. I'm certainly not going to be married soon."

He blew out a gust of air. "Of course. Who in this town would appeal to you, anyway. I'm worried over nothing."

I wondered what he'd have done if I told him that I would marry Dr. Glen Kinnery and not even Dr. Kinnery could avoid it. The poor man might have exploded with frustration and rage on the spot.

I hurried to my room and dressed for the inspection trip through the mills, taking care to wear something rather severe and not unduly colorful. I selected a brown dress, a walking dress, decorated in simple fashion with lace, and with it I wore a matching cloak.

Loran waited at the foot of the grand staircase and escorted me to where the carriage stood outside the door. We reached the mill after driving along Main Street, where women stared and curtsied politely as we passed.

There wasn't a man in the streets, nor a child, except toddlers. This I also noted well. I looked about for a schoolhouse, but saw none. I was about to query Loran about that, but I decided this might not be the best time for it, so I kept my mouth shut for the time being. First I must learn all I could before I reached any kind of decisions or offered any sort of complaints.

The mill offices, where we went first, contained a large number of small desks—about thirty, I guessed —at which men worked, bent over the books, noses close to the pages and never looking up as we passed by. There was certainly a tight discipline here.

Loran's office was large and airy with several windows overlooking the street. No one had said good morning to us; work didn't cease for a scant second. Those who worked in an office should have been the better-educated, the cleverer of the employees who would be more apt to take some small advantage of their positions, yet none did. I wondered what the mill workers would be like.

Part of Loran's office was paneled in dark wood with a wall separating a smaller room behind it and reached through a door and a single window with a barred upper portion, like a teller's window in a bank. Which was what it actually was.

Loran explained the purpose of this room and window. "Every Saturday the workers line up to be paid. The clerk in charge of the payroll checks what each worker owes for rent of his home and what he charged at the company store. This is deducted, and he is then paid the balance, if there is any. If not, he is allowed to let the credit go over until next week. Very few get into debt deeply, and those who do soon learn their lesson."

We left for a visit to the factory itself, though I was taken only through the first floor of the four-story building, which, I had noted, was of solid granite construction with many windows.

Everything was clean. Men were especially assigned for the purpose of sweeping up. "There is always the hazard of a bad fire in a cotton mill," Loran explained.

"The building is of granite; the floor upon which you walk is of wood, but three inches thick and impossible to burn. It's better than metal, because it won't melt. We've had fires, but they never got far. We pride ourselves on that."

I did note that while the interior was clean, as we passed through some of the factory yards, everything outside seemed grimy and sooty. Smoke belched out of several chimneys, and I came across an enormous pile of soft coal which fired the furnaces and drove the machinery.

"We used to rely on water power," Loran explained, "but coal is cheap and steam gives us more powerful machines so we produce three times as much. The carding machines especially were improved by steam power."

At one end of the long building was a tower which intrigued me.

"It used to be a bell tower. We called our workers by ringing a large bell and sent them home with the same ringing of the bell. When steam came, we used a whistle. But the bell tower is pretty, so we kept it. And for a building that was put up in 1825 you can't say it's in a bad state of repair. In fact, it's better now than when it was originally built, what with all the money we've spent on it. Also, the old paddlewheel is still intact and works if we turn it on. It provided the power before steam."

There was ample work for Loran, and he wasn't hesitant about excusing himself and dismissing me to go home alone. The carriage had been waiting, but I sent it on ahead and walked from the mill all the way up the Main Street.

I found that there was a small library and, after all, a school with about sixty children busy at their desks. None of the children seemed more than nine or ten years old. I learned later that at eleven and twelve their education was completed and they went to work in the mill. There was a church which served two faiths and a visiting priest and minister came each Sunday. One service immediately followed the other.

The company store was open, so I wandered in, and all activity immediately ceased. It was a large store selling clothing, meat, canned goods, dry goods, hardware. It smelled of a combination of kerosene and dill pickles.

"Please go on with whatever you're doing," I said. "I only wanted to see what it was like in here. As you may know, I am Joel's Cameron's widow. My name is Maeve."

A neat-looking, buxom woman in a plain gray dress and wearing a dark gray shawl over her head approached me with no sense of shyness.

"You're an O'Hanlon from Mayo, it has been said. And how did the likes of you come to find yourself living with them on the Hill?" she pointed a thumb over her shoulder.

"Irish you are," I said joyfully. "How many of you are there?"

"A hundred at least. None from Mayo. We were never that poor, if you don't mind my saying so."

"I don't mind anything you say. To find my own kind is a joy I never expected. I married Joel Cameron. He was living in Ireland—in our village. The poor man died."

"Joel was not like them." Again she gestured in the general direction of the Hill.

"Thank God for that," I said fervently.

"So you've not joined them, then?"

"I live with them because I'm going to have Joel's child, but I do not intend to stay the rest of my life. Now, what would your name be? If you don't mind telling it to an O'Hanlon, even if she turned Cameron."

"Doyle. Maggie Doyle. My man's a machinist at the mill. Earns better'n most, but he don't put on no airs, and if he did I'd crown him."

"I want to call on you," I said. "Will you do me that honor to invite me?"

"You have but to ask anyone where I live and it will be pointed out to you. You are welcome any time, but as Maeve O'Hanlon, and not as Mrs. Joel Cameron."

"I will come," I said. "There is much I wish to learn."

"Then come to me, Maeve O'Hanlon, for I have a loose tongue and a temper to match, so far as the Camerons are concerned. But if you ever tell what you hear, me and my family will be away from this town half an hour later."

"No one will know," I promised.

"Good day to you, then," she said.

I continued my walk up the street until I came to Glen's office, but a glance in his waiting room showed me how busy he was, so I went on my way. The carriage had dutifully followed me, and now I signaled I was ready to return to the Hill, so the driver pulled up and I climbed in. No doubt, I thought, he would report to Loran every step I'd taken, every place I'd visited and each person to whom I had spoken. It didn't matter to me except that I didn't wish to get anyone in trouble, so if it became necessary I would perhaps lie a bit or evade telling the whole story of my inspection of the village.

Upon my return to the mansion I didn't go inside but roamed about the estate for a while, enjoying the sunlight and air. I came to the family cemetery and marveled at how many there had been preceding those who now live in the mansion. It seemed to me that the Camerons did have a right to be proud of their ancestry and to strive their best to maintain the family tradition in the heights it had always enjoyed. But there were also many things I'd seen this day that I did not like, and I wished to learn more.

I had dinner with Aunt Marcy Tabor, a most correct

noonday meal, while she spoke her mind about all the members of the family. It was a wonder to me that she continued to live here. Or was permitted to.

"I am scarcely accustomed to having a companion for dinner," she began. "I usually eat alone. My sister, Mrs. Cameron, has a tray sent to her rooms. My niece, Helen, goes riding and cares little for the noon-day meal, stuffing herself at breakfast. Her husband rises so late that his breakfast serves as dinner as well and could often also serve as supper. Loran is never home, and neither is Mr. Cameron. Of course, the business keeps them occupied, so I can excuse them. Abner stays home as little as possible. He is off somewhere, probably getting drunk as usual. Joel used to dine with me quite often. I appreciated that, but since he's been gone I am a lonely woman in a house full of people."

"I shall do my best to have dinner with you," I promised. "I hate eating alone, too."

That concluded our conversation. For all her lone-liness, she now devoted her time to berating the maids who served us and turning them into nervous wrecks. Before the meal was over, I began to realize that per-haps the others stayed away from the table by intent— and with reason. This woman was a martinet.

I excused myself as soon as I deemed it reasonable to do so and went at once to my rooms, where I remained for the rest of the afternoon. Just before suppertime a maid tapped on the door and informed me that Loran wished to see me in the library.

I went downstairs, knowing very well what Loran was going to say and not particularly caring. He was affable and invited me to sit down. He was enjoying a pre-supper portion of Madeira, but I turned down his offer of a glass.

"What did you think of our mill, Maeve? Answer me truthfully."

"I would think it a horrible place to work, Uncle Loran."

197

"But you don't mind accepting the money it provides us?"

"I'm not sure whether I do or not."

"I see. And the town itself?"

"I know too little about it to comment."

"Didn't Mrs. Doyle give you a bad impression of it?"

"Mrs. Doyle asked me if I was really Irish, and we talked of Ireland. She offered me tea so we can resume our talk of the country we came from. I will likely accept."

"Then that's when you'll learn that we pay poorly, work our people too hard, and charge them too much rent for our houses and whatever is bought in the company store."

"Is that the truth, then?"

"We are in business. We make profits. That's what business is about."

"No doubt," I said.

"All mills are like this. We are in no respect different from the others. So . . . if you do not approve, perhaps you would prefer that we buy you out."

Then I realized why I had been led on a conducted tour and no effort made to soften the conditions or keep me from meeting other townspeople. I decided not to let Loran realize I was quite aware of his intentions yet.

"I have a personal problem to be settled before I undertake any such important decisions," I said. "I refer to the birth of my child."

"Oh, yes, of course," he said reasonably. "It's nothing to be rushed into. But after that happy event, if you decided you don't care for the conditions that exist here, you might wish to divorce yourself from them. If so, we will pay you the exact value of your one-third share of the firm. It's a substantial sum. A very substantial sum."

"We will speak of that again after the birth of my baby," I said.

"Certainly. I'd have it no other way."

We had a pleasant supper, all the family being there —even Abner, who was quite sober, I thought, and who took a good part in the lively conversation. After supper I excused myself because I did feel tired, and I went to my rooms, where I sat in the waning summer light, not wishing to light the lamps yet.

I looked out upon the green, lovely front of the estate and knew this was a way of life not easy to give up, but from this same window I could see lingering smoke hovering over the town, even though the factory chimneys had gone cold for at least two hours. That was a way of life, too.

Perhaps I would sell Joel's interest if I found I could not tolerate what went on. If I couldn't continue to accept the money derived from the profits created by men who worked too hard, too long, and under conditions that could be readily improved upon. And would not be if the Cameron family lost a dollar of profit on the improvement.

EIGHT

For the next week I became too busy to consider any future plans. The ball in my honor was to be held on Saturday night, and Helen and I were in charge of preparing the mansion for this event. We sent for dressmakers first and selected our new gowns. Mine was a rather startling combination of red and black, with sleeves "as big as skirts," the dressmaker said, "and eight yards of silk for the skirt, the very latest style from Paris."

Helen had no intention of being outdone by me, and she selected material of deep yellow silk, in the same new style. With her fair skin and light-colored hair I knew she would look most attractive. We spent hours at this and became rather close, though only in the details the planning required of us. We never talked about the family, she never asked about Joel or his short life with me. She was entirely ignorant of conditions in Ireland and seemed to prefer it that way.

We consulted with caterers from Portland, with florists, and with an agency that specialized in sending out trained servants and musicians for such lavish occasions.

We also did a great deal of decorating ourselves, knowing that the hundred and fifty invitations would bring at least two hundred people to the mansion by rail, carriage, and even the new gasoline monsters, the ear-splitting motorcars. So we arranged for a large tent to be constructed out beyond the dependency houses; we lined the path with Japanese lanterns and had tables set up so the coachmen and other servants could enjoy themselves and have a place to sleep if their masters were to remain overnight.

Every room at the inn had been reserved. All the bedrooms—sixteen of them—in the mansion were prepared. Four of the older servants in the big house were temporarily transferred to the dependencies and their rooms more lavishly furnished from extra pieces taken from the attic so a few more overnight guests could be accommodated.

There were so many things to do. Mrs. Cameron took charge of the invitations and the communications between the guests and the family. Aunt Marcy Tabor wished the whole affair would be called off and swore all the noise and excitement would be the ruination of

200

her health. Ashley spent his time riding, or gambling with the help down at the stables. Abner made himself scarce by remaining in the town. Loran and Mr. Cameron were, of course, fully occupied at the mill, so almost all of the details fell on my shoulders and on Helen's.

We had the favors to think up and make—the ribbons tied to little silver bells for some, silk bags for others, boutonnieres for the men, details which took a great deal of time. In between there were fittings as our gowns took shape and we had to approve those to be worn by Mrs. Cameron and by Aunt Marcy, who did manage to perk up somewhat after she saw herself in her new somewhat surprisingly low-cut black silk.

We knew we'd never be ready in time, but when the first of the guests arrived, Helen and I were on hand to greet them. In the space of about three hours, a steady stream of guests arrived. There were more motorcars than I thought existed, and there was trouble with the frightened horses, but everything remained under good control. Helen and I had actually drooped with fatigue, but as guest after guest was greeted we forgot our weariness, and when the waltzes, the minuets, and the polkas began, we had our cards filled. We danced until I was sure I'd worn out my slippers before it was time for the dinner.

This was to be served in the dining room and the ballroom, where tables were hastily set up when the dancing temporarily ceased. Everything went well while Helen and I held our breaths. At eight the orchestra struck up a royal quadrille, ending in a grand march as we filed to the tables to take our places.

I had to admit that I enjoyed myself. I was the center of attention, as this affair was supposed to be in my honor. I met so many people I soon lost track of names and remembered only faces. The mansion hummed to the sound of voices and the clink of dishes as dinner was served. I sat between a stately-looking individual with a yellow beard, a ribbon across his chest, another in his lapel, and an austerity that spoke of wealth and power. I learned later that he virtually owned one of the big railroads. The man at my right was about thirty-five, handsome enough but with a face that looked as if it was creased, not by the elements, but by carousing and little sleep. He was paying too much attention to me, and some of his words were slightly slurred as if he'd not only been at the punch bowl too often, but he'd somehow found a supply of brandy or whisky somewhere. If he was a friend of Abner, he'd likely know exactly where.

I disregarded him as much as possible, but it became difficult because Yellow Beard was too rigid to unbend and I couldn't transfer my attention to him. So what should have been a most pleasing dinner turned out to be ruined by this bore at my right elbow, and at the very earliest opportunity I excused myself on the pretext of being required to consult with the orchestra about the dance numbers they would play after dinner.

Mrs. Cameron glanced at me with a disapproving eye as I left the table, but I found it impossible to stand this man any longer. Later I met Abner, and the incident hadn't escaped him.

"I don't know who put Standish beside you, but that person ought to be shot. And I can't for the life of me understand how he ever got invited. He's been crossed off more guests lists lately. He's a stupid bore, and he has an inflated ego that makes him believe he is positively irresistible to all women."

"I certainly don't care for the man," I admitted. "Some of his remarks were not the kind a lady cares to hear, and he has a habit of leering at one as if he has already obtained that person's permission to take her to bed with him."

"If he makes any trouble, let me know. I'll see he leaves at once."

"Thank you, Abner. I hope you'll help me explain

to your mother why I left the table so abruptly. I don't think she approved."

"Mama knows all about Standish. She'll understand. I'll bet he never even received an invitation. He's a bachelor. Not by choice. There isn't a girl alive who'd marry the man. Anyway, I'm sorry it happened. You deserve better."

Oddly enough, when the trouble really did begin, I was dancing with Loran Cameron. Halfway through a fast and lively polka, Standish cut in and before I could prevent Loran from surrendering me to this awful man, I was in his arms and being whirled madly about the floor.

"What makes you dislike me?" he asked.

I was too breathless to be able to reply.

"I'm just a young fellow trying to make everyone happy. Is this dance too much for you? Say, you look positively pale. Are you ill?"

I thought I saw my chance to be rid of him. "I don't feel well. I think I should go to my room for a little while. . . ."

"What you need is air. Lots of air."

Before I could protest he had whirled me off the dance floor and all but carried me through the french doors into the night and the estate outside the ballroom.

There he lost no time. Instead of letting me go or trying to find a bench upon which I might rest, he drew me to him roughly and his lips sought mine in a hideous attempt to kiss me. I pushed at him as hard as I could, but the man was strong, and he began to laugh at my efforts until I delivered a hard kick at his shin. This drew a howl of pain and caused him to draw up one leg. He seemed to lose his balance and in an effort to steady himself, he clawed at my shoulder and tore my gown. Then he was at me again, this time without trying to hide his lust.

Abner put an end to it, but not before several guests saw me struggling in the idiot's embrace. Abner curled an arm around the man's neck and throttled him until his breathing was cut off and he was compelled to let go of me. Abner then whirled him about and drove him off with a solid kick, following him quickly, and I heard the sounds of the brief scuffle and the blows Abner was inflicting upon the wretch.

Meanwhile Helen reached me and Mrs. Cameron, Loran, and Marcy all hurried to help me. I was a sorry-looking guest of honor. My hair had been sadly disarrayed, my gown was torn at the shoulder, my cheeks were stained by the tears of anger and frustration I'd shed.

"My dear child," Mrs. Cameron said, "did that ruffian hurt you?"

"My pride fared none too well," I admitted. "Physically, I'm all right."

"The baby?"

"It wasn't a severe enough fight to have done any damage," I said. "I can't go back looking like this. May I be excused so I can change into something else?"

Mrs. Cameron looked about. "Helen, accompany her and help her. Loran, see to it that Mr. Standish is removed from this property and warn him never again to set foot in this house."

"Who invited him, anyway?" Loran demanded.

"I didn't," Mrs. Cameron said. "He likely came without an invitation. He often does that, but after this I shall make it my business to see he never does again, to any affair. Maeve, I'm very sorry this happened."

"I'll be all right when I catch my breath and restore some of my dignity," I said. "Abner was good enough to warn me about this man, but I was unable to get away from him without creating a bad scene on the dance floor, and I didn't want to do that."

"Next time, never mind the scene—get rid of a man

like that," Loran advised. "He's notorious for his advances toward women."

Helen and I used a rear door to reach my rooms, and there I discovered the gown could be easily repaired by a few stitches, which a maid promptly took care of. I repaired the damage to my hair and face and within half an hour I was ready to go back downstairs.

"Maeve," Helen said, "I'm afraid what happened was partly the fault of my foolish husband. I suspect it was he who brought Standish here. I saw them together. Please don't tell Mama. Ashley is in enough trouble as it is and while I hate him for what he did, he is my husband and I don't want him turned out."

"As you wish, Helen," I said. "I've no reason to hold Ashley to blame if he brought the man here. He wasn't responsible for what Standish did. All I hope is that none of the guests believe I encouraged the man."

"Of course not, dear Maeve. Everyone knows what Standish is like. Now let's go down and pretend this never happened."

We descended the grand staircase and quickly merged with the crowd. If we'd been missed, no one remarked about it. I'd sacrificed three dances, but I was quickly claimed for another quadrille, and the rest of the evening went off splendidly. I almost forgot the unfortunate incident with Standish.

When the last notes faded and the guests either departed or went to bed, I was exhausted. Helen waved to me from halfway up the stairs. She had drooped half an hour ago and was on her way to bed. Abner looked as if the evening was just beginning.

"Standish will never bother you again," he said. "In fact, for the next few days he won't bother anybody except his doctor. I changed the shape of his face somewhat. He has had this coming for a long time. I'm sorry it had to be you he picked on. The man's not fit for decent company."

"Thank you for reaching me in time. I know what he intended, and I'm not sure I could have fought him off."

"I saw you kick him in the shins," Abner chuckled. "If that was a sample, I don't think he'd have gotten far once you were able to fight. Except for that, it was a fine affair. We were all proud of the way you handled yourself."

"Thank you for that compliment, Abner." I kissed his cheek. "More and more you remind me of Joel. I'm lucky you're here. Good night."

In my rooms I examined the several bruises Standish had inflicted upon me. I felt I was lucky that nothing worse had happened. The evening had come off splendidly except for that incident. The first ball I'd ever attended had been a success, and I felt that I'd done nothing to make the Camerons feel anything but proud of the way I had handled myself.

This, I also knew, would probably be the last social affair I'd attend until after my baby was born.

I visited Glen's office next day for a routine examination to discover everything was fine—with me and the baby—but Glen seemed unduly upset after I told him of the incident with Mr. Standish.

"That lout is never invited anywhere, and people who give dinners and balls are always on the lookout to keep him from just walking in."

"Helen admitted her husband may have brought Standish to the affair," I said.

"Ashley's a weakling, a coward. All he wants out of life is to live at the mansion, be part of the Cameron family, and enjoy some of its power. In a left-handed way, perhaps, but that's enough for him. I should think he'd be scared to death to bring a man like Standish around. Especially after Mrs. Cameron was mad at him, anyway."

"Well, it happened," I said, "and it's over, and nobody's been hurt except maybe Standish. Abner beat him up."

"That will get Abner a free visit to my office for treatment at any time. Standish should have been beaten up long ago. As you say, it's over. What else is going on?"

"Uncle Loran took me to the mill for a visit. He asked me how I liked it, and I told him I didn't. I think it's a horrid place."

"No more than any other mill, but that doesn't mean it should not be improved. I'm concerned about the children who go to work there at twelve years of age and spend the rest of their lives in the mill. They don't know what being a child is like. They grow up with the first miserly paycheck they get."

"But why do they do it, then?" I asked.

"Because the family needs the money. The Camerons don't force the children to go to work at that age, but if they want to, there's a job waiting, and the families are told of it. They are paid a couple of dollars a week, and it helps staying out of debt to the company store."

"It's like a serfdom," I said.

"They are not compelled to work there. Anyone can leave the mill and the town at any time. None do because the only place they'd have to go is another mill, and another town like this where things might be even worse."

"Then what can I—or you—or anyone else do about it?"

"Nothing. If anything is done they have to do it for themselves. And if you talk to these people, they'll tell you how bad it used to be, compared to now. And it was. My father used to tell me. Now let's get back to you."

"The family treats me well. They are all concerned for my welfare and my baby."

207

"Joel's baby," Glen contradicted me. "That's whose baby they consider you're carrying."

"Well, they'll come to find out whose it is when the girl is born."

"Girl? What makes you so sure it will be a girl?"

How could I tell him? He'd think me daft if I tried to explain that a worn, ancient mirror could prophesy for me alone what the future held. Of course, there'd come a day when I'd have to explain, but then he would be my husband and there'd be no running. I smiled inwardly.

"It could just as easily be a boy," he said, after waiting vainly for my answer. "Or two boys, or two girls, or a boy and a girl. I won't go further than that."

"Good heavens, man, you don't think there's more than one?" I asked.

"I don't think so. Twins are quite rare. Were there ever any in your family?"

"Not that I know of."

"I can answer for the Camerons—there were none. So it will likely be a single child, but don't go saying it'll be a girl."

"It will be a girl," I repeated. "I have that feeling."

"They'll have a hard time forgiving you. A girl won't carry on the family name."

"I don't care a fig about that. All I ask is a lovely, beautiful, obedient, clever, and very intelligent girl baby."

"Who looks like you, I hope."

"Will you listen to the man, and him with patients to see—and I have a tea to which I have been invited."

"In the town?" he asked.

"Aye, at the residence of Mrs. Maggie Doyle, to talk about home. That means Ireland to us."

"Ummmm," he mused, "wait until they hear about that."

"They already have. I told Loran. He didn't approve, I suppose, but he doesn't run my life. And if the con-

208

versation should unhappily drift from Ireland and turn to this town, I will be glad to listen."

He nodded. "From Maggie Doyle you'll get an earful. All to the good. You might as well learn now."

"Such," I said as I arose, "are my intentions."

I could easily have walked to Maggie Doyle's house, but I used the carriage and had the coachman wait outside. It was well-known to me that he was instructed to inform Loran of everywhere I went and everyone I spoke to, and I was making no secret of what I did.

Mrs. Doyle wasn't shocked to see me, but she was surprised. I found her house to be of four rooms, a fairly spacious kitchen, a tiny parlor, and two small bedrooms. All the living was done in the kitchen, and the parlor was opened for funerals—and visitors like me.

"We shall sit in the kitchen," I told her. "It's more comfortable there, and no need to be carrying the tea tray about. What do you have to pay for this house, Maggie?"

"Half my husband's pay each week."

"Can you live on the rest?"

"Barely, but we get along. Mind you, now, I'm not complaining."

"And mind you, Maggie Doyle," I said sternly, "I'm not a Cameron. I'm an O'Hanlon first, and you will speak to me as an O'Hanlon, or I'll rise up and walk out of here without as much as your leave."

"Glory be," she said, "it's a miracle come to us. We scrape along, but we never save a cent. That's because they know how much it costs us to live and that's what they pay us and not a dime more. That way we can't leave. We couldn't even pay the train fare if we wanted to. My man works from six to six. My son—he's thirteen—works from seven to six. On Saturdays they let him off at noon so he can go to school, because they think he's a little smarter than most and they may make him a foreman. Then we'll move into a better house, but we still won't be able to save a dime."

"Your son did go to school?"

"Aye, right up to the day before his birthday. That day he had off. His present from the company. Next day he was at the mill at seven."

"What if one is sick?"

"Dr. Kinnery comes and does well for us. Like his father before him, he's a good doctor. The company pays him, but it wasn't always so. They didn't pay his father for many a year until he said he'd quit and go elsewhere. They dared him to try that, and he did. They called him back, and he made them pay him double, which they did gladly because sick people can't work and there were too many sick people not able to go to the mill."

"Is Dr. Kinnery beholden to the Camerons, then?" I asked.

"He is not. They pay him, but he is under no obligation to them, and they well know it."

"I can believe that," I said with a sigh of relief. I should have hated to learn that they also held Glen under their big thumb. "What if a man is fired—or refuses to work?"

"They bring in the law, which comes with a dray. The house is emptied, and the dray carries the furniture to the nearest dump and leaves it there. The family can collect it or not, as they see fit, or are able to. A man not working at the mill does not spend that night in a company house. Those are the rules."

"I'm sorry for you, then," I said. "There's nothing I can do, for they will not listen to me and I do not own sufficient of the company to change anything. Yet, I am going to try."

"Maeve, they will hurt you if you do."

"They may wish to hurt me, but they will not, Maggie."

"Please, not until after your baby is born. We have

210

put up with this for lifetimes. Most of us don't even know anything better."

"I will do what I can," I promised. "It won't be easy, and it won't be soon, but it will be done one way or another. Now if you have that tea . . ."

"It is Irish, Maeve. Sent by my brother from Shannon. A pound he sent me, and half of it is left after these eleven years."

"I am that honored, then," I said. "Up there on the Hill it's poor, weak stuff they serve as tea."

"Aye, that they would; and they're deserving of it, I say."

We talked until well on into the afternoon, during which I made up my mind to write my brother to send me ten pounds of Irish tea and I would see that Maggie and her friends got all they wanted of it. For one of the very few times since poor Joel died, I was grateful that he left me with enough money to make me independent and able to buy whatever I wished without asking permission or advice from anyone.

When I returned to the mansion, Helen grumbled a bit because I hadn't been there to help remove the decorations, but as I saw three of the maids busy at that task I didn't think Helen had overexerted herself. If Loran was told of my visit to Maggie Doyle and if he did not approve of it, he never mentioned it to me, and I didn't speak of it to him. I realized that to bring up the matter of improving the lot of the mill workers would be no more than a study in futility, so I didn't try to convince them or even mention it. The welfare of my baby came above all else now, and before long I became acutely aware of it.

My visits to Glen were more frequent, his examinations were more thorough, and the Camerons hovered over me as if I were made of delicate porcelain. I could not have been treated more kindly. They refused to allow me to help with any of the work. I spent hours sitting in the sun, until the weather grew too cold for

211

that, and then they wrapped me in blankets or great-coats and transported me to the greenhouse, where the temperature soared even when it was chilly outside.

Gradually I came to accept all this and revel in it, I suppose. One does get accustomed to such service and concern, especially when there is cause for it. My cause grew ever more prominent every week. I was due in late March, and I kept the schedule intact.

Glen came hurriedly that afternoon. He sent everyone away after ordering the carriage to go quickly to town and fetch his sister. Late that night, after things grew somewhat fuzzy, I heard the wail of my first-born. Thanks to Glen and Jennie, there'd been no trouble and little in the way of real pain.

"Well," Glen said, "you were right. It's a girl. Healthy as you are."

"Ah," I said wearily, "and does she look like me, Doctor?"

"Who can tell? Wait a couple of days and see. Jennie, introduce them."

I held my baby, and I was rightly proud of her. She kicked and fought with strong arms and legs, and her cries seemed almost as lusty as my brother's used to be when we yelled at one another across the Irish fields.

"What will you call her?" Jennie asked.

"No question of that," I said. "She will be Nora, after my mother, but her true first name will be Maeve."

"Nora," Jennie said. "It's a nice name. It's a wonderful name. Well, now, should we let the others meet your little Nora?"

"Tomorrow," Glen said. "Maeve has been through enough, and so has Nora, for that matter. They both need rest. You stay with them, Jennie. See to it no one comes in."

"I'll lock the door after you," Jennie said.

I doubted I'd sleep for days, but I fell asleep within the next ten minutes, and it was sound until the wee hours. After that it was fitful, for I heard Nora cry and then there was the need to feed her. I was that content I believed nothing was wrong with this world and never would be. I was no longer alone. I had my own daughter, Joel's daughter, to love, to cherish, and to raise after my own decisions as to how. It was a wonderful feeling.

Somehow I didn't think it was going to last.

A week later Mrs. Cameron provided the first indication that things were going to be different now that my baby had been born. She did it in a perfectly nice way, but clearly implied she would brook no opposition.

"We must arrange for the baptismal service on Sunday," she said, "when Father Anders comes, as usual, for services in our church. I suggest the baby be named Deborah."

"I was thinking of Nora," I said, with my mind made up that I would not be intimidated by this woman.

"Oh, my dear, that's such a—well, a plain sort of name."

"It was my mother's," I reminded her a bit stiffly.

"Yes, in Ireland. There it would be a fine name, but in this country we need a name more suited to the position the child will bear in life. And Deborah's will be an important one."

"We are, by the way," I said, "speaking of her middle name. She will be baptized as Maeve."

"I see. You are determined on that."

"It is a name that has been in my family for more than two thousand years."

"Yes, I can understand why you wish that name for her, but of course she will be called Deborah."

I sighed because it was so frustrating trying to argue with this woman, or get across to her what your wishes happened to be—if they conflicted in any way with hers. I had no intention of staying here in this house

213

much longer, and when I left, my daughter would be called Nora. So I neither consented nor approved. I would talk to Father Anders at the proper time.

"I would have Abner as godfather and Helen as godmother," I said.

"I think that is splendid, my dear."

"Then we shall consider it arranged."

"We're all very proud of the baby, Maeve. We'd wished for a son, but I'm sure Deborah will carry on the family tradition, if not the name. We will see that she wants for nothing."

"I, too, intend to see to that," I said. "I have missed Loran. Not once did he come to see me or the baby."

"Loran has been in New York on company business for the past week or more. He left before the child was born. It was urgent business. We let him know about Deborah by telegraph, and I'm sure he is as pleased as we are."

"I wondered if he disapproved of a girl so thoroughly that he would not accept her," I said. "I suppose a brand-new mother does get strange ideas sometimes. May I have the carriage this afternoon so I may take Nora to the doctor? He asked that he see her today."

"The outing will do both of you good;" Mrs. Cameron said. "Of course you may have the use of the carriage, or any other conveyance you have your fancy set on."

I felt a rare pride as I was driven along the Main Street with Nora in my arms, wrapped in a pink blanket and sleeping soundly. At Glen's office, patients already there promptly insisted I be next, and they all looked at Nora and agreed she was as beautiful a baby as they'd ever seen.

Glen performed a routine examination of the baby and was satisfied that everything was fine.

"How are they treating you up there since you added to the family?"

"Fine, Glen. They're as happy about little Nora as

214

I am. They can't do enough for her. Or me, for that matter."

"I don't like it," he said brusquely.

"Oh? What do you mean?"

"It's out of character for them to act this way. Whenever they seem to bend over with kindness, they're up to something. Those people plan far ahead, and they're patient, but when it comes time to go after what they want, they're relentless."

"Glen, for months they've been wonderful to me. Why should they change now? I did marry their son."

"Oh, yes—and that fact drove them frantic with anger. When you first arrived, they had the stage set to outlaw you in this town, to drive you away. They'd only begun to make life miserable for you. Then you told them you were going to have Joel's baby and they changed."

"Wouldn't any family under those conditions?"

"Not that abruptly. As soon as they heard the news, they sat down and planned. They always do that. Board meetings, they call them, and any decision they make is carried out with never a failure so far. Now I may be wrong. I'm only going by the history of those people, that entire family, and there's never been a situation up there quite like this one. A new Cameron born into the clan. A new life to carry on the name, something they've wanted and never thought attainable."

"Glen, what can they do? My lawyer has informed me—and them that they cannot take away anything that Joel left to me. Oh, he was suspicious of them, too, as you are, and he took good care to see that the will was drawn so it could never be attacked. Therefore, they cannot harm me or threaten me by taking away my share of the earnings of the mill, nor the cash Joel left. Nor the one-third ownership in the mill itself. If they cannot take that away from me, how else can they harm me? I think they may have intended to do so at first, but when they discovered it was impossible, they accepted it, and me."

"I wish I was as well convinced," he said. "I've known them too long, I guess. Then, too, I take their money, but only because none of their millhands can afford a doctor and they are in need of one here. I do not work directly for the Camerons, and I never will. They can't fire me because the contract I insisted upon states clearly that I take patients on an independent basis and I am free to handle these patients without any interference from the family. And that whatever fee I may claim is never to be part of the wages earned by the millhand in question. My father taught me how to protect myself from the Camerons, and that is why I suspect them so much. Let's hope this time I'm wrong."

"I'm sure you are. However, I don't intend to live on the Hill the rest of my life. As soon as Nora is strong enough and old enough to move, I shall begin considering another place to live."

"Not away from this town, Maeve? You're not intending to leave?"

"No, I have no such intentions." Someday I'd tell him why I knew I'd not leave.

"I'm glad to hear that. Bring Nora back in a week's time."

"Thank you, Doctor," I said.

I returned to the mansion, and if Glen's suspicions worried me, they soon left, for the whole family seemed kinder than ever. A week later I informed Glen his suspicions were wrong, though he seemed to cling to them nonetheless. Loran returned the following week. Nora grew rapidly and was as healthy, strong, and bright as I could have hoped for. The family heaped clothes and toys on her in a profusion which would spoil the girl if they kept it up as she grew older. I settled down, content and happy, busy with my new task of bringing up my child and devoting myself solely to that purpose.

I did take to long walks during the warm spring afternoons. Glen insisted on this for the air and the exercise they provided, and I liked walking. Back home it had been one of my favorite pastimes, and here I could recall the long walks Joel and I used to take during those joy-filled but precious few weeks we were granted.

I thought of Glen, too, and what it would be like, being married to him. Not Mrs. Cameron but Mrs. Kinnery, the doctor's wife. Sharing his life, his bed— I forced my thoughts away. *Oh Joel*, I said in my heart, *I'll never forget you*!

During these solitary walks it did come to me that there were a few changes in the family, Subtle ones, not very noticeable. Joel's father, for instance, rarely spoke to me, appearing to be deep in thought while in my presence. He did make a fuss over the baby, but certainly not over me.

Ashley, Helen's husband, stayed out of my way, but that wasn't surprising. He'd lived in virtual self-imposed isolation since he was accused of being responsible for bringing that boor of a Mr. Standish to the ball. Helen was more casual, I realized. Marcy Tabor never had been overly friendly, so if she changed it was scarcely detectable. Abner was still the same warm, friendly man —when I encountered him, which was seldom. He had taken to remaining in town and even to trips out of town so frequently that he was at the mansion on rare occasions and then for only brief periods of time. No one appeared to object to this.

Perhaps Glen was right and there was something afoot. Something that hung over my head and would fall when the family willed it to.

And perhaps that was the reason I was making my afternoon walks longer and longer. Nora was safe in the care of Helen, who had formed a fast and loving

217

attachment for the baby. Her affection seemed to be returned in measure that sometimes brought out a few mild pangs of jealousy in me.

The late spring weather was strange this year, I was told. It was too dry, and the fields and forests were like tinder. I'd heard talk about the dangers of fires, but it meant little to me. Not until this particular afternoon, when Nora was just over four months old. I had been on one of my longer walks because I felt nervous for some reason. Glen's prodding questions that morning hadn't helped. His suspicions were as strong as ever concerning the Cameron family.

The first sign I had of fire was the acrid smell in the air which made me cough and finally turn about. Well behind me I could see smoke filtering through the trees and rising rapidly in great gusts of gray and black above the treetops. As yet I saw no flames.

The path I'd taken seemed to lead directly back into all the smoke, but I retreated in that direction, anyway, being so unfamiliar with forest fires I thought I could outmaneuver it. Suddenly a great wall of flame appeared to rise out of the earth, and the heat drove me back. I whirled about and started to run. Before I'd taken a hundred steps the fire was to the left of me. I stayed on the path, not daring to leave it. If I got lost, I'd be trapped with rapidly advancing flames closing in on me. I had to keep going.

This was a forest consisting mainly of fir and pine trees. I'd known little about them, but in another moment's time I learned how vulnerable they were to fire. Now the flames at my back had suddenly appeared on my left, but that gave me a chance to try and outrun it. I saw how the wind created by the hot fire to the rear carried firebrands high and dropped them at the foot of a full-grown pine. Small flames licked at the lower branches, there appeared to be a pause, and then the entire tree seemed to explode. Other trees near it caught fire, and now the area to my right was burning.

I could only keep running along the path, praying I'd not find a wall of flame facing me.

Firebrands and sparks were falling all about now. I was out of breath, half choked from the smoke which seemed to be closing in faster than the fire. I couldn't go on without rest, and if I must stop it had to be now, before the fire was too close. I had the wild notion that if it encircled me I would make one mad dash through the flames; I was supremely ignorant at the time of the actual depth of a forest fire. To make this dash I would need wind and strength.

I stopped and sank to the ground. I tried to breathe as normally as possible and to relax my exhausted muscles if I could do so. As I sat there, contemplating my seemingly hopeless predicament, I thought I heard the shrill scream of a terrified horse.

Small animals had been darting across the path from time to time, moving so fast they were hard to identify. I'd seen no large ones, but that sound had come from a sorely frightened horse.

It brought me to my feet. I cupped my hands to my mouth and shouted. There was no response. The heat of the fire was beginning to sear my skin now, and I knew I couldn't wait another moment.

I began running again, and the full realization of the danger that now presented itself gave me a second wind. How long that would last I didn't know, but while it did I had to keep going as fast and far as I could manage.

A stream ran through the forest, but I didn't know exactly where. If I could reach it, I might be able to immerse myself in the water until the fire roared over that area, but the stream might be to my right, or to my left, and if I made a mistake I'd head directly into the flames. It was better to stay on the path and take my chances on running faster than the fire could follow.

I saw a yellow and crimson glow directly ahead. For a moment I thought I'd left the path, but I realized what I saw was a wall of flame that now straddled the path I was on, cutting me off. I was surrounded by fire. I couldn't understand how that could have happened, but there was no question that it had.

I slowed my running steps. All I did now was hurry into the flames, no matter which way I went. Yet I couldn't stand here. I had to determine in which direction the fire was weakest and try to penetrate the wall there. I knew so little about the catastrophe of a forest fire. There must be some way to try to save my life. I had no time to think. The smoke was thick, the heat was getting worse, and the fire was closing on all sides. I was about to remove my skirt to throw over my head and protect my face and hair when I heard the dull boom of a heavy gun.

I cupped my hands to my mouth and shouted. The gun was fired a second time. Someone wasn't too far away on my right. I turned in that direction, shouting every few steps. Whoever it was didn't have much time to save me now. The heat was almost unbearable.

I turned my shouts into screams. Suddenly I saw a dim form lurch out of the heavy smoke. I ran toward the man. I wasn't able to see who it was, but that didn't matter. Something came hurtling my way, and a cool, water-soaked blanket descended over my head. My elbow was seized and I was being piloted back along the path while the man who held me was shouting.

"Go back! I have her. Go back!"

Under the heavy blanket the voice was dull and somewhat distorted. I didn't know who shouted or who fired that heavy gun once more, the sound of which reached me despite the blanket. I stumbled along, still towed by the man who'd saved my life. I could feel the heat lessen, and finally the grip on my arm relaxed and we stopped. I sank to the ground, unable to stand up a second longer. The blanket was lifted from over my head, and I breathed in fairly good air. I stared up at the worried face of Loran Cameron.

His cheeks and forehead were smeared with ash and his hands covered with it. He seemed grim and angry.

"You little fool!" he thundered. "Don't you know better than to wander around in a forest in this dry weather? Didn't someone warn you?"

"No . . . Nobody told me," I managed. "Thank you. You saved my life."

"And damned near lost my own in doing it. Abner is out there, too. We saw the smoke. Helen told us you were walking in the woods, and we knew you'd be trapped. I rode out on horseback. I hope my horse got away safely. Abner took along a shotgun to signal with. He'll find us soon now. I'm sure he's all right; Abner knows his way in these woods."

Suddenly the reaction hit me, and I started to cry.

"You're not hurt . . . or burned . . .?"

"I stayed ahead of the flames, but I—don't think I had much time left. I'm that grateful, sir." I swallowed and blinked and ordered myself to stop crying.

Abner emerged from the smoke and the forest. He reported that he'd seen Loran's horse running away from the fire, apparently unhurt. I was pleased with that news. They helped me up, and we started back to the mansion. I was weak and unsteady at first, but my strength soon returned and I was able to walk unassisted.

"When I discovered you were gone and saw the fire, I nearly went crazy," Abner said. "I didn't know how I'd find you out there, but Loran rode up, and when I told him he started out, too. I never saw a fire travel so fast."

"It circled me before I could escape it," I said. "I didn't realize it could go around that way so quickly as to cut me off."

"I never saw one that did that before," Loran admitted. "Anyway, it all ended well. The fire will burn itself out in the foothills. It won't head for the town —wind's not in the right direction for that. We have these fires often, but this was a bad one. It was lucky, too, I could use the saddle blanket to soak up water from the stream through the forest."

I discovered a slight burn along my right forearm, though I hadn't the faintest notion as to how it got there. Mrs. Cameron insisted I have Dr. Kinnery attend it at once, and I was glad of the opportunity to go to his office.

He questioned me as he cleaned and bandaged the burn. "It's not bad, not deep. You won't suffer a scar, and in a week's time it should be healed. So Loran rescued you? That's unusual. He never seems to be around at a time when he's needed."

"He was this time," I said stoutly.

"With a blanket soaked in water?"

"Glen, what are you trying to say? That he set the fire and then rescued me? What would be the sense in that? And why try to kill me, anyway?"

"I can think of a good reason why your death would benefit the family. As for the rescue—you said that Abner discovered you might be somewhere in that fire and he went to look. Was that before or after Loran started out?"

"I don't know," I admitted. "Glen, Loran's been kind to me. Understanding, too. When I criticized the mill and the town—how they were run—he tried to explain his side and didn't grow angry because of what I said."

"At a time when you were carrying Nora, he wouldn't be likely to."

"Glen, you're talking about murder!"

"I'm talking about a member of the Cameron family. Oh, I'm also probably talking through my hat. Forgive me. I'd no right to bring up a subject like that. You were not seriously hurt, and there's no proof anyone was responsible for the fire. It was put out already, I've heard. All the men were sent from the mill to help check it."

222

"I'm glad of that. It was a terrible thing. I never before lost hope, but for a few minutes while those flames were coming closer, I did. I think you're wrong about Loran, though."

"I hope I am. Have you been doing any thinking about what you'll do when Nora is old enough so you can leave the Hill if you wish?"

"I've thought, yes, but without deciding anything."

"Keep thinking about it," he advised. "Joel's been dead a year now, hasn't he?"

"Aye—a little more than a year. He never even knew he would have a daughter to live after him."

"He'd have been proud of her—and of you. Bring Nora next week."

For another month everything moved with its usual quiet efficiency and I felt no sense of hostility on the part of anyone. Loran was naturally the hero for his rescue of me. I stayed out of the forest. The pathway was blackened, anyway, and I contented myself with wheeling Nora about the estate in the old rattan carriage which had once served Helen, Joel, and Abner.

Ashley stayed in his rooms mostly, or in the village. Abner missed almost every meal, but the rest of us dined quite formally, lingering at the table until almost bedtime. If I'd not had Nora to care for, that existence would have been growing to a frightful bore by now. I listened to the same shop talk. Nothing mattered in this family except the mill and the town. Families discussed over the supper table were sometimes sentenced to instant banishment because the father had been discovered lax in his work. I'd not yet found anyone who was given a second chance. It was a wonder to me that there was an employee left, but always someone appeared to take the place of the family that departed.

Glen maintained there would eventually be trouble and the longer it was in the making the worse it would be. Still, no committee waited on Loran or Mr. Cameron with a grievance, and not a complaint was heard.

The few times I brought up the subject, I was quickly and most deftly talked out of pursuing it any further.

Helen was spending more and more time with Nora these days. Perhaps I should have resented it, but the child did like Helen and she also enjoyed being made a fuss over. I had long since dismissed all of Glen's suspicions as mere fantasies brought about because he disliked the Camerons with such intensity. A certain calm seemed to have descended over this strange household, and everything appeared to be under firm control.

It was mid-September when I awoke in the middle of the night with sharp cramps that brought me out of bed to double up in pain. I walked the floor, waiting for the agony to stop, but it grew slowly worse until I couldn't bear it any longer. At dawn I went downstairs to the kitchen and prepared a cup of tea.

The mansion was silent. Nobody was awake yet, but the kitchen range was never allowed to grow cold, and a kettle was always on the stove, so I was able to quickly prepare the tea. Drinking it made the pain a little better, and I hoped it would continue to improve until morning. Then I would see Glen, for I knew better than to disregard a symptom such as this.

At dawn the agony was unbearable. I awakened Helen and asked her to help me dress.

"I shall awaken Dr. Kinnery. I don't know what has caused this, but it is most severe, and he may not allow me to return at once. Please care for Nora. I'll be so grateful if you will."

"Nora will be fine, Maeve, don't worry. But I am concerned about you. You do seem to be so ill."

"That I am and no lie, but I can manage to reach the doctor if you will have the carriage made ready. And please hurry. Don't awaken the others. No need for that."

Fifteen minutes later I was on my way to town, but halfway along the road I called to the coachman to stop and I was terribly sick. When the carriage resumed its brief journey, I was barely able to sit up. The coachman rushed to Glen's door and pounded the brass knocker until he appeared. Glen strode out to the carriage and, without a word, gathered me in his arms and carried me into the house.

He placed me on his examination table and made several tests and routine examinations. Then he handed Jennie a long red rubber tube and ordered her to boil it for fifteen minutes and be quick about it. I was too ill to talk.

Glen bent over me. "How long have you had this pain, Maeve?"

"Since . . . about three this morning," I managed to say.

"Is it any better now than it was when you awakened?"

"Worse," I said. "Far worse, Glen. Please do something."

"I will. What did you eat for supper last night?"

"I don't remember. I feel so awful. . . ."

"You have to remember," he said sharply.

Suddenly I knew what he meant, and at the same instant I recalled how Joel had been when he was so ill. I tried to sit up in the excitement of my discovery, but Glen forced me back with a firm hand.

"Lie still," he commanded.

"It's like . . . Joel," I said. "The same way he was . . . so sick . . . just like Joel. . . ."

"That's what I was wondering. Never mind about supper. It makes no difference now. I'm going to remove whatever is in your stomach, and then I'm going to wash it out. It will be very unpleasant for you, but it's the only thing I can do that will help. After that you'll get some medicine—lots of it. And then Jennie is going to put you to bed."

"Nora," I said weakly. "I have to go back to Nora."

"Nora will be all right. She's the one person in this

225

business we don't have to worry about. For the moment it's you. How long was Joel ill?"

"About . . . two days, I think."

"And then he died suddenly?"

I nodded weakly.

"Do you understand what I'm saying, Maeve? Does everything make sense to you?"

"Aye, it does that."

"Then let me tell you that you will not die. You will get better, and somehow we're going to find an explanation for all this. What you have to do now is help me help you."

Jennie returned with the length of tubing and I had the terrible experience of having it forced down my throat. Jennie covered my eyes with a folded hand towel then. I heard Glen using some kind of a hand machine that sucked out the contents of my stomach. It was horrible, but I was braced for it. I was proud that I didn't once whimper.

I could feel warm liquid enter my stomach and be removed over and over again. I wasn't feeling any better, but I did have faith in Glen's promise that I would live. After a while I was given cool water to drink, and it stayed down with no trouble. This was followed by a bitter medicine, and then Jennie and Glen suspended me in a blanket, carried me into his house proper, and placed me on a comfortable bed. I was so exhausted that I could only close my eyes and be thankful the pain was gone.

It came back in the late morning, awakening me, but it was not as severe, and Glen seemed much relieved. I looked up at his unshaven, harried-looking face.

"You haven't slept all night, Glen."

"You have, and that's what was important. From here on, we have to depend on medicine and rest. I'm sure we got whatever it was out of your stomach in time. Thanks to the fact that you didn't delay too long."

"I was poisoned, wasn't I?"

226

"Maeve, one does not become that ill from a mere stomach ache. Now, when you took care of Joel, was he as well off—without pain and weakness—as you are now? At the same number of hours after his first attack?"

"I don't know. He had the first one on his way home from Dublin. It was in some wayside inn."

"I see. I forgot that part of it. You appear to be doing well. There may be more attacks of pain. Jennie will stay beside the bed all the time, and when she has to rest I'll be here."

"Glen, you have other sick people," I protested.

"None as sick as you. Understand now, I'm your doctor. I give orders, and you obey them."

"Yes, Glen, that I will. Poor Joel, he would not admit he was that sick. Tell me, has anyone from the Hill inquired about me?"

"No, not yet. When they do, I'll tell them you're too ill to see anyone. I don't want any of that tribe to get near you."

"Bring Nora here, Glen. Please."

"They wouldn't let me. We'd better not take the chance of forcing it. At least, not until you're well and able to defend yourself. And that's enough talking about it for now. Nora is almost as precious to them as she is to you, so there's nothing to worry about so far as she's concerned. The rest of it can wait a few days."

"Do you think they'll take her from me, Glen?" I asked in a fresh surge of fear.

"They can't. The law is very clear on that. Nora belongs to you, not to the Camerons. We've got them there."

"But what if they take her away? Hide her?"

"We'll take them into court. High and mighty as they think they are, they're not above the law. Stop worrying."

"I can't help it," I said. "Now I believe you—that

227

Loran set the forest fire and rescued me only because if he hadn't, Abner would have. That's the way he would think. Loran is clever and sly, and I am deathly afraid of him."

"Loran is just like everybody else when it comes right down to it. He does not scare me. Now stop this jabbering and try to get more rest. You're not out of this yet and it may be you'll need plenty of stamina before it's over."

When he left, Jennie took his place. I talked to her for a few minutes, but weakness was gradually taking over, and I felt drowsy. Finally I slept and when I woke up, Jennie was gone and Glen sat in her place.

Two more days went by like this. I was like an infant, sleeping more than being awake, but I could feel my strength coming back. The pain came back, too, but not with its original severity, and Glen's medicines were doing their work.

On the fourth day I had a visitor. Glen wasn't sure whether he should allow him in, but when I learned it was Abner, I insisted. Then I saw the reason for Glen's reluctance. Abner was gloriously drunk. Hat in hand, he stood beside the bed, swaying a bit, and two big tears rolled down his cheeks.

"I wanted to come before," he said, "but I drank too much. Maeve, clear out of here. Don't go back. Not for anything. Stay away. And for God's sake, don't let them know I came to see you. They'll have my head if they find out."

"I'll not tell them, Abner. Thank you for coming," I said. "Do you know what they're up to?"

"They don't tell me anything. They don't trust me, but whatever it is, it will be bad. Stay away! I've got to go now. I can't stay. Remember, don't tell anyone. . . ."

He lurched out of the room, narrowly missing a collision with the door frame. Glen accompanied him, saw him out of the house, and then came directly back.

"I don't think we have to wonder any longer about the guilt of those people on the Hill, or that they intend to make more trouble for you."

I was sitting up by now and better able to use my wits, for all that insidious weakness had left me. I'd been doing a great deal of thinking during the past twenty-four hours, not giving voice to it, but I thought the time was right to do so.

"Glen, once before Joel made his last journey to Dublin, we were walking along the beach as we did so often. Someone fired a gun at us."

"You didn't find out who it was, or why?"

"We tried. Joel found the bullet in the sand. It came from a modern kind of a gun. I don't know much about those things. At the time there was a man in my village—one Cathal Dolan, with whom I grew up. When he heard Joel and I were to be married, he made threats against me—to my face, at that. Joel wondered about him, so we went to his farm and searched his shack. Joel found a gun, but an ancient one it was, and Joel said it could not have fired the bullet that had been aimed at us. So far as we could even discover, no such gun existed in the village, and that's all we ever did learn. I came to the belief that a hunter, a stranger, fired at some animal and when he saw how close he'd come to us, fled. Now I'm wondering . . . just as I wonder about the forest fire, and now this awful sickness I'm getting over. I wonder about Joel's death, too."

"And do you also wonder—I hope—why I'm asking that you stay away from the Hill?"

"My daughter is up there," I said. "I have to fetch her."

"I'm going with you," he said. "Don't try it yet. You're not well enough. I'll tell you when."

"As you said, Nora can be in no danger, so I can wait. I want to be strong when I face them."

Since it was no longer necessary that I be watched

229

all day and night, Jennie didn't sit beside the bed as often, nor did Glen, so I had time to think. I was far more worried about Nora than I'd let Glen know. People who could arrange for the murder of their own son and try to kill his widow not once, but twice, were capable of anything. I had to get Nora away from them.

I got out of bed, but I was still unsteady on my feet, and the exertion brought on a mild attack of the cramps that had made me so ill. I promptly got back into bed. It wasn't until two days later that I had exercised in secret sufficiently that I felt well enough to make the trip to the Hill. I had decided to go alone, to slip out of Glen's house and face my problem without his help. For if he became too deeply involved, he would also bear the brunt of the Cameron anger. He was, after all, dependent on them for his living. They could, at any time, bring in another doctor and refuse to pay Glen for his services to the employees of the mill.

And rage was growing within me. I realized that the concern and kindness shown me by the family had been only to keep me content until Nora was born. If there'd not been a doctor in the town, or if there'd been some incompetent like the old man who'd tried to treat Joel, I'd be dead by now. Dead of undetermined illness, likely put down as inflammation of the bowels— the same as Joel's death had been listed.

My chance came when Glen was called on an emergency, a childbirth ahead of the scheduled time. He sent for Jennie, as he always did when he needed help.

"I'll be back as soon as I can," she told me. "You're able to fend for yourself quite well, anyway. Help yourself to anything you wish. Please don't overdo, Maeve. You're coming along so well, Glen would hate to have to endure a setback."

"I'll be fine," I said.

Five minutes after she drove off, I dressed as fast as I could. It wasn't too far to the stables, but the afternoon was hot and the distance seemed to stretch itself for miles. I made it, obtained the use of a carriage, and drove it directly up to the mansion on the Hill.

NINE

The door opened before I reached it, and the housekeeper motioned imperiously toward the drawing room. No doubt my carriage had been seen as I approached the mansion, and the family had time to gather. I brushed past her, made no attempt to enter the drawing room, and ran up the grand staircase as fast as I could. I hurried down the upstairs corridor and opened the nursery door.

No one was there. The little crib was made up. Toys were neatly arranged. There was no sign of Nora. Frantic with fear now, I ran to Helen's room. She might help me; we had been friendly, at least after a fashion. She didn't answer my knock, and I went on in. Her two rooms were also empty, and I had a feeling she had not been there for some time. There was nothing to do now but go down and demand an explanation.

I did stop at what had been my rooms, and what fears I'd already accumulated now mounted to a peak. My suitcases and my trunks were arranged in neat rows, all packed. The bureau had been swept clean of my things, drawers emptied, everything gone.

I went downstairs slowly, forcing myself not to hurry, taking time to think. By the time I walked into the drawing room to face Joel's father and mother,

Uncle Loran, and Aunt Marcy, I had guessed much of what must have taken place.

I spoke to them in what I hoped was a steady voice. "I have come back for my daughter. Unless you produce her within a very brief period of time, I shall telegraph my New York lawyer and my attorney in Portland and I shall insist that there be an immediate investigation."

"Of what, my dear?" Loran asked. "Deborah is on a little vacation with Helen. She's quite all right, I assure you."

"Bring her back," I said. "I warn you but once, and I will add this. If there is an investigation, it will include two attempts on my life and the murder of my husband. The murder of your son, you Camerons. Your son! Do you understand me?"

"Maeve," Mrs. Cameron said, "sit down, please. You're distraught and not making any sense."

"All we ask is that you listen," Joel's father added. "It's for your own good, believe me."

I sat down. "No matter what you say, it will change nothing. I will have my daughter back, and at once, or I'll make more trouble than you can handle with all your influence and your money."

Loran's face grew pink with anger. "Now, you listen to me, you ungrateful hussy. You're not going to have Deborah back. Never! We will bring her up as a Cameron should be raised. And you will agree to it, or we'll ruin your name in this town, drive you away, and see to it you are sent back to Ireland in shame and disgrace."

"I am listening," I said. "I will sit here another two or three minutes, and that is all."

Loran picked up a legal-looking document from a table beside him. "I'm recalling the night of the ball when you enticed a half-drunken idiot out of the ballroom so that he could make love to you."

232

"So that's it," I said. "If you've got no more than that, save your breath."

"Oh, there's more. In fact, we are taking a certain risk in adopting Deborah because we cannot be sure Joel is her father."

"And what brought on that bit of nonsense?" I asked. It was so patently absurd I didn't grow any angrier.

Loran handed me the document. "This is a sworn deposition made in Ireland by one Cathal Dolan, a young man who swears you were engaged to him until Joel came along and you discovered Joel was wealthy. The statement swears that you and this Cathal Dolan had intimate relations many times, before Joel arrived and afterward. There are other statements by other villagers to the effect that they all believed you and Cathal would marry and that you were constantly in his company."

"Cathal is a liar," I said. I handed the document back. "I will take the matter up with Mr. Arnold in New York."

Aunt Marcy was smiling. "You're a brazen one, but then your kind always are. It will be a pleasure to publicly expose you as a whore!"

I held back both tears and rage. "I will make no statement now, but this is not the end of it."

"Please," Joel's mother begged, "be reasonable, Maeve. Think what we can do for Deborah."

"I can well think of it," I said. "You've already changed her name, and you would change her personality and mold her after your own small, wrinkled, sour old souls that stink of your scheming and your plotting. That stink of murder."

Loran sat down. "I told you she'd not listen. Throw her out."

"No," Joel's father said. "She did marry my son, and she deserves some consideration. Maeve, we'll buy you out—your share of the mill—for twice its current value. You can go back to Ireland, where you'll be happy and rich. In return we'll destroy all the evidence we have against you, and we'll arrange that you come and visit Deborah at certain times."

"Now that's grand of you," I said. "Generous to a fault you are. I'll have none of it."

"Deborah will grow up to learn her mother is a common whore who carried her practices over the Atlantic right to this house," Loran said. "If you think we can't prove that, test us. Have your great lawyer test us. We're prepared for him. We'll bring this Cathal What's-his-name here from Ireland and anyone else we need to testify against you. We'll have Arthur Standish swear you enticed him into making love to you. Think about it. Every newspaper will pounce on the story. That will be a wonderful legacy to leave to your daughter."

I arose. "I am going upstairs to my rooms for certain possessions I do not trust to remain in this god-forsaken house. I will arrange at once for my bags and trunks to be removed."

I marched out of the drawing room and made my way upstairs. The tears were damming up only because I could not let them see me cry. I closed the bedroom door and sought out the suitcase in which the mirror had been packed. If it was not here, I would refuse to leave until it was produced. But then, there was little reason to think it wouldn't be, for none could possibly realize the value of it. My only fear was that someone might have thought it worthless and thrown it away.

I found it in the third suitcase I examined. I placed it in my handbag and closed the suitcase. As I arose, the door opened and Ashley walked in.

"Go down where you belong with the rest of them," I said.

"They treated you badly, Maeve. I'm sorry for you. Really, I'm very sorry."

He came toward me, and for a moment I believed he was sincere. Suddenly he gathered me in his arms and pulled me hard against him while his hands grew busy and his lips searched for mine. I was so surprised and taken aback that I was too stunned to do anything for a few seconds. Then I managed to raise my right hand and press the heel of it against his chin. I drew it back a few inches and struck him with it at the same time I kicked his leg as hard as I could. When he let go of me I stepped back and struck him again as hard as I could, across the face. He backed up hurriedly, trying to protect himself from my fury, which I unleashed with a will and a vigor that relieved some of the pressure that had built up within me.

I drove him through the two rooms and into the corridor. Suddenly I felt sorry for this poor excuse for a man. I turned away in disgust. In my rooms I retrieved my handbag and then left. Ashley had disappeared. I went downstairs. Martha, at the door, opened it, but I didn't go out immediately. I went into the drawing room.

"If your sorry intentions were to further wreck my reputation by having Ashley rape me, next time send a man, and the devil take the lot of you."

As I passed the housekeeper I said, "That goes for you, too, though I have my doubt the devil would want the likes of you."

I made a grand walk to my carriage and got aboard. I kept the horse moving at a normal pace until I was out of sight of the house. Then I slapped the reins and began to come to pieces with worry and fear. By the time I reached Glen's house I felt as poorly as the night I'd come with all that pain.

Jennie threw her arms around me. "You went up there, didn't you? Glen wanted to save you that, Maeve."

"I had to go. They're keeping Nora. They won't let me have her."

"Glen will take care of that," Jennie said. "The Camerons are not dealing with employees now. Come, sit at the kitchen table. I've made coffee. I don't think it will upset your stomach. Glen will be finished in the office very soon now."

"It's not my stomach bothering me," I said. "It's my head and my sense of reality. I can't believe what's happened. I simply can't believe there can be people like those . . . those . . . up there."

"I know, I know. But it's not over."

"You don't know," I said. "You've no idea what they've done. How they think."

"Maeve," Jennie warned, "please calm down. If you're like this when Glen sees you, he'll make you go back to bed."

"I'll try. Heaven knows I don't want that. So I'll try. The coffee is good. It warms me, and after being in that house I thought nothing in this world ever would again." I held out my arm. "I'm shaking, but I will calm down. Don't leave me, Jennie. I've need of someone I love more than ever in my life."

"I just heard the outer door close, so Glen is probably finished with the patients. Tell him what happened as calmly as possible. Keep in mind that you've been ill—very ill. You also disobeyed him by going up there, and if he sees how upset you are, it will surely be a sleeping draft for you."

"I'm fine," I said. "I'll be calm, but I'll be angry. I'm so mad I could go up there and set fire to the place."

Glen hurried into the kitchen and sat down at the table beside me. Jennie poured him a cup of coffee and refilled my cup.

"You're a wreck," Glen said. "Why did you do it?"

"I had to."

"Well . . . I suppose. . . ."

"They sent Nora away with Helen, and they wouldn't tell me where."

236

"They did? We'll get her back. That's kidnapping."

"Wait, Glen. They will have that Standish man swear I offered myself to him the night of the ball. They have a sworn statement from Cathal Dolan in my village in Ireland that he and I . . . slept together before Joel came and afterwards. They said they weren't even sure Nora was Joel's child but they were willing to risk it."

"Now wasn't that generous of them," Jennie said.

"Maeve, will you marry me?" Glen asked.

"They even were that stupid they sent that nincompoop Ashley to perhaps try and make me surrender to him. I beat him and kicked him and drove him away."

"Maeve, listen to me! Will you marry me?"

"They came right out with it," I said. "They would make me a whore. They would make Nora ashamed of me when she grew up. If I went into court—what did you say?"

"Damn it!" he roared this time. "I asked you to marry me."

"Of course I will," I said. "What made you think I wouldn't?"

"I . . . I . . . don't know. I had to ask. . . ."

"Some good came of it after all," I said, looking directly at Jennie. "This poor man wouldn't have asked me now, except that he's trying to save my honor. To make a good woman of me."

Glen tucked his chin in his hand and looked away with a long sigh. Until I went over to him and bent and kissed his dear lips and told him I'd loved him for ages.

Jennie had somehow managed to leave the kitchen without my noticing it. Glen stood up.

"I didn't ask you to marry me because I felt sorry for you. It was not on my mind to make an honest woman of you, as you said. I spoke because I love you with all my heart, and I have since the first moment we met."

"Aye, darling," I told him, "I knew that, too."

"I couldn't speak to a woman who'd lost her husband so short a time before. But now you're in need of help, and as your husband I can do much for you."

"Glen, it's not true, about this Standish and about Cathal."

"You didn't have to tell me that."

"I know, but I did, anyway. I may be a bit confused, so much has happened to me. I'm in love with a fine man, and we shall be married, which is wonderful. But I've lost my daughter, which is awful."

"You've not lost her," he said.

"Sit down and let me tell you how I feel. Please, darling. We have to talk this out now. I'm thinking of Nora and how they can make her ashamed of me. I couldn't stand that. It would break my heart. If I thought they could use their lying testimony and make a judge believe it, I would do nothing."

"What we need is a lawyer. A better one than theirs."

"I have such a one in New York. He cannot practice here, but he can give me advice. It might be well if I went to see him."

"We'll make it our honeymoon, Maeve."

"Oh, Glen, what kind of a honeymoon would that be?"

"Now, let's get one thing straight. We'll get Nora back one way or another. But if it takes a long, long time, Nora will not suffer for it. They'll give that child the best care in the world."

"They'll turn her into a Cameron, and that's a bad sickness," I said.

"But not a fatal one. Now's not the time for us to talk about Joel, but he *was* a Cameron. By taking our time we can build a better legal case and put those people to shame."

238

"That's what they'll do to me, Glen. There's yet another reason we should not marry now."

"There can't be."

"The Camerons will next drive you out of this town."

"Oh, no. You're wrong. They don't own this house or land. I don't owe them anything. They have to have a doctor here, or their employees will quit and go elsewhere. I can do without the Camerons, but they can't do without me."

"They can bring in another doctor. And what will you do for money if they no longer pay the fees of your patients?"

"I have enough to get by . . . for a while."

I said, "Ah, more than that. There's my money as well. Now don't you start being a man ashamed to take money from his wife. This is different. They can't stop that money from coming to me. They can't drive me out of this town, for I own one-third of it. That's how we'll begin to fight them."

"Only if we can't get Nora back." He stroked my hair lightly. "They could make a great deal of trouble for you. Standish is no good. Everybody knows that, but in court his word will be accepted or, at least, considered. Ashley will swear you enticed him, and that will back up Standish. It's all been thought out. Cathal's deposition can't be argued against without bringing in many witnesses from Ireland, and I have an idea the Camerons could put a stop to that."

"They once mentioned about having me deported. That was when I first came. Can they do that?"

"Maeve, it never crossed my mind. If they win in court—yes, they will have a good chance with their influence, and they'll spend a lot of money to get their will done. I still say we should get married, go to New York on our honeymoon, and talk to your lawyer. Once we are married, there can be no deportation."

239

"We surely cannot be married in this town. No one would dare come. Can you leave your patients?"

"There's no one seriously ill. And if anything happens, Jennie can bring in a doctor from the next town."

"Aye." For a flicker of a heartbeat, I thought of Joel. If there'd been a nearby doctor . . . "I have loved you a long time, darling. Longer than you know."

"Not longer than I have been in love with you," he said.

"Aye, that I will admit. You were in love with me before you ever laid eyes on me, and one day I'll tell you how that came to be."

We made the arrangements quite hurriedly and took a carriage, driven by Jennie, to the nearest town with a depot. There we boarded a train after sending Mr. Arnold a telegram that we were coming and the reason was an urgent one. We stayed over in Boston and were married there as soon as the Church and the Massachusetts law permitted. Glen apparently had some influence, for everything was done in twenty-four hours.

Once away from the town of Cameron, a serenity came over me to replace the anxiety and anger—and the sorrow. I couldn't forget Nora, but Glen was right, she'd be well taken care of. But I didn't feel so secure in my belief I'd get her back after talking to Mr. Arnold. Even Glen became discouraged during that conversation.

"The trouble with this whole affair," Mr. Arnold said, "is that we can quite likely prove their stories of your infidelity to be quite untrue and certainly malicious, but the damage will have been done."

"Which means if I am proven to be perfectly innocent, my reputation will nonetheless be soiled?" I asked.

"I'm afraid so. However, if you wish, I'll send competent lawyers to your assistance, and we'll open a criminal case of kidnapping against them. I doubt it will hold up, but at least we'll initiate the proceedings, and that may help. If you were that evil a woman and unfit a mother, you'd not even start the matter."

"Would we win the kidnapping case?" Glen asked.

"No. In fact, we might not even get an indictment, and if that happened, it could prove dangerous to our side."

"What do you recommend, then?" I asked. "I don't want to lose my daughter. Not to anyone, but above all, not to those people."

"I would suggest caution. As you have indicated, the child will be well cared for and is too young to be permanently influenced. Now you have indicated to me that your first husband may have been murdered and that there was also an attempt on his life with a rifle. Then here in Cameron, there was a forest fire, possibly meant to destroy you by taking advantage of an unusually dry season in the forest. Your death would have seemed accidental. If there was any suspicion, the Camerons could prove beyond doubt how well they'd treated you the previous months and how much they loved you. Next you grew ill, suspiciously ill, like that sickness which took Joel, but here, too, there's no proof of anything."

"The idea," Glen said, "is to wait. People who resort to such measures make mistakes. Is that what you're suggesting, Mr. Arnold?"

"I can't offer much else. We're fighting power and money with little to use as ammunition."

Glen said, "We'll be watching and searching for anything that may lead us to proof that someone in the Cameron family tried to kill Maeve and did murder Joel."

"Then we'll have them where money and influence won't be worth much," Mr. Arnold agreed. "It will take time. I know this is painful to you, Maeve, but

241

unless you wish to take a mighty serious risk with your reputation, which, I know, you could survive but which your daughter might not, I would handle the matter in the fashion I outlined."

"Aye," I nodded slowly. "Given time to think, when the anger softens and common sense takes the place of some of it, then it does become clear what I am up against. I shall be jealous of every day they have Nora, and I shall find comfort only in the knowledge that they will take good care of her."

"You're showing a great deal of common sense," Mr. Arnold told me. "Always keep in mind that you own one-third of their holdings. That's not enough to overcome any business decisions they may vote, but you can slow them down by insisting on full reports, by calling for meetings, by inspections of the mill and, most important, full access to the books of the firm."

"What legal rights I may have I'll use, never fear," I assured him.

"And be patient," he counseled, as he embraced me in fatherly fashion and shook hands with Glen. "This is far from over."

For Glen and me, our honeymoon was also far from over. We spent a week in New York, visited Philadelphia for two days, and then decided to go home, for I sensed that Glen was worried about his practice.

We did enhance the trip by taking a passenger boat from New York to Boston, a steamship of modern style and comfort. Except for my concern over Nora and my missing her, I would have thought these some of the happiest days of my life.

Glen was so much like Joel in some ways. Gentle, thoughtful, and kind. But where Joel was content to drift, Glen was ambitious. Delays annoyed him; he chafed under restrictions he believed to be unfair, and except for Mr. Arnold's advice I'm afraid Glen would have challenged the Camerons at once. The results might have been disastrous. If my daughter grew up to learn—and they would see to it—that her mother had been accused of being a woman of poor moral character, that would have hurt me more than anything else.

From Boston we took the sooty steam train and arrived in Cameron in mid-afternoon. Glen had sent Jennie a telegram, and she was waiting at the depot with the carriage and a somewhat woebegone expression.

"Why Jennie," I asked, "what's wrong?"

"Oh, it's a number of things." She embraced Glen and then broke into tears.

He held her at arm's length, and my own heart began to thump. Would Jennie's tears be caused by something concerned with Nora?

"Out with it," Glen said. "What's happened?"

"Oh, Glen, the Camerons found out that you and Maeve were married and off on your honeymoon. They immediately brought in another doctor. He set up practice in one of the houses along Main Street. They mean to get rid of us."

Glen helped us into the carriage and stowed the baggage. "Well, that's something I never thought they'd dare do," he said. "Were you approached?"

"Only by the new doctor. He's a pleasant enough young man, and I don't think he quite knows what it's all about. He did say the Camerons were going to pay his fees."

Glen sent the carriage rolling toward the town. "Well, that's going to complicate our plans, I'm afraid. But then, it really doesn't do us any harm. I can set up a practice anywhere."

"Can they make you leave town?" I asked.

"Oh, no," Glen said. "I told you before, they have no control over me or the property I own."

"I'm thinking of our patients," Jennie said. "Oh, the

new man will do his best, I'm sure, but this is where we grew up. Father practiced here. It will be terrible if we have to leave."

"Let's not talk about it now," Glen said. "We'll work something out." He glanced at me, squeezed into the front seat beside him, for our baggage filled the rear. "As for you, Mrs. Kinnery, don't go getting the idea we can stay here anyway and live on your money. That won't work. I'm a doctor, and if I don't practice medicine, then I'm not a doctor; I'm nothing. So we'll wait a bit and then make some plans. Meanwhile you can show Jennie the presents we brought back for her."

It was a sad return, no matter how hard Glen tried to make light of it. We passed through the empty waiting room and office. Jennie had a splendid supper waiting, and while we ate well, none of us enjoyed it as we should have.

We were clearing the table, Jennie and I, when Glen said, "I think somebody just came into the waiting room. Be right back."

He was gone for half an hour, and when he returned, his grin was broad and he was chuckling in great humor.

"That was George Prentice. He came for medicine. I told him he would have to go to the new doctor, but he said he would not. I reminded him that the mill wasn't paying my fee for treating him, and he told me he'd do his best to pay whatever I charged. And he said everybody in town will come to me under those conditions."

"Oh, Glen," I said happily, "that's wonderful."

"I'm pleased, too," Jennie said, "but these people can barely buy enough to eat with the wages they earn. They can't afford to pay a doctor and for medicine."

"We've enough to carry us for a long time," Glen said. "By heaven, this is one way to poke those Camerons in the eye. For once they won't get their own way. They cannot compel their employees to use a doctor they select. If the employees and their families want to come to me, there's nothing can be done to prevent that. I'll make my fees so low they can pay—or I'll tell them there is no fee."

"I won't agree to that," I said.

Glen turned to me in dismay. "But, darling, we can do it. . . ."

"You'll charge your usual fees, and the mill will pay them just as before. The money will come out of my share of the profits. Maybe the fees will be paid indirectly, and maybe they won't be fees at all, seeing the money is ours, anyway. But we'll keep books just as if the mill was paying. Have you forgotten that I'm a rich woman?"

"If I have," Glen said softly, "I've not forgotten that I'm a rich man, and I don't mean the riches of money."

We found no further time for discussion that night. The office door opened and closed several times. Glen happily kissed me, embraced Jennie, and went back to work. When I glanced out of the kitchen window, from where I could see the front gate and the path to the office door, people were standing in line. There were seven by count, which meant the office was full. All these people had waited until Glen returned.

"The poor, poor man," I said.

"Who?" Jennie asked. "What poor man?"

"The doctor brought in by the Camerons. The poor man."

After our housework was done, I went upstairs to the room Glen and I now would share. My suitcases were open, but not unpacked. Jennie would not have invaded my privacy by going through my things. I hunted for the mirror.

Lawyer Arnold's advice seemed just and wise. Glen, too, appeared to counsel patience, but I wondered if the mirror could help me. I wanted to know what would become of Nora.

It wasn't quite dark, and I had to light two lamps, for the old mirror required all the light I could provide. I sat down and held it to my breast for a moment.

"This is one of the most important questions I have ever asked," I said in a whisper. "I have lost my Nora. Will I get her back? Will she be my child once again? Or will she be a child of the Camerons? I wish you to show me this child I will love and cherish to my dying day. If you never answer another question, answer this one for my sake, please."

I held the mirror before my eyes, tilting it slightly as I usually did. This time the image didn't flash before my eyes but seemed to grow from within that sorry-looking bit of metal. It took the form of a little girl—but it was not the image of Nora.

"I don't understand," I said. "I asked you to show me the daughter I will cherish and . . . love. . . ."

The image vanished. I sat there for a long time, the mirror again pressed to my breast. Some moments later, quite serenely, I packed my bags. I had just about finished when Glen came in.

"There were fifteen patients," he said. "They insisted on paying something. I took in four dollars. We can live on that."

"Three of us, perhaps," I said. "But there will be four."

"What are you talking about, Maeve?"

"We shall have a girl child, Glen. A beautiful girl child."

"Oh, Maeve, how can you possibly be sure of that? The best doctor in the world couldn't tell if you are pregnant after this short time. You're daydreaming."

"She will be as beautiful as Nora. Perhaps even more so. She will never take the place of Nora in my heart, but I will love her as much."

"Maeve, there's no way of knowing that you will have a child, and absolutely no way of knowing that the child will be a girl."

"The child is within me," I said. "The child is a girl. One day I'll tell you how I am so sure. You will have to come to know me better first, for when I do tell you, I'm sure you'll think me slightly mad. So you will wait, but tomorrow I shall begin making baby clothes, and they will be in pink."

Jennie, too, argued with me over my firm statement that I would have a girl, but there must have been something in my voice or my attitude, because I caught her making baby clothes, too, and they were in pink. Perhaps the influence of the mirror had somehow reached her.

Two weeks went by. Often I would look up at the mansion on the hill and be tempted to go there, but I held back this natural desire to see Nora. I had acquired some measure of strength to resist the impulse because Glen, Jennie, and I were now engaged in showing the Camerons they could not always have their own way.

Then, the new young doctor came to see Glen and informed him he hadn't had a single patient and that he was closing his office. He wasn't angry. Not at us, or the village, but he thought the Camerons could have told him the truth about the situation here.

Glen was, of course, as busy as ever. He didn't take in much money, but we were certainly never in need of fresh vegetables or fruit in season. Each month, regularly, a bank, acting as trustee, sent me the dividends from the mill, and they were remarkably substantial. Glen couldn't deny me the privilege of buying him new equipment and splurging on furnishing the house.

I had little doubt but that everyone in town knew what had happened. I took walks up and down Main Street, but they were not brisk walks, for I stopped often to chat.

It was on one of these mid-morning walks that someone fell into step, coming up from behind me.

"Helen takes Nora in the pram part way down the

road from the mansion," Abner said. "Every morning about eleven."

"Thank you, Abner," I said. "I'm glad to see you."

"I don't go up there much any more. I stay at the inn."

"Nora is all right?"

"Fine. Just fine. She's the princess. Don't worry about her."

"I want to get her back."

"Take your time. Don't make any mistakes. That's important."

He dropped back and somehow disappeared a few moments later. I reversed my steps and went back to the house. I didn't tell anyone what I intended to do, for I wanted no interference. I hitched up the buggy and drove it up the slope toward the mansion, but before I came into view of the place, I drove off the road and left the horse and buggy beneath trees that effectively shielded them from view. I walked then, along the side of the road, trying my best to avoid being seen, too.

My lapel watch told me it was quarter past eleven. One thing about all the Camerons, including Helen, they were punctual, and when they set a routine they followed it almost to the minute. Sure enough, Helen came into sight pushing a large baby carriage.

I stepped behind thick brush. My heart was pounding. I knew the risks I took, yet this was my daughter and I had to see her, to hold her in my arms, if for no more than a moment. I stepped out, confronting Helen, who gasped in sudden fear as she stopped and seemed about to turn the carriage and try to run away with it.

"I'm not here to make trouble or harm you in any way," I said. "I want to see Nora. I'm going to pick her up and hold her in my arms, and you're not going to stop me."

"Maeve . . . you can't. . . ."

"If you try to stop me, I'll take her away with me.

248

If you're sensible, I'll put her back in the carriage, go away, and there'll be no more said about it."

"I . . . can't stop you," she said. "Maeve . . . don't blame me. . . ."

"I blame you and all of them up there." I bent over the carriage and lifted Nora. She began to cry. I held her close to me and cuddled her, and despite everything, the tears came.

"Maeve," Helen said, "if they see you . . . they'll make trouble. . . ."

I replaced Nora in the carriage. She had stopped crying and was gurgling and smiling. I kissed her and covered her well.

"Thank you, Helen," I said.

She seized the carriage handle, turned it about, and went off as fast as the slope would permit. Suddenly she halted the carriage and looked back.

"Never do that again! Deborah is mine. She's my daughter. You can't have her. You're nothing but a common . . . common . . . whore!"

I wasn't even angry. In fact, I felt quite elated. Nora was fine, and I was sure she'd recognized me. A forlorn, foolish idea on the part of a bereft mother, perhaps, but I kept that feeling with me as I returned to the buggy and drove back to my husband to wait my second daughter.

BOOK THREE:

Maeve Kinnery

TEN

Then Patricia was born, but not without danger to both of us. Glen brought us through the ordeal and at the end of it he told me I would bear no more children. I wept at that, though I tried not to let him know.

And the disappointment was softened by Patricia, a strong, healthy baby, as beautiful as Nora had been. She was not a demanding child, but rather, sweet and obedient and truly loving. I saw her through the usual childhood illnesses, and also scarlet fever, which, thanks be to the Blessed Mother, she weathered without being scarred.

Nora, known to the village as Deborah, also proved to be healthy. I had first-hand knowledge of that through Glen, who was called to the mansion on the hill whenever she showed symptoms of being ill. It was a rather unsettling situation, and I suppose the Camerons were as aware of it as I. They had to depend upon the medical skill of the man who had married the mother of Nora, who was denied even the right to visit the child.

"The one thing," Glen told me after he'd treated her for chicken pox, which ran all through the town, "you don't have to worry about so far as Nora is concerned is her health. It must be the Irish in you. Both girls are sound. Not one thing wrong, and both as beautiful as you."

"She is attractive," I admitted. "I've seen Nora a

few times—perhaps as many as ten times—in the last eight years. She looks remarkably like our Patty."

"Well," Glen said, "being Patty's father, I favor her. Nora's hair is darker, and her eyes are brown. Our Patty is fair as a field of wheat, and her eyes look like the sky after a storm. No, Patty's the better looking, but as you Irish are wont to say, Nora is better than a poke in the eye. These have been a strange few years—how many have they been? Seven? Eight?"

"Nora is now nine, Patty seven."

"Yes, that's right. Do you feel the change, darling? We've moved into a new century. I have a telephone in my office, and I can even contact any phone as far as New York City—if I care to pay the price. We'll have electricity in town before another two years are up, and the gas we're using now is some improvement over kerosene, or hauling coal and ashes, I'll tell you."

"The one thing I can't say I care for is that smelly, noisy motorcar you use."

"Dear Maeve, it gets me about ten times faster than the horse could ever do, and I don't have to harness it up every time I get a night call."

"You have to crank it and nearly break your arm. You have to light those awful carbide lamps that smell worse than the car. Oh, I'm out of sorts today, Glen. I have a problem."

It was an early autumn night and we had the fireplace going. Patty was upstairs with Jennie, refreshing herself over her old textbooks, for school was to open on Monday.

"This problem of yours," Glen said, "can I help?"

"No, it's that darned school. You know that the mill children never have enough good clothes. They wear hand-me-downs or something so cheap it's unattractive."

"I know that very well, but they're all in the same boat."

254

"That's the trouble. Nora comes dressed like a brand-new, expensive doll. A different dress every week, new shoes, ribbons; sometimes she wears hats and gloves. I will not dress Patty that way. Nora makes all the other kids uneasy and jealous. They become too aware of the fact that they're poor."

"That's a fact they'd all better learn how to face. The sooner it happens, the better for them."

"Yes, but what about Nora? She's cut off from them; for her there's only the Camerons. Things are changing, I know. The twelve-hour, six-day work week is not going to last much longer. It's already gone in some of the larger cities."

"The Camerons will be the very last to hear of it, you can be sure."

"Eight hours a day is enough," I said.

"Except for doctors."

"That's another thing. Fees are going up, too. Sure, the Camerons did finally agree to pay your fees after they found out not one worker would go to another doctor. Since then they act as if they're doing us a big favor."

Glen stretched his slippered feet toward the fire. "As a holder of one-third of the stock in the mill, Dr. Glen Kinnery hereby petitions you for a fifty percent increase in his fees for medical services to all employees. Take it up with the Board of Directors, please."

I shook my head and joined in his quiet laughter. "You know, Glen, one of these days I'm going to attend a board meeting. Just walk in. I have the legal right. Up to now, it hasn't bothered me because I've been busy with Patty and getting straightened out in a number of other things, but the pressure isn't as great any more. This leisure makes me restless. That's what I was getting at when we began this conversation."

"What were we getting at?" he asked lazily.

"Nora, shining like a rose among the field flowers at school. It would be for her good to bring her down a few pegs. Did you ever see her riding down Main Street in the family brougham?"

Glen chuckled. "She keeps her chin way up in the air and her nose slightly above it. She never looks to the right or left, and if she did, I think she'd raise her hand very languidly and bestow an apostolic blessing on the poor people who pass her by."

"I'm going to do it," I said. "What you just said is perfectly true, and I'm going to put a stop to it if I can. She is my daughter."

He pulled himself up from his sprawled, lazy position because he recognized in my voice a tone that meant I was going to do something drastic.

"We'll build a small school up on the Hill just big enough for her and let Helen be the teacher."

"Oh, no. That would be too easy. They'd love to send her to a private school if they could, but there's none within a hundred miles. There's also a law that says all children must go to school, so they have to send her here. We've a good school, Glen. Ever since we brought in those three normal-school-trained teachers, the kids have been doing very well."

"Thanks to the desks, the books, and the supplies your share of the mill profits have supplied."

"All right. That's as it should be. The Camerons won't see to it, but at least I can see that some of the mill profits do help. Here's what I plan. A girl Nora's age, brought up as she's been, likes to lord it over the other children but—here's my big idea. Uniforms!"

"Uniforms?" He nodded as if he understood right off.

"Blouses and knickers for the boys. Long black stockings, black shoes. Caps and short overcoats. The girls can wear middies, blue skirts, white stockings and shoes, sailor hats—or something like that. Good warm coats, all identical, for winter."

"School starts in a week. How do you accomplish all that in seven days?"

"We have a mill that turns out fine cotton cloth we sell to manufacturers of clothing. These manufacturers will be glad to oblige a one-third owner of this mill. They can furnish the materials, and the mothers can sew the clothing. We'll arrange for the shoes, caps, and other things. The winter things can wait a bit, though we'll order them now. In a week's time, every child will report to school all dressed the same, in pretty dresses for the girls and neat clothes for the boys. Everyone the same. That's what will do it. Nora will come to school all dressed up, but this time things will be different, and before the first day is over, she'll want to wear one of those dresses, too."

"Made of silk, no doubt," Glen commented.

"Perhaps. It doesn't matter. She'll be like the rest of the kids and, in fact, be more like them. These airs she puts on are not natural. They simply couldn't be, Glen, for too much county Mayo blood flows in her veins, and in Mayo, I assure you, nobody puts on airs."

"All right, it sounds good. You will pay for it?"

"Out of the mill profits. Good heavens, man, do you know how much is in the banks? I could dress them all in fur coats and have a fortune left over."

"It's settled, then," Glen said. "I agree it will probably work, and it's bound to make the Camerons dizzy with resentment, which is the main reason why I approve. Also, warm clothes might reduce the number of colds, pneumonias, and diptherias the kids get every winter. Yes, it's a grand idea."

"I'll talk to as many mothers as I can in the morning and get this started at once. Maybe we can be ready by the time school starts." I hugged him quickly. "Oh, Glen, we'll be giving them a better future."

"The future is something you sort of know about, isn't it, Maeve? It's time you told me about that."

"Aye, my love, it is. We've been married long enough now you won't think I've gone daft. I'll fetch the mirror, but if Jennie comes down, or Patty decides to say good night to us, I'll stop right in the middle of the thing. This is between you and me. Man and wife secret."

"All right." He looked puzzled. "But what mirror are you talking about?"

"You'll see. I'll be but a few moments."

I went upstairs softly, not wishing to attract Jennie or Patty. I entered our bedroom and from a high shelf, far back in the biggest closet, I took down the box in which I had hidden the mirror. It had been years now since I'd laid eyes on it. During all that time I'd felt no need for its predictions. When Glen told me that there'd be no more children; when Patty proved healthy and fine and Nora came along so well, my future was all compressed into the present. I'd been content to let it go at that.

The mirror had not changed or deteriorated in any way that I could see. I carried it downstairs with all the reverence I always showed it, and I sat down on the sofa, motioning for Glen to sit beside me. I showed him the slightly curved, oblong piece of metal.

"That's an awful sorry-looking mirror," he remarked.

"No, my darling, it's a wondrous thing. Once, years ago, I told you that you were in love with me before we even met."

"I don't remember that."

"It's true. I did tell you that. When I laid eyes on you, just a glimpse as you passed by the dining room door of the inn one night when I was having supper, I recognized you, though I had never seen you before in my life. When I entered your office the first time, I knew you and I would marry, and after we married I knew we would have Patty, that she would be a girl. I saw your image in this mirror and I saw Patty's image before it was possible she was even conceived. I saw Joel's image—and I saw Nora's image."

"You believe this?" Glen asked. Who could resent the question in his voice?

"I did then. I do now. I saw Joel's image fade, portending his death. When I asked the mirror about my father, I saw a storm at sea. A violent, ugly storm. My father died in such a one."

"You can look into that and see those things? It's not your imagination?"

"Any female descended from Queen Maeve can ask of this mirror a question about herself or those she loves and there will be an answer. Sometimes it comes in a flash, so quick it's hard to be sure what it is, but often it comes slowly and there is no question."

"I could use that in my profession," Glen said.

"Darling, don't laugh at this."

"I couldn't see anything in it?"

"Nothing. Nor could anyone else who is not of Queen Maeve's blood."

"Patty could see in it, then?"

"Aye—and Nora."

"You will tell them of it?"

"Aye, when it is time."

"Maeve, you can't blame me for doubting this."

"No, for there have been times when I doubted it myself. But it told me the truth too often."

"Could you ask it something right now?"

"Yes, I believe so. But it does not always respond."

"You're afraid of it, aren't you?" he asked me.

"Aye. It can bring bad news. I have had no need to consult it these many years since we were married. I have been so happy and content, Glen. Thanks to you."

"If this does work—and I won't disbelieve you, Maeve—it's a treasure beyond description."

"Do you want me to ask it something?"

259

"Only if you really want to," Glen said.

"I want you to believe in the mirror. So, I will ask it this question and when it comes to pass, then you will know."

I brought the mirror close to me, held it against me, and closed my eyes as if in prayer, but I spoke aloud. "I ask of you this one thing. What event is to soon happen which will affect me and those I love? It has been a long time since I asked a favor of you. Do not disappoint me."

I slowly brought the mirror before my eyes, tilting it, gazing into its depths, and there I saw a swirling mass of dark clouds. They grew thicker, more bodied, and suddenly it seemed to me that they became a horde of ugly faces and waving arms which vanished in a fraction of a second to be replaced by a profile. That of a man, indistinct at first, and then taking on a silhouette I couldn't help recognizing. This too vanished, but more slowly, and the mirror was blank.

"Did you see anything?" Glen asked. "You're white . . . trembling. Maeve . . . what is it? You did see something!"

"I don't know. Abner . . . Abner, Joel's brother— he is there, and before him there were many . . . crazed people . . . moving about like an ocean wave."

"What does it mean?"

"I'm not sure. It's evil. I can tell you that. I don't know what all those people meant, but . . . Abner is going to die. It was like the prophecy the mirror told concerning my father. With him it was a wild, angry sea. This is sort of a sea also, but of people."

Glen leaned forward to look straight into my eyes. "The mirror is right about Abner. He is going to die. The mirror told the truth."

"You know this?" I asked in fresh alarm. "About Abner?"

"Abner came to me about three weeks ago. Afterwards he swore me to secrecy, but in this case I have to break my word to him. Abner has sugar diabetes. There is no cure. An ordinary man his age could live two, three, or even four years, but Abner isn't an ordinary man."

"Oh, Glen, he is the only one of them up there I love."

"I know. It's a tragedy, mostly because Abner refuses to do anything about it. Another patient would try to live as long as possible by diet, by caring. Abner doesn't give a damn—and he drinks too much. He has always drunk too much. He isn't going to stop. He said so. In fact, I think he's going on one glorious drunk. And who can blame him?"

"Those people on the Hill are why he doesn't care," I said. "He hates them, never respects them, but he fears them, too. Isn't there anything we can do?"

"He will die in about a year's time—or less. Even if he stopped his drinking, it wouldn't make much difference because of the shape he's in."

Not even the diabetes was going to make any difference. Suddenly I knew what the mirror was trying to tell me.

"Glen, Abner is going to be killed. He won't die of that illness or of his drinking. He will die by violence, and somehow all those people are involved. I don't know how. It doesn't make much sense yet, but that's how it will happen."

"If it does," Glen said quietly, "it may even be a blessing for the man."

I was shaken and nervous from all this. I wished I'd not thought of the mirror or explained it, though Glen deserved to know about its magic. I thought wildly of warning Abner, but there was no object to it. He'd not listen, and even if he did, the prophecy of the mirror was going to come true anyway. It was better Abner didn't know.

"I don't want to talk about this any more. Not

261

tonight," I said. "But while I'm telling you family secrets, there's another thing. It is a torc."

He shook his head. "I've heard the word, but I can't remember what it means."

"It's an heirloom, sort of. A relic—from pagan times, a neck ornament of twisted gold. It has been handed down from one generation to another, always secretly, because it has been made a law that all such relics are the property of the state and no individual shall possess any of them. We O'Hanlons do not defy the law, as a rule, but in this case we have. The torc has a history, somewhat bloody I'm afraid. It now rests in a bank vault in New York City. I put it there the day I came over."

"How'd you get a thing like that through customs?"

"The officer proved to be Irish, which was my great and good fortune, because when he discovered I was from county Mayo, he made a joke of it—though I'm not so sure he was joking—that anyone from there didn't have enough to declare, so he let me through."

Glen laughed, and this broke the tension and the somberness brought about by the revelations of the mirror.

"What are you going to do with it?" Glen asked. "Hand it on? And if so, who will get possession of it? You have two daughters."

"I don't know. The torc is very valuable. It's a link to the past, proof that we were once of royal blood. It has never left the family—and never will if I can help it. I would rather the two girls shared it, but I would be heartbroken if it ever came into the possession of the Camerons, for they'd realize its financial value and be wholly oblivious to the heritage it represents."

"Well," Glen said, "you can't say it's been an uninteresting evening. Your mirror intrigues me. I don't believe it, but it seems to work for you, so I won't say that it's impossible I will believe it one day. But—

there's Abner and that prediction will come true."

"If he dies by violence. That's what you're referring to," I said. "What an awful way to prove something, and yet, we can do nothing about it. What's to happen, will. I hope the mirror is wrong, though it never has been. Not in two thousand years, I have been told, and not in the years I've lived. That I know for a fact."

Any further desire to stay on this subject was at an end when Patty came dashing down the stairs and into the parlor, this lively, blue-eyed whirlwind daughter of mine.

"Aunt Jennie says I'm to kiss you and Papa good night. May I stay up a little longer?"

"For a little while. Come sit with me. I want to talk to you." She promptly settled down beside me, but she was never still. "When school opens, it's possible every girl and every boy will be wearing the same kind of clothes. Like a uniform. Would you like that?"

"I guess so. If all the dresses are pretty."

"They will be. Patty, do you like Deborah, from the Hill?"

"She's too stuck-up."

"Doesn't she speak to you?"

"Sometimes, but I think it's because I dress pretty good. If everybody wears the same kind of dress, she's not going to like it."

"Do you think she'll wear a dress like all the others?" I asked. This was an awful way to obtain information about Patty's half-sister, my first-born.

Patty considered the question. "We'll make fun of her if she doesn't."

"Is Deborah good in school? Is she smart?"

"Maybe like you are?" Glen added with a grin.

Patty laughed gaily. She was such a happy child. "She's smart, all right, but she's not as smart as me. You know why? Because she doesn't have Jennie to

263

teach her and tell her what some of the big words mean and how to say them right."

"Do the other children like her?"

"I don't think so. She comes in that big carriage and it's waiting when it's time to go home, and everybody else has got to walk and the kids don't like that very much. Teacher likes her, though."

Glen made a low whistling sound between his teeth. "Do you mean that teacher likes her better than the other children?"

"Some of the kids call her teacher's pet," Patty said, with a remarkable lack of animosity.

"Do you think the teacher lets her get away with too much? Gives her better marks than she gives the other kids?"

"I don't know," Patty said. At the moment I thought she was seventeen and not a mere seven.

"Think we should look into it?" Glen asked me.

"To what purpose? The teachers are very good. We had a difficult time getting them, and until education became the law, I didn't think we ever would. Remember, the mill pays their salaries."

Glen nodded. "It's a natural weakness. There are times when I feel I succumb to it, too. All right, Miss Patricia. Off to bed with you, and be sure Aunt Jennie hears your prayers."

"You might include Deborah, dear."

Patty slid off the chair. "Why, Mama?"

How could I tell her? Glen shooed her back upstairs to Jennie while I sighed and shook my head over my complete inability to do anything about reclaiming my daughter. As Glen had told me so often—it was too late now. I was too established, and the harm Joel's people could do me would be disastrous. The good people of this town would never quite understand. They might, in their generosity, forgive me, but it would not be forgiveness I'd be after, because I'd done nothing that required it. I wondered if this threat the Camerons held over me would ever go away. It had cost me my first child, and I could never risk losing my second daughter's affection and trust.

In the morning I consulted several mothers and sent them to talk to others until I had unanimous approval for making uniform dresses and boys' clothing out of cloth I would provide. Using my influence as part owner of the mill, I soon obtained all the goods we required, and the women went to work. Time was limited, but by the time school began I watched the children on their way to answer the first school bell of the term. The girls looked quite attractive in their uniform dresses. The boys, freshly scrubbed, with clean shirts and knickers, long black stockings and polished shoes, were a trifle self-conscious, but there was a vast difference in the way the children looked now. Hand-me-downs had never quite fitted, especially after the third or fourth time. The quality of the clothing these people could afford and which they charged at the company store was poor compared to what I had provided. I felt quite elated and satisfied with the result. Not because Nora was going to show up as being oddly different in her expensive dresses, but because the children all had something new and fresh and their faces showed their delight. There was gratification also in knowing that profits from the mill had paid for everything.

Patty, whom I always dressed well, though in a plain fashion, was very pleased with the result and went off flying down the street to join her friends.

Glen had advised it and I'd always made a point of not going out of the way to see Nora. Glen thought the ordeal too painful, and I agreed after that first time I'd stopped Helen near the mansion. Of course, I'd seen Nora since, but only fleeting glimpses. As a rule, any carriage she occupied went through the town as fast as possible, very likely at the Camerons' orders.

Today, however, I wanted to see how the children were reacting after a full day of wearing their uniform clothing, so I took a mid-afternoon walk down to the yellow-painted, frame three-room schoolhouse.

The doors opened soon after I arrived, and the children came streaming out, shouting and screaming, running, or walking with determined slowness, as some had no desire to go home to what was offered them there. Patty didn't see me, and I hadn't intended that she should. I was across the street, standing behind one of the stately elms so I might watch the Cameron carriage unobserved. It was waiting for Nora.

She was one of the last to leave, emerging alone. My heart went out to her. In a pale pink dress with a sash of a deeper pink and matching hair ribbons, with white stockings and shoes, she was by far the best dressed little girl in the town and as pretty as Patty, if not more so.

She walked slowly, her head down. When she reached the carriage and climbed in, she sat there, her head still down. The carriage didn't move. I realized Nora was crying. Without thinking, I ran across the road to the side of the carriage.

The driver knew me well. I looked at him, silently asking him a question he understood.

"I ain't takin' her home, her cryin' like that," he said. "They'll blame me. I don't know what's the matter with her."

I reached into the carriage to grasp Nora's hand, but she jerked it out of my reach.

"What's wrong?" I asked her.

"Never mind," she said, but her determination to treat me with disdain evaporated under her strong desire to cry out her troubles to someone.

"You can tell me," I said. In heaven's name, this was my daughter. Why didn't I climb into that carriage and take her in my arms? Why didn't I tell her who I was and gain her love and, above all, her respect? Why did I allow them to alienate me this way? Nora was only nine. She was a child who needed love and understanding. Not from a houseful of stiff-necked, rigid-spined, cold-hearted people interested more in preserving a family line than in loving this beautiful little girl who needed it so.

She raised her head. "They teased me," she said. "They made fun of me."

"Because you weren't wearing the same kind of clothing all the children wore?"

"Yes."

"Then wouldn't it be wise to dress as they do? You're a very pretty girl, and you're certainly wearing an attractive dress, but the uniform dresses are pretty, too. You'd look nice in one."

"Mama won't let me have one."

"Mama?" I gasped. "Your mother?"

"Yes."

This time a cold rage almost made me do something I'd certainly have regretted. So they'd not only taken Nora away from me, but they'd presumed to make her believe Helen was her mother.

I calmed down with considerable effort on my part and tried to take her hand again, but she stubbornly moved away from me.

"Ask her again. Say you'll feel better if you wear one because then you won't feel out of place among the other children."

"You get away from me," she said. "I know who you are. You're a bad woman. Mama said I was not to talk to you. Grandma said you'd try to kidnap me and I was to scream...."

I stepped off the footrest on the carriage. "No one is going to kidnap you." I looked up at the coachman. "Take her home. You need not mention this meeting if she doesn't."

"Yes, ma'am. It's none of my business anyway."

The carriage pulled away, and I watched it go off.

I had brought this encounter on, and I was to blame for what had happened, but I was angry. By the time Glen's office hours were finished and he came into the house proper, I was at work in the kitchen and seething at a temperature rivaling that of the gas oven where I was baking a cake.

"I'm sorry I didn't have time to come in for a few minutes during the day," Glen apologized. "There was a pretty big patient load this afternoon."

"It's all right. I was better off alone, fit company only for myself."

"What happened?" he asked, with his customary concern.

"I did a fool thing. I went down to the school to see how Nora was taking the new uniform dresses, and I found out she'd been teased to the point of tears because she wasn't wearing one. You know how the children are. Well, I couldn't resist my motherly instinct, if that's what you call it. I went over to the carriage where she was crying and I tried to comfort her. She told me her mother would never agree to her wearing one of the uniform dresses."

"Mother? Are they causing the girl to believe one of them is her mother?"

"It has to be Helen who is taking my place. Nobody else up there is young enough to convince even a little girl she could be her mother. Yes, that's what they've done. And"—I swallowed, dangerously close to tears—"Nora called me a bad woman and said her grandmother had warned her I might try to kidnap her."

Glen sat down at the kitchen table. "They're a damned arrogant bunch, but that about does it. I'm going up there. . . ."

"No, Glen, please don't. They have Nora convinced I'm not a good woman. Don't make them prove it to her with those stories and that terrible document from Cathal Dolan."

"Maeve, we can't let them get away with this."

268

"I don't intend to, my dear."

"Maybe," he said gently, "you'd better tell me what's on your mind."

"Yes, of course I will. I think they've just about forgotten that I own a one-third interest in the mill. It may not give me too strong a voting power, but they can't keep me out of board meetings. I've never gone to one because I don't care to be in their company. Now, however, I'm inclined to think I've been doing them a favor and not one to myself. So there's a meeting day after tomorrow and I'm going to be there, and I intend to make my feelings known. To put it short—in a nice, nasty fashion, I'm going to raise hell."

Glen got up to embrace me, avoiding the serving apron I held in one hand and caring not a whit for the perspiration on my face from the kitchen heat.

"Now you're talking a language they'll understand and won't like. We'll go over this and figure out what's the best way to get their goat. I wish I could be there."

I kissed him and hugged him. "I don't, because I might not be ladylike, and I wouldn't want you to see me that way."

I scarcely slept that night, going over and over in my mind how I would greet the ice-cold reception I was bound to get at the mill office when I came to the meeting.

More than once I almost weakened, but on the day of the regular business meeting of the stockholders, I dressed simply but well and topped off the tan silk street dress with a new hat in the Parisian style, big enough to require four long hatpins to keep it securely in place. Patty thought it dazzling, but Glen shook his head in dismay and said he'd have to widen the doors to our house.

I would have driven our autocar to the factory if I'd been able to crank the thing, but that being hopeless, I gave up the idea and used the buggy instead.

The meeting was always held in Loran's paneled office, highly polished for the occasion. Although the stockholders consisted only of the family, they nevertheless insisted on formality because it impressed the workers. When I entered the main office a slender man with a thick mustache stood up to block my way, but he recognized me and apparently knew of my legal status and sat down again very slowly and somewhat reluctantly, I thought. A buzz of conversation began immediately among the office workers.

I opened the door to Loran's office, walked in, and surveyed the room for a moment. The family was there. Helen, Loran, Joel's father and mother, and Aunt Marcy Tabor. Helen's husband was not present. I presumed he was at home making certain no one ran off with Nora, for this was not a school day. Abner was not there.

All heads turned at my entrance, and hostility gleamed in all eyes. They were seated at a long table and, as there were no vacant chairs, I carried one to the table and sat down. Before anyone could comment or I could say a word, Abner burst into the room, and the hatred expressed for me became annoyance with him.

"Well, I'll be!" he said, in tribute to my courage, I suppose. He noisily dragged a chair over and sat down beside me. "Good morning, my good Irish colleen. And may I say you look better each year."

"Thank you, Abner," I said. "It comes of being happy. If not entirely content."

Joel's father arose. "It's time to open this meeting. As there have been few changes in the past month and business is holding up well, there is nothing to report."

"Move the meeting adjourn," Helen said promptly.

"Wait a minute!" I said sharply. "There are matters to be discussed, even if you don't seem to think

270

so. What of the petition sent you since the last meeting asking that our employees be given a raise in pay?"

"Do you wish to take that up?" Joel's father asked.

"I believe it to be important," I said.

"We will vote. Those against granting a raise signify by raising their hands."

All hands went up except Abner's and mine, and then, slowly he raised his.

"I'm going to say something." I spoke in anger I couldn't control. "So long as I speak, you cannot close this meeting. All of you are blind as well as deaf. You don't see what's happening all around you. There are strikes, there are unions forming. Whether I'm against or for them doesn't matter. They're small now, but they won't be for long. Wages are going up in defense against them, but we do nothing. The eight-hour day has been mandatory for several years in factories that handle government business, and many industries are following that schedule. Yet we work our people twelve hours a day six days a week. Our profits have been fine—excellent, in fact. They are making all of us wealthy, including me, but I don't especially care for more money than I need when it is earned by the sweat of others. I move to put the workers on an eight-hour day."

Joel's father gave a contemptuous shrug of his shoulders. "Those in favor raise their hands."

I did, but nobody else.

"The motion is not carried," Joel's father said. "I heard a motion to adjourn, and it has been seconded. The meeting is adjourned."

"One moment, please." Loran stood up. "There is danger in being too hasty in these matters, and Mrs. Kinnery has a right to be heard on the strength of her shares in this mill."

"Thank you," I said. "I was about to announce that I would take this up with a lawyer."

"Let me, first of all," Loran went on, "say that we

would still like to buy your share at any price you may wish to name. Within reason, of course."

"The answer is no," I said.

"Very well. Do you think our employees would enjoy having their wages cut by one-fourth? They would be if we changed to the eight-hour day. They'd be then working only three-quarters of the time they put in now to earn what we pay."

"The wages should remain the same," I said. "They must not be cut."

Aunt Marcy greeted that idea with a loud laugh. Even Helen seemed amused, and Joel's mother merely shrugged the idea off as if it was too preposterous to consider. Joel's father scowled but remained silent.

"Have you considered what that would do to the profits of this mill?" Loran asked. "I'm trying to be reasonable, Maeve. What differences there are between us are personal and do not concern the mill. I'm speaking to you now as an important stockholder. You have already stated you've been getting rich. Is that a crime?"

"In her case it is," Aunt Marcy shouted. "It's family shares she has. She's not entitled to them."

"Marcy, if you've nothing more intelligent to offer than that, please don't say anything," Loran said. "Maeve—everything we have is in this mill. Without it our employees wouldn't have a job."

"I'm going to say something," Joel's father spoke up. "The way you talk, it seems you believe our workers are not satisfied and may cause us trouble. Am I correct?"

I didn't anwer him.

He glared at me. "I asked a question."

"Of me?" I said innocently. "It's customary to use the name of the person one addresses a question to."

"Mrs. Kinnery, then."

"Eventually there will be serious trouble."

"Then let me tell you that should there be a strike,

272

every person who does not report for work will be fired and immediately ordered to move out of his home and to settle whatever outstanding accounts he has at the company store. Those who are in debt and cannot pay will have their possessions attached."

He strode out of the room. Loran waved a hand to indicate the meeting was adjourned. Abner touched the back of my hand lightly and shook his head in dismay before he abruptly left. I could feel nothing but compassion and sorrow for this man who was so dominated by this family that he was afraid of them even while he slowly died.

Loran sat down beside me. "You know, I agree with you, Maeve. I can see trouble coming, too."

"Then why don't you try to head it off?" I asked.

"I'm one person. I haven't even any voting power. Gabriel is thick-headed, and the rest of them go along with him. I have to, but I've enough common sense to realize this can't last forever."

"Perhaps between us we could force something," I suggested, still quite amazed at Loran's attitude. I'd have thought he'd be the sternest and most formidable one of the lot.

"I can't do that. My power is scarcely above the point of nonexistence. You forget, Grandfather Cameron left his estate in three parts. I didn't get any of it, and my right to be here lies only in the fact that I handle all the business of the mill."

"I had forgotten that," I admitted. "Apparently there's nothing we can do except wait and let the trouble begin."

"There might be one way to soften them and get some kind of a concession."

"I'll listen to anything, Mr. Cameron."

"I understand you talked to Deborah the other day."

"She was crying. I'm her mother. I have a right to comfort her, and that brings up something else. She seems to believe that Helen is her mother."

273

"No one told her that. She assumed it."

"Because Helen was with her from babyhood, and naturally she'd think of her as mother. Why didn't someone tell her the truth?"

"We didn't believe it wise. Not at her tender age."

"You thought it wise enough to let her believe I'm a loose woman. Someone she shouldn't even speak to."

"I had nothing to do with that," he said quickly.

"You could have prevented it. Frankly, I'm tired of this conversation. If you have something to offer, please say it so I can leave."

"As I told you, they'd likely soften their attitudes if you would be willing to sign a document giving up all rights to Deborah."

I leaned back in the chair, too amused to be angry. "You are asking me to legally give up my daughter and in return the family may, or may not, grant their workers a small raise. What kind of a transaction is that, Mr. Cameron? It's the most absurd thing I've ever heard. Nora is my daughter, and I shall have her back one day. There will come a time when she is old enough to understand the truth and be able to see what sort of people have been sheltering her, and to what purpose. As a human machine to perpetuate the family. All of you have forgotten that she is Joel's child and mine, and she will think as Joel did and as I do. This offer is an insult, and I reject it."

I pushed my chair back, arose, and walked out. I'd accomplished literally nothing.

ELEVEN

Winter came with a vengeance, though not as severe a one as that of 1904, which was one of the coldest in history. We did have a great deal of snow, and Glen fashioned a ripper out of three bobsleds, a wide plank, and various nuts and bolts.

As there was but one hill steep enough for sliding, everyone utilized the road to the mansion. I half expected the Camerons to post an objection to this, but so far they'd not done so. In previous years the workers wouldn't have dared to let their children use that road, but they were taking a few more liberties year by year. Precious few, but they were mounting up. And the Camerons were not making the fuss they used to make. Life was changing, slowly perhaps, but the change was definite and permanent.

Patty, Jennie and I hauled the ripper to the top of the hill and glided swiftly down on the fairly well packed snow. It was a good ride, worth the long uphill haul. The ripper was not a flimsy affair.

There were twenty others like it, a horde of sleds, some new, some home-made, but they all served the purpose, and on this crisp, cold moonlit winter night it was inexpensive fun for people who enjoyed little of it during their humdrum days.

Children without sleds were welcome to ride the rippers. Encouraged to, because the more weight on them, the better and faster the ride. We had a few hair-raising near misses at tipping over, and Patty romped in the snow and shouted for more and more speed.

We were getting children aboard for another downhill slide when I saw Nora standing well back, watching us. There seemed to be no one with her.

I said, "Patty, Deborah is back there, and I think she'd like a ride, but she's too shy to ask. Why don't you invite her?"

"Oh, Mama, she's so stuck-up."

"Maybe that's because nobody ever asks her to share in your fun. It won't hurt you to ask her."

"Oh, all right."

She went flying off. If I'd approached, Nora would have run away, but she listened to Patty, and they both came running down to the ripper. In the excitement and the semi-darkness I suppose Nora didn't recognize me, or if she did, decided she wanted to ride that ripper more than she feared me.

"You sit here, right up front," I said. "I'll be right behind you, and I'll help steer. You hold the ropes in both hands. When I say pull to the right, you pull. Or to the left. All right," I waved to Jennie. "Give us a push."

The ripper was crowded, the hill was now slick, and the ripper went noisily flying down the incline. It was a dizzying ride at best. Nora began to squeal with delight. I shouted to pull right and she tugged obediently at the rope, though I did the actual steering without her being aware of it. We came to the bottom without mishap, and I sat there for as long as I dared. My daughter, my first-born, was held in my warm embrace and she was happy and shouting with glee. I bent forward and kissed the back of her head, exposed below the stocking cap which had slid perilously close to falling off.

"Want to do it again?" I asked.

She turned to look back at me. "Oh, yes, please! May I steer again?"

We managed to enjoy four more rides, even though I was that exhausted I could hardly do my share in pulling the ripper up the hill.

Then I saw lanterns swinging in the dark as people from the mansion were coming our way searching for Nora.

"I'm afraid they're looking for you," I said. "Did you have fun?"

"Oh, yes. It was such fun. May I come again, please?"

"Any time you hear us sliding down this hill, you're welcome."

"Thank you."

"How does it happen no one came with you this time?"

"I ran away."

"Well, if this is as far as you ever go, there's little harm in it. Run along now. Go back and meet them before they freeze to death searching for you."

She regarded me solemnly, as if she was judging me, making up her mind about something. "I think you're very nice. I don't think you're bad at all. I like Patty, too."

She threw her arms around me; then she was gone, shouting to those who searched for her.

I settled a sleepy Patty on the ripper, wrapped a blanket around her, and joined Jennie at the rope to drag the thing back to the house.

"Nora is a dear girl," Jennie said. "They haven't completely spoiled her."

"Tonight she was having fun," I said. "She forgot everything they've taught her about staying away from riff-raff like us. Tomorrow she'll be their daughter again but, by heaven, tonight she was mine. Not for very long, yet, while it lasted, she was mine."

"I saw her kiss you. Do you think she somehow recognized you as her mother? As someone she should love?"

277

"No, Jennie, it was only impulse brought on by the joy of the moment."

"Still, it's a good sign the child is capable of natural love and isn't selfish and stuck-up like the rest of the tribe up there."

"Stuck-up is the word Patty uses when she talks about Nora. I don't suppose Nora can help that. But I'm hoping that stuck-up veneer they've painted on her doesn't run too deep."

Jennie looked back, left my side while I kept tugging at the rope. Patty, sound asleep, had almost fallen off the ripper. Jennie arranged her in a safer position and returned to help me pull.

"The two girls look much alike. Have you noticed?"

"Oh, yes. How could I help it?"

"Of course, I think Patty is the prettier. Oh, Maeve, I hope that some day they'll come to know they're sisters and learn to love one another. It's heartbreaking this way. They could be having such good times together as they grow up."

We rounded a corner and saw the welcome lights in our house. I'd been cheered by the evening's fun with Patty and Nora, but I was worried, too. Without knowing why. I thought back and recalled that I'd felt this way before—when my father drowned, and just prior to Joel's return from his last and final visit to Dublin. I wondered if the mirror would tell me anything, but I decided against consulting it. The last time had been enough.

Jennie put Patty to bed while I gratefully drank the steaming coffee Glen had brewed when he heard us approaching the house. I told him what had happened.

"All to the good," he said. "In one evening you wiped out the impact of the story they told Nora about you. If they try to convince her again, she'll find it harder to accept."

"I'm very happy about it. Call it a crumb if you

278

like, but to me it was important and something big. Important and wonderful." I went to his side and kissed him and placed my cheek against his. "You're wonderful, too, my darling."

"And lucky," he smiled. "And tired. This cold weather brings on a lot of sick people. I've three cases of pneumonia right now. None of them elderly, so they have a good chance."

"What of Abner? Have you seen him lately?"

"I stopped him on the street yesterday. He was quite drunk and happy. So far, he claims, he's having no trouble, but it's brewing and when it comes he won't last long."

"Darling, you forgot, Abner is going to die by violence."

"You really believe that, don't you?"

"You seemed to after I told you about the mirror."

"I know, but since then . . . time makes believing a little harder each day. Forgive me."

"I don't blame you," I said. "It's not a natural thing, this bit of ancient metal being able to foretell the future to me alone."

"Will it really work with Patty? With Nora, do you think?"

"Aye, I know it will. When Patty is grown, I'll explain it to her, and we'll see. About Nora, who can tell? They failed to make a monster of her so far, but over the years anything is possible."

"Let's go to bed. I'm exhausted."

I went to sleep happier than I'd been in a long, long time. I slept soundly, too, and it was only Glen's stirring and his groans that brought me half awake. Glen was getting dressed, blundering about in the darkness.

"Martha Berrett sent someone to tell me she's in labor," he said. "A month before her time. I'll wake up Jennie, for I'll surely need her help. You go back to sleep. There's nothing you can do."

279

"If you don't mind, I will," I said.

I didn't even hear them leave the house, and I was only vaguely aware of hearing the motorcar start up, sputtering madly because the motor was so cold. Glen must have had to crank it a dozen times, I thought, and then I went back to sleep.

I have no idea how long I slept, and I was never sure just what awakened me, but suddenly I sat up in bed because I'd heard some alien sound. The old house had a tendency to creak in this cold, dry weather, and it had creaked very loudly. I thought Patty must have awakened, possibly gone to the bathroom, but that idea was eliminated by another creak, this from the direction of the stairs.

Perhaps Glen and Jennie were back already. I lit a match to see what time it was. They'd not been gone twenty minutes. A slow fear began to creep around me, engulf me. Someone was in this house, moving stealthily. Someone who didn't belong here.

The bright moonlight which had illuminated our sledding was gone, and in its place was only an intense darkness outside and no light entering through the bedroom windows. I couldn't even see the foot of the bed.

I found the box of matches again, removed one, and felt about the small bedside table for the lamp. Before I could strike the match, I felt a cold wave of air sweep across the bed. It was a draft, caused by the open windows and ... the opening of the bedroom door.

I swung my legs off the bed and started to get up. At that moment there was a rush of feet, not a stealthy approach now. Someone threw me back onto the bed. A heavy body came down on mine, and two hands encircled my throat. My wide-open eyes were unable to distinguish the identity of the man who was choking me. His breath stank of brandy. While his hands sought to take my life, his mouth came down on mine in a brutal kiss.

All of this had happened in the space of a few seconds, and I was that surprised I'd offered no resistance up to now, but that monstrous attempt at a kiss replaced some of the terror with a cold rage. I reached up, grasped his hair and pulled as hard as I could. The hands at my throat relaxed a bit, and I was able to draw in a good, solid breath. I managed to bring up a knee, and I drove that into the man while I kept tugging at his hair.

It was an insane thought at that moment, but I was hoping all of this was not making so much noise that Patty would awaken and come to see what was wrong. This man was bent upon murder, and I had no doubt he'd kill her, too. I continued fighting, but it was hopeless. I wasn't a match for him, and his fingers were at my throat again, throttling me. I could feel myself getting weaker, and I was unable to hold onto his hair any longer. My arms fell limply to my sides, and I thought I was about to die. Once again, while my life ebbed, my brain wondered why Queen Maeve's mirror had never warned me of this.

The intense darkness was growing even darker now. I felt my nightgown being savagely ripped down one side, then a hand rough on my bare breast. The other hand was still tight on my throat. I had no strength left. It was over. In a matter of a few more seconds, I'd be dead. There could be no way by which I'd be saved. Yet I felt the man's weight rise off my body; his hands relaxed and I could breathe. Suddenly I realized I was alone. He'd fled, and I didn't know why.

I sat up, dazed, breathing precious air, not caring why he had gone, nor even who he was—content only in the fact that by some miracle I still lived. I heard voices, and panic seized me once more until I recognized the voices as those of Glen and Jennie. I tried to call out to them, but my tortured throat could produce no sound. There were quick steps in the corridor, Glen entered the bedroom with Jennie behind him. As she lit the gas lamp on the round corner table, I tried to cover my breasts with the torn edges of my gown. Glen gave a sharp cry and rushed to my side. Jennie darted out of the room. I knew she was going to see if Patty was all right.

"Maeve . . . what happened?" Glen asked. "Wait . . . I'll get a glass of water. . . ."

I felt a little better after I drank the cool water, and my throat was soothed enough that I could manage to speak in a voice that sounded more like a croak. Glen drew a robe over my shoulders.

"Someone came into the house and attacked me. I was being strangled . . . murdered. I don't know what made him stop. . . ."

Glen said, "God. Oh, my Maeve . . ." He looked over his shoulder. Jennie had returned. "Patty?" he asked.

"She's sound asleep. What happened?"

"Maeve was almost killed by an intruder. Run down and fetch a drink of brandy."

Glen's gentle hands felt of my neck. He had me swallow water while his fingers touched my throat, following the muscles I used in swallowing. He nodded slowly.

"You're going to have some bruises, no doubt, but whoever it was evidently didn't have murder on his mind."

"Glen, I couldn't breathe. . . ."

"I know, but he exerted only enough pressure so you'd fall unconscious. If he had intended to kill you, he'd have crushed your throat, inflicted severe injuries. He only cut off your breath. And now—have you any idea who it was?"

"No. Glen, he tried to kiss me. I smelled brandy on his breath."

"Are you sure you didn't get even a glimpse of him? A profile, perhaps?"

"I was only half awake when he came into the room and he just . . . just lunged at me. Then I was smothered under him, and he was choking me. I seized his hair. I may have torn some of it free. . . ."

"Let's see." Glen lit the bedside lamp to augment the illumination from the gas mantle of the table lamp. He found nothing.

"By the time I was able to defend myself that way, most of my strength was gone," I admitted. "I thought I'd held onto his hair and pulled it. Yes—I did—he even stopped choking me because of the pain I inflicted, but then he was at it again."

"Was he a big man or small? Heavy or light? Was he bearded?"

"I don't know. As I said, I was half asleep, and after that everything happened so fast. Oh Glen, I thought I was going to die. I still don't know what made him run off."

"I do. The call I had about Mrs. Berrett being in labor was false. Someone threw pebbles at the window, woke me up, and called out from the street. I didn't recognize the voice but, like you, I was too sleepy to really be able to recognize anything. When Jennie and I got to the Berrett home they were all asleep, and I knew we'd been lured away from the house. What happened, I suppose, is that whoever did lure us away and then came in to attack you forgot how much faster a motorcar is than a horse. I was back here in only a few minutes. He heard the car approach and ran for it. I expect he used the kitchen door to get away."

"I shall never again complain that the motorcar smells to high heaven," I said, with an attempt at lightness.

"That's the only clue," Glen said, refusing to be diverted. "You did say his breath smelled of brandy."

"Reeked of it, I would say."

"Are you pretty sure it was brandy?"

"Pretty sure."

"Brandy is not a drink common in this town, because nobody can afford it. But it's a common drink on the Hill. Do you see what I'm getting at?"

"Someone up there . . .?"

"It was an attempt to disgrace you again. With the lies already circulated over the years, it could be expected some people might believe you were not the victim of force."

"I can't conceive of such a thing, Glen. They're evil people, yes, but such a thing—"

"They developed these lies, they refused to surrender your daughter, they changed her name, they let her believe Helen is her mother. All those things are evil—as evil as what they tried to do to you just now. You saw Nora last night, and she came to like you. She must have told them so, and this is in the form of a warning that unless you stop trying to see your daughter, this will happen again. Or something worse."

Though I'd now donned the heavy flannel robe, I shivered at the thought. "Is there nothing we can do?"

"I can't think of anything now. We've no proof. Not even that this happened, and of course they'd deny knowing about it. There are four men up there. Let's consider them. How about Loran? He's a big man, heavyset."

"It could have been Loran, but he's the only one, except for Abner, who is taking my side occasionally. He does drink brandy, I recall."

"They all do. What about Gabriel, Joel's father?"

"He's an arrogant man and I believe capable of any sort of evil, but this . . . I don't know."

"Ashley, then? Helen's husband?"

"It might have been Ashley. Yes, it's quite possible. Because even while I was too weak to resist with any sort of strength, I did make him stop choking me for a second or two. Ashley isn't a big, strong man, but it could have been he."

"I wouldn't put it past him. He's been accused of more than one peccadillo in the village, and I suspect that when he goes off on company business he doesn't grow wings and achieve sainthood. There's one more."

"Abner? Oh, Glen, I can't believe that."

"Abner is a strange man. He's always been kind and gentle, but since he discovered he has a fatal illness, he's changed. He doesn't care what he does. Also I think Abner has secretly been in love with you all along. He may have gotten drunk—as if he's been sober—and lost control of himself. Abner drinks only brandy."

"You mean if it was Abner, what he did was not at the behest of the family?"

"I don't know about that. Under the right conditions, it wouldn't have to be. Mind you now, it's all conjecture. We've no proof of anything."

I sipped the brandy Jennie had delivered before going off to see that Patty was still asleep. "What can we do?"

Glen stroked my hair gently. "Not much, but from now on I'm going to be much more careful about leaving you alone. You'd better try to sleep now."

"Yes," I said. "Those awful, ugly-minded people!"

For quite a long time afterwards, there were times when I awoke in the middle of the night and pressed a fist to my mouth to keep from screaming.

I had no more contact with Nora that winter, though Patty, Jennie, and I often dragged the ripper to the hill and spent hours there. Apparently Nora was being carefully watched. I did see her a few times being driven to or from school in that elaborate carriage, and I noted with some satisfaction that she wore a uniform similar to those worn by all the girls. Hers was no doubt made by some clever dressmaker, and it seemed to be of finer material, but it conformed. I'd broken down that much resistance to Nora's training.

I didn't attend the next regular meeting. I was still angry and upset over that attack, but after six monhs passed, I went to the summer meeting.

I was greeted with a distinct chill. Abner wasn't there and in fact didn't show up at all. Ashley, too, remained absent as before, for the same reason I supposed. Nora had to be guarded.

I wasted no time. "I move that there be a general pay increase beginning with the next payday in keeping with the trend of other manufacturers who have raised wages. And, shortened hours."

No one was courteous enough to even flatly reject my motion. They merely paid no attention. I might as well not have spoken. I sat down, seething again, and asking myself why I had bothered to attend.

Loran addressed us. "Beginning on Monday, this factory will go on an eight-hour shift, six days a week. Such a move requires approval of the stockholders, and I now put it to a vote."

"Just a minute," I said. "I'll vote, but not until I'm told what else is involved. I know you too well to think you're giving in out of plain kindness."

"Wages will be raised two percent, and they will be hourly."

"That means every worker will receive far less money," I said.

"For far less work," Joel's father reminded me sarcastically.

"Which means less production and less profits," Loran added.

I said, promptly, "I vote no."

"You're voting against a proposal you yourself have been trying to put through for more than a year," Joel's father reminded me.

"Our employees can barely scrape together a living

now. If they are paid less, shorter hours are not going to be of any benefit to them, except to give them a little more leisure time to realize the hopelessness of their predicament. And their hunger."

"A majority vote will carry the motion," Gabriel Cameron said. "It is carried and so ordered."

I couldn't stop them, but I could annoy them. "What brought this on? Not the goodness of your hearts. You don't have any. There is something else behind this. I wish to see the books."

"Not granted," Joel's father said sharply.

I arose. "I shall have my lawyer send in accountants. It's about time the books were audited, anyway. Good day."

"Business is off," Loran said. "There's not enough work to keep the mill going on a twelve-hour six-day shift. And don't be in such a damned rush, Maeve."

"Why must you explain anything to this hussy?" Joel's mother asked. "Finish our business so I may get away from her presence."

"Evelyn," Loran said, "she is legally entitled to be here and to vote. Maeve, you get about the village. Have you heard any whispers of impending trouble?"

"They are not whispers I hear," I said. "They are loud, clear voices, Mr. Cameron. There's a storm brewing which you had best head off before it breaks."

"The woman's trying to frighten us," Marcy Tabor said with a sarcasm not lost on me.

"Think what you like, all of you," I said. "It's still not too late, but next week it may be. If business is bad now, there may not be any in a short time. You cannot open your hearts, but you can open your eyes. If you remain blind, I swear you'll be sorry for it."

"With this woman present," Joel's father said, "we cannot conduct a proper meeting. So it is adjourned."

They all filed out, leaving me there alone. I wondered how much more of this frustration I could put up with. And I wondered why Abner had missed this

287

meeting. It was the first time. Was it possible that he'd been the man who invaded my bedroom and he was too ashamed to face me? I'd studied Joel's father and discounted him as the assailant. Loran could have been the man. I hadn't seen Helen's husband in a long time, so I couldn't be positive about him, but if he hadn't changed, I doubted he could summon enough courage to even enter a darkened house, let alone commit a crime there.

I left the office. The workers kept their eyes down as I passed through. It was a terrible way to have to work, being so afraid of their superiors. I wanted to move between the desks, talk to them, be friendly, but I'd only embarrass and scare them, for they'd be filled with apprehension that the Camerons would take some sort of revenge on an employee who so much as smiled at me.

I returned home and put our telephone to use. I called several manufacturing plants to whom we sold much of our products, and by the time I was finished I had learned that cotton fabrics were diminishing in demand. Woolens, silks, and linens were taking their place. Women were fascinated with silk hose and buying in ever increasing quantities, which meant our mills wove less and less cotton for that purpose.

There was also a somewhat stationary condition in all business. Nothing prospered as it had during the past five or six years. Possibly the markets were saturated with too much of everything—including cotton fabric.

"They'll go on eight hours because they'll be forced to," I told Glen and Jennie. "But there's sufficient money in the company to not cut wages to conform with the shorter hours."

"There's another item," Jennie said. "They've raised prices at the company store. Butter went to twenty cents, bread to eight, eggs to eighteen. Everything children and hard-working men need has gone up."

288

"When did that happen?" I asked.

"This morning. At the same time the factory bulletin boards changed working hours to from eight to five."

"There's going to be trouble," Glen said. "I've smelled it coming for some time, and this is going to bring it to a head. I can tell you something else that happened and was kept secret. The company could have obtained a very large government contract six months ago if they agreed to accept a little less profit, reduce working hours, and raise pay. They turned down the offer."

Jennie said, very quietly, "If anybody wants to burn down the factory, I'll supply the matches. That's how I feel, and I don't even work there or depend on the mill."

"It's a horrible situation, and what concerns me is the fact that I'm part of it, but I can't do anything."

"Everybody in town knows that," Glen said. "They also know you spend your share of the mill profits very generously all around town. Nobody blames you."

"Do you believe there will be trouble soon?" I asked Jennie.

"From what I hear, the men are past the grumbling stage and are very angry. Almost anything could start it, and what happened today can very well be the fuse that will set off the explosion."

"The family will stop all paychecks if a walkout begins," I said. "They threatened that some time ago. And if the men aren't paid, they can't provide food because the company store will refuse to sell them on credit. They won't be able to pay their rent. The family has always arranged for it to be paid by the week and the sum deducted from each pay envelope. If the rent isn't paid, they'll begin legal proceedings and have the families put out of their homes."

"It might be well if that happened," Jennie said.

"They'd go elsewhere and work for someone other than the Camerons."

"No, Jennie," Glen said. "All they know is mill work, and from what Maeve has been learning all day, the other mills are also in trouble. There won't be any jobs elsewhere. It's not a time to strike and, I'm ashamed to say it, defy the Camerons."

"Should they meekly accept this and starve to death?" Jennie asked hotly.

"They won't starve," I said. "I'll see to that."

"If they wait for the right time, they'll get somewhere," Glen went on. "But to act out of weakness, against that bunch on the Hill, means defeat all down the line. They'll be licked before they begin."

"They're not to be denied," Jennie said. "I can tell from the talk I hear. It's coming, and soon. They'll march on the Hill, and they'll march on the mill. There'll be scores of them, angry men past the point of thinking clearly. I'm afraid. For one of the few times in my life I'm really afraid."

And I was far more frightened than Jennie, for I suddenly knew what the mirror had meant. There was going to be a riot, and Abner was going to die. I could do nothing to stop it. Not even Abner would listen to me. He'd scoff at the very idea of the mirror prophecy or, if he should believe it, probably welcome the fulfillment of what it had foretold.

Glen was worried, too, but mostly concerned with our inability to stop the violence which was so evidently impending.

"There have been many times when I've felt we should get out of this town, and this is one of them. What good are we doing? The Camerons won't listen to you, Maeve, even though you're an important stockholder. The men won't listen to me, except when I give them medical advice. This is going to blow up, and we'll be right in the middle of it."

"He's talking through his hat again," Jennie said

in mild reproof. "He's had a hundred chances to leave and better himself in doing it, and always refused."

"This time I mean it," Glen grumbled. "Almost, anyway. We've battled the Camerons for many years now and gotten nowhere."

"My daughter hugged me and told me she liked me," I said. "That's a big step forward, in my opinion. I don't think we should do anything rash. Besides, if we leave, the Camerons will consider it a complete victory and likely impose all sorts of new regulations on the mill hands."

Jennie said, "I'm going to see old Matt Simon, Glen. He needs more medicine."

Glen nodded and went to his pharmacy to prepare a pain-killing medication for an aged man who was slowly, and painfully, dying. Jennie turned to me.

"Maeve, some talk has been coming out of the mill office, based on what must have been heard at one of the family conferences. The Camerons have been considering putting a stop to paying Glen for his services to the mill hands again. I haven't told him because he's upset enough now."

"It won't matter," I assured her. "That won't make Glen leave, nor me. The mill profits will pay his fees."

"No doubt, but this is just another way to bring pressure on the workers. The Camerons believe if they scare them enough, they'll be afraid to demand more money or threaten to strike."

"Do you think they'll scare that easily?"

"It bothers me mostly because I know they won't. It will only make them angrier."

Glen returned with the bottle of medicine, and Jennie went off with it at once. Glen had apparently been waiting for us to be alone.

"Trouble at the mill may result in a riot if things go badly. That's what worries you most of all, isn't it? That's what the mirror meant when it showed you angry faces and waving arms."

"And Abner. Yes, the prophecy is going to come true. There will be a mob and great violence, and Abner will die. We cannot prevent it, Glen. We're but two helpless people. The mirror will not be denied."

Yet for a week everything remained peaceful in town. Each morning the steam whistle screeched its command for the workers to be at their posts and at five, for a welcome change, sent them home. They had a little more time for leisure, but a little less money for food. Any cut in pay was a serious matter when the original sum paid them was already inadequate. Before long, this quiet was bound to be broken.

It was, in fact, being shattered even while I thought everything was peaceful. I first heard of it when Jennie told me there was a notice on the bulletin board posted near the main gate to the effect that production was down and the workers were being warned that unless it improved, measures would be taken.

I got out the buggy. We'd not yet come to depend entirely on the motorcar, and I was unable to handle that monster, anyway, so we kept our horses. I drove down to the main gate and read a fresh notice that even Jennie hadn't heard about yet.

There were half a dozen men reading it. As I got out of the buggy, they sullenly walked away, as if they were now associating me with the Cameron family. Only gray-haired Mike Fallon, one of the senior foremen, remained.

He took off his cap and nodded, but his face was grim. "It's a bad day, Mrs. Kinnery. They've gone too far this time."

I stepped closer to the bulletin board. The old notice was there, warning that production levels must be increased. Beside it was this fresh notice; the mill was going to close for one week to grant a vacation period. There would be no pay. I turned to Mr. Fallon.

"They're fools, Mr. Fallon."

"That they are and forever will be. All the men haven't seen this yet, but you saw a few who did, and they're now spreading the news."

"Is it true that production is off?"

"Sure it is. The men were cut. They couldn't live on what they made before, and with that cut there's nothing ahead but debt, and that means the company is going to own them body and soul. So they quit working hard. The poor, fey creatures should have known better. The Camerons don't take orders, they give them. But there's an end to it, Mrs. Kinnery, and it's about here now."

"Can you think of any way to head this trouble off?" I asked.

He wagged his shaggy head. "I'm not that clever a man. I don't think anybody is. The only way would be to bring the pay back to where it was with eight hours instead of twelve and drop this vacation idea. It's to be laughed at, Mrs. Kinnery. In the hundred and more years this mill has been in business I'll bet this is the first time the word 'vacation' was ever on that bulletin board or even spoken aloud in the presence of a worker."

"I know. It's cruel. I only hope this can be headed off. I'm going to see Mr. Loran Cameron now. He seems to have a little common sense. Perhaps I can get this rescinded."

"You can tell him if it ain't, there might be a very long vacation for everybody, including the Camerons. They might have a mill to rebuild. The men are mad and getting madder every day."

"I'll do what I can in a hurry," I said.

I drove the buggy around to the office entrance to the mill and went on in, passing the secretary who tried to stop me but decided against it after a look at

293

my face. I walked into Loran's office without knocking. He was seated behind his massive desk, lighting a cigar and looking comfortable and quite pleased with things.

"I can see trouble," he said as I approached his desk.

"Mr. Cameron," I said, "I own a considerable interest in this mill, and I don't want to see it destroyed. I'm not going to ask anything of you or of Joel's father. I'm going to tell you something, and you had better listen."

He settled back and exhaled a cloud of smoke.

"This vacation notice is a punishment because the men have slowed down. They did that because what they are now being paid doesn't warrant any more work than they are now being paid for. That's not the point. At this moment they are just learning of the week's vacation. That's as cruel a punishment as any satanic mind could devise. The loss of a week's pay will wreck any hope these families have of ever getting out of debt. That's not the point, either."

"Then you're rambling," Loran said patiently. "Like most women, but go on. Of course I know what you're going to say."

"I don't believe you do. You and the others sit here serenely unaware of what's going on. Unions are getting stronger. They watch for situations like this, where workers are angry and frustrated. Then they come in and have an easy time establishing themselves. You won't be facing a lot of men who are in your debt, but a union that will defy you and even take you into court. Then, too, there is a labor board expressly set up to examine instances of this kind. I think the mill is in violation of the law."

"We can take care of that. There are no unions anywhere around here yet, and there won't be. They'll never hear of what's going on. Even so, we own the factory, and we can do what we please."

"The union *will* hear of it," I said.

"If any worker calls on them for help, he will be fired and ejected from his home on one hour's notice."

"It won't be a millhand. I'll notify them and, as a stockholder, I can also call upon any government agency to investigate conditions here. You've had your way with me for many years. You've taken my daughter from me, you've told her lies, you've held falsified evidence over my head. You've done unspeakable things, and I've had enough. In one more hour— the same amount of time you'd give a worker before you threw him out of his home—I shall go to the bulletin board at the gate. If there is not a new notice to the effect that the vacation without pay is rescinded, I shall immediately contact union representatives and whatever federal agencies are required to bring some semblance of justice to this town. One hour!"

I walked out before he could deliver a word of argument or threats. I didn't drive home. I drove down to the gate and sat in the buggy within sight of the bulletin board. I had already checked the time by my lapel watch, and I kept referring to it. I'd grant them not one extra minute.

Thirty-five minutes after I left Loran, an office worker came rushing to the board. He tore down the vacation notice and tacked up a new one. I went over to the board, joining Mr. Fallon, who had apparently also been watching. The new notice rescinded the vacation.

"It helps," Mr. Fallon told me. "Maybe we've put off the trouble for a while, but the slowdown ain't going to stop, ma'am. They're giving fair labor for the amount of wages they get, and no more. Even so, unless something is done pretty soon, there'll be trouble. It won't take much to set it off."

"I know. But at least it won't happen tonight," I said. "And that's comforting."

By suppertime, Glen and Jennie had heard all about what I'd done. Neither was very optimistic.

"You made them kowtow," Jennie said. "They don't like that, and they're going to do something about it. You'll see. They never let anybody get the best of them.".

"I'm afraid I agree with Jennie," Glen added. "From now on, either she or I will be with you. Don't go out alone, keep the doors locked, and I'm going to put a loaded pistol in the drawer of the table beside the bed. If anything happens like that attack on you, use the gun if you get the chance."

"That's the only way they can harm me," I said. "They've done everything else and not put me down. Things are changing. They're fighting a war they're now bound to lose unless they alter their ways."

"They won't. It's an inbred habit of the family to exploit the millhands," Jennie said.

"I'm not afraid of them any more," I said. "Even if they bandied about that pack of lies concerning what they call 'my moral character', I don't think the people here will believe them. They're losing their grip on me, and when it loosens a bit more, I'm going to get my daughter back."

"Darling, don't depend on that too much. They're still powerful and rich. If the right moment comes, we'll take advantage of it, but it has to be exactly right."

"The moment will come," I said confidently. "So will the riot, no matter what we try to do."

Jennie looked up. "What makes you so sure of that?"

"It's a feeling we both have," Glen said, heading off the risk of my having to explain about the mirror.

"Well, in fact," Jennie said, "I share it, too."

"Where do you get all this information?" Glen asked. "Seems to me you know more than anyone."

"She goes walking with that handsome Willie Markham," I said, with a sly look at Jennie, who instantly blushed, she was that shy.

"So that's it!" Glen exclaimed. "I wondered why you were going out so often. Willie's a very good man."

"We just . . . go walking," Jennie said.

"As head of the office, he certainly knows what's going on," Glen said. "Be careful and don't get him in any trouble with the Camerons."

"We're careful they don't find out. We would, I think, be married except that if we did, he'd be fired. Isn't that an awful thing, Glen?"

"You tell Willie to begin looking for another job somewhere else," Glen said. "I hate to lose you, but this situation can't go on."

"Trouble is, jobs are scarce in this field," Jennie said. "We have to wait."

The waiting proved to be not long. It was next day when four men of the town conveyed a fifth man, struggling and squirming in their grasp, to Glen's office. His efforts to get free brought on a few kicks and blows with fists until he grew docile enough to submit without any further persuasion.

I saw them coming, and I hurried to Glen's office to find out what it was about. By the time I got there, the stranger had been roughly pushed into a chair, and he seemed somewhat bewildered by it all.

One of the men—Alice Dowell's husband—assumed the role of spokesman. "This here bozo," he said, "came to town this afternoon, and he's been goin' around askin' fool questions about you, Mrs. Kinnery. They ain't nice questions he's been askin' either, like he thinks you're not a good woman. Ain't nobody in this town don't know how good a woman you are, so we thought we'd bring him here and you could find out what the runt is up to."

The man wasn't very big. He had pale brown hair, small blue eyes that were full of fear at the moment. He didn't look very dangerous to me.

Glen said, "Who are you? What do you want here, and why are you asking questions about my wife?"

"I work for the *State Graphic*," he said, as if that explained everything, which, actually, it did. The *State Graphic* was the yellowest of the current yellow journals that devoted themselves to exposés and gloried in matters concerned with morals.

Glen said, "Thank you, men, for bringing him here. I'm sure he meant no harm, and we'll get to the bottom of this."

"Long as he don't go around askin' more fool questions," Dowell said. "He's lucky he didn't get his face busted."

They left us. Glen and I sat down.

"You're a reporter?" Glen asked.

"My name's Roscoe Kane. I got papers." He produced identification. "I came here because we got a letter saying there was a woman in this town who thought she was pretty swell and she was nothing more than a whore. Excuse the word, ma'am. It was in the letter. I got it here."

He showed us the letter. It had been mailed in town. The envelope was plain; it had been typewritten. The note was brief and unsigned, of course. It stated that I was a woman seeking social importance, I was wealthy, and I was hiding an unsavory reputation.

Glen placed the letter on his desk. "The only typewriters in this town are in the mill office, so we know where it came from." He turned his attention to the still somewhat confused man eyeing us with considerable apprehension. "You, sir, what do you intend to do about this?"

"Do? Am I crazy? I'm not going to do anything. I came here to see what it was all about. I asked a few questions, and I was told Mrs. Kinnery was as fine a woman as there ever was and she was married with a little girl, she led a respectable life and had never been in any trouble in her life. Next thing I know, I went into a tavern and asked just one question, and I was dragged here. Somebody sent that letter because they had it in for you. Hated you."

"What a dirty trick that was," Glen said. "Will they never stop persecuting you?"

"Glen—there is a story here." I glanced at the reporter. "You've been asking the wrong questions. Never mind me. Even if I was a woman of the lowest morals, my story would be nothing compared to what's really here to be written about."

The reporter began to lose some of his apprehension and showed interest. "You tell me, Mrs. Kinnery, and leave the rest of it to me. I can track down a story if there is one."

"It concerns the people who own businesses and grow wealthy from the work of other people, like those who live in this town."

Glen whistled sharply. "You're opening a big box this time, darling."

"Yes, I'm aware of that, but nothing will sway those people, except publicity perhaps. They can't stand a strong light being turned on the way they do business."

"You're right, of course," Glen agreed. "Mr. Kane, ask about the reduction of hours at the mill because business is slow, and how the pay was reduced in exactly the same proportion."

"Pay that was meager to begin with," I added.

"Ask about an enforced vacation without pay which was nothing more than a way of retaliation against the workers because they slowed down somewhat in resentment over the treatment they were getting. You can go around this town asking those kinds of questions and be perfectly safe. You'll get all the help you need."

"There's a mansion on a hill at the end of Main Street," I said. "The owners live there. I'd stay away if I were you."

"I'll check in at the inn," Kane said. "Tomorrow I'll get about. I'm sorry I caused you any trouble, and I thank you for putting me right."

He left us, none the worse for the rough handling he'd received. Glen seemed disturbed by what had happened.

"This is really going to bring things to a head," he said. "I don't know what form of vengeance the Camerons will contrive this time, but it's not going to be pleasant. I still don't know if what we did was right."

"It had to be done, darling. We've exhausted every other way. If this town is to continue to exist, it has to change. There must be a civil government, not a barony headed by the Camerons. People have a right to be heard, to be paid for a day's work, and not live in constant dread of losing their jobs and their homes at a moment's notice."

The story would be printed in two days, Mr. Kane told us before he left town. He'd obtained overwhelming cooperation when he explained what he was after, and he'd been informed that while I shared in the profits of the mill, I spent most of it in helping the town. I prevailed upon Mr. Kane not to mention my name or that part of the story.

Glen and I were having supper next day. Jennie had gone for a drive with Willie Markham and wouldn't be back until later. A thought struck me suddenly, and I felt myself growing pale. I actually began to tremble, and Glen, observant as always, noticed instantly.

"Are you ill, Maeve?" he asked.

"No, darling. I thought of something. You were right. I shouldn't have asked that reporter to do a story about conditions here."

"Why not? I agreed with it. You were sure it was proper then."

"No, darling. We weren't thinking. The paper will

300

be out tomorrow. Copies are sure to be sent here. Don't you see what that means?"

"Maeve . . . my dear . . . what if the Camerons do read it? That's what was meant. Maybe it will force them to change their ways."

"It's not the Camerons, Glen. It's the millhands. They'll read it. That newspaper makes everything seem ten times worse than it is. The men here will grow angry. They're bound to. All they needed the other day was something to bring them together. This story will do it. They'll resort to violence."

"Now, Maeve, how can you be so sure? They'll likely take some action, yes, but not necessarily violent —" He went limp. "The mirror prophecy!"

"Why didn't I think of it before? What I've done set the stage for the trouble."

"Knowing it's to happen, maybe we can do something—"

"I'm worried about Abner. It will be his time to die!"

"I don't see how the man will find the strength to even be there. He doesn't come to see me any more, but I seek him out when I can. Last week I gave him —in my mind only—not more than a month. His kidneys are gone, his strength is wasting away, and so is he. All he does is drink."

"The mirror never lies," I reminded him.

"I will agree, but it may be a matter of interpretation, darling. It didn't come right out and tell you Abner would be killed. There were two images, remember? You didn't see Abner being killed."

"It did not show my father being drowned, or Joel dying the way he did, but it came true. As this will come true. Yet, it would happen no matter what I or anyone else did. If I was used in this manner, to bring about the conditions that will lead to his death, it was foreordained that I should."

"Then there's nothing we can do about it, no matter how we try."

"Nothing," I said. "There are times when I have wondered whether the mirror is more evil than blessed. All we can do is wait now."

The waiting wasn't long. The newspaper published Mr. Kane's story, and he saw to it that a supply was sent to our town. Everyone had a chance to read it and, of course, someone saw to it that copies were delivered to the Hill.

That night I sat waiting for the first sounds of the trouble, but the town seemed quieter than usual. Glen was on a case, Jennie was with Willie Markham once again, and I was unable to bear the loneliness. I drew a shawl around my head and shoulders and went out into the night.

The streets were deserted. I walked along, and the only sound to be heard was the clicking of my heels against the flagstones. I kept thinking of a lull before a storm. I passed the tavern, where many of the men were accustomed to gather even if they had no money with which to buy a drink. The doors were closed, and only a faint light appeared from somewhere behind the bar.

It wasn't until I reached the Town Hall that I discovered the reason for all the silence and the deserted appearance of the town. The hall was well lighted. Four men stood on the steps outside, and they seemed to be on some sort of guard duty. I started up the stairs.

"Evenin', ma'am," one of the men said.

"What's going on?" I asked.

"Meetin', ma'am. Every man jack in town is in there, 'cept me and . . . these others."

"A meeting about what?"

"The mill. The article in the newspaper stirred everybody up. They know tomorrow something will be posted on the bulletin board and we'll get it in the

302

neck again. So we're going to be ready. I'm out here in case somebody from the Hill comes down and tries to get into the meeting. We don't want them."

"I'm a Cameron," I said.

"You are Mrs. Glen Kinnery, ma'am, and there's no place, no house, in this town where you ain't welcome."

"Thank you. Will there be trouble tonight?"

"No, ma'am. I don't think so, unless somebody gets too fired up. We're waiting to see what the Camerons will do first."

"I won't go in, then. I hope there won't be trouble. I sincerely pray there won't."

"You better do your prayin' to the Camerons, ma'am. The men ain't goin' to listen to anybody after this."

I turned away and walked back in the direction of home. Halfway there I heard Glen's sputtering motorcar, and I waved to him. He stopped the car and I scrambled onto the seat before he could get out and help me.

"They're holding a meeting," I explained. "They're going to wait and see what the Camerons do tomorrow. If they post anything on the board that hurts these people, the trouble is going to start."

"Will you see the Camerons and advise them of this?" he asked.

"No. It would do no good. I've done my best to tell them how things are, but they won't listen. I shudder to think of what they'll do now. Tomorrow it will happen."

"I'm afraid so," Glen said.

"Tomorrow Abner is going to die. That's what tears at my heart. That and the fact that we can do nothing to prevent it. Take me home, Glen."

TWELVE

I was in and out of bed that night, pacing the floor, heedless of Glen's advice that I was only working myself into a nervousness that wouldn't help me or anyone else next day when, surely, the disorders were going to take place.

He was right, of course. At breakfast I was that upset I grew cross with Patty and sent her off to school in a near state of tears and bewilderment. As soon as the breakfast dishes were done, Jennie walked down to the store for supplies, but I knew very well she'd continue on to the mill so she might study the bulletin board, where all the factory news was posted.

Glen was too busy to join me in my worries. I did suspect some of his work was done so he'd not be near me in my present state of mind, something I couldn't blame him for.

Jennie came back in an hour, looking puzzled. "There's nothing on the board. Nothing has been said. The mill is running as usual."

I poured two cups of coffee, saturated as I was already with the beverage. "Did you see anything of Abner?"

"No. He's rarely about any more, staying close to his room at the inn or even closer to his stool at the café bar. The poor man is wasting away."

The morning went by, and so did part of the afternoon. Jennie called me with the first of the bad news. "Three drays just drove down the street. From out

304

of town. That's what the Camerons send when they throw someone out of their home."

We went out as we were—no wrap or hat—and hurried down the street to where the first of the drays had backed up across the sidewalk. By the time we got there, two brawny men were already carrying out the furniture of the Holden family while Mrs. Holden and her elderly, infirm mother looked on, stunned at this sudden turn of events in their lives.

Standing by the gate was a man in a makeshift uniform consisting of a Western-type hat, boots, and a shiny badge pinned to his shirt.

"Afternoon, Mrs. Kinnery," he removed his hat. "It's a real pleasure to see you again, but it gives me none to do what I have to do."

"You're a county deputy, aren't you?" I asked.

"Yes, ma'am. The court gave me papers to serve on three families. Eviction papers. I hate to serve them, but I got to keep my job, too."

"I know. Will you arrange that all the furniture be taken to a warehouse in Bakersville?"

"Can't do that. Seems these folks owe money and the furniture has got to be sold."

"You must first make a demand on them for the money owed, isn't that true?"

"Yes'm, but they never have it."

"They have it. I'll pay whatever they owe, in cash. I'll need a few minutes to go get it. Just tell me how much. And I'll settle for the other families, too."

He consulted his legal papers and gave me a figure that should have made the Camerons ashamed of themselves. It was a pittance, actually, yet I knew, as they did, these families could not pay it.

"Ma'am," the deputy said, "you just take your time. I can slow the men down if need be."

"Thank you," I said. I hurried over to where Mrs. Holden was trying to comfort her mother. "Everything is all right," I told her. "Your furniture will go

305

into storage for the time being. You take your mother to the inn. When your children return and your husband comes home, tell them that's where they're going to live until we find a house in another town—and a job for Mr. Holden. There's no need to be sorry. In the end you'll all be better off. While Mr. Holden is out of work I'll pay all expenses. Now run down and tell that to the other two families."

"Oh, Mrs. Kinnery, they'll be very angry with you for this," Mrs. Holden said.

"The Camerons? They've been angry with me for years, and I haven't been hurt by it or lost much sleep. Now you do as I say. I want all of you installed at the inn before the Camerons know about it. To-morrow you'll have plenty of time to straighten everything out. Meanwhile you're not going to lose anything except a job that's no good anyway."

I hurried back to the inn and made the necessary arrangements with the clerk, who was very leery of the whole matter.

"I don't know what they'll think about it, ma'am. I work for them, and I don't want them mad at me."

"You listen to me. This is a public place. I have just paid for the rooms. If you turn these people away, they can take you into court. There's no need for the Camerons to find out, anyway."

"Ma'am, they'll know about it five minutes after you leave here."

"How?" I asked quickly.

"They got ways. I don't know how, but they got ways, and they know what's going on always. I'll do like you say. I know what's going on, too, and I wouldn't be proud to turn those families away."

"That may not earn you a place in heaven," I said, "but it does in my heart, and I won't forget it. See that they are well fed, too. If they ask for extras, give them whatever they want."

Glen was in his office when I returned. Jennie and

I joined him there after making certain he was not with a patient. "Well," I said, "they've done it. Three families are being evicted and their furniture possessed. I shall need some cash to give the deputy so he'll release the furniture and to pay for having it brought to a warehouse for safekeeping until we find work for the men, who have no doubt been fired by now."

"You're taking on an awful lot, Maeve," Glen said.

"I'm trying to prevent a riot. If the men who were fired are not seriously damaged, even if we help them and the Camerons do not, perhaps the anger won't rise quite as high."

"It's dangerous," Glen insisted.

"That may be," I said, "but you know what the consequences will be if the men march."

"Abner," Glen nodded slowly.

"What's all this?" Jennie asked. "I keep hearing little things that mystify me. As if you two know something that I do not."

"Maybe it's better you don't," I said. "We carry an awful responsibility, Jennie."

"Have you consulted the mirror since?" Glen asked.

"I haven't dared go near the thing."

"What mirror?" Jennie persisted. "What are you two talking about?"

I said, "Glen, my love, you tell her while I fetch the mirror. Now that the time of trouble is at hand, perhaps the mirror will be clearer in what it foretells."

Jennie was listening in complete fascination as I went upstairs to get the mirror and in even more awe when I returned. She looked at the bit of metal in my hand.

"Can this really be true? Oh, what am I saying? Glen believes it, and he's as hard-headed a man as I know when it comes to believing such things. It has told you there will be a riot and Abner will die? Maeve, I don't dispute you, but . . . but . . ."

"Jennie, it is not possible for anyone to believe what this mirror can foretell until they have experienced it. I will look now and ask that I be shown what is to happen."

"Does it always work?" Jennie asked.

"No." I brought the mirror closer to my eyes. "I ask that I be shown what will happen this day, or during a few days to follow. So I may be guided and no harm come to those I love."

Something, like a miniature cloud, began to swirl about. It took shape quickly and vanished all in the space of three or four seconds. I lowered the mirror and closed my eyes.

"Abner lies on the ground, face down. He is dead. All about him are moving shadows. Many of them. Abner's fate has not changed."

"I feel as if I'm sitting here in the presence of some kind of a ghost," Jennie said with a shiver. "Until this moment I wouldn't have believed a word of this, but I do now. Something tells me it is true."

"No matter what we do, Abner cannot be saved?" Glen asked me.

"He cannot," I said. "Jennie, please see that Patty does not go outside the house until this is over. Please walk with her to and from school. She won't understand, so don't try to explain, though I suspect she knows there's something bad brewing in this town."

"All the children know," Jennie said. "They've grown quiet these last two or three days. There's no running, or shouting, or playing games. They know."

"One more thing," I said. "The clerk at the inn told me the Camerons always find out quickly what is going on. Do they have spies among the towns-people?"

"They've always had spies," Glen said. "In the

past these people were eventually discovered and they left town in a hurry. At this moment nobody knows who is giving information to the Hill, but there's no doubt it is delivered."

"Can't Abner be warned . . . something be done?" Jennie asked in desperation.

"No," I said, "nothing can be done. That doesn't mean I won't try if I see a chance to help the poor man. If he is there—when it all begins—I'll stay as close to him as possible."

"It might be dangerous," Glen warned.

"That may well be, but I will do what I can. When do you think this will start?"

"It may not begin at all, since you were thinking, cleverly enough, to see that the three families were taken good care of."

"Unless they come up with something else," Jennie said. "Which they are well capable of, especially when they hear that getting rid of these three families didn't do much harm."

In the afternoon Jennie escorted a somewhat puzzled Patty home. At the supper table I told her, as frankly as I could, considering her age, about what was going on.

"The Camerons own the mill and think they can do as they please. When they become angry at any of the workers, they sometimes fire them and make them leave their homes. It's been going on for a long time."

"Mama, if they own the mill, why can't they do as they please?" Patty asked.

"They can," Glen answered for me. "But the workers are not slaves. They should be shown kindness and understanding. When they have a complaint, it should be listened to, and if it's justified, something done about it."

"The Camerons won't listen?" Patty asked.

"That's about it, darling," I said.

"Deborah is like that, too. She thinks because she's a Cameron we all have to do as she says."

"And do you?" I asked.

"Some of the kids do. I don't."

"Good for you," Jennie said. "That's what I've been teaching you. They don't own anybody, especially Patricia Kinnery."

"I think I like her, though. I wish she wasn't so stuck-up."

"She can't help it," I said. "That's the way they've taught her to be. There's no Aunt Jennie up there. Only a lot of people who are too proud for their own good."

Gradually, as the evening progressed, I became calmer. We went to bed that night grateful that there'd been no violence.

If it had not been for the dismal prophecy of the mirror, I would have increased my hope for peace, but I knew better. It was coming. Before long something would set it off, a spark would fly, and the seething anger would burst into an uncontrollable flame and fury.

I was, however, that content and peaceful of mind that I spent part of the afternoon in the front yard flower gardens weeding, a task that I'd shamefully neglected lately. During the morning I'd sent the three dispossessed workers to the next town to look for homes and work. They were skilled in their line, and there was a fair chance they'd find something. If they did not, they were to move to another town and keep this up until they were located. I gave them sufficient money for the trip, and meanwhile their families could stay at the inn and the children attend the school as before.

I heard the rattle of a heavily laden wagon coming down the street from the direction of the depot. The afternoon train had just departed, and I could still hear it puffing in the distance. When the big dray

310

came into view, I saw that it contained several burley men in city clothes. They were all strangers.

I ran back into the house. Glen had a woman patient in his office, but I took the liberty of breaking in after a warning knock on the door.

"Excuse me," I said to the patient. "Glen, eight or nine men just came in on the afternoon train. They look like guards to me. The Camerons must have sent for them."

Glen shook his head. "That's a sure way of asking for a fight. As soon as I finish with my patients, I'll see what's going on."

I said, "As a stockholder I'm going to the mill office to try to find out what I can."

I dressed hurriedly in a street dress and had Jennie harness the horse to the buggy. "Be sure to bring Patty straight home," I warned. "I have a feeling it might be dangerous to be on the street before too long."

"I'll see to it. I heard a couple of women calling to one another just now—the houses down back of our stables. They were using the word strikebreakers."

"There's no strike," I said.

"It looks to me like the Camerons expect one."

"I intend to find out, Jennie. I'll be back as quickly as I can. They'll likely tell me nothing anyway, but something might slip out to give us a hint."

I drove directly to the mill office and tied up the horse. There was a certain air of nervousness in the large office. The workers kept glancing up, almost covertly. Nobody spoke, and I could feel the tenseness. Trouble in the village of Cameron was a rare thing. These people were unaccustomed to it, and they were going to feel it immensely when it came. No one tried to interfere with my brisk walk to Loran's office.

He was standing at the tall window behind his desk, peering out of it at the employees' entrance and exit to the plant. He turned as I entered and nodded, not unpleasantly.

"I'm glad you came, Maeve. Can you tell me what's going on in town?"

"I came to you to find out what goes on here, Mr. Cameron. The men you sent for were observed coming into town."

"They are private detectives. To guard the plant."

"Why should the plant require guards?" I asked.

"Well, as you heard at the last board meeting, business has fallen off. Also the men are getting lazy. Doing half the work they should be. We are, therefore, compelled to do something drastic. Beginning day after tomorrow, seventy-five men will be laid off indefinitely. Those who remain will have to increase production to maintain the present sorry levels. If they do not, fifty more will be laid off. We are going to bring the mill to a profitable point, no matter how we have to do it."

"What will these families do without wages coming in?"

"What will we do without profits coming in? Have you ever asked yourself that? We could be wiped out. We have to protect ourselves."

"I'm ashamed to own an interest in this mill, Mr. Cameron."

"We'll pay you a fair price whenever you wish. Of course, with business the way it is, you won't profit as much as before . . . if you don't like our way of doing business. . . ."

"To tell you the truth, Mr. Cameron, I don't like you, either," I said. "Good day."

I drove back as fast as the horse could take me. Glen listened to what I had to say with growing concern.

"It will happen, then. The three men whose families were dispossessed yesterday—they headed up the meeting at the Town Hall the other night. The Camerons fired them to avenge what they call treachery to the mill. Now with seventy-five out of work and perhaps fifty more laid off . . . the millhands won't accept this. They can't, because it would be impossible to live with. I don't know but the best thing we can do is stay home and get ready to care for injuries."

"And death," I said. "Don't forget that."

"Yes, I know. I'm not making any sense. Of course we have to go out and try to reason with them, even though it can't really help. On one hand we have desperate millhands who believe they've little to lose now. On the other hand there are the Camerons, too stiff-necked and greedy to give way an inch. When those two forces meet, there's only one end—an explosion. Where's Jennie?"

"Fetching Patty, I suppose. I asked her to, anyway. This might begin at any time, and it's nothing for children to take part in. Or be close to."

"When she returns, tell her to stay in the house with all windows and doors locked. She is not to leave Patty's side under any circumstances. I'm going out now to try to talk sense. You'd best see what you can do."

I had a horrifying thought. "Nora is at school. If anything starts before school is out, and they see her . . ."

Without another word I fled from the house. I'd left the buggy in front, fortunately, and I quickly climbed aboard to drive it down to the school. Classes were still in session. Jennie saw me coming at that great speed and believed something drastic had happened.

"I'm worried about Nora," I said. "Things may begin to happen at any moment, and the men will be blind with anger. Nora might be a tempting target for their hate."

Jennie nodded. "I heard loud voices down at the

mill a few minutes ago. They're quiet now, but I'm scared."

"The Camerons are laying off many men. They've brought in guards, strong-arm men to fight the workers if trouble starts. And it's going to. At any moment."

"Let's go in and see that school is dismissed this instant. We can't wait, Maeve."

We ran toward the entrance to the school. Jennie sought out Patty and whisked her out of there. The teachers, to whom I whispered the news, ordered the children to go directly home without stopping to play. Nora was among the last to leave. As it was an hour before the usual end of school time, the Cameron carriage wasn't waiting.

I touched her shoulder, and she whirled about nervously, as if she was already afraid.

"It's all right," I said. "I have a buggy waiting. I'd like to take you home if you'll let me."

"Thank you, I'll wait for the carriage," she said.

"You can't. In a little while, there's going to be some trouble, and I don't want you involved in it. Come with me, Nora."

"Why are you calling me Nora? My name is Deborah, and I'm not going with you." Her eyes that were flashing in anger were my eyes. The resemblance was remarkable. I had no trouble holding my temper.

"You were certainly happy to ride with me when we were sliding down the hill," I reminded her.

"That was different. I'm not going with you now."

I said, "Listen to me, you silly girl. There is a good chance you might be seriously hurt if you stay here. The carriage will come too late. You have to leave now."

"I'm not going. You can't tell me what to do. Nobody can tell me what I must do."

I secured a firm grip on her arm. "You're coming with me if I have to carry you. Now, be sensible!"

314

She tried to pull away from me. I seized her in a firmer grip and hustled her out of the schoolroom. When we reached the buggy, she balked and began to struggle.

"You're a selfish, stupid little girl," I said. "I've half a mind to——"

A great shout went up from the vicinity of the mill gate. It grew louder, and we could see the first of the mob, for that's what it had become. Nora gave a cry of alarm. Perhaps she'd been warned something like this might happen. She finally knew I was right and this mob was in a mood to spend their fury on anyone. Young as she was, Nora realized that. She suddenly clung to me.

"Get in," I said briskly. "Hurry!"

She climbed into the buggy. I removed the whip and for one of the few times in my life I used it, turning the buggy sharply and sending the horse running at full gallop in the opposite direction from the mob. Nora was crying now, huddled close to me.

"We were in time," I said comfortingly, wishing the reins didn't require both hands just then. "They can't catch up with us now. Everything is all right."

She straightened up a little at that, and tried to stop crying.

"Did your grandfather tell you there might be trouble?"

"No, but I heard them talking. They weren't going to let me go to school today, but I guess they didn't think anything would happen so fast. Where will you take me? My house is back of where they are. I'm afraid of them."

"I'll get you home safely, dear. Don't worry. What we'll do is pass my house, continue on toward the depot, and cut off on the side road that leads through the woods. It's a back way, and by taking it we can circle them."

315

"I guess so. I wish they'd sent me away like they were going to."

"Send you where?" I asked in alarm.

"I don't know. Some school."

"Oh, I see. We don't have to worry about that now." I slowed down the gait of the horse. "Remember, not so long ago you once said you were afraid I was going to kidnap you."

"Yes, I remember."

"Do you realize how silly you were?"

"Yes, I guess so." She looked up at me, and those clear blue eyes sent shafts of pain through my heart. "Did you know my father?"

"Yes, I knew him well."

"Nobody ever talks about him. I thought you knew him. What was he like?"

I pulled up the reins. Danger or not, this was a time when I needed to talk to this daughter of mine who had no idea I was her mother. If I could not reveal to her my true identity, I could at least tell her about her father.

"His name was Joel. He was a handsome man. Oh, yes, it's easy to see where your beauty came from. He had eyes like yours and hair . . . well, his was a mite lighter. He was a kind man. He thought of others much more often than he thought of himself. And he was a clever man. Very intelligent. There was little he couldn't do well. He liked people, and he liked to learn about things. He liked children. He would have loved you, my dear. Oh, how he would have loved you."

She suddenly threw her arms around my neck and kissed me. I didn't try to hide the tears.

"Does remembering my father make you sad?" she asked.

"Very sad. We were special friends. One day I'll tell you all about it, and then you'll know. . . ."

From the town streets came a roar of voices. Nora

316

cried out in fear again, and I got the horse going. We reached the foot of the hill by using the side road, and we were far ahead of the mob, if they were coming this way. I couldn't tell what they were doing. I pulled up in front of the house.

"Go in, dear. Don't be afraid. No one is going to hurt a pretty little girl like you."

"Thank you," she said somewhat stiffly. She'd changed the moment we came into sight of the mansion. She slid off the seat and ran straight to the front door without looking back. The door opened. They'd been watching. I turned the buggy around and headed back to town. I didn't know what kind of a situation I'd find there. But Nora was safe. I'd accomplished that much.

Halfway down the hill, I saw the forward fringes of the mob. From higher up I could see enough to realize every man in town was there. None would dare not be. They moved in silence. If they made any sound with their steps, the noise of the horse and buggy was sufficient to drown them out. It was an awesome sight, several hundred men all moving in a tight group. No shouting, no cheering, no threats being called out. They were deadly serious, and that mood was the most dangerous of all.

I slowed down. The crowd recognized me. They asked no questions as to what I'd been doing on the Hill. They trusted me sufficiently to know I'd not done anything against them. They parted ranks to let me drive through. The buggy was barely moving now. Suddenly a man grasped the side of it and with an effort hauled himself onto the seat beside me. My momentary panic vanished when I saw that my passenger was Abner. I scarcely recognized him.

He'd been a big man, strong-looking. Now he was thin and frail, his cheeks sunken. His hair was unkempt, he was shaven but carelessly, and tufts of

317

beard remained. His skin was sallow and about him was the look of death.

"I couldn't keep up with them," he said. I realized he was panting for air. "Can you turn this buggy around?"

"Abner, do you trust me?"

"Of course I do."

"Then please drive the buggy back to the stable behind my house. I want to try to stop these people if I can."

He laughed bitterly. "Glen tried that. They won't even listen. Nobody can make them, but maybe up there . . ." he pointed back toward the mansion, "maybe they will if I can get there before the mob."

"They're as stubborn as these men," I said. "You'll never make them understand."

"I can try," he insisted grimly.

"Abner, you're sick. You say yourself you can't even climb the hill. Please believe me, you can do no good there. Drive the buggy back and wait for me. Jennie's at the house with Patty. Wait there. Please, Abner."

Even as I spoke, I knew how wasted the words were. He shook his head and suddenly dropped off the buggy. I called to him, but the crowd had already swallowed him up.

I got down, too, leaving the horse to fend for herself. I joined the crowd and battled my way through it so I might be in the forefront where I could do some good if there was the slightest chance of it. I looked vainly for Abner. If Glen was here, I couldn't find him. There was a cloud of pinkish dust over everything. The afternoon was hot and dry. My face was already dripping perspiration, and my voice had gone hoarse from entreating the men I passed by to go home. None paid any heed to what I said.

By the time I reached the front of the crowd, they were slowing down because facing them, in a line across the road, were eight burly men in some sort of uniform. They wore holstered pistols and carried billyclubs. Directly in front of them stood Gabriel Cameron, Loran, and, surprisingly, Ashley. These three had rifles, held at a ready position, and all of them looked as grim as the men they faced.

"The damned fools!" someone said.

It was Abner. He'd found me again and now stood at my right elbow.

"I'm glad you're with me," I said. I still entertained a thought I might save this man, forlorn as the idea was. "Don't leave me, Abner. I'm very frightened. I can't do anything with the men."

"Nobody can, but up there, facing us, is the potential for some real rough business. My father should have known better. All right—he should be there, perhaps, but not carrying a gun or standing in front of those hoodlums he hired. I wonder if he actually thinks all of them can stop all of us?"

"Just stay at my side." I grasped his arm, slipping my hand under it to cling to him. It was like clinging to his life.

"Stop where you are!" Gabriel Cameron shouted. The little man with the small voice, so inconsequential at this tense moment. Loran could have issued the order with more authority.

"We come to tell you we don't stand for the lay-off," someone in the crowd called out.

"Whoever said that, step forward," Gabriel shouted. "If you have the nerve."

One of the men, I didn't know his name, moved out ahead of the others. "I said it, Mr. Cameron, and I meant it. I spoke for all of us here."

"You are fired," Gabriel said.

He couldn't have made a worse decision. Even Loran began to move forward to warn Gabriel, but it was too late for that. The man he'd just fired stood his ground.

319

"We took enough, Mr. Cameron. We don't take any more. Tomorrow nobody will report for work."

"Then all of you are fired," Gabriel yelled.

Loran dropped back to his original position. It was no use now to interfere. Gabriel had issued a challenge, and these men were in no mood to back down.

Several of them broke free of the crowd and moved farther up the hill. Their manner was aggressive, though they carried no weapons. Ashley—it would have been he—raised the rifle he held.

"My God, the idiot is going to shoot," Abner said.

"Stay with me," I implored. "Don't leave me, Abner."

But Ashley didn't fire. He didn't have the nerve for that, apparently, though the gun remained in that threatening position. There was a shot. It came from somewhere behind me, from the crowd of workers.

"I knew there were guns," Abner said. "I've got to go up with them. That's my family, Maeve. They are my people. I can't stay here."

He tore himself free of my grasp and stumbled up the hill. I started after him, but men closed in around me and I couldn't get through until it was too late.

When that shot was fired, Loran and Gabriel both raised their rifles, and the men behind them quickly drew their pistols. It was a tense and very dangerous moment. Abner was stumbling up the slope, waving his arms and shouting something. All I could think of was that I was watching a dying man going to his death.

Another shot was fired from the crowd. Abner looked over his shoulder. He was close to his family now. He must have seen the flash of the gun, for he summoned strength enough to lunge toward his father to bring him down before a bullet did.

He didn't quite make it. I knew he wouldn't. Another shot. Abner seemed to come to a sudden stop. Then he swayed and pitched forward, falling face

320

down. Exactly as I had seen him lying dead in the image of the mirror.

I hurried up the slope. I reached Abner and knelt beside him. He was mercifully dead. An instantaneous, merciful death I was sure. Someone knelt beside me. Glen was at my side. I stood up to face Abner's father.

"Take you and yours, and go back into your house. There's been sufficient blood for this day. If you stay here, there'll be more. After the men have gone, your son's body will be here."

He stared at me, dazed for the moment.

"Get out of here!" I screamed at him. "Get out . . . all of you! Get out!"

They turned slowly. I thought Loran was going to say something, but he made a helpless gesture and left along with the others. I went down to face the silent crowd of workers.

"It isn't important which one of you fired that shot, because when it comes right down to it, all of you did. I don't know what's going to happen now, but you just killed a man who would have given his life to help you—and he did. Go home! Please go home!"

There was a mighty shuffling of feet as the crowd turned. I went back to join Glen. We both sat there, in the dust, beside a dead man we had loved.

"The damned fools!" Glen said. "The goddamned fools!"

"Don't curse them, darling. They were in a state of mind . . ."

"He was trying to save his father. He knew some idiot in the crowd was aiming at Gabriel."

"I didn't think he'd even make it up the hill, he was that sick," I said. I looked about. "The men are gone. We can't leave Abner here like this. I'm going to the house to tell them to send down for him."

"Yes," Glen said. "You do that. I'll not risk facing

321

any of them. There's still too much anger in me, and my tongue is too loose because of it."

I arose and brushed the dust off my dress. I wiped my eyes quite inelegantly with the back of my hand, knowing full well I smeared more dust over my cheeks. I walked slowly to the mansion. Loran came out.

"Maeve, I was not responsible—"

"Be quiet, man," I said. "All of you are responsible, as all of the village men are. It doesn't matter now. There's a fine man lying there in the dirt—dead, because he was trying to save the life of his father, who hated him. Abner was one of the finest men who ever lived. All of you in this house put together couldn't equal him. Now send some of those brawny men down to carry your nephew into his house for the last time. A house he disliked to enter while he lived, but in death he belongs there."

"I will see to it," Loran said.

I turned away. Four men passed me before I reached Glen. They picked up Abner, and Glen and I stood, hand in hand, watching them carry him up the hill and into the mansion. The big door slammed shut.

Still holding Glen's hand, I walked with him down the slope to where the horse and buggy waited. Someone had led the horse off the road into a field, where the mare grazed contentedly. Glen drove the buggy home along Main Street, where not a sound could be heard, where no one stirred and the afternoon heat simmered off the flagstone sidewalks.

It was next day before I felt human again. Glen had no patients, no calls. In the morning the factory whistle blew as always. People were on the streets again.

Glen had gone down to Town Hall to see if he could learn anything about Abner's funeral. School

322

was in session, and Patty had gone off to classes. Jennie and I sat at the breakfast table, neither one of us caring to get up and do the dishes.

"I wonder what they'll do," Jennie said. "About burying Abner. Do you think townspeople will go to the funeral?"

"I hope not. Abner might have welcomed it, but there might be more trouble, a confrontation. There's still a great deal of hatred."

"I'm afraid that if the layoffs are not rescinded, what we saw yesterday will be small compared to what's coming."

"We can't let it happen," I said. "I don't know how to stop it, but something must be done."

Jennie refilled our cups. "I wonder how Nora took it."

"I doubt she really understands, any more than Patty does."

"Nora is two years older—almost. Very soon now, she's going to be a young lady."

"Yes, I know."

"Patty won't be far behind her, and they're a pair of rare beauties, Maeve."

I nodded. "I'm not going to wait forever to tell them they're sisters. They have a right to know, and Nora must come to realize Helen is not her mother and I am."

"I know this may not be the right time to say it, but something good came out of yesterday. Willie came to call last night, if you remember."

"Jennie, he didn't!"

"He did. We're going to be married right away. But not in Cameron. He wants to leave here, and I don't blame him. He's had offers, and there's a good job waiting for him in Boston."

"Oh, Jennie, I'm delighted. We'll miss you, but it's lovely news. What did Glen say?"

"I haven't told him yet, but Willie is probably

323

doing that right now. Willie said he'd go down to the meeting at Town Hall and get Glen on the side. We're going to leave right away. As soon as we can."

"Boston's not so far," I said. "But how will we get along without you? Especially Patty."

"I don't know how I'll get along without her. Will you break the news? I don't think I can."

"Of course."

"I wish Glen would come back. The men went to work this morning as always, depending on the Camerons rescinding the layoff order. I don't know what happened."

"The whistle blew," I reminded her. "That means they were being asked back." It had surprised me, but it sounded comforting, too. I'd been afraid the Camerons might close down the whole plant.

"Yes, I heard it. I suppose if the gate had been closed there would have been a lot of excitement and noise going on by now. To think, someone had to die to make them see reason—and one of their own, at that."

"Jennie, do you recall the prophecy of the mirror?" I asked.

"I don't want to talk about it. Please don't bring that up, Maeve. It's unnatural. It's ghostly, eerie."

"It tells the truth without fail."

"Do you consult it often?"

"Only when I feel there is a need. It is not supposed to be used like a fortune teller's crystal ball. Will you attend Abner's funeral?"

"I don't know. They may not let us in. Do you think they'd call in the police? It was a murder."

"I doubt it," I said. Glen and I had talked that over before going to bed. "They'd have too much to answer for, and any investigation would surely involve them."

"I can tell you one thing for certain, they can question every man and woman in this town, and

324

none will ever reveal the identity of the one who fired the shot."

"It was a wanton act, Jennie. He should be punished, but I know very well he never will be. With that in mind the whole thing should be forgotten as quickly as possible."

Glen returned half an hour later, right after we'd cleaned up the kitchen. He was in an exasperated frame of mind as he sat down at the kitchen table.

"All the talk in town is about burying poor Abner and what should be done. Well—nothing has to be done. The family buried him in the family cemetery last night. Almost in secret. They brought in a coffin from somewhere. Those men they hired must have helped. At any rate, Abner is now in his grave. There was no funeral, as I understand it. Perhaps he didn't want one. And the so-called private detectives are gone."

"Darling," I said, "you have to file a death certificate, don't you?"

"Yes. I'll list death as by gunshot wound, but I won't give the reason why he was shot. Nobody reads those statements, anyhow. They're just filed away. I doubt there will be any repercussions."

"How long would he have lived if he'd not been killed?" I asked.

"Not more than another month. In his wasted condition, I'd probably have given him two weeks."

"Would you mind if I went to his grave and prayed for the man?"

"Do you wish me to go with you?" Glen asked.

"I would rather go alone. If too many of us do, others will want to, and there could be the beginning of more trouble. I won't be long."

"As usual, you're right. Besides, I just found out my sister is deserting us, and I've a few things to say to her."

I didn't try to hide my visit to the graveyard, about

325

a quarter of a mile behind the mansion. I drove directly past the house and entered the cemetery by the metal gate that needed oiling badly. The new grave seemed separated from the others until I realized that the resting places next to the grandfather were reserved for Gabriel, Evelyn, and Loran. I'd often wondered whether I should arrange to have Joel brought here, but I'd decided long ago that he would surely have preferred to be where he was, in the shady quiet of a peaceful village with my father and mother for company.

I knelt at Abner's grave and bowed my head in prayer. I knew someone had walked up behind me before I was finished, but I paid no heed and kept on with my prayers until I was done. Then I arose to face Loran.

"If it's a comfort to you," he said abruptly, "Abner didn't die in vain."

"He saved his father's life," I said. "What more can a man do?"

"We revoked the order to lay off men. The mill is working as usual."

"That is a blessing, but it's a shame someone had to die to bring it about, Mr. Cameron."

"I agree, it's a shame. Abner was very ill, wasn't he?"

"Yes, he was that sick he wasted away."

"I almost didn't recognize him. He hadn't been home in weeks."

"Do you wonder why?"

"All right, Maeve, we'll dispense with all matters except business. When we laid off those men, we considered it necessary. Orders are growing smaller and fewer. And in my estimation things are going to get worse. Not tomorrow, or the next day, but in four or five years, these mills may even be idle. The men have to understand that."

"They'll understand it if you treat them like human beings. If business is bad, what harm does it do the

326

mill to let the families remain in their homes? Even if they can't pay the rent? Or if they go into deep debt at the store? You're not going to close up completely, and you'll need them when things get better. They always do. There are other lines of textiles you can investigate and experiment with."

"We're thinking about that. Are you familiar with the financial status of the family? I mean the fact that with Abner's death there are no changes in the mill holdings?"

"I know that Joel's father owns one-third of the stock, Helen a third, and I a third, having inherited it from Joel. I know Abner was not included in the will."

"He was too lazy and indifferent."

"And neither were you," I added.

He smiled. "That hurt a bit. Yes, the old man left me out, too, but he did so because he knew I could make my own way. What I'm getting at is the fact that with Abner's death you have no more say in proceedings than you had before."

"I can accept it," I said.

"Another thing. Deborah told us how you brought her home. Thank you."

"I don't need your thanks for doing what I could for my own daughter. I am going to insist that I be permitted to see her."

He shook his head. "She's not here any more."

I felt my heart sink. "Where is she? What have you done with her?"

"She is being well cared for. Helen has taken her abroad. She will be given a Continental education and turned into a lady."

"I think I could put a stop to that, Mr. Cameron. I'm thinking that's what I'll do."

"Maeve, the situation hasn't changed. Right now Deborah thinks you're a good, friendly woman, and she likes you. But if you make one move to interfere with her education or our handling of the girl, she will be informed of your trysts with that Irishman with the fancy name. She will be told how you lured a noted philanderer away from a ball so that he might fondle you and kiss you. We have the evidence, and it's foolproof. What of Deborah? Shall we tell her we kept from informing her you are her mother because you were not the type of a woman she should call her mother? And show her why?"

"You can stand here at the graveside of your nephew, in whose death you had an important part, and threaten me with these lies. You've neither heart nor soul, Mr. Cameron. You're not fit to be this close to the grave of a fine man—who left his own home because he knew what you were. For Abner—and for myself—I'm ashamed of you."

I walked away from him. He made no attempt to follow me. I returned to where the buggy waited, boarded it, and drove home, so angry I couldn't shed a tear. I was bubbling over with rage when I walked into the house, but Jennie was upstairs getting ready to pack, and I didn't want to disrupt her happiness. Glen was on a call, and Patty was in school.

I was still nursing that rage when Glen returned and I told him about it. "They spirited poor Abner's body into a secret burial and now they've spirited my daughter away without a word to me or anyone else."

"Do you wish to risk fighting that false information they have over your head?" Glen asked. "If you do, we'll go into it together. I know it's all a pack of lies. Maybe we can prove it."

"No, Glen. I refused to do it before because of Nora. Anyone else doesn't count. That hasn't changed. The last time I was with her, she kissed and hugged me. A crumb of affection for a mother from her daughter, but better than nothing. I cannot take the risk."

"At least no harm comes to the girl."

"No, that's true. I swear, though, that one day she'll learn the truth. I'm not done with it, Glen. I'll find a way eventually."

"The town has settled down. I hope it stays that way. Nobody talks about strikes or burning. Abner's death put a stop to that."

"Loran tells me there may be bad times because orders are getting scarcer and we're having more and more competition. What's to be done then?"

"I don't know. If the factory has to go on short time because there's no work, the men will have to understand that. I think they will. We'll have to wait and see what happens."

Everything seemed to be changing. Not just here in Cameron, but all over the world. You could almost feel it. There seemed to be an undercurrent of activity that portended great things. This country had grown up, suddenly realized it, and was expanding its muscles.

In our personal lives, Jennie was leaving us. Glen's medical practice was just the same. He'd never be a rich man, but it didn't matter to him or me. Dividends from the mill profits still piled up in the bank, and we wanted for nothing.

Patty was growing up so fast we were constantly amazed at her progress. There was so much to look forward to. Perhaps Abner's death, sorrowful as it was, may have put an end to the turbulence and unhappiness which had beset the town and brushed off on us to some extent. I hoped the mill would prosper, for the sake of the town, not for my sake. I hoped that Nora would find happiness and one day discover the strength to face the truth I was bound to tell her.

So Glen and I—and Patty—settled down to wait for whatever was in store. Once—only once—a week after Abner's death, I consulted the mirror. It remained dark and blank. It told me nothing, and therefore I could live unafraid. I had my love, I had one daughter, at least, and I knew my first-born was safe and well.

It was a good time, a peaceful, quiet time, and we set out to enjoy it at its fullest.

BOOK FOUR:

Danger in the Mirror

THIRTEEN

It was 1913, and the years had ceased to be long and endless to become frighteningly short. I was thirty-seven and Glen well into his forties. He'd grown a bit heavier, but then, so had I, though it wasn't very noticeable, and I began eating less. My hair was still dark, while Glen's had begun to turn. He wore it as before, parted on the left, and it was a luxurious crop.

Patty was fifteen, a strong, bright, happy girl content with herself and all things. To me she was a perfect delight. The town had no high school, so we'd sent her to boarding school in Portland, not so far off she couldn't return frequently. Also the journey by car— Glen was fascinated by them and bought a new one each year—was on good roads for the most part and an interesting drive during good weather, though a decided risk during winter.

The house was lonely by day. Where there'd been Jennie and Patty both for company, now there was only Glen, and while he spent every possible spare moment with me, he was nevertheless busy and away much of the time. So I tried to keep busy by learning more about the mill, and textiles in general.

Dividends had fallen off considerably. More mills had started up, bigger ones, far more modern. It was expensive to ship cotton from the South all the way to New England, so the newer mills set up where the cotton fields were, in the South. Our men quickly understood that they were lucky to have any sort of job. At first there'd been a slow exodus, though those who left rarely did any better elsewhere and for the most part found conditions even worse. But these desertions had frightened the Camerons into using some common sense. They'd lowered rents and the prices at all the commercial establishments they owned, and had grown far more lenient in the collection of debts. They'd even gone so far as to provide improvements in the houses they rented. Electricity had been brought in, the old iron sinks were now porcelain, bathrooms had been installed and the application of paint had gone far to brighten both the village and the disposition of the workers. Greedy as they were, the Camerons finally realized that even though business was not good, at least the mill was paying its way and if the workers were that disgruntled they left town, there'd be no mill at all. Glen said the wisdom came to the Camerons by a blow from a sledge hammer otherwise named "more modern times."

Jennie and Willie Markham had prospered well, had a family of three lively sons, and we saw them on an average of twice a year. Glen found it hard to take vacations. Doctors were scarce, and there was none to relieve him even for a few days. He was that wonderfully conscientious he'd leave only for short periods.

During all this time I'd not once consulted the mirror. It could have depicted no greater happiness than that which I enjoyed, and I had no desire to see in its dim reflection anything evil or dismal.

Nora was back from Europe. She and Helen had stayed there for several years and returned only a few months ago. When I learned she was on her way back, I almost consulted the mirror, for that was when the *Titanic* sank, and during all those anxious hours while the telegraph brought in the only news we heard, I was beside myself with worry that Helen and

Nora were aboard. It turned out they had taken the *Lusitania*, so all my fretting had been for nothing.

I hadn't seen her. They'd gone to New York for a number of weeks, and I understood Nora had been at the mansion on the Hill only the last two or three weeks. If she'd come into town, I'd not seen her or heard of it.

I prided myself that I'd turned into a rather good business woman of late. I could make them listen at the stockholders' meetings, and I knew what I was talking about. My information came directly from customers whom I'd visited, from trade journals, and from salesmen who were constantly in the field.

"I don't like the way things are going," I told Glen one evening. "The mill has accumulated too large an inventory, and orders aren't coming in as they should."

"Is there anything can be done?"

"I'm not sure, Glen. I've been thinking about it."

"Have you considered the idea that there's going to be a war in Europe?" he asked.

I nodded. "It's come to my mind. The newspapers seem to think it inevitable."

"One war was fought last year, and now the second Balkan war is beginning. The whole area is ready to go. These little countries—Serbia, Montenegro, Bulgaria, Greece . . . the Turks . . . there's been hatred between them for centuries."

"Can their war be any of our business?" I asked, showing, I suppose, my total ignorance of the problem.

"Not their war—no. But the Germans have armed heavily and won't need much encouragement or reason to go in. The French will try to stop them. There'd be a real war going on then, and bound to grow even bigger."

"Even so, will it involve us?"

"I can't say as to that. We're not a warlike nation. I mentioned the chance of a big war breaking out because if it does, Europe is going to need many things

335

from us, and among the necessities, it's obvious there will be all kinds of dry goods. Cottons, woolens, everything."

"I'm going to read the war news far more carefully from now on," I vowed. "How long do you think it will be?"

"A year—not more than that."

"What they'll need is woolens," I said. "Far more than cottons. Anyway, the manufacture of woolens is a more profitable business. Better than cottons. There's another thing. Our machinery is almost worn out, and they're considering buying new. So why not the kind that will turn out woolens?"

"Military uniforms are woolen," Glen said. "There'll be need for ten million, at least. Once this gets going, so many men will be drafted, the European factories won't be able to produce what they should and they'll have to depend on us. If there was ever a chance to bring business back to where it was, or even better it, the time is now."

"I'm going to suggest it."

"It will likely take a great deal of money. Will the Camerons come up with it?"

"They haven't got it," I said. "They are thrifty people in some ways, scrimping in fact, but they also spend on certain things. The years Nora and Helen were in Europe cost a great deal. Gabriel invested heavily in the stock market just before the slump last year. Loran may have some, but not enough."

"Good heavens, Maeve, you can't handle it. You'll need half a million at least."

"Aye," I said slowly. "That I will, and I know where I can get it."

"Half a million? Do you know how much that is?"

"Aye, it's a deal of money, but I've a deal in the bank already, and my shares in the mill to use as collateral for the loan, and good Queen Maeve to provide the rest."

336

"What are you talking about?"

"The torc!" I said.

Glen shook his head vigorously. "I forgot about that, never having seen the thing. I don't know what it will bring, but even so, you can't sell it. It has to stay in the family. Not even to save the mill must you part with it."

"I won't have to. Oh, I'll be gambling a bit, but from what you say, the odds won't be too bad. We will need money only for a short time. Two years— or three. A bank will lend it if I put up the torc and my part of the mill as security."

"My dear, naive wife. A bank won't know a torc from a zulu headdress."

"I think this can be managed," I insisted, because I'd thought of it for some time now. "We have to help the mill. Mind you now, it's not for those people on the Hill, not even Nora. It's for the people in the town who have given their lives to the mill and will never manage without it."

"Now how do you propose to handle this financial transaction, my dear?"

"Mr. Arnold will know. I will go to New York and talk to him. Do I have your consent?"

"Of course you have. My help, too, for whatever it's worth. Hadn't you better see if the Camerons will go along with this proposition first?"

"They'll have to."

"All right, darling Maeve, but remember this. It will be your money and your risk. What will you get out of it?"

"Two things," I said serenely. The thought of them had just come to me. "I will insist on fifty-one percent of the stock so I control the company. And I shall see Nora."

"Very well." He smiled slightly. "Now which of those do you consider the most important?"

"I wonder," I said. "Tomorrow I'll try to find out.

So long as you believe in what I'm about to do, I'll chance it gladly."

"They'll never agree to giving you control."

"Perhaps not. I've become good at the art of compromise."

"They'll not let you have Nora back, either."

"We shall see."

"Perhaps you should consult that mirror?" Glen suggested.

"I think not. If it showed disaster, I believe I'd try anyway. Because I have come to the conclusion this has to be done. After what you told me about the war in Europe, I can now see that the time is perfect and any further delay will be almost as bad as failure. Tomorrow I go to the Hill."

I drove the motorcar next evening to the Hill. We'd long since disposed of our horses. The livery stable in town was still in business, but it sold more gasoline than it rented horses and carriages. With self-starters a woman could now operate a car with no difficulty except when the car suffered a flat tire or became mired in mud. I took care not to drive any great distance, only over solid roads, and never so far I couldn't walk back or find someone to give me a ride.

I pulled up before the mansion. It seemed strange to me how little it had changed. I didn't think even a rose bush had been replaced or moved. I didn't have many good memories connected with this house, though while I carried Nora there, I'd been treated like a princess.

Martha, who had aged greatly, it seemed to me, opened the door and with her customary hospitality greeted me not at all. Nor did I favor her with as much as a smile.

They knew I was coming. I'd telephoned beforehand to make certain they were all present, and they were, all but Helen and Nora.

338

It wasn't greatly different from the first time I'd walked into their drawing room. Joel's father was completely gray now, but his face was unlined with not even crepiness around his throat. I couldn't say that for Evelyn, Joel's mother. Her hair was dark, kept that way with the use of the contents of a bottle, I suspected, and the wrinkles around her mouth and throat gave away her age, and no dye could change that.

Loran was bulkier, his face florid. Maybe he drank too much brandy, I didn't know. Except for a monk's fringe of mousy-colored hair, he was bald. He was given to smoking fat cigars these days, and he puffed on one now while he regarded me with that ever-lasting amusement he seemed to acquire whenever he glanced my way.

Ashley hadn't changed a great deal, though he had developed a considerable pot which his trousers couldn't hide despite the suspenders that pulled up on them considerably.

I sat down without an invitation. I'd long ago ceased to stand on formality with these people. "Well, now," I said, "I've come to dispel some of the gloominess which appears to have afflicted all of you. But I'll not talk of it while you stand there."

They sat down. Loran, who'd already been seated, leaned forward, and the amusement was gone from his eyes. He seemed to recognize the seriousness of my visit in my tone of voice. Possibly he saw some hope that I'd found a plan that might help.

"Go on, Maeve," Loran said. "What is this magnificent scheme of yours?"

"There is a war going on in the Balkans. It's getting bigger, and it's going to spread. Before long, half of Europe may be involved."

"The girl's mad!" Marcy Tabor had entered the drawing room without my noticing, and she approached us with a dark frown of disbelief. "We'd be idiots to

339

listen to her. What does she know about Europe?"

"Sit down, Marcy, and keep still," Loran said. "I think I know what she's driving at."

"This war is between beggarly nations that have nothing else to do," Marcy insisted. "Except kill one another."

Loran said, "Ashley, go up and fetch Helen. She spent years over there. She ought to have an opinion."

So Helen was here. Perhaps Nora was, too.

"Have Nora come down, as well," I said. "She was also there and I'm sure she is old enough to have observed and listened."

"No!" Evelyn arose to stop Ashley. "Deborah is not to come down."

"In heaven's name," I said, "may I not even see my daughter? I have no intention of running off with her."

"Absolutely not!" Evelyn said. "I forbid it."

Ashley looked about, bewildered, not knowing whom to take orders from. I arose, too. I adjusted my hat and began putting on one of my gloves.

"Good evening, then," I said.

"Ashley," Loran commanded. "Fetch Helen and Deborah."

"Loran, you can't—"

"Evelyn, I don't know what Maeve has to tell us, but she does not come here on a whim. When she has something to say, it is important, and we are at our wit's end. We are in danger of losing the mill and everything we possess."

"Mrs. Cameron," I said, "I give you my word, I'll not tell Nora she is my daughter. Not now."

Evelyn sat down again. She reached for a palmetto fan on a table beside her and began fanning herself energetically, though it was not overly hot in the drawing room. I sat again in my chair.

Helen came down first and began to approach me in what I could only construe as a friendly fashion,

340

but she stopped short, veered off, and approached Loran instead.

"Good evening, Maeve," she said to me. "You are looking very well in spite of the years."

Helen didn't seem to have changed. She was slim, youthful-looking. I envied her.

"They've been kind to you, Helen."

"Thank you. How is your daughter?"

"Very well. She's at boarding school."

"Oh, yes—she's younger than Deborah, isn't she?" Helen didn't wait for an answer. "Uncle Loran, you wished to see me?"

"Yes. Sit down, this may take some time. We've been discussing the war situation in Europe. Maeve believes it is ready to spread. You were there for several years. Do you have an opinion?"

"The trouble will be confined to the Balkans," Helen said. "It will not spread. The larger nations have more sense than to start another war."

"Did you spend time in Germany?" I asked.

"A great deal of time. An entire year. We were guests at a ball in honor of Kaiser Wilhelm, in fact."

"Tell me," I went on, "is business good in Germany?"

"Better than in this country. It's booming. They know how to manufacture things over there."

"The Krupp plant was busy?" I went on.

"Of course. It was working all night."

"Tell me," Loran was suddenly on my side, "what does the Krupp empire manufacture, Helen?"

"Why . . . why . . ."

"Guns," I said. "Weapons of all kinds. They don't manufacture motorcars, or plows, or trolley cars, or baby carriages. They make guns! To what purpose?"

"You're right, Maeve," Loran said. "What's your opinion, Gabe?"

Gabriel nodded. "I have to agree."

"These small wars are going on all the time," Joel's

341

mother protested. "There's no indication larger nations are going to get involved."

Helen spoke before I could challenge that remark. "Maeve may be right," she said, "now that I think of it. The formal affairs we attended were almost military, there were so many officers there. And there seemed to be soldiers everywhere. I heard they'd been calling up the younger men. Everyone believed it was just routine."

"Maeve," Loran said, "I accept your theory. Thank you, Helen, for your help. First-hand information is the most reliable of all. Let's assume there is going to be a big war. Now, Maeve, you know where the mill stands. We could profit richly if we could get orders based on war conditions, but we don't know how soon war will break out."

"What good are war orders without more machinery than we have?" Gabriel asked sadly. "And we don't have the money to replace it."

"All right, Maeve," Loran said, "you came here with some idea in mind."

"We must go into woolens, perhaps other materials, and we must replace all our machinery with new, modern types. It will be very expensive and take some time."

Gabriel leaned forward to object, and Marcy Tabor snorted in contempt of the whole idea. Evelyn merely shrugged as if the whole thing was beyond her, but Helen and Loran were attentive.

"Before you begin your objections," I went on, "hear me out. I've more to say, and it's important."

"You have the floor," Loran conceded.

"If this war breaks out, it may last a long time. Manpower in Europe will be at a premium. Factories will not produce as they should, and America is going to be called on for everything it can furnish. Woolens will be in the most demand. We may have several months to prepare, to buy the machinery, have it

342

installed, train our people to handle it, and produce enough to have at least a small inventory on hand."

"Madness." Marcy Tabor used her favorite word.

"What do you think, Gabe?" Loran asked.

"She's right," Joel's father admitted. "But to buy this machinery, to switch over . . . what's it going to cost?"

I said, "I guess half a million."

"Dollars?" Ashley gasped. It was his first contribution to the meeting.

Nobody paid any attention to him. "All of that," Loran agreed. "To be perfectly frank, Maeve, we can't handle it."

"I'm quite aware of that," I said.

"Well, then, what's the purpose in coming here with a scheme that's impossible to follow through?" Gabriel wanted to know.

"I may be able to handle it," I said, and my moment of triumph had been fulfilled.

"You? Half a million?" Loran scoffed.

"I said I may be able to handle it. The chances are good. If I can raise half that amount, any bank will advance the rest. Isn't that true?"

"Yes—but a quarter of a million dollars!"

I saw her enter the room. My grown daughter. I'd not seen her since she was a child, and here she was, almost a woman. Tall, graceful as she crossed the room, a beauty Patty would measure up to but not without two or three more years and much, much work. Here was poise, confidence, a quiet assurance and—a haughtiness she could not conceal.

"You remember Mrs. Kinnery?" Helen asked.

"Yes—somewhat," Nora said. If you placed her in one room, Patty in another, and one spoke, you'd not know which had spoken. It was a soft voice, highly cultured. Whatever else they'd done to this girl, they'd turned her into an astonishing lady at seventeen. I expected she could glide across a dance floor with an astounding grace, act as hostess at a large gathering, sit at the head of the table during an important banquet.

And she remembered her mother—somewhat.

"You're looking very well," I said. "Did you enjoy your European stay?"

"Of course. May I ask what this gathering is about?"

"Mrs. Kinnery is about to inform us how she can furnish half a million dollars to the mill so we can begin full-time work and make some money," Loran said.

"Is this possible?" Nora asked. "Mrs. Kinnery and half a million . . .?"

"My dear," I said, "if it were not possible, I'd not be sitting here talking about it."

"I beg your pardon," she said stiffly.

"That'll be enough out of you," Loran said. "Maeve, we now come to the important part. What do you want?"

"Two things," I said. "One I will not mention now, but I'm quite sure you understand what I mean. The other will be in legal form before I do anything, and it will put me in possession of fifty-one percent of the stock."

Loran arose. "Good night, Maeve."

"I told you she was mad!" Marcy said.

I pulled on my gloves. "Good night, Mr. Cameron . . . all of you. It's been my pleasure."

I walked out with just one more glance at Nora, and I prayed that none of the longing I felt was in it. I reached the motorcar. Behind me someone opened the mansion door again and came down the marble steps. I turned around to wait until Helen approached. She was alone.

"Maeve, I don't know what all this is about, but I want to explain a few things. Back there you hinted about something you would demand. I suspect it is the return of Deborah."

344

"It is," I said.

"The girl is beautiful. Don't you agree?"

"Yes, she's my daughter. She is beautiful."

"I sent her to the best schools all over Europe. She has had an education very few girls have ever enjoyed. She speaks French and Italian. She is fluent in German and Spanish. She knows all the graces. She has met so many important people I couldn't begin to name them. Right now she could handle a castle staffed with fifty servants. She's proficient in everything."

"I've no doubt of it."

"Could you have done that for her?"

"I could have given her a mother's love."

"I did that," Helen said.

I turned away from her, climbed into the motorcar, and when it started my touch was that angry on the throttle the engine all but tore loose. I suspect it startled everyone in the mansion. I drove away, seething. Angry enough to let them all go to the devil. Why should I risk the loss of the torc to help such of these? Let the mill fail, and let them go down with it.

I was entering Main Street, and the lights in the cozy houses were lit. A few people were sitting on the front steps, or in hammocks and swings on their porches. They called out greetings and I waved.

Let the Camerons go down—but these good people would go with them. Sanity came back with a painful stab. I drove home. Now I had need of Glen's wisdom and his quiet assurance when we reached a decision. I had need of his cheek against mine, his lips pressing sweetly to mine, his arm about me steadying my soul and quieting my nerves.

I began telling him about my experience before I had the veil untied from under my chin and my motoring hat off. He helped me with the duster and hung it in the hall closet for me.

"They're bluffing," he guessed. "They know you

345

well enough to realize you can get the money, but they can't give in to your terms without a fight. Well, let's give it to them."

"We have to be sure, darling," I said. "There's so much at stake."

"They'll wait a day or two in case you come back. If you don't, they'll come to you. My advice is wait."

"I'll need it, my dearest Glen. In this and all things."

"Perhaps we can think of a compromise."

"I'm thinking of what will happen if this does not go through. It came to me as I drove along Main Street. I was that angry I was ready to let it all go. They infuriated me, and Helen came out to tell me once again, ever so sweetly, that she was Nora's mother. Can you imagine? I drove off before I did something I'd be sorry for."

"You did see the girl?"

"Oh, yes. Glen, she's a wonder. Oh, not a whit more attractive than our Patty, not a shade smarter, and Patty is a million times warmer. But Nora has been that educated she's a real lady. Oh, yes—very ladylike. She speaks several languages, which is of course a valuable asset in this town where the folks are lucky they speak one. But regardless, they have done well by her. Not as I would have, but well in spite of that. I'm going to have her back. I told them so. They can't afford to deny me this time. I know the condition they're in."

"And the condition the town is in," Glen reminded me.

"Yes—the town and the people we love. Oh, Glen, I don't know what I'll do. Help me! Don't let me go off like a crazed woman. Hold me back so I will do what is right and proper."

"The initiative is not ours. You presented a proposition, and it's now up to them to accept or reject it."

"What do you think they'll do?" I asked.

"Offer some kind of a compromise. They'll never

346

grant you control of the mill, but you'll get something out of it that will give you more to say about its operation and be all to the good."

"Also concerned with Nora? Oh, Glen, I'm losing hope there. They seem to have enclosed her in a shell I'll never be able to penetrate. Even if I get her back, how will I gain her love and keep it? With her high-falutin ways in five languages and all that education. She's been taught by teachers with all those degrees. While I was taught by my father and by an ancient woman, herself who never saw the inside of a schoolroom."

"Patty is my daughter, and I favor her," Glen said. "Put the two of them together over some good problem that requires sound judgment, and neither will outdo the other. From what I've seen of Nora, especially when she was a child and I was her doctor, those two girls might have been twins, they're so much alike in temperament and intelligence."

"They are much alike," I admitted. "They could be so happy together. I'm going to insist they let go of her."

"They won't. That's where they'll hold out no matter what you offer. Nora represents the future to them. Something more important than the success of the mill."

"Yes, I suppose she does. But isn't it fair to say I should share in that future? That some of it should be mine?"

"Without a doubt. All of it should be yours. There's one thing I begin to believe you've failed to see. In reference to Nora you're thinking like a mother and not considering motives."

"Now what motives are you talking about?" I asked. He was right about me. I was at a total loss to know what he meant.

"They sent Nora abroad to keep you away from her, but there was likely another reason. When Nora is grown and ready for marriage, they can see that she marries into money and power, all to further the interests of the mill."

"Oh, my sainted aunt! They'll marry her to a prince or a duke. All the social climbers are doing that these days."

"There'll be a difference with the Camerons. If it is a prince or a duke, he'll have to have a great deal of money. Unlike the socialite mothers who look for only a glamorous title for their daughters, the Camerons look for wealth and power to enter the family."

"I will not have it," I said.

There was great truth in what Glen had just told me. I'd never considered this before, or even thought of it momentarily. Yet that must lie behind their intent to make such a lady of Nora. They wanted wealth and power, and Nora would be the magnet to draw it.

"We'll wait and see," Glen said. "There may come a time when you'll have to risk their using all that false information, the mass of lies."

I told myself I would not break down. This was not the time for it, even though I had the most sympathetic shoulder in the world to cry on.

"Glen, I remember when she was small she called me a bad woman. She was afraid of me. I think she's forgotten that, but I never will. If she called me that again, I'd die where I stood. Oh, those people! How well they trained her. How well they know me."

"Not as well as I do, Maeve. If it becomes needful that you oppose them, you will. No matter what the consequences."

I moved behind his chair, bent, and kissed his forehead when he tilted back to look up at me. "Darling, I'm going to see what the mirror will say. I swore not to do this, for often it will destroy my happiness, but I feel now that I must know if there is trouble in store for us."

"It's been so long since you consulted it perhaps it's lost its powers."

"Darling, the mirror is more than two thousand years old. If it lasted all that time, surely it will not fail me now. Will you wait until I return?"

"Of course. Bring it down here, why don't you?"

"Yes, I'll do that," I said, and I hurried upstairs. As usual, I kept it deep in the darkest closet, completely wrapped. I carried it downstairs and there, in front of Glen, I removed the wrapping reverently. I never failed to give this bit of metal all the respect it deserved.

"It looks the same," I told Glen. "It shines, but only in the very center; yet the images do seem to appear where there is no reflection. Darling, hold my hand tightly. I'm going to do what I swore I would not. I'm afraid of the answer."

He grasped my hand. I breathed lightly on the surface of the mirror and then pressed it hard against my breast. I closed my eyes, and I spoke in a whisper my entreaty to the spirit of a woman dead for twenty centuries.

"I ask this of you. Will my daughter be restored to me? Is there danger for her?"

I slowly brought the mirror before my eyes. The image had already formed and was in the process of fading, but there was no mistaking what it was. Once again there was water. Not the boiling, angry sea this time, but a placid surface of water with not so much as a ripple upon it. As it faded, the profile of a young girl came into being swiftly. It was gone before I could positively identify it, but I'd seen enough to be fairly certain.

I turned to Glen. "Once I saw an angry ocean and my father died. Then I saw an image that faded as a man might fade at death—and Joel died. I saw an angry mob and Abner died. Now I see water again —and the image of a girl."

349

"Nora?" he asked. "Is she in some kind of danger? Or will be?"

"It is not Nora, Glen. It is Patty. I'm sure."

"If I were you," Glen said in a voice gone cold, "I'd destroy that thing. It's a menace!"

"Ah, no, my dear, it is the truth. We are warned now. We can be careful."

"As your father was careful?"

"My father did not know of the prediction of his death. I never told him. Nor did Joel know that he, too, would die. We shall not tell Patty, either, but we shall watch over her from now on."

"It was Patty? You asked about Nora."

"It was Patty. Yet," I said hesitantly, "there was a difference. I mean between this and the other evil predictions. In the other cases, the profiles of Father and Joel had little substance, while this of Patty was plain and clear and it did not fade but vanished instead. That may have a meaning. I don't know. No matter, something bad lies ahead for our daughter, and it will be our responsibility to see that it does not happen."

"We'll do what we can," Glen assured me. "Has there ever been an instance that you know of where the prediction was interfered with so it didn't come true?"

"No. I never head of such an instance."

"We'll watch over her."

"The water—it was quiet, still as a small pond. Darling, there is no water around here."

"Except for the river, which isn't really a river at all. It used to power the old mill. When the new one was built, the Camerons diverted the stream so it wouldn't come close to the factory. That was after they began operating with steam, of course.

"Is there a pond? I've not been down there often enough to remember."

"Of sorts. I used to swim in it when I was a boy.

350

We didn't do any diving because it was too shallow, but we used to hear our fathers tell us how they swam in the river, too, and how they'd see how close they could get to the mill wheel. It was all paddles and pulleys. It's all there still but hasn't been turned over in many years."

"Then Patty must be warned not to go near the mill where the pond and the stream are located," I said. "I'll think of some excuse to keep her away from there."

"She'll do exactly what you say. Patty is an obedient child who doesn't have to be threatened or even coaxed with promises."

At the supper table I questioned Patty about her knowledge of the old part of the mill and the pond.

"I ask because about all you could possibly do there is wade. It's far too shallow for swimming, especially for a girl as old as you."

"It's not that shallow, Mama," Patty said. "I used to swim there. It's a nice place, all shady and cool in summer. Lots of the kids go there to swim. I told you."

"It must have slipped my mind," I said. Prior to the prediction of the mirror, I wouldn't have given the mill pond a second thought. Patty was a strong and skillful swimmer.

"We don't go there any more because it's mostly for kids," she said serenely. "I'm too old now. Besides, the water's kind of dirty sometimes. I saw Deborah Cameron this afternoon."

"Oh? In the village?"

"She was driving an automobile. All by herself. A red one."

"You didn't speak to her?"

"I waved, but I guess she didn't see me. She never did see anybody very often. We used to tell her she was blind."

"I saw her at the Cameron mansion," I said. "She looked very well and very attractive."

"I guess so. Honest, Mama, what makes a person so stuck-up? What makes her think nobody else is as good as she is?"

"Her bringing up," Glen said. "That's what she was taught. All the Camerons are stuck-up."

Patty nodded. It really didn't matter a great deal to her. "I guess so. Well, if she keeps on living here, she won't have many friends."

"Do you like her?" I asked. I hoped my voice was casual.

"I don't know, Mama. I never knew her well enough."

"Well, don't blame her for being aloof," Glen said. "That's all she knows how to be. They've never let her be anything else."

"Gee, I'm glad I don't live up there."

"So am I, dear," I said. "And your father and I are so pleased you are not jealous of Deborah."

"What's there to be jealous of? I'd rather be me, anyway. May I be excused now? I've an awful test in geography when I go back to school."

"You're excused," Glen said. "And don't fail the test, or hate geography because it seems to be dull. By the time you grow up, there will be so many new roads all over the country you'll have to know where you're going and how to read a map. So off with you."

We heard her door close upstairs, and Glen smiled. "I don't think we have to worry about Patty going swimming in that mill pond. She's too old for that nonsense. She says."

"I'll worry anyway. But I am relieved, I must say. I wonder how long it will take the Camerons to make up their minds?"

Even with Glen's reassurance I didn't sleep well that night. I felt burdened down with far too many problems. I was about to undertake an extremely risky business in furnishing capital so the mill could convert. Unless I was exceedingly careful, the Camerons would cheat me out of all they could.

It was the next afternoon when I returned from a brief shopping trip in the village that Glen told me Loran had telephoned and I was to call back. Our phone was in Glen's office, and when he finished with his patient, I picked up the receiver.

"Alice, get me the mill office, please," I said. Someone answered and I asked for Loran. He came on at once. "You wanted me to call you," I said.

"Oh, yes. I'd like you to come by as soon as you can. We have a generous offer to propose."

"I'll be there within the hour, Mr. Cameron. The sooner we get the preliminaries over and start to get ready for the change-over at the mill, the better for everyone."

I hung up. "He has an offer," I told Glen. "Would you care to come with me?"

"You can handle them, Maeve. Don't sign anything. Just listen."

"Yes, you can be sure whatever we decide upon will be reviewed by Mr. Arnold in New York."

I changed into a tan skirt, trimmed with dark brown, and a matching shirtwaist. I tilted a small sailor straw well forward and held it down with a narrow veil. I put on my duster and gloves.

Glen would not be using the car, so I drove it to the mill and an hour after I'd phoned Loran, I walked into the office to find Gabriel Cameron also present, but no one else. I was grateful that Evelyn and Marcy Tabor were not there, though I would have appreciated it if Nora had been in the room.

"We'll get right down to business," Loran said. "First of all, are you certain you can raise this money?"

"Quite certain, Mr. Cameron," I replied.

"Where will you get such a sum?" Joel's father asked.

"I prefer not to divulge that at the moment. Let it be sufficient to state that it will be honest money, and if necessary I shall account for every penny of it."

"Very well," Loran said. "We cannot grant you controlling interest. That's out of the question, and I believe you know that, too."

"What is your proposition, then?"

"We will give you forty-nine percent."

"I will have fifty, with no more dickering. Take it or leave it."

Loran shrugged. "You have the money."

"You mentioned another demand," Joel's father said. "I take it you refer to Deborah."

"I refer to my daughter, yes."

"Listen to me, Mrs. Kinnery," he said. "We will allow the mill to go bankrupt, the entire town to fail and pass out of existence, if keeping the mill and the town depend upon our giving up Deborah. Under no circumstances will we turn that girl over to you."

"I am her mother. Must you be reminded of that?"

"You are also an immoral woman with a history of immorality in Ireland and you have carried on here in a manner to shame us all. I will not have this child exposed to such a woman as you, madam."

I stared at him, for this had suddenly taken on a new tack. "You actually believe that, don't you, Mr. Cameron? You really do."

"Of course I do. We have documentary proof of it. Enough to convict you in any court of justice. If you force our hand, that's where it will wind up. If Deborah has to find out the truth, I prefer it be that way. Not from you. I hope I've made myself clear."

I saw any chance of getting Nora back now go glimmering. I was reconciled to it, thanks to Glen's repeated warnings. What surprised me was the way these people had convinced themselves those absurd stories were true.

"I shall have my attorney prepare an agreement

354

giving me fifty percent interest in all the stock," I said. "This agreement will also provide certain measures you may not approve of but I insist upon. The foremost of these is that every worker be granted each week the equivalent of his last paycheck during the change-over until the mill is ready for them to take up their duties once more."

"What else?" Joel's father asked.

"All indebtedness owed the mill by its employees be wiped out. All rents, all debts at the company stores, all loans, if any were ever made. When the mill begins operations again, it will be with a clean slate. For the mill, and for its employees. That way they'll work harder and be more interested in what they're doing."

"You may include such provisions," Loran said. "When will you know about the money?"

"Possibly by the day after tomorrow. I will telephone the office or, if the factory is closed, your home."

Joel's father walked to the door. "Then our business is concluded. Good day, Mrs. Kinnery."

Loran said, "Don't leave yet, Maeve. You know, I believe we'll make a go of this. I've investigated the field of woolens, and it's going to be very big. So is the war over there. Yes, a lot of uniforms are going to be needed."

"Are they ever going to let go of Deborah?" I asked. "I know all about our prospects for success, but I place my daughter's future on just as important a basis."

"If you attempt to take her away, they'll immediately inform her of what they call your immorality, past and recent past. They can make this harm you and surely turn Deborah away from you, even if she is convinced you are her mother. If you begin any action, or begin insisting she be returned to you, my brother will use the proof he has. It's sufficient, and you know that as well as I do, because you consulted

355

your lawyer about it. If he had indicated there was a chance of getting the child back, you'd have started a legal battle a long time ago."

"Mr. Cameron, has it ever occurred to you—or to those others of your family—how a mother feels when she loses her daughter through no fault of her own?"

"Of course it has. On the other hand, do you realize how much we've done for Deborah? And never forget, her father was one of us."

"Oh, no," I said promptly. "He never was that, and you know it. Neither he nor Abner wanted anything to do with you and your ways. Abner remained because he was compelled to, being without funds. If he'd shared in his grandfather's will, as Joel did, Abner would have gone away, too. Oh, no, they were not of you."

"Your opinion," Loran said, and he arose as a signal the conversation was over. I had no objection to that. I left him and drove home where Glen was waiting to hear what had happened. I outlined the offer they'd made.

"If I control half the stock," I said, "I may not be able to have my own way, but they won't, either. And they are much more anxious than I to regain the money losses they've endured these last months, or perhaps years. I can object if I don't like their suggestions, and I can hold out, whereas they can't."

Glen nodded. "They went pretty far in trying to accommodate you. That's a good indication of how desperate they actually are for capital funds. So it may be you made a wise decision, but I'd have it drawn up in precise legal form."

"I'm going to New York tomorrow to have Mr. Arnold take care of the matter and advise me as to what I can and cannot do with one-half the holdings. While he studies this and draws up the papers, I'll see about borrowing on the torc."

"Does it bother you to be forced to do this? You

said some of your ancestors would have chosen to starve rather than sell the torc."

"True, my dear, but I'm not selling. I'll get it back quickly enough, though I would worry about that if the Camerons knew how I was getting the money. Or why the torc is so important to me. They'd attempt to see that I couldn't meet the payments so I'd lose the torc. I wouldn't put anything past them."

"I wouldn't, either. I knew they'd be firm in denying you, Nora."

"The way Gabriel Cameron spoke, I'm beginning to think he really believes Cathal Dolan and I were guilty of misbehavior. And that I actually enticed that boor of a man out of the ballroom that night. Heaven knows what else they believe I did."

"It's more likely they've been telling themselves this fairy tale for so long a time it's become the truth to them. They have to know, deep in their hearts, it's all a lie. Some day we're going to prove it."

"A blessed day that will be," I said. "I'm worried over the prediction of the mirror. Please, darling, if Patty should return from school for any reason while I'm in New York, watch over her every moment."

"Yes, you can be sure of it. I doubt she'll be back, though. Remember, she's taking her examinations now, and they'll last all week and into next."

"Thank heaven for that. I'll be back long before she returns for the summer. Now I've got to pack. I won't be gone but two or three days."

The train ride to New York wasn't much of an improvement over the same ride the years before when I'd come to this town I now called home. From Cameron to Boston it was equally sooty, though the Pullman from there to New York was reasonably clean but extremely hot. The little fans in the cars didn't help very much.

I checked into the new Waldorf-Astoria, an even more resplendent hotel than the older one had been.

This done. I telephoned Mr. Arnold's office and proceeded directly there. He listened to my story of the torc and my need to place it as collateral for a large loan. He was well versed in artifacts and he knew exactly whom to call for the proper information.

The following morning I unwrapped the torc to place it on the desk of the Chairman of the Board of one of the great banks. He was also a devoted fancier of relics, and he recognized the torc instantly as being genuine.

"It's a privilege to even look at this," he said. "There's nothing quite like it except in the Dublin museum."

"How much could I borrow on it, Mr. Bishop," I asked.

"Mr. Arnold talked to me at length about this, Mrs. Kinnery. I took the liberty of doing some investigating on my part, too, even in the brief time before your arrival at my office this morning. The Cameron Mills are situated to make a great deal of money. Confidentially, the Balkan war is worse than ever, and the prospects for peace are bleak. We bankers make it our business to know these things. At this moment, any incident of even moderate importance will bring Germany into it and I cannot see how this country can stay out of it indefinitely. Do you follow me, Mrs. Kinnery?"

"I'm aware of what goes on. My husband keeps up with such things. I know woolens are going to be in heavy demand, and if we have a stockpile of them we can make a great deal of money, for the price is surely going up."

"Way up! War has a habit of making everything cost more—including human lives. Now—getting back to the business at hand. I am willing to advance you, as an individual, the sum you require with this wonderfully handsome and rare object as security. It's unusual for a bank to make this kind of a transaction, but in this case we won't quibble about that. Now, if you then invest this sum entirely in the mill, get it ready to start producing, we shall be happy to lend the corporation a similar sum."

"Mr. Bishop, I'm that grateful—"

"It's a business deal, Mrs. Kinnery. The bank will make money on it, and I'll have the pleasure of knowing this wonderful piece of jewelry has been in my possession, if only for a brief period of time."

I spent the rest of the afternoon with Mr. Arnold while he dictated a legal agreement which the Camerons would have to sign.

"It's not the best of agreements," Mr. Arnold told me. "But I expect the most advantageous you could get under the circumstances. To run the mill it will take unanimity on all sides, but sometimes without it, things work well enough. Now I wish to talk to you about your daughter—the one the Camerons took from you. As I recall, they hold a deposition made in Ireland from some man who swore you and he had intimate relations over a period of time. And that you married Joel only for his money."

"That is what the paper said, Mr. Arnold."

"Also there was an incident in which you were placed in an embarrassing position by an uninvited guest at an affair held by the Camerons."

"Yes, that, too."

"No doubt this man was urged, or even paid, to perform that cruel act. It's been some time now. He may have had a change of heart. Some do. It's possible he might recant his story and tell the truth."

"I have my doubts, sir," I said.

"All right. Now about this man in Ireland. Do you have any means of checking up on him?"

"I have a brother who is a surgeon—and an important one—in Scotland. He might find out about Cathal Dolan."

"Why don't you have him do that? Perhaps talk to

the man and, by chance, persuade him to make another deposition recanting the first."

"I have thought of it often," I said. "I dare not risk it. Cathal is that thick-headed he would never recant. If I opened such an investigation, surely Nora would hear of it. I cannot bear the thought of having her further convinced that I am an unfit person to be her mother. It would break my heart."

Mr. Arnold had grown quite old and very wise. His advice was sound, and he understood my feelings because of his long experience in the field of human emotions.

"I realize how you feel, my dear. But if they ever box you in, and it becomes needful to defend yourself, then have someone go to this man and at the same time, see what can be done about learning what happened to Joel that he died so mysteriously."

"That has worried me, too," I admitted. "But after all these years, I see no way to prove that he was poisoned."

"No medical means, surely, but there are other ways of looking into it. Someone had to give him the poison. Either someone was hired to do it, or it was accomplished by a person who went to meet Joel with the deliberate intention of killing him. Find out, if you can, whom Joel saw during his last trip to Dublin. There are ways, my dear Maeve."

"I will write my brother," I said. "If it becomes necessary, I shall go back myself." I closed my eyes for a moment. "I would not mind seeing my old house again, and the graves of those I loved so well. You have planted an idea, Mr. Arnold."

"But make the solving of the mystery the main objective," he warned. "Don't let sentiment cloud the real purpose of your visit."

"I'll remember what you have told me. But of course I cannot go now. There is the mill and all the work involved there. I shall let you know how things fare, and I'm that grateful once again. Something I seem to say every time I come here."

After I left his office all of my big city business was concluded, so I made arrangements for the journey home. I was able to get a night train to Boston, and in the confines of my drawing room, as the train sped through the night, I had time to contemplate what Mr. Arnold had told me and to realize how wise his advice had been.

At the time of Joel's death I suspected he'd been poisoned, but it never occurred to me—a girl grown up so naively in that little Irish country village—that murder had been done. Rather I thought only that somewhere he'd been accidentally given spoiled food to eat. Now, older and far wiser, I knew the possibilities that he'd been poisoned deliberately, by some slow-acting chemical that killed by degrees.

I knew also that if I could face Cathal Dolan I could force him not only to recant the testimony of his deposition, but to make another stating it was all a lie induced by the request of someone else who might very well have paid him to swear to this outrageous story.

As the night progressed and my thoughts were that busy I couldn't sleep, I worried again over Patty and the portent of the mirror's prediction. The porter knocked to ask if he might turn down my bed. I asked him to return later. I was in no mood to sleep.

The mirror had shown me a placid body of water followed by Patty's profile, but somehow, because the profile didn't fade away like those others had when the mirror proclaimed a death, I felt that Patty's danger might be overcome. Not averted, because the prediction would come true, but Patty would be safe at the end of the ordeal, whatever it turned out to be.

I did my best to fashion some sort of idea how that quiet body of water could threaten her, but it was impossible. The only pond was at the old part of the factory where the original mill was located. It seemed a most unlikely place to present any great danger.

I couldn't dismiss this easily, though I did manage to turn my thoughts to the Camerons and the mill. When they signed the document I carried with me, I would then own fifty percent of the stock. With no one enjoying a voting majority they could stop me if they chose, but I could also stop them. Now they would have to bargain with me, and I did hold the great advantage. I controlled the money.

They'd give way to me now, but when the mill began to regain its old prosperity—and a far greater one was all but insured—they'd change to their old arrogance for they'd no longer have to look to me for financing. I'd still own an even amount of stock, but they'd find ways to outwit me unless I was very careful and very clever. I meant to be both.

FOURTEEN

I stopped in Boston for a day to visit with Jennie and Willie Markham. They were doing very well indeed; their children were a delight, and I spent an enjoyable evening talking over old times and informing Willie about what was going on.

"Never forget," he warned, "that family is full of tricks. They sit by the hour and scheme. They wait until they're sure these plans will not fail, and then put them into effect. Maeve, there isn't anything they

362

wouldn't do to further their own ambitions. I worked in their office a long time. I know them."

"Willie told me some time ago that their plans for Nora are to marry her to someone of great importance and wealth," Jennie added. "They've always had that in mind. Nora, to them, is an investment—an asset—to cash in on at the right time. Maeve, get her away from them if you can."

"You can be sure I'll try," I said. "Glen, by the way, has exactly the same opinion. I'm going to discuss this with him. Perhaps there is something to be done about Nora, after all."

"I'm glad. Nora and Patty belong together."

"If I have my way, they will be, I promise you."

I felt better, lighter in heart after my visit, and I was overjoyed to find Glen and Patty waiting for me at the depot. Patty hugged me and shed a few happy tears. I did love her so. Glen enveloped me in a bear hug and kissed me with an abandon that showed me the longing in his heart and quite took my breath away.

That night, as we relaxed after supper and Patty had gone to her room to study, I told Glen about Mr. Arnold's advice, and concluded, "As soon as it is possible for me to do so, darling, I want to go to Ireland. I want to go home."

"I'll go with you if I can. If you wish me to."

"Oh, Glen, I didn't want to ask, but I do wish it so. I'm going to see Cathal Dolan face to face and make him back down. I know I can do it. He's a vengeful man, but the years may have softened him. If not, I'll be as hard as he and make him tell the truth."

"How long will it be before we can go?" Glen asked.

"I wish it could be tomorrow, but we'd come back and find the Camerons in full control. It won't be for weeks, I'm sorry to say. However, I've waited

363

this long to get my daughter back, I can wait a bit longer."

"I've a feeling we're going to win this time," Glen said. "Now I've some news. Good news, though it worried me some when I first heard it, because this is not like the Camerons."

"Now what have they schemed?" I asked.

"After your telegram was received, Loran immediately posted a notice on the bulletin board that the factory would close down in one week and remain closed for an indefinite time. That all employees would receive their pay as usual, and that all rents would be suspended, all arrears forgiven, and all debts at the company stores in town be wiped out. Now that's like the sky falling down. I'd have considered it an impossibility."

"I have brought back with me, in legal form, an agreement they are to sign. It includes what you have just told me. I made that part of the bargain."

"They're going to get the credit for it unless you insist otherwise."

"Let them. It may be a good thing. There's so much animosity between the workers and the Camerons, a little friendship can't hurt."

Glen came over to sit on the sofa beside me and to take me in his arms. "You sacrificed a great deal and took an awful risk to help this town. No one will ever be aware of it, but I am, and I have never loved you more than I do right now."

"Ah, then it's all worthwhile and all right with me," I said with a sigh of contentment. "Tomorrow we'll begin the change-over. It will take two months, I'm guessing. Then another two or three months to see that everything goes well. After that, we'll begin planning our trip to Ireland. I'd take Patty along if we could keep from her the real reason for the journey."

"I'm sure we can, Maeve."

"Then she comes, too. It will be good that she sees where some of her ancestors came from. We've much to do now. It's going to be very busy, what's left of 1913."

Next day in the factory office Gabriel Cameron and Helen Easterly signed their names to the agreement transferring sufficient stock to my name that I now had exactly fifty percent. There was no quibbling or argument. They didn't even show any sign of reluctance, which worried me, but once the document was signed, what could they do?

I presumed the following days would be busy ones, but I underestimated that by far. First the old mill machinery, for the most part, had to be removed and room made for the new. While our employees were furloughed with pay, we did ask them to help with some of the work, and they were eager and willing to do this. The inside of the mill was painted, cleaned up, and put into fine condition. Toolmakers came to measure and to consult with us, and the railroad began bringing in supplies and, eventually, the new machines. We purchased a motor truck and kept it busy.

Christmas and New Year's came and went, and we were scarcely aware of it. The winter and the snow slowed us down, but not very much, for it had been planned that during those bad months the inside work would be done.

The Balkan War was still going on, though there didn't seem to be much interest in this country. We were too occupied here to worry about it, anyway. The mill began turning out our first woolens in April and, with the best modern machinery and our skilled workers, the product was of excellent quality.

Our money was almost exhausted, but there was enough left to see us through. We'd begin selling now. The sales force had been reorganized and were already in the field, supervised by Loran. Our old reputation for fine quality assured us heavy orders, and we were on our way.

During this period the Camerons and I got along well. Any arguments were quickly settled. At times I gave in, other times they did. Gabriel and Loran worked very hard. Ashley did little or nothing. I understood that Nora spent a good deal of time in Boston and had wintered part of the season in New York. In June Helen took her to Saratoga, and after a few weeks there they would go to Newport. I prayed more than once that she'd not marry someone urged upon her by the Camerons. She was far too young to think of marriage.

By mid-June Glen and I began talking about our journey to Ireland. I was suddenly homesick after all these years. I thought about seeing my village again, discovering what had happened to the folks I loved so dearly, and walking once more on the sands of Clew Bay.

Late in June a madman assassinated Austria's Archduke Ferdinand and his wife at some place called Sarajevo. Austria promptly blamed Serbia and issued an ultimatum.

"It won't stop with that," Glen said. "This may be what Germany has been waiting for. And perhaps some other countries, as well. I don't like the look of it."

While Glen hated the idea of war, even that far away, Loran and Gabriel Cameron gloated over the prospects. They, too, had followed the course of events over there and were agreed with Glen that this was but the beginning.

"Just as soon as it breaks open," Loran said with ill-concealed happiness over the situation, "we'll begin getting massive orders. If it goes on for six or seven months, this country is going to build up its armed forces and there'll be further need for cloth. Everybody will begin to realize there will certainly be shortages,

366

and they'll start buying. We're in for the greatest wave of prosperity we've ever known."

I should have been happy, too. We'd probably pay off the indebtedness before its due date. We were already financially sound.

Loran sat behind his new desk, twice as large as the old one, in a leather chair with a high back. He touched the tips of his fingers together and looked saintly. Not a usual expression for him.

"You taught us one thing," Loran told me. "We were wrong in dealing with our employees as we used to. Giving them all that time off with pay—"

"They worked hard helping put the mill together again," I reminded them. "After they'd taken it apart and cleaned it. They weren't exactly on an extended vacation."

"We did cancel all debts," Gabriel reminded me.

"What are you getting at, Loran?"

"Very soon now we'll probably have to hire more help, and put our present people on overtime. There won't be many hours for relaxation, so I suggest we hold a picnic. The biggest and most lavish picnic this town has ever seen. Maeve, you can be in charge of buying the food. Only the best—and lots of it. Along with drink, toys for the children . . . everything to make one weekend something they'll remember."

"Why, Loran," I said, "I never thought you had this in you. It's a marvelous idea."

"It's going to be very expensive," Gabriel complained.

"You're right about that," I told him. "This picnic is going to be a banquet. Give me time to organize things, and then we'll post a notice about it. Maybe weekend after next."

"That would be fine," Loran approved. "I'll bring Helen and Deborah back for it."

I left with the warmest feeling for the Cameron clan that I'd ever had. Maybe they were softening. If with the mill, one day, perhaps, with Nora.

Glen didn't think so when I told him about it. "No —this will be costly, but they've learned, thanks to you, that being kind to employees produces more every time. And there may be another reason. I talked on the telephone to the head of a pharmaceutical company while you were gone. Their main office and plant is in Germany, and the man I talked to just came back. He says the shooting will begin within a month, certainly before the summer is out, because they have to have dry ground for cavalry and infantry maneuvers when the war begins. The Camerons may have heard war is this close, and they'll need hard-working men."

"Will it involve us, Glen? Do you think we'll get into it?"

"Not unless things change drastically. It's not our fight as it stands now. But you never can tell what'll happen. All we can do is wait and depend on President Wilson."

"I'm not going to let it interfere with the picnic, and I do think we should make the trip to Ireland as soon as we can. Great heavens, you don't think the war will reach there . . .?"

"Hardly—it's a long way from the Balkans. Maybe they'll confine it to just those little states. I doubt it, but maybe. We can still plan our trip."

First, though, I had to plan the picnic. The town was beginning to change. New houses were being built; some old ones were razed and modern homes erected on the sites. More workers were being brought in; wages were not good, but compared to what they used to be, there was considerable improvement. As the town limits began to extend, it grew beyond the point where the mill owned all the land, and when an independent grocery store sought to go into business at the edge of town where the Camerons couldn't control it, I was not averse to the idea. Soon now the company stores would have competition. I was feeling very well satisfied with myself for my part in this improvement of conditions.

I enlisted the help of several men skilled in carpentry. I provided the lumber, and they created picnic tables which would be set up. I'd not yet selected the spot, though it came about that Loran seemed to have.

"We should make it a permanent park," he suggested. "Tables and benches to be there from now on. With facilities for campfires and outdoor cooking. What about the pond and the old mill? The ground is level there, and the kids can swim if they like. Lots of the old people remember the mill as it once was, with the big wheel churning the water, the long leather belt carrying power to the mill itself. You can't deny there's no better setting."

"No, I admit I can't," I said. "That's where it will be. And the town is as excited about this as it's ever been about anything."

"I'm looking forward to it. So are all of us."

The picnic was scheduled for the first weekend in August. On July 28th Austria-Hungary declared war on Serbia. Three days later, Germany declared war on Russia and invaded Luxemburg almost simultaneously. The next day, Germany declared war on France, and her armies entered neutral Belgium. England promptly declared war on Germany and began mobilizing as France was doing. Other, smaller, countries entered the war, choosing sides like a baseball game, it seemed to me. The whole of Europe appeared to be engulfed in this madness.

It didn't interfere with the plans for the picnic. After all, the war was still far away and not of our concern, except in a business sense. My plans were all made. The women baked pies and cakes, but most of the food was being sent in. I arranged for an ice cream man to bring his truck and freeze his product on the spot. There would be games for the children, baseball for the men. It would begin early Saturday morning and, with time out for church, end Sunday afternoon.

A bar had been set up with enough kegs of beer, I thought, for a small army. We decorated the old mill with bunting, hung more of it from trees, and suspended Japanese lanterns from any place that would let them swing free with their firefly light. We strung wires from the mill and arranged for electric lights, for the festivities were not going to stop at darkness. The town of Cameron might not remember many things in its existence, but this picnic it was going to recall for years. Nobody was going to be neglected.

Friday night before the picnic, Patty came home. The moment she sat down to the supper table I suddenly dropped my fork and it clattered against my plate noisily so that Patty and Glen looked up at me with curiosity filling their eyes.

"I'm sorry," I said. "I guess I'm that tired my fingers can't hang onto a mere fork. Now, let's enjoy our supper. And while we're doing that, Patty can tell us how her marks have been."

"Not if it's going to spoil the meal," Glen said in a good-natured warning.

"Oh, Papa." Patty was indignant. "My marks are very good."

"Of course they are, dear," I said. "Your father's joking."

"I saw Deborah," Patty said.

"In town?" I asked.

"She was driving that noisy little car of hers. Oh, my, is she snooty! I hollered at her and waved, but she didn't even look at me. I felt like throwing a stone at her."

"You get that kind of idea out of your head," I said. "I told you before that Deborah can't help it. That's how she was brought up. It's wrong. You and I know that, but Deborah doesn't."

"She must not be very smart, then," Patty said. "I won't holler at her again, you can bet."

Later, when Patty was off to bed and the house settled down for the night, Glen came to sit beside me in the parlor.

"You were very nervous at supper. Is something wrong?"

"Yes, Glen. It's wrong, and I can't do anything about it. The picnic is going to be held down at the old mill, where the pond is located. Do you recall what the mirror told me? There was a quiet bit of water. The pond is quiet and calm. Patty would somehow be in danger, and Patty is back. I wish now I'd not let her know anything about this. Let her remain at school. But I didn't think. All the excitement and . . . the prophecy was made so long ago."

"Well, if it helps you, now I'm worried, too," Glen admitted. "But let's look at it this way. You saw nothing to really associate Patty with the millpond. Now did you?"

"No, that's true, but it was like the prophecy that foretold how my father would die. Oh, my dear, I'm so tired of living under these threats. These awful predictions."

"Some of them are good. You saw Joel. You saw me and had me married to you before I even knew you existed."

"Aye, thank you for reminding me of that. It wouldn't be so bad if I had Nora. If I wasn't so constantly afraid of the Camerons. They seem to threaten me wherever I am, whatever I do. I fear them terribly. They are capable of anything, and they hate me. Now more than ever, because I've put them partly in their place."

"Have they been giving you any trouble?"

"Very little, and it worries me, because their like usually make all the trouble they can. They've given in too easily, and it seems to me they do this because

371

they believe they'll have their own way soon. I feel that I'm always threatened by them. As if their scheming is always aimed at me, their plans have me in mind and I must be done away with somehow, so they can exist as they once did. Absolute rulers of this town."

"They'll never be able to do that again," Glen told me. "Not a chance of it. As for the prophecy, I'll make certain Patty stays out of any danger."

I took his hand and walked with him upstairs to our room. There I went into the closet to bring out the wrapped mirror. I removed the wrappings and walked over to the bureau light.

"I'm going to look once more," I said. "I don't want to, but I must."

I moved the mirror into the best light and studied its concave surface. Before I could utter my usual supplication to the long-dead queen, the same scene appeared. The quiet body of water, with nothing near it to identify its location. It faded and the profile of Patty came into view, just as it had before. I was about to give up when a second image appeared. Beside Patty, the profile of another girl materialized. She moved slightly and gently placed her cheek against Patty's, just before the image vanished.

"You saw something?" Glen asked.

"Aye. The pond again." I was wrapping the mirror. "Patty again, as well."

"Nothing changed, then?"

"Nora was there, too. I know it was Nora. She and Patty are so alike, but it was Nora. She did a strange thing. She placed her cheek against Patty's."

"What could that mean?"

"It was a gesture of love. If the image of the water had not first appeared, I would have been pleased beyond any measure. Now I do not know what it means. Part of it portends evil, part only the good I have prayed for. That Patty and Nora come to love

372

one another as sisters should. Can you make anything of it?"

"Not me," Glen said. "But I'll not relax my watch over Patty, I can tell you."

The Saturday morning of the picnic was heaven-made for the occasion, bright and clear but not too hot. I was there early, with Patty to help me with the final touches on the decorations. We made certain the food already delivered was of the quality I'd insisted upon and that there was a small mountain of ice in an especially prepared icehouse for use in drinks and to preserve the more perishable foods.

Patty surveyed the scene from the edge of the grounds with the old mill in the distance. "Mama, it's perfect. It's beautiful. Everyone is going to have such a good time."

"See that you do, too," I said. "You've done enough work. When everything gets started, you concentrate on having fun."

"Don't worry, I will. Do you suppose Deborah will unbend enough to come?"

"I believe she will."

"She'd better behave herself and not lift her nose too high in the air. Some of the kids just might not like it and get mad at her."

"See that you don't," I warned her. "That girl needs special consideration. She needs help and kindness, not ridicule."

"All right, Mama, but why doesn't she let us be friendly? Nobody wants to hate her. We just do because she makes us hate her."

"I don't like the word, Patty. Hate is causing a lot of trouble in the world right now. Let's try to forget there is such a thing and see to it that everyone is happy—even Deborah."

"I'll try. I can't speak for the other kids, though. Well, I guess all we need now are people."

373

"They'll be here soon enough. Let's start slicing tomatoes and cucumbers. The bread has to be sliced, too, but not yet."

I put my arm around Patty's slim waist and stood quietly surveying the scene. "Isn't it perfect?" I asked. "In all the years this town has existed, nobody ever gave a picnic, so this one positively must be the biggest and best on earth."

The first arrivals were understandably shy. Nothing like this had ever been done for them before. They were not inclined to trust the Camerons, and some had even doubted the picnic would ever come off. As more and more arrived, everybody scrubbed and nicely dressed, the shyness vanished, and the affair began to grow noisy and fun-filled.

Glen had a few house calls to make, each one accompanied by a picnic basket of food for those patients who were too ill to attend. We weren't overlooking anything if we could help it. Patty joined the young men and women she'd grown up with, and amidst giggles and laughter they exchanged confidences, made plans that would never come into being, and finally gave it all up for a game of basketball.

At late afternoon, just before the food was going to be served, the Camerons arrived. All of them. I was sure Marcy Tabor and Joel's mother were not enjoying themselves, but Loran seemed to be, and even Joel's father moved about talking to some of the men whom he otherwise wouldn't have even glanced at.

Ashley and Helen mixed, though Ashley was that superior no one bothered to talk to him very long, and he eventually drifted off to be by himself. Marcy and Joel's mother sat at a smaller table, especially made for the Cameron family, and fanned themselves energetically. I didn't see Nora, though I looked for her.

Down at the millpond some of the younger children were wading, and a few older ones were showing off their swimming skills. Most of the children played noisy games, and the general attitude was a carefree one throughout the gathering. There had been a brief lull in the excitement at the appearance of the Camerons, but that soon ended and the fun resumed.

Nora finally did arrive, just before everyone lined up for the picnic food. She wore a white silk dress with a pink sash and a wide pink ribbon to keep her hair in order.

"She's a looker," Glen said. He'd joined me moments before.

"So much like Patty. It's surprising no one has ever noticed."

"They are alike," Glen admitted, "but Patty is two years younger and isn't quite the young lady Nora has become, so I doubt the resemblance is that compelling."

"It would be nice if they could become friends," I said, knowing how impossible that was.

"Maybe they will someday. They are sisters; they could be drawn to one another. At least that's my opinion. Come on, let's get something to eat. I'm starved."

We lined up with the others. There was roast turkey, fine roast beef, and ham. There were baked potatoes, yams, cubed turnips. There were salads of varieties these people had never before seen, let alone eaten. And, as I had insisted, the servings were very generous. No one was going to leave the picnic tables hungry.

I had bowed to the authority and standing of the Camerons to see that several girls brought their food to the special table. Glen and I ate with the others, but I kept an eye on the Camerons. Even Marcy was eating heartily, though Nora picked daintily at her food and maintained that terribly aloof attitude which was beginning to infuriate me. I realized why the kids didn't like her, and while she angered me, I also felt sorry for her. To me she was a pathetic, lonely girl in need of a mother's love, while I sat there looking at her, unable to do anything about it.

Patty, meanwhile, was eating with the gusto of a healthy, hungry teenage girl. Eating and jabbering to her friends at the same time. Patty maintained a host of friends, and there wasn't an iota of selfishness or aloofness about her.

During the meal, which lasted two full hours and finished with a variety of sweets and all the ice cream one could eat, the orchestra I'd hired played chamber music. Once the tables were cleared, the Japanese lanterns lit, and the darkness had set in, the music changed to livelier tunes. Few of these people had ever danced, or knew how, but the engaging melodies soon had them paired off and doing their best to the tunes of "Bill Bailey," "Ida," "Sunbonnet Sue," "You Beautiful Doll," and, the most liked of all, the slower waltz time "Moonlight Bay."

Illuminated by the lanterns and a three-quarter moon, it was a sight Cameron had never before seen. I felt great pride in having fashioned such festivity. It was going to help change things in this town.

A few minutes previously, Glen had been called down to the area on the other side of the mill where a boy had fallen out of a tree and been injured. It was apparently nothing very serious. Patty, excited and gloriously happy, came out from the dancing group to join me.

"You looked lonely," she said. "Where's Papa?"

"Oh, you know a doctor never stays put very long. A boy was hurt—not badly, I think—and your father went to bind up his abrasions. Isn't this a wonderful party?"

"I've danced until my feet hurt," she confessed as she sank to the grass beside me. "We should have put up a dance floor. The grass is too slippery for polkas and things."

"Have you seen Deborah anywhere?"

376

"No, she didn't come down off the special place you built for her family. Last I saw, they were getting ready to leave. Old Marcy and old Mrs. Cameron left some time ago."

"Now, you watch out who you refer to as old," I said. "Next thing, you'll be calling me that."

"I didn't mean anything by it," Patty declared placidly. "Just to distinguish between Mrs. Easterly, Deborah's mother, and . . . her grandmother, I guess."

There it was again, the reference to Helen as Nora's mother. I hated it as much as ever, and I was more determined to put a stop to it as soon as I could.

A boy about twelve came running through the crowd, obviously on a mission of importance, and when he saw me, he came straight in my direction.

"The Doctor wants his bag," he was able to say while panting for breath. "He wants you to bring it, Mrs. Kinnery. Right away."

"Thank you," I said. "Where is he?"

"You go down to the mill and cross over the little bridge by the paddle wheel. He's right on the other side. That's what the man told me."

"I'll go, Mama," Patty said. "Is Papa's bag in the car?"

"Yes . . . you fetch it to him. You're quicker than I'd be, and he may need it in a hurry."

She sped away, the boy promptly ran off, and I sat alone, still glorying in the results of my work. It was after eight, and the excitement hadn't subsided. Some were still stuffing themselves with what was left of the food, some were dancing, others lay about too tired or pleasantly lazy to do anything else. They'd talk about this day for the next ten years.

Suddenly I gasped and jumped to my feet. Patty—crossing near the millpond—the prophecy of the mirror! I began to run. People tried to stop me, to tell me how much they were enjoying themselves. I put them off as quickly as I could. I was within a hundred yards

377

of the millpond when I heard someone scream. It wasn't loud, for the slow and creaky turning of the mill paddles drowned it out, but there was fear in that cry, and it was taken up by others. Something had happened.

To reach the other side of the stream it was necessary to cross a narrow bridge that ran directly above the turning paddles. Below them the water was churned white, and the pond wasn't quite as placid, but certainly not approaching anything like water gone wild in a storm.

People were running toward the other side of the pond. I passed the millhouse, left the bridge, and saw a terrifying sight. People were gathered at the edge of the millpond. Some men were removing their shoes, but moving through the thin crowd was Nora in her white silk dress with its immaculate pink sash.

She reached the edge of the pond in a dead run and continued on into the water until she was swimming. I pushed and elbowed my way until I was at the edge of the pond, and I saw Nora swimming back, holding up someone's head above water in the most expert life-saving technique I had ever witnessed.

I knew it was Patty. I waded out into the water, but before it grew deep enough to swim, Nora had brought Patty close enough so I could raise her in my arms.

Nora waded out ahead of us, bedraggled, with none of her finery intact. Patty, in my arms, was beginning to moan and move. On dry land I put her down and asked someone to bring Glen. I unloosened her clothing and made sure she was breathing well and there was likely no water in her lungs. She opened her eyes and screamed briefly from some dark memory.

"It's all right, darling," I said. "You're fine now. There's no need to worry. Everything is all right."

"I . . . I . . . fell in the pond. Mama, he pushed me. . . ."

I drew in a sharp breath. Before Patty could speak again, Glen was at her side making a rapid examination.

"She's not harmed," he said. "You can tell us what happened later, Patty. Right now I want to get you home and out of those clothes. Look after her while I get the car, Maeve. I'll be quick."

He went off at a run. I held Patty's head in my lap. "Don't talk now," I said. "Save your strength. You can tell us all about it when we're home."

Someone beside me said, "Is she all right?"

I looked up at Nora. She was pushing back her wet hair, and she seemed more angry than pleased that she'd saved a life.

"Yes," I said, "she's fine now. Thank you, Deborah. It was a brave thing. You saved Patty's life."

"She should have known better than to fall into the millpond," Nora said, and she turned and walked away.

Patty began to laugh. "Isn't that like her, Mama? She saved my life, and I'm to blame."

"Yes, dear," I said. "But she acted when everyone else only thought about it, and I saw her go into the water without the slightest hesitation."

"Well, why does she have to be so mad about it, Mama?"

"She's not mad, dear. I think she's secretly very proud of herself, as I am of her. But she's too shy to admit it. She would like to, but she can't. That's how she was brought up."

"Well, gosh, she ought to do something about that."

"She will," I said. "And I'm going to help her. Never forget, she undoubtedly saved your life."

"Mama, he just grabbed me—"

"Don't talk about it here," I warned her. "It's important you do not. And here comes your father with the car. Are you in any pain?"

"Only my chin. Gosh, that hurts."

"Well, your father will take care of it. I'll help you up now."

The people who had crowded about gave way, and I assisted Patty to the car as it pulled up. Glen lifted her onto the seat beside him. He looked at me with a question in his eyes.

"I'll be home soon," I said. "There's something here . . . I have to do. . . ."

"I'll wait for you at home, then. Don't worry about Patty."

I nodded and moved away from the car. For the next fifteen minutes I moved through the crowd, looking for one person. I found him watching the dancing, which had resumed. He was seated on the grass, and I dropped down beside the boy who had brought me the message that Glen wanted his medical bag.

"Are you having a good time?" I asked.

"Yes'm, I sure am. It's grand. It surely is."

"Tell me, who asked you to find me and tell me to bring the doctor's medical bag?"

"Deborah's pa."

"You mean Mr. Easterly?"

"Yep. He gave me a dime."

"Thank you," I said. "What's your name?"

"Billy Martin."

"Thank you again, Billy. Now you stay up as late as your folks allow and have all the fun you can."

I walked over to where a few buggies and carriages were tied up, and I asked one man to drive me home. He was eager to oblige and regaled me with compliments about how delightful the picnic had been.

Glen was in his office, gently applying an antiseptic to Patty's chin. I sat down.

Glen said, "Patty, tell your mother what you told me."

"Well, I got the medical bag and I ran down to the millpond and I began to cross the bridge. You know, over the paddle wheel. Mr. Easterly was there. He grabbed me. It was dark, and I didn't recognize him at first. He . . . tried to kiss me, and I kicked him and he hit me and . . . I think he threw me over the bridge. Maybe I fell. Everything got dark. It all happened so fast."

"You're sure it was Ashley Easterly?" I asked.

"Yes, Mama. What's the matter with him? Is he crazy?"

"Perhaps he drank too much. I think you ought to go to your room and lie down for a while, dear. After you rest a bit, you'll feel better, and you can come down again."

"I guess I want to lie down for a little while," she admitted. "It was wonderful the way Deborah saved me, wasn't it?"

"Absolutely wonderful."

"May I thank her later on, Mama?"

"Yes, I think you should. We'll talk about it tomorrow. Come along now."

She had removed her wet clothes and wore a bathrobe, so she was ready for bed when we reached her room. I sat with her for a few minutes until she was drowsy. Then I kissed her and returned to Glen's office, where he sat in thoughts angry enough to show on his usually happy face.

"Do you think she was right about Ashley?" he asked.

"Yes. A boy came to me saying you needed your bag. Patty took it instead. I found the boy later, and he told me Ashley had given him a dime to ask me to fetch the bag. I think Ashley intended to harm me, but Patty went in my place."

"I don't care who he was after. I'm going to break his jaw. He struck Patty a very hard blow. No doubt she was all but unconscious when he threw her into the pond. Maeve, if she'd slipped under those paddle wheels . . . this was an attempt at murder! Do you realize that?"

"I know, Glen. I also know I was to be the victim. I can't say whether Ashley did this on his own— or was inspired to do it by those others. I've had a feeling for some time now that they were biding their time, waiting for a chance to do something drastic. I didn't dream it would be attempted murder."

"That damned idiot tried to kiss her. Did she tell you that?"

"Yes. I think I know what happened. He was waiting for me with the full intention of throwing me into the millrace, under the paddle wheel. I'd surely have been killed. But it was dark and he seized Patty instead, probably identifying the medical bag I was supposed to be carrying. When he found he'd made a mistake, he may have lost his nerve. I don't know what to think about that. But he didn't throw her under the paddle wheels. At least there's that much in his favor."

"There is nothing in his favor. We've enough evidence to send that fool to jail, and he's going there. I refuse to let this pass off as just another incident. It doesn't matter to me how many were involved, or whether Ashley did it entirely on his own. I'm going back to find him."

"We certainly can't sit back and do nothing about it. I'll stay here with Patty."

"Good. I'll enlist the help of everyone in town to find Ashley. If he's fled back to the Hill, I'll go into that mansion after him. I've had enough."

"Just one blessing came of it, darling," I said.

He glared down at me, still fuming in his rage. "Now, what blessing could possibly come of having our daughter nearly murdered?"

"The prophecy of the mirror came true."

Glen's anger subsided rapidly, to be replaced by

a look of awe. "There was the quiet water. There were the two girls, and Nora showed affection toward Patty. Maeve, that thing is uncanny. It's haunted! I had to make myself believe in it, but no more. Oh, no, never again. And it was a blessing, of sorts. I agree."

"Not of sorts, a real one. The prophecy has been fulfilled, and no great harm was done."

"Thank God for that. I'll be back as soon as I can."

I tiptoed upstairs and looked in on Patty. She was sound asleep. I went down to the parlor and sat there to await Glen's return. I didn't know what he'd do if he found Ashley. I hoped there wouldn't be too much violence. An hour went by, and I began to worry. I went out the front door to look down the Main Street for any sign of Glen. What I saw was at least two-score lanterns swinging in the hands of men who were moving rapidly about. They were searching for Ashley. He must have somehow escaped. I didn't know if I was glad or sorry. No doubt Glen had informed the people at the picnic of what had taken place and the affair had ended on the somber search for a man they'd probably be talking about hanging if he was caught.

I returned to the house and put on coffee. When Glen returned I poured two cups and we sat at the kitchen table while Glen described what had taken place since I left the picnic.

"Ashley must have guessed Patty recognized him, so he got away before we knew what had happened. There's no trace of him, but I had word sent out to all neighboring towns to be on the lookout for him. He'll be caught. I almost paid a visit to the Hill, but I was too angry. I might have said more than I should. Tomorrow's another day. We may have Ashley by then and get his story. Heaven help those people if they ordered Ashley to do this thing."

"I'm glad you didn't go there. I don't want Nora

upset about this, and I don't want her to hear the story they'll tell about me if we press too hard."

"I thought of that, too."

"Now I won't rest until Nora knows the truth about me. It will take time, I know, but when she is told, the proof must be there so she will have no doubts whatsoever. I am going to Ireland. I'll write my brother first, and then I'll make the journey. Alone, because you must remain here with Patty just in case what I intend to do meets with failure. Never forget, there's Patty's peace of mind we have to consider, as well as Nora's. Oh, these people on the Hill hold a terrible advantage, darling. They can lie, and we can't prove they are lying. Not yet."

"I agree," he said. "We do have to keep the two girls in mind most of all. Of course, when Ashley is caught, I don't know what will happen. I can't promise he won't tell the whole miserable business."

"That's a chance we have to take. Don't go to the Hill tomorrow, please. Patty wants me to take her there so she can thank Nora again. If we set up a turmoil beforehand, Patty will wonder and ask questions."

Glen brought me to my feet and held me close to him. "I married a clever woman. I love you. I suppose I loved you before I met you, but that's all right, too. Now, what about the mirror?"

"You want me to look into it again?"

"Not unless you believe it will help."

I took his hand. "Come, then. Maybe it'll tell me something pleasant for a change."

Upstairs I made the mirror ready and sat down in the best light. "I have asked many things," I said in a half whisper. "What you have told me has always come true. Tell me now what will happen as I go about obtaining the proof of my innocence of the lies told about me, so that my daughters will never be harmed by these falsehoods. My intention is to go back home, to our Ireland. What will happen? Will I be successful?"

I brought the mirror before my eyes. Somehow I was afraid of what I'd see, but what flashed before my eyes made me gasp in fear. I saw clouds of smoke, flame from guns, men reeling back and dying. I saw war! It didn't fade, it vanished in a twinkling, leaving me stunned.

"Once again," I said to Glen, "there is a prophecy I don't understand. I saw war. Guns firing, men dying. I can only assume that a war will prevent me from finding the truth I seek. The mirror has warned me I will not succeed because of the war."

"And a likely prospect that is," Glen said. "In Europe things are rapidly developing into the greatest war the world has ever known."

"Ireland is not involved. It will not come there. Why can't I go to Ireland as I planned? I will not be near the war itself. Perhaps the mirror meant something else."

"Let me check into it," Glen said. "I'll learn what I can as quickly as possible. First there's Ashley to be accounted for. We've had enough for tonight. Put the mirror away, and let me say now that I will never again disbelieve what it predicts."

"I'm waiting for the day, darling, when I can show the mirror to my two daughters and tell them the history of it. And then let them look into it while I pray they will see only that which is good."

Glen let his practice go next morning while he directed an intensive search for Ashley. He was away when I heard a motorcar arrive. Loran came toward the house. Patty was upstairs. I would have to be careful about what I said and somehow cut off Loran if he began speaking of Nora.

"Good morning," Loran said. "I came to congratulate you on the picnic and to offer the apologies

385

of my family for what happened to your daughter last evening."

"You know it was Ashley who was responsible?"

"Yes, I've been told. Ashley has been acting strangely of late. I don't know what's come over him. I didn't expect anything like this, or I would certainly have seen to it that he was sent away. I am very sorry."

"Do you know where he is?"

"Unfortunately, I do not."

"He will be found, you know."

"I hope so. That is, in a way I do. You see, Ashley might bring up certain matters we have successfully kept quiet these many years."

"You're counting on that, aren't you?" I asked bitterly.

"Ashley is not only a fool, he's a coward. If he's caught, he'll use any means to get off, and that includes the subject to which we have just referred. I don't want that to happen any more than you do."

I granted him a short, sardonic laugh. "Come now, after you've been using it all these years to gain your own ends."

"I mean it. This has gone so far now we'd damage innocent lives. . . ."

"Loran, please stop your pretending. It doesn't work with me. I know that in all likelihood, Ashley did not do this on his own. He was told what to do but, being a stupid man, he made a mistake. I was supposed to cross that footbridge over the millwheel—which someone had caused to turn after all this time—"

"You're mistaking the whole thing, Maeve. Yes, we had the wheel turning. It was a bit of nostalgia for the folks who remembered it when the wheel was the only source of power the mill had."

"The wheel was turning, and it presented an added hazard to anyone who happened to fall—or be pushed—or thrown—into the water from the footbridge.

386

Ashley was there waiting . . . for me. The false message that Glen wanted his medical bag was delivered to me —but Patty took my place, and when Ashley attacked her and discovered his mistake, he had a situation on his hands that he had to deal with. He struck Patty and threw her into the water, but beyond the mill-wheel so, fortunately, she was not killed."

"I don't know what you're talking about," Loran said with none of his customary aplomb ruffled in the least. "We want Ashley found and punished as much as you do. If he shows up at the mansion, we'll turn him in. What he did was unforgivable."

"On all counts," I said. "Patty wishes to thank Deborah in person for her heroism in saving her life. Patty and I will call upon her soon, unless you have objections to that."

"Why should I? Deborah is, actually, a heroine. You can see now that we raised her and educated her properly. When your daughter was in danger of dying, not one of scores of people at the scene had presence of mind enough to rescue her, but Deborah never hesitated. You have to give us credit for that."

"I do not," I said promptly. "She is the kind of person she is, not because of anyone in that house, but because she is the daughter of Joel—and me. That you will never change."

"And you will never accustom yourself to the fact that she will never be yours," Loran said with a deep sigh of resignation. "Too bad. Well, there's nothing I can do about the situation. I'll tell the family to expect your daughter's visit."

I saw him silently to the door. Years ago, even one or two years ago, I would have sobbed my heart out after such a cold-blooded interview with this man, but I'd grown used to his ways now and he had ceased to surprise me or send my spirits plunging downward. I was just as certain I would have Nora back with me as he was that it could never happen. As I had right on my side, I felt I would eventually win and I'd never stop trying.

"It could be dangerous," Glen warned. "If there's a confrontation, something might slip and make the girls suspicious."

"It's a risk I'll willingly take," I said. "The girls must have some sort of good contact so that later on, when we prove the truth even to their satisfaction, they won't be such strangers to one another."

"Yes, you may be right. It's coming to a point where things are going to happen soon, anyway. I wish you luck up there on the Hill. There is a chance they'll be mighty subdued after what Ashley just did."

"I doubt it," I said. "They even take the credit for Nora's heroism. Now, what can be done about an attitude like that?"

"Nothing, I suppose. However, we'll sleep on it. Perhaps things will seem clearer in the morning. Nothing is going to prevent me from resuming the hunt for Ashley. He must be found."

I could only nod agreement. I was tired and upset. I didn't sleep well, and I wished I'd not agreed that Patty could go to the Hill. Yet the promise had been made.

By the time she was out of bed, Glen was already gone, to head up one team that would scour the woods for Ashley. This was Sunday, so the factory whistle didn't draw anyone away from the hunt, and from the way the men turned out it seemed just about everyone was taking part.

Patty made no special attempt to dress for the visit to the Hill. She wore a simple cream-colored dress and a plain hat befitting her age, but she insisted on silk stockings and her best patent-leather shoes.

We attended church first, and then I drove up the long slope to the mansion, which had become such an important part of my life. I disliked that house intensely because of the people who occupied it. And yet there lingered a small portion of love for it because this was where Joel had been born and where he grew up. Joel was my first love, and I adored his memory still, although that in no way interfered with my whole-hearted love for Glen. I did long to return to Ireland, if only to kneel at Joel's grave.

"Why don't you like Deborah?" Patty asked me as I pulled up in front of the mansion.

"What a question!" I said. "I don't dislike Deborah. What on earth made you think I did?"

"Well, you certainly don't like her folks."

"No, I do not. That's something entirely different. Deborah has nothing to do with it."

"I can tell you one thing, Mama. I don't like Deborah's father. Is he out of his mind, do you think?"

"Obviously there was something wrong with him, dear. We'll not go into such matters. All you will do this morning is tell Deborah you're grateful that she saved your life."

"Mama, I was drowning, wasn't I?"

"Yes indeed, you were."

"Deborah's father meant for me to drown, didn't he? That's why he hit me so hard."

"I suppose so. He was afraid you'd tell about the way he stopped you and insulted you. He must have lost his head, or he had been drinking too much at the picnic. We don't know what the answer is. All we do know is that Deborah acted quickly, while everyone else stood around wondering what to do. For that we owe her our fervent thanks."

The now-aging housekeeper opened the door for us, stone-faced as always. As I'd told Loran we would be calling, they were waiting for us. All of them.

"Good morning," I said. "May I present my daughter Patricia? Patty, you may greet Mr. and Mrs.

Cameron, Mr. Loran Cameron, Miss Marcy Tabor, and Mrs. Easterly."

Patty, in the most ladylike manner I'd ever witnessed, curtsied, shook hands, and spoke in a clear, bell-like voice without a trace of shyness. Truly my second-born was grown up, and I'd never been prouder of her.

Moments later Nora entered the room, pale, obviously unnerved, and I knew instinctively we shouldn't have come here.

Patty approached her. "Thank you very much for what you did yesterday," she said in that earnest way of hers when she was dead serious. "You saved my life. And I'm sorry you ruined that pretty dress you were wearing." Some of Patty's girlhood was still there, I thought.

Nora said, "You don't have to thank me. It was my father who threw you into the millpond. You don't owe me anything, and I wish you'd get out of this house and never come back."

Patty stood there in shocked silence. Helen had sense enough to hurry to Nora's side, lead her from the room, and prevent any further outburst. Patty's adulthood now completely dissolved in a flood of tears, and it was my turn to lead her from the house.

It was my fault for not remembering how Nora might feel, since it was the man she believed to be her father who'd been responsible for what happened. Yet, that had been no factor in Nora's act of bravery, for when she went into the pond, she had no way of knowing her father was guilty. And, as for me, I'd not even associated her with Ashley—because he was not her father and I never thought of him as such.

What to do now was beyond my poor ken to judge. Patty's tears subsided, and I comforted her as best I could, but she was not easily consoled.

"I wanted Deborah to be my friend," she said. "She hasn't any friends, and I like her. I thought we could do things together and see one another once in a while. I could have made the other kids like her, too. You said she's not really stuck-up."

"She isn't. I can assure you that, actually, Deborah is a warm, loving girl who would want nothing more than your friendship but . . . if there was any chance of that before, that man destroyed it by what he did. Deborah is now ashamed, and her aloofness will get more pronounced because she's going to use it in self-defense. Don't judge her harshly, Patty. Perhaps in time we can break through to her. We'll keep trying."

Glen was inclined to blame himself for what had happened. "I should have realized how Nora would think. It never occurred to me."

"What of the search for Ashley?"

"He's vanished. It's hard to believe, but that's what happened. Right after we learned what he'd done, men went out in all directions to block any chance of his escape. They even filtered through the forests to stop him. But he's gone."

"On foot?" I asked, incredulously.

"Obviously. No horse is missing, no motorcar stolen—unless he took one of the three up at the Hill."

"All three were there this morning. I saw them in the garage."

"Do you think he could be hiding in the mansion? Or even the garage? The old stables?"

"There's that chance, but I doubt it. If he was found there, and the family had been hiding him, the people of this town would be bound to grow very angry, to the point of losing their heads. And the Camerons are smart enough to know that. The law would come down hard on them, even though they are rich and important."

"You're probably right. As a matter of fact, some of the men slipped up to the hill during the night and searched the garage and stables. Ashley would

391

hardly be hidden in the mansion, so I doubt he's there at all. I've come to the conclusion that he made good his escape, by a stroke of luck perhaps. There is, however, a warrant issued for his arrest, and sooner or later he'll turn up."

"By then the hot-heads will have cooled down," I said, "so it's all for the best. I was afraid there'd be a lynching if they found him last night."

"Not if I could stop it," Glen said stoutly.

"You're one man against many, all of them unwilling to use reason. I feel sorry for Patty. For what she went through because of him, and for what occurred this morning when Nora turned on her."

"We'll keep searching. The men are organized into groups and assigned to areas. Ashley, if he's around here, will have to dig a great big hole to escape now."

But the search for Ashley, over the next three days, proved unproductive. Either he had made a successful run for it, which everyone believed unlikely, or he'd found a remarkably good hiding place.

The excitement died away; the mill was working full-time, and the town resumed its customary calm, quiet way of life. Conditions were better now. Not as good as I wanted them to be, although I had managed to see that wages were raised and I had proved, beyond any doubt, that this had increased production, so the Camerons were satisfied.

We were at loggerheads most of the time during stockholders' meetings. Either side could cancel out the plans of the other, so things got done only by the force of sheer necessity. There was, however, a bright future for the mill. Orders were coming in from traders in foreign markets which could only have originated from warring countries. The promises for more and larger orders were excellent. In Washington there was talk of increasing our armed forces, and that would result in more work. Soon now, dividends would more than equal what they'd been before the slowdown struck us.

Patty went back to school on Monday, as usual. Glen finished his afternoon office visits and because he had been having trouble with his car he decided to drive it to Branborough, the larger town where he'd bought it and where repairs could be made.

That evening he telephoned he'd miss supper and I was not to wait for him and to keep the office closed. The car had been partially dismantled, and he had no idea when they'd put it back together again. He would surely be very late.

"I'll have something when you get back," I told him, "but be sure to have your supper there."

"I will," he said. "Any news about Ashley?"

"Nothing that I've heard."

"Well, I think he's around there somewhere. Keep that pistol I gave you sometime back, handy, and use it if you have to. Ashley may be half-crazed by now."

"I'll be careful," I promised. "I don't think he'd come here. Come home as soon as you can, darling."

I ate my solitary supper and, being alone, my thoughts began to ramble. Into wrong channels, as they often did. Glen's remark about keeping a gun handy had frightened me.

By eight o'clock, with the dishes done and the kitchen cleaned up, my worries grew even greater, and I did remove the loaded pistol from the cabinet near our bed to place it in the large pocket of my apron, where it hung heavily and uncomfortably.

Then I had this inspiration. No one knew where Ashley was hiding, but the mirror might be able to tell me. It was well worth the try. I had to be rid of the potential danger he presented. If I could find him, I could turn him over to men from the town if Glen wasn't back. I hurried to unwrap the mirror.

"I have great trouble and danger," I said. "You will understand that, good Queen Maeve, for your

393

life was full of both. There is a man who threatens me. He is hiding, and I would learn where he is so that I may have him taken and rightfully punished for what he did. If this is not too trivial a request, please show me the way to be rid of this peril."

I waited a full minute and then I looked into the mirror, and I saw a familiar sight. The old millhouse. It was as clear as if pictured on a penny postcard. The image was momentary and vanished, but I had my answer. I put the mirror away in its customary place and untied my apron after removing the cumbersome pistol. I dressed hastily and placed the gun in the handbag I carried.

I made up my mind I would go down to the millhouse quietly and look about for some sign of Ashley's presence, then go get help. I certainly could not explain to the search parties that I knew he was there because a two-thousand-year-old mirror had told me so.

Perhaps I should have waited for Glen, but he had been so uncertain when he'd return. Ashley might take it into his head to leave at any time. Obviously he was hiding until he felt the vigilance of the men had died away before he chanced making a run for it. I would be in no danger, because I'd not go near the man. If, by some ill luck, he found me, I had the gun in my handbag and I knew how to use it.

I walked the length of Main Street, hoping no one would stop me even for a brief chat. The street was quite deserted, so I encountered few people and they went about their business after waving or calling a greeting. It was after nine when I reached the old mill. I had crossed the picnic grounds, well-concealed by darkness. Afoot I made very little sound as I approached.

The old mill had been searched, I knew, but probably no one had climbed among the rafters where the upper part of the drive shaft that ran the mill wheel was located. There was room to hide up there. Possibly other places as well, which a none too careful search had not revealed. I was nearing the short bridge where Ashley had stood waiting for me to cross and where in the darkness, he'd mistaken Patty for me and tried to destroy her.

Then I saw the runabout. The red car, the little car Nora drove about with such grand airs. There was no mistaking it, of course, for there wasn't another car like it in the entire state. Ashley was here, and the girl who believed him to be her father was secretly paying him a visit. I sank to the ground behind a large oak where I could watch the door while I wondered what on earth I would do now.

I couldn't bring the men while Nora was there. Trouble might begin, and she could be hurt. I could do nothing but wait.

I have no idea how much time elapsed. Perhaps it was half an hour or half a minute. Then something moved down near the mill. I came to my feet quickly. A figure emerged and headed toward the runabout. It was hard to identify who it was. I took several steps forward. I must have made a noise, for the figure came to an abrupt halt.

"Debbie," Ashley's voice whispered hoarsely, "is that you?"

I brought the gun from my handbag and I walked right into the open. Ashley, while he couldn't make me out any better than I could see him, did become alarmed. He got into the runabout. The motor started. I leveled the gun as the car began to move. He would pass within thirty or forty feet of where I stood. I could stop him now. The car hadn't gained enough speed to make the target difficult. My finger rested hard on the trigger; the hammer was back. A little more pressure now . . .

The car was closer and beginning to move faster. I followed it with the gun, but then I gave a bitter cry and lowered the weapon. How could I shoot a man? Even one such as this. I shook my head to clear my wits and turned away—to find Nora standing ten feet behind me.

"Nora!" I gasped, without thinking.

"Is that my name?" she asked in the coldest voice I had ever heard from the throat of a lovely girl.

"What are you doing here?" I asked, roughly, to cover my own astonishment.

"Let me ask the questions, please. Why didn't you shoot him?"

"I couldn't. I . . . couldn't."

"You're lying. He was driving away too fast, and you knew you couldn't hit him."

"If that is what you wish to think."

"Are you going to spread the alarm?"

"Not if you gave him permission to take your car."

"What has that to do with it?"

"Everything. You have committed a crime. I do not wish you involved in this."

"Why not?"

I didn't know what she was leading up to, though I should have. All I could keep in mind was the fact that I was facing my daughter and above all else I wanted to take her in my arms. Yet I had to stand here like a ninny, holding a pistol in one hand, even if it was held down at my side. I thrust the gun into my handbag.

"You helped your father escape. I can't hold that against you, even though others would."

She stepped closer. Her features were impassive, her eyes gone dead. "He is not my father."

I exhaled slowly. So the truth was out at last. I should have realized it when she challenged my use of her real name.

"He told me that you are my mother," she went on.

"Yes, I am your mother. There is no point in

denying that now." I was numb and filled with fear. I knew she was not going to accept me.

"Who was my father? Or shouldn't I ask that of a woman like you?"

I felt as if I'd been slapped across the face. "What are you saying? Your father was Joel Cameron. He was a lovely, fine man I adored with all the love I had."

"Are you sure Joel Cameron was really my father?"

I nodded slowly. "I understand now. Did he tell you that? The man you believed was your father all these years?"

"He said I had a right to know."

"Yes, you did have. If it was the truth. He lied."

"If I asked my grandfather and grandmother; if I asked Loran and Aunt Marcy; if I asked Helen, who has been my mother—would they, too, lie?"

"Every last one of them," I said.

"Would the man in Ireland have lied? Or the man you carried on with in public during a dance? Or all the other shameful things you have done?"

"I am going to tell you, in as few words as possible, what is the truth."

"I will not listen. You can't make me."

She was turning away when I seized her by both arms and held her fast.

"You are the daughter of Joel Cameron and me, Maeve O'Hanlon. The people who raised you took you from me by threatening to make public all these lies because your father had willed to me his share in the mill and I would not give it back to them. Everything they say is lies. I will prove that one day . . ."

"If there was any proof, you'd have come up with it long before now. You're the liar. I am not your daughter. Helen is my mother. Ashley is my father. I will not have it any other way. I despise you with so much hatred I could take that gun from you and kill you."

I let go of her. I opened the handbag and took out the gun. I held it toward her. She stepped away, looking at the gun, then up at me.

"You're not worth it," she said. "No whore is worth it. I never want to see you again as long as I live. I will never consider you as my mother. Never!"

"Nora," I let the gun fall to the ground. "Nora, please—"

"If you try to make me accept you as my mother, I'll kill myself!"

"Very well, Deborah," I said, as evenly as I could. "I give you my word I will not interfere with you in any way. Until I have the proof I seek. Then I will present it to you, and you will either acknowledge how wrong you are, or continue to be the silly, foolish, headstrong girl they have made you. I owe you but one thing. Your sister's life. You saved Patty. She does not know you are her half-sister, and she will not know until you are willing to acknowledge her as such. I think that's all I have to say."

I turned around, walked several steps, recalled the gun on the ground, and went back for it. Nora had disappeared into the night. I placed the gun in my handbag and walked home, slowly, holding back my rage against those who had poisoned my daughter's mind with their vicious lies. I didn't weep. I was beyond that stage.

When Glen returned, just before midnight, I told him what had happened, leaving nothing out.

"I have a feeling she isn't going to tell the Camerons what happened," I said. "She's going back to them, and she wants things to be as they were before. I believe Ashley took it upon himself to tell her because he was angry with us, with the town, and especially with the family he married into. He was trying to make all the trouble possible."

"We could easily have him arrested if he's still

using that car. He's as conspicuous in it as if he was riding an elephant."

"Please don't," I said. "What does it matter now if he escapes? He's wrecked his own life. There'll be no coming back for him. Let him go."

"As you wish, my dear. And what are your plans? I know you better than to believe you're going to let this go by without a fight."

"I haven't changed them. In the spring I intend to go to Ireland. I'll get the evidence I need, and then I'll present it to Nora. What she does then is up to her. If she still feels the way she does now, then I can do no more. Oh, Glen, it will break my heart."

I was apprehensive next day when I entered the mill office for a regular business conference. Neither Loran nor Gabriel showed any indication that they knew Nora had been told the truth. As I'd guessed, she'd said nothing about our encounter. I wondered how they were going to explain the absence of her red motorcar. Eventually they'd have to say something about it.

The meeting was brief. Things were going along so well there was no need to argue about matters. The latest report showed the orders were stockpiling faster than we could produce and more were coming in. We talked a little about expansion, but I objected because much of our work was brought on by war, and wars do end, usually with a great slump.

"It is better," I said, "to be satisfied with less now than lose everything in the future. I will vote no expansion, though I will not object to the installation of more machines if there is room for them now. And I will agree to more help. The most important matter—and I insist upon it—is steadily adding to the fund which will enable me to repay the personal loan I contracted."

I was tempted to leave for Ireland at once, as I'd originally planned in the heat of anger, but on second thought it would be best if Nora had a chance to cool off. Also, a voyage across the Atlantic in winter storms, while not dangerous, was certainly not pleasant. Jimmy, too, had written for me to postpone my trip until things settled down some. The war was still spreading. There was talk of submarine warfare, something quite alien to me, but Glen knew about it for what it could be, and he agreed with Jimmy.

"Germany has defeated Russia already," he said. "They're pushing right up to Paris, but they have to conquer England if they hope for any sort of success. To do that they have to invade, which is not likely because it's too hazardous and uncertain, so my guess is that they'll try to starve England into submission and the only way to do that is by submarine blockade."

I said, in mild protest, revealing my own abysmal ignorance of matters of war, "But our ships could bring food and supplies."

"My dear, the Germans won't care whose ships they torpedo, or how many neutrals die in the sinkings. They've already coined a phrase for it— unrestricted U-boat warfare."

It sounded fantastic and scarcely worthy of belief to me until May, when the news came that the *Lusitania* had been sunk with the loss of more than a thousand lives. My trip to Ireland would be impossible until the war was over.

"Such a waste," I said to Glen. "Such senselessness in the taking of so many human lives, of people who were certainly no threat to the Germans."

"The ship itself was, and there's talk of cargo the Germans insist would be carried to and from British ports. Who knows what anyone thinks during these wars?"

"Will we be into it soon, do you think?" I asked.

"It's hard to say. Almost anything can bring us in. Even a bayonet in the hands of some stupid German soldier could be used in a manner that would be the

400

turning point. My guess, however, is that the U-boats will start sinking too many of our ships and taking too many American lives. Then we'll have to get in."

I looked up from my sewing with a sudden start of fear. "I never thought of this before. Glen, will you have to go?"

"I don't know. Not at first, I'm sure. Not at my age, though doctors are going to be in demand. Still, some of us will have to stay home and tend to the sick among the workers who keep the troops supplied. One is as vital as the other. It would be anybody's guess what will happen to me, though I would suggest... nothing very much."

"There's no word of Ashley?" I asked, in an effort to change the conversation.

"Nothing, but unless he abandoned the runabout, he's going to be caught. Even if he does, I think they'll find him. After that there'll be the question of what to do with the man."

"I hope he's never found," I said.

"One thing I have to tell you. This morning Helen and Nora left on the morning train, and the afternoon train carried out a big load of their baggage. I snooped enough to find out it was being shipped to Philadelphia —no address, but to be called for."

"That means they're going to stay, but they don't know where. It suggests to me that Nora wanted to get away and contrived some excuse. I'm at a total loss what I can do about that girl, Glen."

"If you do anything now, you may alienate her forever," Glen warned. "You have to rely on one thing—and a significant and important matter it is. Nora is your daughter and Joel's. The characters of you both are bred into her and they exist, but for the present they're dominated by what the Camerons have told her. And the manner in which they raised her. Bide your time, darling Maeve. It's all on your side."

"If only I could fully believe that, it would sustain

me, Glen. I've had too many disappointments. When she told me she knew who I was, she was so hate-filled I felt like someone dragged through mud."

"Imagine how she's going to feel when she learns her hatred was based solely on a pack of lies."

"I dread that, too. Almost as much as her hatred. But I do have Patty, and she is such a comfort to me. I'm sorry I was unable to give you more children, darling."

He looked at me with a smile. "Good heavens, we've enough trouble between the two of these. And speaking of children, here's something I'll bet neither you nor the Camerons have thought about. If we get into the war, many of the millhands are going to volunteer, and others may be drafted. The mill can operate efficiently with older men working longer hours, and the government boards are going to know this, so the younger fellows are going to find themselves in uniform. It would be best to prepare for it."

"We haven't thought of it," I confessed. "I'll bring it up at the next meeting. We're holding them every week now, instead of once a month, because of the pressure of business."

"What of the loan you insured with the torc? It might be well to settle that before the war begins to regulate and mix up all sorts of financial transactions. I don't say it will, but the franc and the pound aren't precisely free."

"In another two or three months I shall be able to reclaim the torc. We've also been paying on the bank loan. The mill is in excellent condition financially."

"At least you don't have to worry about that. You're doing a good job, darling. In fact, you're better at business than I."

"Being good at business doesn't allow me to set bones or remove an appendix. In my estimation, that's far more important."

Over the next few weeks we could feel the pressure

growing. There was war talk everywhere; the newspapers were full of it, and at the movie houses the news films were showing some of the heroics—and the horrors. We were becoming acutely aware that we were living in a world where changes were coming so swiftly we were ill-equipped to cope with them.

It was a month after Ashley had disappeared when we heard about him again. The search had died off except for the wanted notices that many police departments had posted. Loran, soon after Ashley had vanished, informed the State Police that Ashley had apparently stolen Nora's red runabout. I had an idea that he had done so only after he'd heard from Ashley secretly and could afford to divulge this information because it would no longer be effective in Ashley's apprehension.

I was positive of this at the board meeting when Loran began the proceedings with an unbusinesslike statement.

"I am quite proud," he said, "to announce to you, Maeve, that Ashley fled to Canada and for some time now has been enlisted in the British Navy as a volunteer. He was an expert boatsman and this experience will be of benefit to him."

"May I ask what you intend to do about this information?" Mrs. Cameron demanded. Joel's mother had been taking an increasingly passive role in the board meetings, but asking me this question, she was belligerent.

"It would be possible, I'm sure," I said, "to have Ashley arrested by the Canadian authorities. However, since he is fighting in this war, even if only to avoid being arrested and tried, I am not inclined to prosecute him. I hope that he will serve with honor."

"That," Marcy Tabor said sarcastically, "is extremely kind of you."

"Yes," I said, "isn't it? But I take into consideration the fact that I doubt very much Ashley instituted the

403

attack on his own. And you may construe what you wish from that statement. Now, shall we begin this meeting before we grow too angry to conduct it?"

We were making a great deal of money, but they were never satisfied. Invariably our weekly board meetings ended in arguments that the men were paid too much, that they didn't work hard enough, or long enough, and the company stores were not charging sufficient to show more than a niggardly profit.

My repeated suggestions that the families be allowed to apply this so-called rent toward the purchase of their homes rolled off the various Cameron backs as considered insults to their intelligence. They refused to heed the warnings that if an election were held today, the union would come in tomorrow and, unless there were raises and benefits, we would be unionized soon. Laws had now been passed to make this easily possible. Yet the Camerons held out and my dismay grew greater.

Then, early in 1914, I entered the board room for a meeting to find everyone oddly subdued.

"We have grave news," Loran announced. "Ashley Easterly's destroyer was attacked by a submarine, torpedoed, and sunk with the loss of all hands. Ashley died a hero. Whatever he did in the past has now been wiped clean."

The war had come home to us!

FIFTEEN

Violence and war seemed to be everywhere around us. There was trouble in Haiti, and we landed marines. In Mexico a man named Villa, designated a bandit, was being pursued by our soldiers. We landed more marines in the Dominican Republic. A great civil war raged in China, and what saddened me most was the news of an Irish rebellion, put down with the result of executions of Irish leaders. In 1917, there was a gigantic revolution in Russia, and in April we declared war on Germany.

These hectic times had passed peacefully enough in Cameron. The town had prospered. The workers had been granted raises and privileges that rankled the Camerons but pleased me. So far the union had not been able to make any headway. Every time they seemed about to, the Camerons were wise enough to surrender something more to keep the workers satisfied.

Whatever my plans had been before this storm of violence came into being, they were still in abeyance. My brother Jimmy had written that he'd been unable to do anything to prove my innocence for, just as he was about to undertake the problem, he'd been ordered into the British Army and was now serving in France. I hadn't heard from him in many months, though, as Glen pointed out in his calm and quieting way, Jimmy never was one for letter writing, anyway.

Patty was now nineteen, graduating from a private

school in Boston and contemplating entering nursing school so she'd be of some value in the war effort. I heard little of Nora. The Camerons made it a point never to mention her name, though some little news did filter back to us that she had entered a business college, an idea that surprised me. But not Glen.

"Why not? Men haven't a monopoly on business. Look at the success you've made of it. And you must remember that the Camerons are completely devoted to the idea of perpetuating their ownership of this mill. Nora is the only descendant of their children, the only person in line to inherit both family name and the mill. She may have to give up the name some day, but not the mill. And she'd better know how to run it."

"They'd hardly dare to bring her back here now, while I'm on the board."

"That family would dare anything to maintain their hold on the town and the factory. What will you do if Nora comes back and they give her an executive position?"

"What can I do? I'll face it, though I'm not worried, because it won't happen."

"You've forgotten one thing, darling," Glen said. "The Camerons don't know that Nora is aware you are her mother."

"I'm not going to concern myself about it. If they bring her in, I can't do anything, so I'll accept it."

The Camerons, in my opinion, had grown over-confident concerning the attitude between the workers and management. They were now sure the family was not only respected, but actually loved. Why wouldn't they be? That's how they'd argue the point. Hadn't they granted all kinds of concessions, made the workers happier, given them four times the pay they used to get? Everything was better.

Marcy Tabor died late in the summer of 1917. Glen had been called in the middle of the night, but she was dead by the time he arrived, and there had

406

ensued a stormy scene between Glen and the family, for Glen had learned she'd complained of heart pains two entire days before she lapsed into unconsciousness and yet he had not been called.

"They are so damned superior they don't even recognize death," he grumbled. "I might have saved her. We do have methods to help heart attack victims if we reach them in time. Two days! Imagine that! Two whole days they let her suffer and didn't get scared until she became comatose."

"It's over," I said. "It was not of your doing. They are what they are."

Very unexpectedly I was involved. I was called to the Board Room, and there a brief meeting was held where a formal announcement of Marcy's death was to be made and posted on the factory bulletin board. The funeral was to be held the following morning.

"I want the mill closed for the day," Loran said. "I want—"

"Mr. Cameron," I said, "you can't close the mill. The War Labor Board won't permit it. We're at war!"

Loran's enthusiasm subsided somewhat. I wasn't certain if what I'd said was true, but I wanted to save the family an embarrassment.

"Well," he said, "we will close down for three hours at the time of the funeral. They can't object to that. If they do, we'll work three overtime hours to make up for it."

Joel's mother, as haughty as ever even in the sorrow of her sister's death, asked the question I hoped nobody would come up with.

"Do you think they'll turn out for the funeral, Mrs. Kinnery?"

"I don't know," I said. And really I didn't know, but I had my suspicions.

"I'm sure they will. Marcy was associated with the mill and the town most of her lifetime. Marcy's memory will be respected," Mrs. Cameron declared.

"I'm convinced of it," Gabriel Cameron added.

"Will you be present?" Loran asked me, practically in the way of a demand.

"Yes," I said. Nora might come back for the funeral . . . and it had been a long time since I'd last seen her.

The notice was posted on the bulletin board. While no one uttered a word of condemnation of the dead woman, no one expressed any sympathy, either. I couldn't tell whether they'd attend the funeral mass and the graveside ritual.

The whole town seemed tense next morning. The men reported for work as usual. The hour was seven. At ten the power would be shut off and the mill would close down for three hours.

Glen and I drove down empty streets. When we entered the church we were the only ones there.

"Nobody's coming," Glen said. "I told you that last night. I think of all that clan on the Hill, Marcy was disliked the most. These people are not inclined to turn out to say goodbye to someone they didn't care for."

"I wish they would come. There's no telling what the Camerons will do if they get angry enough, and this is going to infuriate them."

"You lived up there for a year. If you were not on the board of directors, would you be here?"

"No, I would not."

"If you worked in the mill for years, would you attend?"

"I'm sure I wouldn't."

"They won't come," he repeated. "And they won't care a hoot what their bosses think. Including you."

We sat well up front. When the family entered, following the casket, they seemed to deliberately seat themselves on the other side of the aisle. But Nora was there. For more than two years I'd not seen her. She walked down the aisle well behind the family, and

408

I had a surprise that shocked me so that I drew in a startled breath that Glen heard. He turned his head and saw what I had seen. Nora, tall, an attractive girl even dressed in somber black, walked with Patty. We'd sent Patty word by telephone, but I'd not expected her to come home. And above all things, not in the company of Nora.

Glen bent so his lips were close to my ear. "You might say, peas in a pod."

It was true. As they came opposite us the resemblance was startling; they could have been twins; the only significant difference was in the color of their hair. I thought Patty seemed the more relaxed and far less haughty, but attitudes had nothing to do with it.

"If they ever stand side by side gazing into a mirror," I whispered, "they're going to wonder."

"Nora won't," Glen said.

"If she's told Patty . . ."

Patty left Nora's side and came to join us. She sat beside me and reached out her hand to grasp mine. We didn't speak, for the services were to begin. Not one person from town was in the church. Across the aisle the Camerons, except for Nora, looked angry. Perhaps she didn't understand the situation.

After the services the procession to the cemetery began. Glen, Patty, and I were the last in the two-car cortege. It rolled slowly along the street though what looked like a ghost town. The stores were closed, all doors were shut, and many window curtains had been drawn.

"What's the matter with everybody?" Patty asked.

"Well, dear," Glen said, "you didn't really know Marcy Tabor, but the townspeople did. They didn't like her, and apparently they chose not to go to her funeral."

"That's just silly," Patty said. "She can't hurt them now."

"That's true."

"Anyway, I'm glad you and Papa went."

"You came in with Deborah," I said. "How did that happen?"

"Oh—we met on the train. I decided to come home, and when I got on the train she and her mother were in the same car, so naturally I said hello and Deborah said hello and we began talking about things."

"What things?" Glen asked.

"All sorts of things. Mostly the war."

So Nora hadn't informed Patty they were half-sisters. I wasn't certain whether I was sorry or pleased.

At the graveside Nora moved away from her family, or those she accepted as her family, and Patty moved away from us—as if these two young people felt they had a need to be together at this moment of sadness. I didn't know how the others felt, but to me it seemed beautiful. Quite suddenly Nora began to weep, and Patty's arms enfolded her, and I brushed away tears that were not caused by my mourning Marcy Tabor, who was being lowered into her resting place.

Loran nodded curtly to Glen and me. Joel's parents never so much as acknowledged our presence. Helen, who had not been in church, had joined us at the cemetery. She seemed upset over the way Patty and Nora had been drawn to one another, and as we all turned away, Helen went to Nora's side and whispered to her. Nora obediently went away with her, but she did turn to look back and offer a wan smile. Patty waved before she dropped her arm and walked over to intercept us.

"I guess she liked Marcy," Patty said.

"I hope so, dear. Will you see her again?"

"I don't think so. Her family probably won't let her see anybody. She finished some kind of business school, and I think she's going into the mill office."

"Then I'll likely see her from time to time," I said.

"I guess so, Mama. If you do, please tell her if she

410

wants to see me any time at all, I'll be glad to meet her. I like Deborah."

"I thought you considered her stuck-up," Glen said.

"I used to, but she's not stuck-up any more. Maybe on the outside she'll act like she is, but . . . well, I just like her, that's all. We could be very good friends."

I drew an arm around Patty and squeezed her shoulders before we stepped into the car. "I'm glad. Friends are precious. I'll tell her."

Nora didn't enter the office, but returned to school instead, accompanied by Helen, who had never come near me. I was grateful that Nora had not informed anyone on the Hill that she knew her true identity. I wasn't ready for that under the present circumstances, and I was certain Patty couldn't possibly be.

Patty also returned to finish school and from there went immediately into nursing school in Boston. Jennie saw her often and relayed news of her, for Patty became too busy to write.

At the mill everything went smoothly. The war was the cause of it, to be sure, but we were now on a steady basis, the reputation of the mill's products well enhanced, and we felt that even after the war we had a fine opportunity to continue our success— possibly to branch out into the production of other products, now impossible because of the conflict.

And the war was roaring in full frenzy of guns and the dead and wounded. The new mechanical monsters called tanks came into being; airplanes turned into formidable weapons of attack and defense. Fortunes shifted from one side to the other, but the Allies were slowly gaining the upper hand, and there was speculation about a supreme drive to break the Hindenburg Line soon.

Glen had not been called up because of his age and the fact that his skills were essential to the civilian population that produced the goods needed to fight the war. He had become increasingly busy, for younger

411

doctors had been taken, and Glen was required to extend his practice to two neighboring towns. There were weeks when I saw him for only a few minutes a day. I kept busy with Red Cross work and with writing letters for some of the townspeople who had difficulty in constructing a letter, so their sons abroad would be kept up to date on family affairs. Everything was upset by the war, of course. Prices were sky-high, and shortages had become familiar to us. We had "victory gardens" growing in profusion, and I even tended one, with reasonably good results, in our backyard.

In early summer, after school graduations, I heard that Nora had been given an office at the mill and was living once again on the Hill. At the next board meeting she quietly joined the group at the table. I tried not to look at her too frequently, but when her eyes met mine briefly, expressionlessly, I felt a flicker of the old pain. Still, Nora and I had at least this contact now.

After the formalities were over, Loran announced, "I can see the end of the war coming soon. We should be prepared for the changeover from war to peace. Deborah has been preparing a campaign to be undertaken by an enlarged sales force to sell our products in as great a quantity as we do now, or better than that. And I'm proud to report that Deborah is one of the first young ladies to enter business fields on an executive basis. We have placed her in charge of sales. I'm sure you have no objection, Mrs. Kinnery?"

"No objection," I said with a smile. "I think Deborah will perform in a manner to give us all cause for pride."

Deborah didn't comment or even glance my way. The meeting ended soon afterwards, and I left without approaching her. I wanted her to know that I was not interfering with her life in any way.

She, however, caught up with me along one of the long halls down which I walked.

"I have learned that your generosity actually saved the mill from bankruptcy," she said. "I'm indebted to you for that, but I still wish to have nothing to do with you."

"As you wish," I said. "I'm sorry we have to be in contact like this, but there is no avoiding it without telling these people the truth, and you have indicated you do not wish that."

"I haven't changed my mind."

"Very well, but you don't have to be so cold, my dear. I'm playing this awful game your way. I always have."

"Because you had no other choice," she said tartly.

"We have just terminated that phase of the discussion. Patty asked me some time back to give you a message if we met. She likes you and wants you as a friend. That's very fine. I approve with all my heart. However, if you intend to hurt me—and Patty—by telling her one day what your true relationship to her happens to be, I'll not forgive you. Please understand that."

"How could I tell her without destroying everything? Without hurting Helen and the others?"

"I'm glad you realize that. When I'm prepared to announce the truth, I'll do it, under my conditions. They're simple enough. When that time comes, I'll have the proof that I've been maligned and lied about, so that even you will believe me."

"Good afternoon," she said curtly, and marched off. My daughter! Joel would not have been proud of her today.

As if she wasn't content with that abrupt and chilly parting of the ways, she telephoned me not long after I returned home.

"I neglected to inform you, Mrs. Kinnery, that your daughter and I have exchanged letters and we intend to write often. So there is no need for you to act as a messenger, for I know the only reason you do this is

413

because you wish to see me. And I shall pray that Patty will never turn out as you did."

Beyond speaking a greeting into the phone, I had no chance to say another word. I hung up slowly, close to tears.

Not until the war ended and the passage to Ireland was safe could I go there and confront Cathal Dolan. It had occurred to me that he might have been lost in the war, but I didn't think so. Cathal would never have served in the British Army, nor in any other. He would be planting and harvesting his barley, shearing his sheep, and cleaning the mud from his boots from time to time. He was a man not even a World War would change.

I was that concerned and confused, however, that I considered asking help from Queen Maeve's ancient mirror. I confided this to Glen that night after telling him the unsatisfying events of the day.

"I don't see why you can't use it more often," he said. "While it's still hard for me to believe in the thing, it hasn't failed you yet."

"Ah, my dear," I said, "it is not to be used indiscriminately. It is no ouija board, or pack of fortune telling cards. It has a power to be drawn upon when necessary, true, but not on whim alone."

"In that case, I'd say you need its advice now."

I went upstairs to fetch it. Glen sat beside me after arranging a table lamp with a bright bulb behind the sofa. I unwrapped the mirror and made my plea.

"During my lifetime, whenever I have consulted your mirror, I have been told the truth without fail. Now I am once more in need of knowing what is to be. Tell me then, what next in my life I should look for."

I brought the mirror before my eyes. An image was there, fleetingly. It was clear when I first looked, and vanished in the space of a second or two, as it some-

414

times did. What I saw made me shudder and close my eyes tightly.

"What is it, Maeve?" Glen asked anxiously.

I rewrapped the mirror carefully. "For the first time ever, I saw myself. Only my head, but it lay back; my eyes were closed, and I seemed to be deathly ill. I do not think I was dead. Would the mirror show me that? Yes—I suppose it would. Yet I have a feeling I was not dead."

Glen said, "In the morning, first thing, I'm going to put you through a physical examination such as you've never had before. And from now on, I'll be checking your health every day without fail. That mirror may accurately foretell things, but this time I'm going to give it a real battle."

"My peace of mind is not the best," I said, "though I know you will help me. Yet, physically, I don't think I've ever felt better in all my life."

"You're not to be worrying yourself ill over that ungrateful Nora Cameron, either," Glen warned.

I moved closer to my husband and rested my head on his shoulder, content once more in knowing I could draw upon his strength and his skill.

"Darling," I said, "I do not worry about Nora. Perhaps I once did, because of what they were turning her into. They've succeeded to some extent, but not completely. She's a girl with much common sense— though it's somewhat clouded by her hatred of me. She has a mind of her own, and she has ability. Nora is a girl I shall never have need to worry about, and when I am able to furnish her with all the evidence I need to prove those people on the Hill lied, she will accept that, too, and become my daughter finally. I have never been more certain of anything in my life."

Glen examined me next morning, thoroughly, as he'd promised. I was in sound health so far as he was able to determine. My work with the Red Cross and the little I had to do with the mill kept me so busy

415

that gradually the vivid memory of what I'd seen in the mirror had softened and finally been all but forgotten. It came back to me sometimes in the night silence, yet I was able to shake off any feeling of doom.

Patty wrote regularly and often said she'd heard from Nora, though what the two girls had to write about were secrets shared only by them. I was gratified by this growing closeness. With Patty it was a natural thing, for she was, by the very nature of the girl, friendly and warm. Nora, on the other hand, had been cold and scornful of friendships with those not on her exalted social level. She knew Patty was her half-sister and was drawn to her because of this. That was true, as I saw it, but this also made Nora's inherited warmth and compassion evident. I longed for the day when they could openly admit to being sisters.

The Fourth of July that year was not celebrated in the town of Cameron with fireworks and a parade as had been customary. Flags were flown, and there was a band concert in the little newly created park, but it was not well attended. Too many local names had been on the casualty lists, and too many young men were fighting their way across Europe. Nobody felt like celebrating anything, not even the birthday of their nation.

The next morning I was quite surprised to receive a telephone call from Nora.

"I believe we have some urgent factory business to discuss," she said. "Uncle Loran and grandfather have asked me to take up the matter with you."

"I'm available whenever you wish," I said, mystified.

"I suggest we meet this evening for supper at the inn. Would that be satisfactory to you, Mrs. Kinnery?"

"If that's what you wish, of course. About seven?"

"That will be fine. I will make the arrangements. Thank you."

She hung up. At noon Glen returned from making

house calls, and while we ate our noonday meal I told him about the telephone call.

"She actually asked you to dine with her at the inn? Just the two of you?"

"That's what she said."

"There's trouble brewing," he warned. "There has to be. I can't for the life of me see Loran letting that girl take over any important matter to be discussed between you two alone. Besides, how does he know you won't tell the girl you're her mother?"

"I'm sure he believes there's no possibility of that. Loran made up his mind long ago that I'd never get her back. As for discussing business, she did study at a business school. Did you know she was one of two females in a class of three hundred students that year? She's highly competent, and Loran knows it."

"What's there to discuss in private? That's unusual, too, isn't it?"

"I don't know. Perhaps Nora wants to try her wings. They may have one of their little propositions for me to agree to that will deprive the workers of something and line the Camerons' pockets with more gold."

"They've been dwelling on such matters?" he asked. "With a war on?"

"Their ideas are for the future, when there's no War Labor Board to clamp down on them. No, they wouldn't dare change things now, because they are sure I'd not stand for it and, positively, the government would not."

"What of afterwards? When the men come home? The mill is running short-handed now, but once everybody is back, there'll be too many for too few jobs. What then?"

"We'll have work for everyone if they listen to me. That's one reason I want to talk to Nora. She does have sense, and she's been educated in modern business methods, so she'll see the idiocy in cutting wages and adding working hours."

"Is that what they want to do?"

"Only a part of it. They want to raise prices as soon as they legally can, raise rents, too. But these company towns and company stores are things of the past. The Camerons can't get that through their heads. They'll be asking for labor trouble, and they'll get it. Oh, my, they'll get more than they can handle."

"It might be a wise move to talk to Nora then—unless her head is already armor-plated with Cameron pig-iron."

When I entered the dining room at seven, Nora was already there, seated at a table in one of the far corners, obviously at her request.

She was, indeed, a daughter to be proud of. Somehow that haughtiness seemed to enhance her quiet beauty.

"Good evening," she said, with somewhat less coolness than usual, perhaps for the benefit of the elderly waiter who drew out a chair for me.

"Hello, Deborah," I responded. I couldn't be angry with this girl.

"We'll order at once if you don't mind, Mrs. Kinnery," she said.

"Fine. It isn't hard to order a restaurant meal these days. What's on the menu, Walter?"

"Baked chicken and fish," Walter said. "No beef. Ain't been any beef in two weeks now, and I forget what bacon tastes like. The coffee ain't much, either, but I guess you know that."

"I'll have the chicken," Nora said. "And red wine."

"Make mine the same except the wine—mine to be white. The usual kind, Walter."

"I remember," he said with a smile. "We got a few bottles left. I got orders to pour it in the kitchen so nobody can see it comes from Germany. First time I ever knew we were having a war with Moselle wine."

He tottered off on legs long made weak by his years

418

of service in this restaurant. I turned my attention back to my daughter.

"I think we can begin our discussion now," I said.

"Whatever is personal between us," she said, in a thoroughly businesslike way, "has nothing to do with what we must discuss. Is that agreed?"

"Naturally," I said.

"I'm glad we do understand one another. Now—while I do not especially believe in this, I feel that what grandfather, Loran, and my mother wish, I must agree to."

I nodded. "Namely, cut wages, increase working hours, shorten sick leaves, raise prices at company stores and increase the rentals."

"I see you've anticipated this."

"Anticipated it? I've been fighting it ever since they began to realize the war was going to be over one of these days."

"Will you tell me, please, what the workers' re-action will be to these changes? You're far more aware of their attitudes than I."

I wondered if she'd found it hard to admit that. "The first thing to happen will be a strike, brought about by a vote to join a union. We cannot prevent that vote. The law is on their side."

"If the strikers are warned they'll lose their jobs after a specified length of time away from work, we can legally bring in other men."

"True. And if the war has ended, there will be a big pool of unemployed to draw upon."

"Then why are you concerned?"

"Because there'll be trouble. More than you can imagine. Remember now, this is not on a personal basis. I'm only telling the truth. When I first came to this town, it was so dominated by the Camerons that it was like serfdom. They gave any orders they wished and they were obeyed or—that was the end of those who disobeyed. The townspeople have come

419

to resent and despise the Camerons. They work for them because this kind of work is all they know and their roots are here. They don't want to move. This kind of hatred doesn't need more than a tiny spark, and it will flame up beyond control."

"Workers who strike and make trouble can be legally forced to leave Cameron. Isn't that true?"

"It used to be. Probably it still is, but with a difference. The Camerons used to send drays and a deputy sheriff with eviction writs they would serve with one hand while dragging out the furniture with the other. Today they couldn't get away with that. There are appeals, hearings, all manner of legal ways to slow down an eviction."

"What then do you propose?" she asked.

"Haven't they told you, Deborah?"

"Of course they have. I want to hear it directly from you."

"Very well. Change nothing except from now on allow all rentals to apply to the purchase of each individual's home. The houses are old, well-worn, and not worth a great deal, so they should be paid for in a brief span of time. That gets the responsibility for renovation work off the back of the company and will likely save money in the long run."

"No changes in pay or hours?"

"None. There's no need for that, my dear. The mill is making a great deal of money. We can afford to maintain the present wage level, and we'll profit by doing so. There's going to be a great demand for our woolens after the war ends. People have been deprived of good clothing as a war measure. They'll be eager to replenish. For full production we'll need cooperation from the workers. Nothing less will do. You've studied economics. In heaven's name, if you don't agree with me, you've wasted your schooling and learned nothing."

"What I believe won't influence them. My schooling

also taught me to obey those who pay my wages."

We postponed further talk while Walter served us. When he left, I raised my glass of white wine in a silent toast to my daughter. She looked at me without wavering, but she didn't reach for her glass of red wine. During dinner we spoke only of mundane matters that were boring to both of us. Walter came back to replenish Nora's wineglass and to take mine back to the kitchen so no super-patriot would see that the inn served German wine.

Walter also had a message for me. "There's a phone call for you, Mrs. Kinnery. In the lobby."

"Excuse me," I said to Deborah. "It's probably my husband about to go out on an emergency. I'll be right back."

She nodded coldly in that manner which made her so hard to like. I went out to the lobby where the phone waited, but nobody seemed to be on the line. I jiggled the hook and got the operator.

"There sure was a call, Mrs. Kinnery," she said in answer to my query. "I guess whoever it was hung up."

"You know the Doctor's voice. Was it he?"

"I don't think so. I didn't recognize the voice at all. I'm sorry."

"It's all right. Not your fault," I said.

I returned to the table. "Whoever it was hung up. It couldn't have been very important."

"Do you get many calls like that—away from your home?" she asked.

I pushed aside the refilled glass of wine. I was no longer interested in food or drink.

"Deborah, that was as vicious a remark as you could possibly make. I know what you insinuated—that I get calls from men secretly so my husband won't know. Your imagination is running away with you. I thought you were at least getting away from those people on the Hill and there was some hope for you. Apparently I was wrong."

She said nothing, but there was no softening of her brazen attitude. I gave up.

"What were we talking about before this silly remark of yours? I want to get this over with."

"We were discussing the attitude of my grandfather, and especially of Loran. I promise you they won't accept your ideas."

"They won't put theirs into effect, either," I said. "Because I own exactly fifty percent of the stock. They can stop me, but I in turn can stop them."

"You obtained that much influence by blackmailing them, didn't you?"

"Is that what they call it? I saved the mill with a personal loan, a secured one. Using that as a base, I negotiated another quarter of a million on the strength of the refinanced business. If I'd chosen to hold out, I could have forced them to grant me fifty-one percent, because they could not deny me. The mill was on the verge of bankruptcy."

"The personal loan to the mill is now on deposit for you to accept at any time," she said.

"Good. I'll see that it is transferred to a New York City bank tomorrow. Thank you for the information."

She gathered up her gloves. "I think that about concludes our talk, Mrs. Kinnery."

I leaned back and looked at her with a sad shake of my head. "You are a wonder, darling. You've accepted what I just told you about a business affair. I know you have, but you refuse to take my word about a more personal matter that concerns us far more than business."

"One regards facts, the other requires proof. They are two different things, Mrs. Kinnery. I cannot confuse them."

I slowly drew on my gloves, watching the cold, pretty face across from me. "I see. But our meeting has been worthwhile if you can persuade Mr. Cameron and Loran to accept what I believe and what I'm sure you do."

"No one can do that," she said. "They make up their own minds."

I smiled and nodded as if we had just concluded an important business matter successfully, and we walked out of the dining room together. Nora didn't offer to drive me home, and I would have refused if she had. I preferred to walk because it gave me time to think.

I still didn't know why they'd sent her. Not to obtain information; they knew everything I'd told her—knew exactly how I felt about their greedy plans. We'd be together, only the two of us, and if one broke down, the other might follow and the whole black tale come into the open. The entire affair didn't make sense. Loran, particularly, did nothing that was either risky or unnecessary. There was something wrong, though I couldn't determine what it was.

Somewhat to my surprise, Glen was not only at home, but already in nightshirt and robe, sitting in the parlor reading a medical journal. He greeted me with his usual hug and kiss.

"How'd it go? I've been sitting here listening for the sound of the riot."

"No riot. No trouble. Did you phone me at the inn?"

"No. It's been a very quiet evening. If you'd called me, I'd have driven down to pick you up."

"I liked the walk. Someone called me, but by the time I left the dining room and reached the lobby telephone, whoever it was had hung up."

"That's strange. Well, it will probably be explained in the morning. Did you have any trouble with Nora?"

"No, not at all. She was very cool and businesslike. She's going to be very good at running that mill when the time comes." I didn't think it worthwhile to mention her malicious remark about the phone call.

"If she runs it in the same manner the Camerons

always have, there may not be a mill to run. Things are changing. Automobiles are beginning to let people be on the move—to go elsewhere to look for jobs if what they have at home doesn't suit them. Half the West is only sparsely settled, and that would be a place to grow along with the country. I tell you, Maeve, they won't be staying in one place any more. Not very often."

"For the Camerons nothing has changed," I said. "It never will if they can help it. What if the town dwindles down to, say, half the people now here? What will you do?"

"Well, I've heard talk that I might make a pretty good medical director at the new hospital going up in Bridgeton."

"Oh, Glen!" I said joyfully. "Why don't you take it now?"

"For the special reason that the hospital exists only in blueprint form as of this moment, and it will take a couple of years to build. But it will be a three-hundred-bed, five-operating-room place. I don't like leaving this town after all these years, but if there's a chance the town isn't going to be here much longer, I have to look out for myself."

"I say you ought to begin campaigning for it now. Give me the word and I'll do some arm twisting myself."

"Let's wait a little while longer."

"If there are two years to wait, we can chance it. Oh, yes—before I go to bed, I'm going to give you the papers concerned with the loan on the torc. And I'll sign a check on order at the local bank where the entire loan is collected and ready to be returned to me. I'll see to it, but in case I can't, will you take care of it for me?"

"Of course I will. What's this business about not being able to handle it yourself?"

"It's nothing, darling Glen. Papa taught me to take

no risks with anything concerning legal matters or money, so this will be placed in your hands and mine. Either one of us can conclude the transaction."

"Then," he said lightly, "there's nothing left to do but go to bed."

Halfway up the stairs I reached for the bannister. "It's nothing," I told Glen, who also stopped. "I felt a little dizzy. I drank some wine. Perhaps that and the excitement of the evening was too much for me. Go along. I'm all right."

I was fine, and I went to sleep promptly, as I usually did, but I awoke sometime during the night and I felt nauseated. I lay quietly, hoping it would pass over, but it seemed to grow worse. Finally I sat up, and the exertion made me gag. I jumped out of bed this time and hurried to the bathroom.

Glen, always a light sleeper, awoke instantly and followed me. He stood by while my stomach rebelled. I didn't feel any better afterwards, and I didn't want to lie down. Glen made me sit in a rocker close by the open window so I'd be cooled by the night breezes. They didn't help, either.

"What did you have at the inn?" Glen asked. He was holding my hand lightly but exerting just enough pressure over my pulse that he could study it, hoping I'd not be aware of that. I didn't let him know I realized what he was doing.

"Just the usual. Nora had the same thing. These days, it's always chicken or fish. We had chicken. There's a war on, you know."

"Yes," he said, "I seem to have heard that. The grocery bills say so aloud. Do you have any abdominal pain?"

"A little. I suppose it must have been caused by the attack I just had."

"Possibly. I want you to lie down on the bed."

"Glen, I'll be all right. This is just a stomach ache."

"You have your appendix," he reminded me. "They

425

can be treacherous sometimes, and it's very easy to find out."

I obeyed him, and he made an examination with negative results. There was no pain in the region of the appendix.

"It puzzles me," Glen said. "What else did you have beside the chicken? Was there stuffing?"

"Yes, and we had a baked potato with it. We also had wine. You know the German kind I like. Nora drank a red—could wine make me this ill?"

"Well, maybe . . ." He sounded doubtful. He took my temperature and when he didn't tell me what it was, I thought it must be high. A few moments later, I didn't care. Glen had to help me into bed. Then he lit all the lights, went down for his medical bag, and made a more careful examination.

My abdomen seemed to be on fire. My mouth and throat were painfully dry. I was breathing in rapid, shallow breaths, and suddenly I didn't want to move a muscle in my body because I knew it would give me pain.

The next thing I knew, Glen was wiping perspiration from my face and neck, and he seemed terribly worried. I managed to reach up and touch his face and bring forth a smile of sorts.

"Darling," he said, "I want to take you to the hospital. I don't know what's wrong, but you're not getting any better. I can make tests there I can't do here."

"All right," I said in a whisper.

"Do you think you can make it? There's a twenty-five-minute ride. I'll be as fast as I can. . . ."

"If you're with me," I managed to say, "I can make anything. Please help me, darling. I am so sick."

Without another word he dressed hastily, wrapped me in blankets, and carried me out to where the car was waiting. He bundled me into the front seat and to make certain I wouldn't fall out, ran the isinglass curtains down as if he expected rain.

I knew he was driving very fast. He honked the horn at every sharp bend and never slowed up. I was so jammed in with the blankets I didn't slide off the seat.

I began to giggle in a half-hysterical way. "One . . . good thing. . . ." I said.

"What?" he asked. "What good thing?"

"This time when I'm sick . . . I'm not pregnant."

Then I gasped and cried out in sudden terror. "It's like Joel," I said. "Like Joel, darling. Just like Joel . . . and like last time—with me!"

"Hang on," he said. "We'll be there in a few minutes."

"I've been poisoned. Joel was poisoned. Now I've been . . ." I moaned in fresh dismay. If I'd been poisoned, only one person could be responsible. Nora, my own daughter. I tried to tell this to Glen, but the words wouldn't come. My tongue seemed paralyzed, and then everything left me as I left the world temporarily.

When I awakened again, my stomach was so sore I knew I'd been pumped out. Glen, in a white coat now, looked down on me anxiously.

"She's coming out of it," he told somebody. "Darling . . . everything is all right. It's fine."

"Yes," I managed. "Yes, my dear Glen, my dear husband. . . ."

He clasped my hand between his own. "You'll be fine. You're in the hospital now. Maeve, do you hear me? Do you know what I'm saying?"

I nodded. I had something to tell him, but I couldn't recall what it was despite the fact that I knew it to be of great importance.

"You had your white wine at the inn. Did Nora have the same wine? Just nod or shake your head. I don't remember what you told me before."

"Red," I said. That was what I wanted to tell him. "Red . . . wine . . . not white . . . obstinate, maybe . . . or doesn't, like white. . . ."

"All right. . . ."

"She . . . poisoned me." I closed my eyes tightly, and I felt the tears start from the corners of them. Glen stroked my face gently, and I stopped those tears to look up at him. His face was grave, very serious, but it seemed to grow somewhat older, too, and his still quite dark hair was turning white before my eyes. Then he spoke again, but it wasn't Glen's voice. It was my father's voice, and that was my father looking down at me.

"Get up, you sleepyhead. Time to get up. Is it the whole day you'd be sleeping away?"

"Yes, Papa," I said. "I'm getting up." I was out of bed with no difficulty, and I was in my own darling bedroom in my village in county Mayo, among the people and the places I had known so well.

My red-haired brother Jimmy was trying on a new cap of which he was very proud, and though the knickerbockers and the woolen jacket he wore were threadbare, he regarded that new cap as something fine to wear with them.

"Cathal came by, smellin' like a stable, he was," Jimmy told me. "He was askin' when you'd be comin' down to see him."

"Cathal, my eye," I said. "When he gets himself cleaned up, like a man should, then let him come asking me, and maybe I'll say yes and maybe I'll say no."

"Listen to her," Jimmy derided. "Listen to the girl when she's achin' for any lad to take her walkin' down by the sand."

"Why don't you take her walking down by the sand?" Father asked.

"Me?" Jimmy asked indignantly. "Be seen with me own sister? What d'ye think I am, Father? A lad who can't get a lass of his own? That's what you're sayin'."

"All right," Father said. "I'll take her down to the sand, and we'll stop by to see Grania on the way."

428

I shivered just a little because I was a trifle afraid of Grania. She was very old. Some say she was eighty if she was a day, and they said she would live forever because she was blessed with the power to foresee the future and probably had been born under several veils. Or whatever it was the bewitched were born under. I did like Grania, though. She would tell me things that were going to happen to me, and sometimes they did. Father said they always did, but I was too much a dullard to know it. Which was likely true.

It was good to be that young. And free without cares. And happy because I loved everyone and I knew of none who didn't love me. My shoes might be heavy and clumsy, as were those of all the other children, and the grownups as well. My dress might be too long for a child of my years and of a drab and not very lovely color, but it covered me, and it detracted not one whit from my joy of being alive.

The green hills and the smell of the thyme and the clover were the only perfumes I knew, and they sufficed. I thought that if there'd be any change ever in my life, I would fight it until I could battle no more.

Father brought me out of my reverie. "Pack Grania's food basket. What are you waiting for, lass? Ah, but you're young, and it's a time for dreaming."

"I was not dreaming," I said stoutly. "I was . . . just thinking, and now I will prepare Grania's basket."

I heaped it with the things she loved, and Papa and I walked briskly over the dusty street to the little cottage where Grania had been born and where she vowed she would die.

She got out very little any more and liked to spend her time at the fireplace even when the weather was hot, for she claimed the summer's scorching temperature didn't reach the depths of her bones where she was constantly cold.

Grania didn't want for visitors. All in the village were her friends, and she was well and kindly taken care of. But it was to me alone that she would grant her morsels of wisdom, or her tea-leaf prophecies.

As always, she knew we were arriving before we set out, and she would call to us to enter as we set foot in the outer room of her cottage. Father had accepted this years ago and admitted she was gifted with some extra sense he could not explain.

"Come sit by the fire," Grania said. Father dreaded these invitations, for he often said he came near to suffocation from the blast of heat. I suppose I didn't mind because I was younger, so while Papa took it upon himself to visit some ill person close by, it was left to me to entertain Grania, or be entertained by her.

She had finished the pot of tea. She removed the lid of the pot and dumped some of the wet leaves onto the saucer, then let enough of the remaining dregs of tea dribble onto the leaves so they would float a bit. Then she stirred them up with the back of her spoon, and finally she placed the saucer on the little table beside her and bent over it to study the leaves. Every few seconds she would look up at me, and I would invariably succumb to a tremor of fear. Grania's predictions were not to be ignored, and sometimes they spelled misfortune.

"You will not die in the village where you were born," she said. "You will not even die in Ireland, worse luck. It will be across the sea, child. Far from here. It will not be for a long, long time. You are strong of body and mind. You will have a life that is pleasant and yet worrisome. The leaves tell me there is danger and disappointment."

"Will I marry, then, Grania?" I asked.

"You are too young to talk of such things, child. There will be those who hate you and cause you grief. There are those you can never trust, and those you should but will not because you are blinded by anger and untruths. Yet your enemies will not prevail and

430

you will win over them, but only with sorrow, and there will be death all about you."

By now I was actually shaking with fear. Grania, affected by her own words, covered her face with both hands and rocked from side to side for a few moments wailing softly.

Finally I arose and backed out of the room. Grania didn't stop me or remove her hands from her face. I was happy to reach the sunlight.

I told Father what she'd said, and he said not to worry. He took my hand and we went running down the path to the sea where we waded out into the cold, cold water.

Finally we went up onto the green slopes rising from the beach, and there we dropped onto the grass and lay back to close our eyes and rest. I must have fallen asleep, for when I opened my eyes, Father was not there and everything seemed different somehow.

There was a great roaring sound from the sea. I sat up to find the water churning wildly and the wind howling in great wrath, and though the waves created clouds of mist I could see through them and watch a tiny *currach* pitched and tossed in the high winds.

Then it changed again and there was peace and quiet and I was lying side by side with a man. I turned my head and smiled at Joel. My darling Joel, who lay on his back and seemed to be fast asleep. I leaned over and kissed him lightly, for fear of waking him up. Then I closed my eyes, too, for what seemed to be an instant of time.

When my eyes opened again, someone stood over me, looking down. Everything was unclear, hazy as a sea fog coming in at dusk. I tried to speak, but I was unable to open my mouth. I struggled for the strength to clear away the mist over my eyes, and when I finally succeeded, the fog parted to show me Glen's anxious face peering down at me.

"She opened her eyes," he said to someone. He

431

touched my forehead and then caressed my cheeks so tenderly I felt like crying.

"Her fever seems to be down a little," Glen was telling somebody. I could see no farther than Glen's face. I felt my shoulders supported by a strong arm, and I was gently lifted. A glass tube was placed between my lips.

"Please drink the water, Mother," a voice begged. "Please, Mother. . . ."

Another face came into focus. It was Patty, and when she asked me again to drink, I obeyed her. The cooling water felt good in my throat, and I heard someone give an exclamation of joy, apparently because I had been able to drink. I was eased back on a pillow, still confused and still unable to respond. It seemed to be that I'd exerted myself to the utmost, and I gratefully closed my eyes and went to sleep.

When I again awoke the whole room was in focus. I knew at once it was a hospital room by its starkness and its practical furnishings. I seemed to be alone. I didn't know what I was doing here. Memories of my father, and Grania, and poor Joel returned. But Joel was dead, and my father, and Grania . . . I started to weep quietly.

I could feel a draft and hear the swish of a door opening. Then someone came swiftly to the bedside. Patty looked down at me.

"Mother . . . you're awake." The discovery seemed to excite her unduly. "Oh, Mother . . . I've got to get Papa. . . ."

Glen came immediately, and both of them stood at the bedside. I was able to fashion a smile and raise one feeble hand which Glen took tenderly, to lower it to my side again after only a moment.

"Can you understand me, Maeve? Do you know what I'm saying?"

"Of course I do," I said indignantly. Was that my

voice? It seemed to come from a distance and be so weak I could scarcely hear it.

He grinned this time, buoyed by my indignant answer. "That's wonderful. Now, you've been very ill. It's going to take some time before you're strong enough to even sit up. Please don't try. And this is not the time to ask questions. Apply yourself to getting better soon. That's what is most important."

"When . . . did Patty . . . come?" I promptly disregarded his advice not to ask questions.

"She's been here for two weeks."

"Oh, that's nice," I said, and then I did try to sit up, though it was a hopeless attempt. "Two weeks?"

"It's late in August, darling," Glen said. "You were unconscious for days."

"But—I don't seem to understand. To remember . . ."

"You will in time. No matter whether you do or not, we can't talk about it until you feel much better."

"Mama, please get better first," Patty said.

I didn't try to fight the sudden desire for sleep. I merely closed my eyes and drifted off. Perhaps, I thought, I'd go back to that once-again land with Papa and Joel, with Jimmy and Grania and all the rest of them.

When I awakened again, I remembered what had happened. I was fully oriented this time. Glen and Patty were no doubt close by, but I didn't try to call them. Instead, I wanted time to think.

I must have been very close to death, I realized. This time the Camerons had almost succeeded. Now the questions began to take shape, but when Glen and Patty came in to see how I was, they smothered me with their delight so that I asked nothing, but took great comfort in their kindness and the loving care they gave me.

"I've something to thank you for," Patty said. "You're my first patient. Oh, I'm not a nurse yet,

433

but the last two weeks gave me more training than a year at nursing school. Besides, Papa gave me some lessons, too."

"You must have done all the proper things," I said, "because I feel much better today. Glen . . ."

"Call me Doctor," he said. "Otherwise you'll ask too many questions. As a doctor, I don't have to answer them except as they concern your condition. Which is good and will improve very rapidly from now on."

"You do realize we have to talk?"

"Indeed I do."

"When? Please, Doctor, when may I question my husband?"

"I would say in about three or four days. Patty, bring in a tray of something special. Soft food, the kitchen will know what. It's time your mother began eating again, instead of being fed through a tube. Run along."

"How has she been, Glen?" I asked.

"As a nurse? A bit clumsy, but she shows ability and an aptitude for the work. Give her a little time and more training, and she'll be the best."

"How has she been as a girl, not a nurse?"

"Angry, like I've been. Look, we're not going to talk about it now."

"It was Nora?" I asked.

"Who else? And that's all for now. Later on, Patty will fill you in on what's been happening while you slept the days away. There's a letter from your brother that's interesting, too."

Patty returned with an excellent custard and a small bit of finely chopped beefsteak—and I wondered where they'd ever obtained it. There was also milk—a heavy meal for me, the way I felt, but I ate all of it.

Patty was so eager to tell me what had happened. "There's been news that the Kaiser is asking to talk to some official from Washington. I guess he wants

434

to ask for peace. The papers say we have far more than a million soldiers in France and they're doing very well. The Germans are being pushed back every day. Some say it will be over by late next month."

"Let's hope so. The mill?"

"Nothing changed there. Not yet," she added significantly.

"What do you mean by that?" I asked.

"Oh, it's all so complicated to me. Papa can explain it better."

"Have you seen Deborah?"

"No," she replied curtly. "There is a letter from Jimmy. I hope I can meet him someday. He sounds like he's a lot of fun. Is he, Mama?" She produced the letter, written on official British Army paper. She read it aloud.

"Dear Sister: First of all the good news. I've been wounded. They shelled a hospital area and some of the shrapnel caught me a clip in places not to be mentioned in a family letter. Nothing serious. The bad news—I had been hoping for leave so I could go home and choke the truth out of that blackguard of a Cathal Dolan. Now it has to wait a bit. But then I'll go without fail because I'm on furlough and the way things are going the war won't last much longer. We've got the Boche licked good and proper. Don't worry about my wounds. They won't interfere with my work. However, my red hair has turned gray and that's a change I find it hard to abide, though of course it makes me look handsomer than ever—and older, too, be damned to that part of it. I hope you and yours are well and that we can soon meet once again. If your problems are not solved by the time I get to see you, I'll tear into them with my bare hands."

"That," I said, "is the longest letter Jimmy ever wrote in his life."

"What's he talking about—your problems, Mama?"

"When I'm home once again and on my feet, we'll

435

talk about them. There's so much to tell you. But you're a sensible girl, and I know you'll understand."

"I've always known there was some kind of mystery about you. Nobody ever said anything, but sometimes when I walked into a room you and Papa would stop talking in the middle of a sentence. And I know whatever it is, the Camerons are mixed up in it. Oh, Mother, I despise them. All of them—and especially Deborah."

"You know about her, then?"

"Papa told me. He said if I was old enough to be your hospital nurse, I was old enough to be told what had happened to you. It's awful. How could she have done such a thing?"

"It's all one big, mixed-up problem. Be patient, dear. I wish I didn't have to tell you, but it is time. You have to understand, because there are going to be changes. After what happened, there must be."

"I'll not mention it again," she promised. "And it's doing you no good to be talking so much, either. Now let me raise you a bit while I change pillows . . . and then you're to sleep."

That's how I spent much of my time for the next four days. From then on, my recovery was rapid and complete. When I had my first look in the bureau mirror I was shocked, but Glen told me I'd fill out the hollows in my cheeks, and the sun would change my paper-white skin back to its normal color.

I didn't dread the day I'd go home, but I didn't look forward to it. I felt as if I'd been away from the mill town for months, though it had been just short of a single one. How drab the town looked! It was as if I saw it for the first time—really saw it as it was, and its ugliness not tempered by my wanting to like the place.

Being home was good. I'd kept a pleasant house, and Patty saw that it was as neat and tidy as when I managed it. I came to the conclusion that my daughter was a full-grown, capable, and quite clever young woman.

The evening of the day I returned, Patty, Glen, and I had our supper as usual and then, with a large pot of coffee on the back of the stove, we drifted to the parlor with our cups and saucers and drank our coffee while we seemed to gather our thoughts.

Patty got up and placed all the cups on a tray. "I'll get some hot," she said, and off she went to the kitchen. Perhaps she'd sensed Glen and I needed a few moments to talk.

"Do you think she should be told now?" Glen asked.

"Yes," I said. "She's not a child any more, and she certainly must know about Nora so she can guard against her."

"Those are my opinions, too. Of course, she realizes something is up and it concerns not only us, but her as well. You were undoubtedly poisoned by Nora. Patty figured that out for herself."

Patty returned and came over to embrace me fondly before she sat down. "I'm not a little girl any more, Mother. I think you know that."

"Yes, we both know it, your father and I. Now I'll tell you what I recall about that night I became ill. Nora asked me to meet her. . . ."

"Nora who?" Patty asked.

"I'm sorry, dear, I forgot. Deborah's right name is Nora. I'll explain later. So when I call her Nora I mean Deborah. Now—the matter was not that vital that I had to meet her over a supper table. I remember wondering just why she'd arranged it. Glen, were you able to find out whether whatever it was that made me ill had been placed in the wine?"

"We're quite sure it had been, yes."

"Nora saw to it she had red wine when I ordered white, so there'd be no mistake, I suppose. Glen, I

437

just thought of something. Perhaps Walter—the old waiter—he might have seen something. . . ."

Glen said, "Walter had a habit of draining the wine from glasses left partially full. He drank your wine—and Walter died the following day."

"Oh, dear God!" I said. "That poor old man."

"You were younger and able to resist the effects of the drug. Walter had no stamina at all. Now, I saw to it that every possible test was made on his body, but we were unable to isolate any drug that could have caused his death. We analyzed what we pumped from your stomach, and we checked your body fluids—with the same result. Nothing."

"It was the same substance that killed Joel," I said. "The symptoms were exactly the same. Joel, too, wasn't the strongest and ruggedest of men. He resisted a long time, but finally he died."

"The drug seems to be slow-acting, depending on the size of the dose. I could tell you more about it if we knew what it was. Unfortunately, we do not have any proof that you or Walter were deliberately poisoned. The general opinion—and the police are satisfied with it—the medical examiner, as well—is that something in the food was bad. Spoiled, but not detected by either smell or taste. Because you and Walter became ill at the same time, it was accepted that both of you ate the same food. In these days of shortages, slow shipment of perishable foods, it's a wonder more people aren't struck down by some sort of poison."

"Tell me how it is that Deborah has two names," Patty said.

"Helen is not Nora's mother," I said. "Nora was born to Joel Cameron, the youngest son of Gabe Cameron, and his wife. I am Nora's mother. Joel and I were married in Ireland, and he died there of a poison."

"We suspect he was murdered by one of the

438

Camerons," Glen explained. "No proof again—all done quite cleverly. He left your mother, Patty, one-third of the stock in the mill. The Camerons didn't want her to have it. She came here to claim her inheritance and discovered she was pregnant. The Camerons took her in, after first banishing her from the Hill. When they discovered Joel would have an heir, your mother was accepted and treated well until Nora was born. Then they took Nora away from her and made her leave. By that time, your mother and I were deeply in love and we married."

Patty listened to the explanation without interrupting either of us. "Nora is my sister then?" she asked finally.

"Your half-sister," I corrected her.

"And she tried to kill you? Because they believed that if you died, the part you own in the mill would go to her?"

"Perhaps that's what they thought. In fact, it will all go to your father. I arranged that long ago."

"I liked her," Patty said. "Mother, I liked her so much." She suddenly bent over and buried her face in her hands. "Why did she have to spoil it all? What made her do such a terrible, ugly thing? You are her mother. Doesn't she know that?"

"She knows," Glen said. "The Camerons don't believe she knows, but she does."

"But . . ." Patty raised her head and looked straight at me. "Why didn't you take Nora? Why did you let them keep her?"

"Now comes the part I pray to heaven you'll understand, because I cannot keep it from you."

"Mother, I don't care what it is. I love you. Nothing is going to change that. Nothing in this world. You don't have to tell me anything."

"My dear," I said, "it's all lies. They say a man in Ireland has sworn I slept with him and married Joel only for the money Joel had. This man swore to the lie because he hated me from the time I refused to marry him—the great oaf that he was and likely is—and married Joel instead."

"Is that what Uncle Jimmy wrote about in the letter I read to you?"

"Yes. Jim is going to see this man and make him retract the lie. Jim is a great surgeon now, and no doubt he has influence. He is also going to try to find out what Joel really died of. It's been many, many years, and I have no hope he'll learn anything, but he is going to try."

"Did you believe this would make me think less of you?" Patty asked.

"I hoped it wouldn't. There was another matter. At a ball long ago, a well-known roué tried to"—I looked at Patty doubtfully—"to take advantage of me. He swore I had . . . cooperated. The Camerons said that, that I was no more than a common woman of the streets."

"Mother, if anyone had ever told me that, I'd have had hysterics, it's so impossible and crude. . . ."

"In those days—" Glen began.

"And I'd have scratched open the face of whoever told such a lie."

"Thank you, Patty," I said. "You've no idea how relieved I am to have this off my mind."

"Your mother accepted their terms," Glen said, "because she wanted to protect her daughter, even if only lies threatened her. It was also possible that if a court action was taken, your mother would have lost, for the Camerons were influential. Then she married me, you came along, and the need to remain silent doubled. We're waiting now for word from Jimmy. If he learned nothing, your mother and I will go to Ireland and do our best to spike that lie."

"I'm afraid this attempt on my life wasn't the first. I'm sure now they tried to poison me before," I said. "There was even an attempt in Ireland when someone shot at Joel and me. Then, after Nora was born, I was caught in a forest fire that spread so quickly I think now it was set to close in on me. Loran saved my life that day, but I wonder, sometimes, whether he did that because I would have been rescued anyway, and Loran could make himself out a hero."

"You can't convince me any Cameron is heroic," Patty said.

"All this I've been longing to tell you, Patty. There were times when it almost burst out of me, because I was deathly afraid someone else—someone on the Hill—would tell you, and I might lose you."

"You need never have feared that," Patty said. "But what will you do now? They failed to kill you. They may try again."

"There's still a great deal to discuss, darling," Glen said to me. "First of all, one of the last things you did before you became ill was to give me a signed order on the bank for money on deposit there by the company, to repay the loan you made. Do you recall that?"

"The torc!" I exclaimed. "Glen ... did you ... ?"

"As soon as I felt you were out of danger I got a draft from the bank, I went to New York, and I reclaimed the torc. It is now in a safe deposit box at the same bank from which you were able to borrow on it."

"Thank heaven," I said. "It's been so long since I saw the thing it slipped my mind."

"What on earth is a torc?" Patty asked.

"It's a relic, two thousand years old. . . ."

"Maeve," Glen broke in, "hadn't you best tell her the whole story of her ancestry. Mirror and all?"

"Yes, it's high time. Patty, you're in for more surprises. Glen, will you excuse us?"

He nodded. "Mother and daughter, I know. That's how it should be. That's how I want it to be. Afterwards come down again. There's more to tell."

"Save it," I said. "First there will be the pleasure

441

every woman descendant of Queen Maeve has enjoyed for these two thousand years. Come, Patty, and bring your doubts with you."

SIXTEEN

Patty stared at the ancient mirror. I didn't know how much of what I'd told her she really believed.

"I think I'm afraid of it, Mother."

"No need to be, dear. What it will tell you happens anyway. It will prepare you."

"What should I ask of it?"

"Perhaps you are too young to ask it whom you will love. When the time comes for that, you will know."

"Should I ask what lies ahead for me?"

"I think so."

"I'm almost afraid to touch it." Patty accepted the mirror from me and, as I was accustomed to do, pressed it close to her and closed her eyes.

"Your mirror has now come to me," she said softly. "I cannot ask that it show me only the good and happy things of my life, but I pray that there will be less evil and less sorrow than my mother suffered. What is there I should know about?"

She brought the mirror before her eyes, moved it about to obtain the right angle. Suddenly she let go of it, and her face turned deathly pale. She arose and threw herself across my bed and began to cry.

I picked up the mirror and placed it on the bureau before I sat down on the bed beside Patty and raised her so that I could look into her tearstained face.

"What did you see?" I asked. "Tell me! It may not be as bad as you think."

"Bad? Mother, it's awful. I don't want that thing. I don't want to touch it again. All I saw were dead people. Bodies . . . all over. Dead and dying."

"You are a nurse in training," I reminded her.

"This was nothing that would happen in a hospital. I don't know what it was like. I can't imagine anything like it ever happening. The mirror lies. It must. Nothing like what it showed me could ever happen."

"Bodies . . . dead and dying. It has a meaning. Were any faces familiar?"

"I saw no faces, only bodies. So many of them . . . It was awful. You can't imagine. . . ."

"Yes, Patty. Yes, I can imagine. I have seen ugly things and wondrous things. Remember this—they come true. Without fail, they come true."

"But so many . . ."

"Perhaps it's part of the war?"

"It was not war, Mother. It was . . . worse than war, if such a thing could be."

"We'll go down and see what your father thinks of it. There will be an explanation somewhere. I promise you that."

I wrapped the mirror and put it away. I'd been tempted to look into it myself, but after Patty's reaction I decided it might not be wise. For her state of mind—or mine.

Glen was as puzzled as we. "If I didn't know the power of that mirror, I'd say forget the whole thing. But I can't. Whatever it is will come true, yet we don't know what to expect or where—or how."

"Papa," Patty said slowly, "I think it showed a great many sick people. Not injured or wounded, like a war . . ."

"What I had in mind was something different," Glen said. "I was about to tell you, Maeve, about some

443

information that came to me confidentially. It could result in what Patty saw in the mirror, but it wouldn't be people dying of an illness, but perhaps dying of injuries and wounds."

"Papa, I saw no wounds," Patty insisted.

"How long did the image last?" I asked her. "Sometimes it's no more than a flash."

"Long enough for me to be certain of what I saw."

"Glen," I said, "go on with what you started to say."

"Gabe and Loran haven't been too discreet in some of their plans for when the war ends. Some of their figures and estimates have come into the hands of office workers who were able to figure out what it all meant. Everything you're against is going to be instituted."

"I thought as much when I came to realize they were trying to be rid of me with this last attempt. Do you have the details?"

"From both sides, and it will scare you half to death. After a reasonable length of time, Loran will take charge of the change. All wages will be drastically reduced, hours will be lengthened, men will be assigned to perform twice as hard as they do now."

"Then the plant will be unionized in a matter of days."

"They're counting on a relaxation of rules by the War Labor Board. Since the war will be over, the rules won't apply—so they hope. They know the workers will strike. By that time, enough soldiers will have returned to create a big pool of unemployed—men who will be glad to take any job if it gives them and their family a living. And these ex-soldiers will be tough, trained to fight. If our workers try to stop them —what Patty saw may actually happen."

"The Camerons will never listen to me," I said. "I own half the stock, but I can't prevent this. They'll go about it in a way we can't stop."

"I know. But what the millhands intend is even worse. They know all about strikebreakers and the type of men who will be brought in. They know they'll be no match for them, so the millhands have made plans of their own. When they walk out of the mill, they're going to burn it down behind them. And that's not all. They plan first to move most of their belongings out of Cameron in secret. Then, after the plant is burning, they'll go through the town and put the torch to every company house."

"Dear God," I said. "Can't you talk to them, Glen?"

"Nobody can. They've been lied to, cheated, and exploited too long. Only the war provided them with fair wages which the Camerons were forced to pay."

"What are we going to do?" Patty asked. "Maybe they'll burn the mansion on the Hill, too. And everybody in it."

"Oh, no," Glen said. "They won't be caught in that kind of a trap. The Camerons won't be hurt physically, but when it's over, they'll be sitting up there with nothing but a pile of ashes to look down upon."

"Deborah . . . she'll be safe?" Patty asked.

"Are you concerned about her?" I asked coldly.

"We are sisters. I hate her but—we are sisters. She is your daughter."

"Yes," I nodded. "I'd not wish any harm to come to her, either."

"It won't," Glen said. "The men are counting on that. If they burn the mill and the town, they'll have enough sympathizers on their side so there'll be few, if any, repercussions legally. But if anyone on the Hill is hurt or killed, there won't be much sympathy, and the hands know it. They'll take special pains that Nora will not be hurt."

I had toyed with a plan while I recuperated in the hospital, when there was so much time to think. "Glen, I've something to say. You have told me you are in line to become the medical director of the new hospital in Bridgeton. I suggest that we leave Cameron for good. I'll sell my stock and be rid of all connections with the mill and the Cameron family."

"We might as well," Glen said. "If the prophecy of the mirror comes true and there is all that violence, the town will certainly be destroyed. There'll be nothing to stay for."

"I'll talk to Loran soon," I said. "He'll assume I've had enough and I've surrendered. There'll be no need to try to kill me again."

"Papa," Patty said earnestly, "I did see people dead and dying in the mirror, but . . . but . . . none of them showed any signs of violence. I've had enough nursing experience to recognize wounds and contusions. There were none."

"The mirror didn't show any of the victims at close range, did it?"

"No, but the whole thing was plain enough. . . ."

"You saw a panorama of the scene, too spread out to show such details. It has to be the riot that's going to take place when the war ends. What else could it be?"

"I agree with your father," I said. "Glen, is it now agreed that we'll clear out?"

"Yes. We'll know in plenty of time. The soldiers have to be returning by the hundreds of thousands before Loran can put his scheme into being. Meanwhile we'll look for a place to live close to where they're building the new hospital. It's going to have a nurse training school, Patty, so you can transfer there if you haven't completed your training by then. And there's the hospital to work in. As medical director I'll make certain all the interns right out of college are handsome."

"I hate to think of Cameron being destroyed," Patty said. "I love it here. I don't know why. There's surely not much to like, but. . . ."

"It's home," I said. "I've grown to love it, too, but

446

we'd gain nothing by remaining if the men are going to destroy it. The mirror, my dear, was meant to grant us warning so we could take advantage of its predictions. The things it prophesies are not often of a type to take advantage of, but this one is."

"We'll begin working on it at once," Glen said.

"I'll begin by paying a visit to the Hill," I said. "Just as soon as I feel up to the ordeal."

"What will you do if you meet Nora face to face?" Patty asked.

"Nothing. Beyond, perhaps, telling her I never want to see her again as long as I live."

"I wish—" Patty began, but she jumped up and hurried out of the room without finishing the sentence.

"I know what she wishes," I said. "It's not going to happen. Nora tried to kill me. Oh, perhaps she didn't know how lethal the drug was. But she obeyed them, knowing that she was harming her own mother. She could have refused, but she meekly obeyed and very nearly became a murderess—oh, God!" I exclaimed. "There was poor Walter—the old waiter who died."

"It was murder," Glen agreed.

"Then Nora is no daughter of mine."

Driving up the hill to the mansion was one of the most agonizing things I had ever undertaken. Not because I was about to apparently surrender to the Camerons and, in return, receive full compensation for my half interest in the mill. I knew there was enough money to buy me out.

What they planned would wreck everything, make all the stock worthless, but it was of their own doing, and I'd fought against it as strenuously as I could. What I regretted was severing all connection with what Joel should have had.

Glen and I had carefully talked it over and examined our resources, and we knew we were not only

447

financially sound, but with the sale of this stock, we'd be wealthy. My visit was strictly a business matter, not one during which I should issue warnings they'd never believe anyway.

Martha had opened the door for me the first time I ever came to this mansion, and now she opened it again for what would surely be the last time I would ever visit here. She had grown very old, shrunken and wrinkled, but age had made her no more friendly than she'd been the first time. She said nothing as I walked past her into the drawing room. I'd telephoned ahead, so they were all there—except Nora. I was glad for her absence. Evelyn Cameron was frail-looking these days, no longer the austere, cold, commanding woman so erect and domineering. Gabriel had aged, too, but not to the extent she had. Helen, my age, seemed to have flourished and looked well. Loran, his face somewhat lined, had not yet given way to time. He was as stern and formidable as ever—a man to be wary of.

"My dear Maeve," Gabriel said. "We're delighted to find you looking so well after your serious illness."

"I'm here on a matter of business," I said. "I think all of you know what happened to me, so we shall let it rest right there. I am here because I'm tired to death of your manipulations, greed, scheming, and your persistent refusal even to listen to me. Therefore I have decided to give in and sell you my shares of stock at a price current to the earnings of the mill. There will be no bargaining—no dickering. You will either accept now, or I shall sell the shares in the open market for what I can get."

"We'll buy you out," Loran said promptly.

"So your stubbornness finally gave way after all these years," Helen said. "Frankly, I didn't think you'd ever do it, Maeve."

"When will you have the money ready?" I asked Loran, disdaining to comment on Helen's statement.

"It will take at least a week. There's a rather large sum involved," Loran said.

"That will be satisfactory." I opened my purse and removed the legal document I'd had prepared. "Here is a written intent to buy at the terms we have just agreed upon. If Gabriel and Helen will sign it, I'll leave this house forever."

"I don't think I'll sign," Helen said.

"Don't be a fool," Loran snapped. "Of course you'll sign. That is what we've wanted for years."

"She never was entitled to a penny of our money," Helen insisted.

I picked up the legal document. "In one minute I'll tear this to pieces and before the day is over, my stock in this company will be offered for sale on the open market. One minute."

"Sign it!" Loran shouted angrily. "You idiot, Helen, sign it! She means what she says."

"I can be obstinate, too." Helen grew angrier under Loran's shouting.

"If she puts the stock up for sale, we'll have fifty people telling us how to run the mill. Damn it, Helen, do as I say."

Helen finally accepted Loran's fountain pen and signed the agreement, followed by Gabriel, who was more eager to affix his signature. I folded the document and put it in my handbag.

"I shall give this to the bank this morning along with my agreement to vacate my interest. When you have the cash ready, the bank will undertake the exchange of documents and cash. I think that's quite all the business I have with you. It's been a long time. I came here young and trusting, wanting to love all of you and to be loved. I was tricked out of my daughter, whom you have turned into a monster. You tried to cheat me out of Joel's inheritance. Behind this house lies the only person in this family I ever respected. I loved Abner almost as much as I loved his

449

brother. And I'm happy that Joel is buried elsewhere. I do not care to be associated with any of you again."

Not a word was spoken as I walked briskly out of the room and through the door Martha held open for me—and slammed behind my back. I walked down to my car. I hesitated a moment, for someone was inside. I pulled open the door. Nora sat there, looking straight ahead.

"Get out," I said.

"I will talk to you," she said firmly. "Get in!"

Sheer surprise made me curious enough to obey. I slipped behind the wheel and closed the door.

"They do not know I was waiting for you. Please drive down the hill and stop halfway along it."

"I'm not inclined to take orders from you," I said.

"Will you please do as I say? Don't be as obstinate and stupid as they are."

"Oh, so it's dawned on you, has it? All right, I'll talk to you. You won't like what I have to say, but I'll talk."

I drove the car to a suitable place off the road, halfway down the hill overlooking the town. There I shut off the motor and set the handbrake. I turned to look at her. She was still rigid, erect, frozen-faced, but ah, she was attractive and so much like Patty.

"I'm listening," I said.

"I may be wrong about this, but I believe you think I tried to kill you. Is that true?"

When I didn't answer at once, she hurried on.

"I went to the hospital to see you and . . . someone there advised me not to go to your room. Word got around that you'd been poisoned while dining with me at the inn."

"I can well imagine it might have."

"Do you believe that?"

"If you wish the blunt truth—yes. And I also believe you are responsible for the death of the old waiter, a dear and inoffensive man."

450

"I couldn't accept it at first," she said. "It was so . . . so horrible to even imagine." She opened the door beside her. "I won't keep you any longer."

"Let me say this first. I never want to see you again as long as I live."

She began to close the door, but hesitated a moment. "You have asked me to believe that you were innocent of the things we have said about you. You had no proof, but you begged me to believe you. I refused. Now you won't believe me because I have no proof. Is there any difference? Must a mother have absolute proof of her daughter's innocence more than a daughter needs the proof that her mother is not a wanton and evil woman?"

She slammed the car door and fled up the hill back to the mansion while I sat in stunned silence for several minutes. What she'd said was the truth. But then, I knew I was innocent and that made a difference—unless Nora was as innocent as I.

I released the brake, allowed the car to roll down the hill, and shifted into gear before I took my foot off the clutch pedal so that the motor caught without using the starter. I was traveling quite fast by the time I reached the bottom, but slowed to a crawl when I reached Main Street.

When I'd first arrived in Cameron, the houses had all been unpainted, sad-looking structures. Now they were neat, in good repair, nicely painted. We'd forced the Camerons to provide all that. And the company stores had competition. A grocery had been set up on the outskirts, also a garage, a hardware and feed store, and even a small restaurant and café. They were on land the Camerons didn't control, and they had no way of blocking these intruders, as they called them.

It was, actually, a nice little town. The six hundred people had grown to seven hundred and fifty, though the population was somewhat decimated by the war and the draft. There were few young men in the town these days.

Now it was going to be destroyed. What the Camerons wouldn't wreck with their greedy schemes, the millhands would complete with fire and violence. All these houses were old, but no matter, they were livable, could be renovated even more, and were now comfortable enough. The mill, run properly, would provide them with a good living for years to come. The postwar years were bound to be profitable.

The streets were no longer dusty deserts in dry weather and quagmires in wet. There were flagstone sidewalks everywhere, a boon during the years when skirts had been long, but not so vital now that they were shorter, though not the less welcome.

Electricity glowed in every home, and there were a surprising number of telephones. Glen had counted forty motorcars in town, with the prospect of many more once the war was over and cars would be again in production.

I pulled to the curb in front of our house, but instead of getting out, I sat there a few moments, thinking about Nora. All my memories of Cameron and what the town had been and become were no more than an effort to cease considering Nora's argument.

Yet, she had brought me to the supper table with little reason for the meeting. She'd disliked me, so why had she agreed to handle this interview? Why not Loran, or even Gabriel? She could have refused. If she'd not actually placed a drug in my glass of wine, she must have realized something evil was at hand and I would be the victim. Therefore, I could see no reason why I should change my attitude toward her, painful though it was for me.

I went on into the house. No one was at home. Glen must have had an urgent call and taken Patty with him to assist. I set about dusting, though the parlor didn't really need it. I wanted to keep occupied.

I finished this chore and decided the carpets would have to be taken out to hang on the line and be beaten. I could obtain the services of two local boys to take care of that.

I had consumed the first glass of wine. In no manner could Nora have administered a drug to it, and this I was positive of. I'd finished the wine, worse luck for me, and then been lured away from the table by that false telephone call. Nora could easily have poisoned the second glass of wine, but—I'd not touched the second glass to my lips. So how could she have administered the drug?

I sat down heavily at the kitchen table. No matter how hard I tried, I could not avoid thinking about her and the possibility I had been mistaken. About her having actually given me the poison. But if she knew about the plot, she was as guilty as if she had put the drug in the wine. So why should I grant any doubt of her guilt?

I heard Glen's car pull up and the outer door to the waiting room slammed noisily as if he was in a great hurry. I made my way to the office, where Patty was already bent over one of several thick medical books she'd taken from the shelves. Glen, his face flushed with excitement, hat thrust to the back of his head, was searching through yet another medical book.

"Well, you two seem unusually busy," I said. "When you have time, I'd like to tell you—"

Glen glanced up. "Later, Maeve. Please, not now."

"What's happened? What's wrong?" I asked.

"I don't know for sure. We're trying to find out. Anything, Patty?"

"No, Papa, nothing. It certainly wasn't any ordinary form of pneumonia."

"I didn't think it was." Glen looked up again. "Oh, I'm sorry, darling. We're upset, I guess. We were called out by Arnold Philips, who said his wife was very sick. She'd returned from visiting her sister in

453

Boston only yesterday and came down with chills and fever very suddenly. I took Patty along, and we found Mrs. Philips on the verge of death. It was due to some kind of pulmonary infection. I'm sure of that, but it was so fast . . ."

"And so deadly," Patty remarked, still studying the medical books.

"We did our best for her but . . . she just expired despite all our efforts to save her."

"Glen, if you did your best . . ." I tried to comfort him.

"There was more to it. When Arnold came for us, he wasn't feeling very good, either. Right now he's in bed, just as sick as his wife was. We didn't tell him she had died. Just as in her case, nothing we do seems to help. He was on his feet one minute and collapsed the next."

"Is it some new and strange illness?" I asked.

"I don't know. It seems to start as a cold and go into pneumonia. A particularly virulent kind. My first impression was influenza, but no flu ever acted this fast, or was anywhere near as severe."

"Do you think Mr. Philips is going to die, too?" I asked.

"Yes. A neighbor is sitting with him now. I'm going back soon. . . ."

Patty straightened up from the book. "I think I heard someone in the waiting room."

She opened the door, and an exclamation brought Glen and me into the room after her. A man was slouched in a chair, breathing with great difficulty. He was conscious, but apparently too weak to speak.

Glen picked him up and carried him into the examination room, where he placed him on the table. The man seemed a little better.

"I'm awful sick," he said in a trembling voice. "Awful sick. I woke up this morning feeling poorly,

454

but I felt good enough to start for work. I couldn't make it. All I wanted to do was lie down."

"Who brought you here to my office?" Glen asked. "You're John Porter, aren't you?"

"Yes—John Porter. I walked. Nobody brought me."

"In this condition?"

"I wasn't too bad till I got here, and then I had to sit down quick. What's the matter with me, Doctor? I never been sick before in my life."

"I'm going to try to find out," Glen said. He turned to me. "Maeve, I don't know what this is, and I don't want you to stay here. Go into the house—"

"If you and Patty stay, so will I. There might be something I can do. Don't send me away, Glen."

"Get me a tongue depressor," he said.

I handed him the wooden instrument and he examined the man's throat. Even my inexperienced eye could see how terribly red and inflamed it was. Suddenly the man began to shake with a hard chill.

"My legs hurt. My arms ache like a toothache. Doctor, do something for me. I'm awful sick. I feel terrible."

He began to cough violently, the spasm wracking his body until perspiration stood out in great drops on his face and forehead. The chill had gone. Patty took his temperature and reported it as a hundred and five. He wasn't complaining any more. He'd lapsed into unconsciousness.

"I don't know what to do for him," Glen said. "I'm going to telephone for an ambulance and send him to the hospital. Patty, watch him."

Glen made the phone call, talked for several minutes, and hung up with a frown. "There are seven ambulance calls ahead of ours," he said. "Everybody's coming down with something."

"We were looking up influenza," Patty said. "The books say it's more like a bad cold. . . ."

Glen read the brief description of the disease. Then

455

he was on the phone again, making a call to the health department in the City of Boston.

"This is Dr. Glen Kinnery in Maine. I have a patient with a remarkably strange set of symptoms. Another patient with exactly the same symptoms just died after returning from a visit to your city. I was wondering . . . Yes . . . yes, mouth and throat bright red. Yes . . . chills . . . fever—this one has one hundred and five. Yes . . . yes, aching . . . he's in what looks like coma now . . . I see. So that's it! Oh, my God! That bad? Thank you. I'll do what I can here."

He hung up. "I don't know what to do. There's no precedent. This man is suffering from Spanish influenza. It's caused by a germ we breathe in. Patty—you'll find surgical masks . . . you know where they are. All of us will begin wearing them now, and wear them even while we sleep. I'm not sure how much good they'll do, but maybe some."

We tied each other's masks while Glen kept telling us what he had heard from Boston. "There were two hundred and two deaths in Boston yesterday and so far today more than a hundred. This is spreading all over the United States and all over the world. It's a killer influenza they say started in Spain. Boston is full of it. They expect thousands of deaths there. So many people have it they've lost count. What we have to do is try to check it before it begins here."

"It's already begun," Patty observed.

Glen nodded. "You're probably right. Maeve, call the mill and have them blow the whistle. Stop the machines, and send everybody to a meeting in front of Town Hall. In front of it, in the open, not inside. It spreads ten times as fast inside. Quickly now . . . this goes like wildfire, from what they told me."

I hurried to the telephone and finally persuaded the mill superintendent to blow the whistle and send everybody to the meeting as fast as possible. I would take the responsibility if the Camerons objected. A

456

minute after I hung up, the whistle blew as if for a major fire.

The whole town would turn out for that. Glen seized a large packet of sterile gauze pads and adhesive. Our supply of surgical masks was pitifully limited. I scurried about finding more gauze in rolls. Glen told Patty to stay with the patient. If he grew worse, she was to come for him at once. Then Glen and I hurried out to his car and got in. He drove down the street, with the horn blowing all the way. People were already assembling, and the army of workers was hurrying up the street. As we alighted from the car, a woman grasped Glen's arm.

"My Willie is terrible sick, Doctor. When you got time—"

Glen heaved a great sigh. "I'll be with him as soon as I can. Go back and stay with him. If he's feverish, put cold towels on his forehead." She left to obey his instructions, and Glen turned to me. "It's here. We're too late."

He left me and mounted the Town Hall steps so he could address the assembled people, all of them mystified but somehow aware that there was a serious reason for calling this meeting.

Glen said, "Listen, everybody. Listen well, because your lives could depend on it. Throughout the world a new kind of influenza germ is running rampant. It's a killer germ, and we don't know how to combat it. I talked to the Health Department in Boston, and they said there's an epidemic all over the country and it's growing worse. One person died here just an hour or so ago. Another is in my office now, deathly sick. There's a child come down with it. The disease is here, and it's bound to spread. All I can tell you is this. I'll give out as many gauze pads as I can, and I'll send for more. Wear them all the time over your mouth and nose. If anyone in your family gets sick, don't let anyone else near the patient. Just one person, who will act as nurse. The patient should be given all the water he wants. If the sickness isn't severe, a little light food can be given. Don't take any blankets, sheets, pillow cases, or clothing out of the sickroom. When the nurse gets a chance, I'd advise burning everything that came into contact with the patient. Remember, this is a killer sickness. It's going to hit young and old, and no matter how healthy you seem to be, this will lay you low in a matter of hours."

"How do we know we got it, Doc?" someone called out.

"You'll feel weak. Your legs won't be able to hold you up. Go to bed, arrange for your nurse. You're going to be mighty sick. I'll come as quickly as I can. There are a few things I can do, but I warn you, the fight is almost entirely up to you. I'll obtain information on the telephone every chance I get. Now, no more work at the mill. Everybody go home and stay there. No visiting, no assembly. Just go home, and if you know how to pray, start doing it. Speaking of prayer, no church services—not inside the church."

"What if somebody dies?" he was asked.

"There will be a prompt burial without a service. That can come later. What we're after now is to preserve lives. So—go home as I said."

The Cameron phaeton came rumbling down from the Hill with Loran driving. Glen held up his hand and stopped him. Before Loran could get out of the car, Glen stood beside it, telling him what he'd told the townspeople. He must have been very effective, for Loran turned the car around and drove back at a fast clip.

I was kept busy handing out the gauze squares and cutting rolls of gauze into pads. But I did see Loran's car come racing into Main Street again. Nora was at the wheel. I turned the gauze supply over to someone else, took one square with me, and ran to meet the car before it reached the dispersing crowd.

"Did Loran tell you what's happening?" I asked.

"Yes. I want to help."

I stepped onto the running board of the car without opening the door. I leaned forward and touched Nora's cheek.

"You're my daughter, and I'm that proud of you. Nothing else matters now. Drive to Glen's office. I'll meet you there. We don't know what to do, but you will be of help, I'm sure. Even more important, I don't want you coming down with this awful sickness. Tie on this mask—now—and then drive to the office. Patty is there."

Nora said, "Mother—"

"Off with you," I said. "We can talk later."

She tied on the mask and drove away. I went back to the crowd. Before long I had given out everything made of gauze, and we were still short. Women hurried home to fashion masks out of anything porous enough to breathe through. The afternoon train came in with Boston newspapers that headlined, for the first time, the enormity of this epidemic. More people were dying of it each day than soldiers were being killed in the war.

I looked for Glen but I was unable to find him, so I drove the car to the curb and left it there for him. I hurried home on foot. Nora was there, but Patty had gone with the patient in the ambulance.

"We had a very sick man, and he's been taken to the hospital," I told Nora. "Patty went with him. You and I will do the best we can. I'm not too certain what that will be, but Glen will tell us. Nora, we may be in for a catastrophe such as neither you nor I have ever known."

"I didn't think influenza was that serious," she argued.

"This kind is. Oh, I'm as ignorant as you, but my dear, I know what is going to happen. I'll tell you one day—soon, I hope—how I know this. For now, please

. . . please take my word for it. A great many people are going to get very sick, and many of them will die. We have to do the best we can. It won't be much, I'm afraid, and there's even a fine chance we'll come down with it."

"Where shall we begin?" she asked.

"We'd best act according to our ability to do the most good. With so many people sick there'll be need for food. Simple, nourishing food. Prepared in large quantities and taken to those who are ill and have no one to provide for them. The patients will have to be watched over, but we can't be everywhere, so relatives will have to care for them. Remember, entire families may come down with it. And become our responsibility. We'll set up sort of a center here."

"Coordinate things," Nora said. "I'm good at that."

"Nora, you may be sorely needed on the Hill. Your people are not going to be immune."

"My people are down here," she said tersely. "If they get sick up there, I'll do what I can, but my place is working with you. Aren't you afraid?"

"Of what? Dying? Yes, I'm afraid of that. I'm afraid of even becoming ill. But until I do die, or I am too ill to be of any use, I'm going to keep doing what I can."

"Up there . . ." she pointed vaguely over her shoulder, but I knew what she meant, "they're terribly afraid. Gabe and Evelyn have locked themselves in their room and won't let anyone in. Loran ordered all the servants to leave at once. He has a gun lying across the table in the reception hall, and he says if anybody tries to get in he'll use it."

I shook my head in sorrow at their ignorance. "Loran won't see the intruder who will make him sick. Germs cannot be seen except under a microscope, and there's no way to keep them out."

"Loran thinks they won't dare come up there."

I moved toward her and held her gently by the

460

shoulders. Our eyes met above the silly-looking gauze masks we wore.

"Nora, whatever happens, I want you to know that I was wrong. I'm sorry and I'm proud at the same time. Sorry I misjudged you and heartbroken that I refused to believe you. But oh, so proud I have two daughters like you and Patty."

"It wouldn't do to kiss one another," Nora said. Her wide eyes were brimming with tears, though none fell. "Or even come closer than this."

"And no time to carry on a conversation unless it concerns this damned bug that's going around killing people. Now, you start boiling water in every pot you can find while I run down to the market and bring back everything needed to make soups and broths. The epidemic hasn't struck hard here yet, but it's going to. Glen thinks so, and I'm positive it will. So if we can have things ready, we can move about helping others when it gets worse."

"I'm not very good in a kitchen," she confessed, "but I can boil water, I'm sure."

I drove to the market, explained what I wanted, and came back with all the meat and soupbones I could manage. Between us, Nora and I cooked broth and soup. We filled every dish we could find and then from the cellar brought up Mason jars and filled those.

Patty came home just before dark. She sank into the chair behind Glen's desk. "Mama, it's unbelievable. The hospital filled up overnight, and today the corridors are full. There are no empty beds until . . . someone dies. Those who get better are sent home as quickly as possible. They're too weak and helpless to do anything. How is it here?"

"I'm not sure. I can only guess it must be serious, because your father's not been back. . . ."

"Who's in the house? I hear someone—"

"Your sister," I said. "She's helping."

Patty jumped up and ran into the house. I heard

461

the two girls greet one another warmly and, being intelligent enough not to embrace, they talked about working together.

"You're a nurse," Nora said. "You can do far more good than I. Oh, if there's anything I can do—"

"I'm only a student nurse, Deborah."

"Nora," she said. "My name is Nora. Around here, anyway. You have had training, and I've no idea how to care for a sick person. All the education I've had isn't worth a penny at a time like this. But I'll help. . . ."

"Remember one thing," Patty said in the voice of authority, "don't let yourself get tired. That's when you're most apt to come down with it. If you feel any weakness, no matter how little—or dizziness, or you start to cough . . . go back to the Hill. It may not do much good, but you'll be away from most of it. . . ."

"I'll take care of myself," Nora vowed. "Don't be worrying about me."

"I will, you know. I'll worry my head off, but right now I'd better worry about the rest of the town. I'm going out to see how bad things are. Watch out for Mother, Nora."

"Yes, but it will more likely be Mother watching out for me."

I hurried into the kitchen. "We'll need to make other things . . . I'm not sure what, as yet, but Glen will return soon, I hope, and he can give us suggestions."

Glen didn't return until after ten, and he sank wearily into a chair at the table. Nora brought him a dish of food I'd kept hot. He pulled down his mask and managed to fashion a smile.

"Hello, Nora. You are Nora? These masks . . ."

"I'm Nora, Doctor."

"She's come to do what she can to help," I explained.

"That's fine. We need all the help we can get. Even so, you're more than welcome. Where's Patty?"

462

"Outside, going about," Nora said.

Glen shook his head. "I wish she didn't have to, but . . . I doubt I could stop her."

"How are things?" I asked. "How serious is it?"

"Beyond comprehension. There are more than sixty people down with it."

"Oh, dear God!" I said. "As bad as that."

"This is only the beginning. I telephoned Portland and Boston from the mill office. Statistics are beginning to show how terrible this really is. The latest count shows that eight million people are sick. Theaters are closed, church services are being held outside. They've run out of coffins long ago. Burials are out of hand . . . the situation is regarded as being far worse than the war. The losses are heavier—far heavier."

"What of the village? Right here?" Nora asked. "Will it get much worse?"

"I believe it will. I've men bringing beds from every house that can spare one, to the corridors in the mill where I've set up sort of a temporary hospital. They get filled almost as fast as we get them there."

"But how did it spread so quickly?" Nora asked. "We're so far away from big cities. . . ."

"The first to die in this town visited in Boston and came back two days ago. With the germ. Before she became really ill, she'd spread it everywhere. Oh, it wasn't her fault. How could she know? But it happened, and now we're as badly off as a big city. Worse, in fact, for we don't have the facilities to handle it."

"Glen," I said, "Nora and I have prepared broth and soups. Can they be safely given?"

"They'll do more good than all the medicines I can prescribe, none of which are doing anything so far as I can see. But I don't want you or Nora—"

"We're not listening," Nora said.

Glen nodded. "I didn't think you would. I'm going to prepare a gargle—use it every chance you get. If you come into contact with a sick person, wash your

463

hands thoroughly. Cleanliness seems to be most essential. Whatever you do, don't bring any sick person into this house. It may be your only refuge when you need rest. You have to be heartless sometimes."

"I learned how to be long ago," Nora said in a mild voice.

"Please, Nora." I moved toward her. A gesture from Glen stopped me.

"Don't get close to anyone," he warned. "Thank you for a fine supper. Keep a pot of coffee going if you can. I don't know when I'll be back. Do the best you can."

He smiled before he raised the gauze mask and then he was gone once more. I sat down. Nora poured me a cup of coffee and another for herself. She sank wearily into a chair across the table from me as we lowered the masks.

"We can make custards," she said. "I heard they are good for sick people."

I nodded. "I'll get milk and eggs. Right now, I'm going to take a large container of broth down to the mill. Some of the sick may need nourishment."

"We'll take two containers down," Nora said. "You're not leaving me here."

We took the time to dress warmly, for the October nights were chilly. Nora had brought no clothing, but Patty's fitted her very well and, encased in heavy coats, we set out for the mill with two large containers of steaming hot broth in the back of Nora's car.

We both flinched at what we saw when we entered the corridors at the mill. All beds were full; several very ill people were sitting in chairs; others had made crude beds out of two larger chairs. We went to work at once. Patty was there, in full charge of a dozen girls she had recruited and trained as best she could. The smell of sickness and death overpowered the odors of the ancient mill, and when I moved toward a closed door, Nora arose to intercept me.

464

"Don't go in there, please. I did. It's . . . where they put the dead."

I said, "Oh, thank you for telling me," in a voice that sounded as if I'd just been informed the room had been recently painted and I might ruin my clothes if I ventured into it.

By midnight Nora began to droop with fatigue. Patty came to me and gestured toward her. "Take her home, Mama. If she gets too exhausted, she'll come down with this."

"Yes, I will, Patty. You're quite wonderful, you know."

"I'm so incompetent I could cry," she said. "Besides, even if I wore a cap, there's not a thing I could do to help. They either get better or they die. It's awful."

I had to grasp Nora's arm to get her away from a woman so ravaged by this sickness I didn't recognize her. I led Nora out of the mill to where her car was parked.

"Drive home," I said. "We've had enough. We must rest."

"But there are so many sick——"

"Patty's orders."

"I wish I had her strength and skill," Nora said. "I can speak in four languages, but these bloody germs wouldn't understand that, would they? I am tired."

I felt of her forehead, disregarding the command that we should not be in physical contact. She had no fever.

"We'll eat something and go to bed," I said. "I'll get you up early."

"I hope you will. We've so much to do."

One of the Cameron big cars was parked at the curb outside the house.

Nora said, "Damn!"

"Yes, I know," I said. "Who is it?"

"I can't tell yet. One of them must be sick."

465

"I'll go," I said.

"After what they did to you?"

"At this moment, what difference does it make what anybody did? I see now, it's Helen."

She was standing beside the car when we parked and then approached her. "I've come to take you home, darling," she said to Nora. She disdained to favor me with even a glance.

"I'm not going," Nora said. "I'm needed here."

"Your grandmother and grandfather are both very ill. They want you, Deborah."

"I'll go, Helen," I said. "Nora is close to exhaustion."

"I don't recall asking you," Helen said tartly.

"Doesn't even this bring you down?" I asked. "What difference does it make? If Nora goes with you in her state of exhaustion, she may come down with the disease. I'm not that tired. I may be able to do something. . . ."

"Are you coming, Deborah?" Helen asked.

"No," Nora said. "My place is here."

"Your grandfather and grandmother are ill. . . ."

"There are scores who are ill here. I go where I can do the most good. I don't see you feverish or sick. Can't you care for them?"

"Deborah, I demand that you come back with me at once."

Nora's shoulders slumped, and she heaved a great sigh. "I'm not very clever at the moment, Helen. I can think of only one thing to say to you. Go to hell!"

She walked toward the house. I stepped in front of Helen to prevent her following.

"She's that tired she doesn't know what she's saying, Helen. How bad are your father and mother?"

"I think . . . they're going to . . . die."

"Go back. I'll follow you in Nora's car."

I hurried into the house to change clothes and do a careful washup job on my hands and face. Nora, stretched out on my bed, was trying to get to sleep, but she was that exhausted all she could do was toss and turn.

"Your grandmother and grandfather need care," I said. "We can't just dismiss them, so I'm going up there for a while. I want you to take off your clothes and get in bed properly."

"Yes, Mother," she said sleepily.

I'd never before heard two words I appreciated more, but she didn't abide by them, for as I left she fell, fully dressed, into a sound sleep, and I didn't disturb her except to cover her with a blanket.

I brought along some of the broth we'd prepared, and I drove to the Hill. This time Loran let me in.

"Martha's sick," he explained. "Half the world is sick. What's come over all of us?"

"It's a tiny, invisible germ," I said. "But powerful enough to bring down the biggest of us. Beware of it, Loran. You're no exception."

"Deborah is with you, I understand."

"Yes," I said, but I gave no further explanation. I went on by him and upstairs. Helen was there with her father and mother.

Evelyn lay in the large double bed, and a smaller single bed had been rolled in for Gabriel's use. They were both deathly sick I could see at a glance. I'd brought along an extra thermometer, and I took their temperatures first. Neither saw fit to welcome me with even a word, though they were quite capable of talking. Evelyn was running one hundred and two, Gabriel was a hundred and four.

"Is there ice?" I asked Helen.

"I suppose there must be."

"Then fetch me enough to make two ice packs. I want to bring their temperatures down if I can."

She hurried to obey me, though taking orders from me didn't sit well with her. I soaked a washcloth in cold water and cleansed Evelyn's face and neck. I patted her dry and did the same for Gabriel.

She said nothing. He murmured something that sounded like thanks. Helen returned and I fashioned ice bags, applied them, and asked about Martha.

"She's in her room upstairs," Helen said.

"When did you look in on her last?"

"I don't remember. Before I went down to bring Deborah back. Maeve, you cannot take her from us. I forbid it, and I will use every means at my command to prevent this."

I made a third ice bag, filled a basin with cold water, dropped a washcloth into it, placed a towel over my arm, and went up to the servants' quarters on the top floor. Martha lay in her bed.

Helen had followed me. "She wasn't bad off when I last saw her," she said.

I handed her the basin, towel, and ice bag. "She's not bad off now, either. She's dead."

When Helen gave a scream of horror, I pushed her out of the room. I went about doing what was necessary. I covered Martha's wasted form with a sheet, pinned it, covered her with a blanket, and went downstairs. Loran was waiting for me. Helen had apparently given him the news.

"She brought the sickness here," he said. "She went into the village yesterday."

"A pity she didn't stay there," I said. "We might have saved her life. Here she never had a chance. No one even looked in on her."

"I'll telephone the undertaker."

"No one will answer. The undertaker is too busy, and there are no coffins. I'll see what's to be done when I go back to town."

"Seems to me," he said, "you're taking on a great deal of responsibility."

"I will surrender it to you, gladly," I said. "I'm

sure you won't mind sitting with your brother and his wife while they die."

"Are they that bad?"

"They are old. Evelyn is frail. The disease has a strong grip on Gabriel. There is a good chance they will not live through this."

"By God," he said, "I'm going to get in some doctor—"

"None are available," I told him. "Neither are nurses. If you were worried sufficiently you might have investigated the situation a little more, Loran. Right now half the town is in bed and the other half is trying to care for them and growing exhausted in doing so, while this exhaustion makes them easier prey to this germ. There's not enough of anything to go around. The hospital in Bridgeton cannot accept another patient, no matter who it may be. The only thing to be done for those two sick people is to try to bring down their fever, warm them when the chill comes, and give them a little nourishing food. They cannot feed themselves. They have to be fed. Do that and trust in God, and maybe they'll get better. I have left broth in the kitchen. Heat it and give it to them if they are able to swallow."

"If I fill myself with brandy, will that help?" he asked.

"It might. Nobody has any answers. However, I might remind you that Helen alone cannot care for Gabriel and Evelyn. She will have to sleep sometime. So it might be well—and wise—on your part not to get drunk. You are going to have to take your turn before long."

"The devil with you!" he shouted. "I'll do as I please. I think you're exaggerating the whole thing."

I returned to the sickroom and instructed Helen how to give her patients nourishment. I took their temperatures again. They were down slightly, but not enough to be significant, and they would soon rise again.

"Loran may become too intoxicated to help," I warned her. "I'll try to find someone to come for Martha."

"We need Deborah here. This is her place. This is where she belongs."

"She doesn't think so, Helen. If she changes her mind, she may return whenever she pleases. I'll be going now. There's nothing more I can do here."

How large and ostentatious this mansion was—and how silent and dreadfully filled with apprehension and death. I walked through the rooms downstairs to find Loran at the sideboard, where he was drinking from a tall glass nearly filled with brandy. He said nothing, and neither did I.

Outside I felt that I was breathing free again. It was very late now, but time stood still in the town of Cameron. Nobody cared what the hour was. Day or night, those on their feet were busy caring for someone they loved who was either slowly getting better or far more quickly dying.

When I returned home, Nora was still sound asleep, and in another room Patty had taken off her nurse's uniform and fallen across the bed to rest. I didn't disturb either one of them, though I did look closely at their faces for signs of sweat and the beginning of fever. I found none.

Glen came home shortly before three in the morning. By then I was curled up in a parlor chair, and he had to shake me awake. He dropped wearily into one of the other chairs.

"It's not improving," he said. "Last count I had forty-two more definite diagnoses and about a dozen probables. It's so fast, Maeve."

"It's what the mirror told Patty."

"I hope to heaven when she looks again there'll be something more pleasant than this. I've got to sleep.

470

If I don't, I'll fall down. Give me two hours. No more than that, darling. There are too many sick people. . . ."

He arose and lay down on the sofa. His feet hung off it, but that didn't matter; he was asleep in seconds. I managed to raise his legs and cram his feet onto the sofa before I covered him. Then I went into the kitchen and drank coffee before I cleaned up, made fresh coffee, and sat in a semi-stupor until dawn.

I didn't do any thinking. My mind was incapable of it. Instead I fell into a half-sleeping, half-conscious state wherein I knew what was going on but I didn't much care.

I gave Glen four hours instead of two, because he was so surely in need of it. Even if someone suffered for that, others would benefit, I knew. He was angry at first but quickly cooled down and saw the logic of my decision.

"The girls," I said, "went to sleep two or three hours before you did, and they're still sound asleep. I'll wake them presently."

"After which you're to get your own rest," he said sternly. "You're not made of iron, either, you know."

"Martha—you remember the housekeeper on the Hill? She died last night. I've not been able to do anything about her. Frankly, I don't know what to do or what can be done, though certainly something must."

"I'll send the undertaker. A truckload of plain coffins were coming in this morning, and if they want her buried on the Hill, I'll try to send two men to dig the grave. No service, however."

"That has to wait. I know. I'm afraid Gabriel and Evelyn are in serious condition, too. If you could go up there—"

"My first visit."

I served him eggs and ham with several slices of toast, for he ate like a famished man. "How bad is

471

the situation, Glen? In the light of day, and when you are rested, how does it look?"

"It's unbelievably bad. In wild fancy I couldn't have envisioned anything like this, and we're not as bad off as they are in the cities. I don't know when this will run its course. Nobody does, for there's no precedent. All we can do is fumble about and try to do the right thing. There were six deaths last night. I expect I'll find four more this morning. Are you watching the girls?"

"Yes, as closely as I know how."

"Good—and be sure to watch yourself, too. Keep in mind how fast this strikes. The longer you fight it on your feet, the worse the attack will be. Give in the moment you feel out of sorts. Stop whatever you're doing and go to bed at once."

"Yes, Glen. I'm afraid you're going to overdo."

"There are times when you can't stop, darling. I'll be careful. Thank you for breakfast. I'll look in whenever I find the opportunity."

Patty came down first, rested, in a clean uniform, and in a hurry to have breakfast and go.

"How did Nora do?" she asked.

"Fine. Not as well as you, naturally, because she hasn't had the training, but as well as I could do."

"Papa is all right?"

"He had four hours' sleep and was off again about half an hour ago. He seems to be bearing up."

"If he gets too tired, that bug will get him. Make him rest."

"What about you?"

"I'll be all right. Were there many deaths last night, do you know?"

"Your father said six, and he expects four more by this morning. It's no better, perhaps even worse. Martha—the housekeeper on the Hill—died, too. Evelyn and Gabriel are very sick."

"This is the most vicious disease. What about Nora? I mean . . . Nora and the Hill?"

"She refused to go back. She felt she was needed more here. Anyway, Helen seems all right, and Loran decided that enough brandy would keep the germs away from him."

"I think they'd be afraid of him without the brandy." She had quickly eaten eggs and ham, drunk half a cup of coffee, and was ready to go. I went to the door with her.

"Mama, I'm glad Nora's back," she said earnestly.

"Yes, so am I. She'll be down presently, and I'll send her to the mill to help you."

"Believe me, she's needed."

Someone from the hospital called to announce two deaths of local people. This doctor had more information about the overall picture of the epidemic for me to relay to Glen.

"It's spread nationwide," he told me. "Fatalities are so numerous there's been no time to make an accurate count. Tell Glen the Department of Health in Washington says every precaution must be taken. No assemblies, schools to be kept closed, theaters, racetracks, churches, all kinds of meetings are advised against. The only advice they give is to stay in the open as much as possible when you are well. Breathe in as much fresh air as you can, eat lightly, and rest often. Don't overexert. That can be dangerous. Whiskey is of no value; people should be cautioned against spitting or coughing; and masks must be worn whenever a sick person is approached."

"We're following those suggestions quite well already," I told him. "I'll inform Glen as soon as he finds time to come home."

Glen returned in the middle of the afternoon, in need of a shave and clean clothes, tired, but exhilarated because there'd been no new cases since mid-morning.

"It may be waning," he said.

I told him about the call from the hospital. "They say it's going to grow worse, Glen."

"Damn," he said bitterly. "Well, I saw the Camerons this morning. Gabe seems a little better. Evelyn is weaker. It's a gamble whether they'll come through."

"Helen isn't down with it?"

"No, not yet. Loran must have bathed in whiskey or some spirits, though he was lucid enough, and he's very much concerned with what this is doing to the mill business."

"He would feel that way. What of the housekeeper's body?"

"I arranged for burial on the Hill. Have you heard from the girls?"

"No. They're too busy to send any word or come home. Patty was up early. Nora left two hours ago. We didn't even take time to talk."

"I never did have a chance to ask you what happened when you offered to sell out."

"They accepted promptly. They were to have the cash in the bank today, I think. I've lost track of time, sort of. It doesn't matter. I'll not do anything about it until this epidemic is over."

"I doubt you'd be able to, anyway. How did it happen Nora came down?"

"She told me she had nothing to do with the poisoning. I didn't believe her, and I said so. We parted on a grim note, I'm afraid. But when she came down after the epidemic began, she swore she didn't know anything about it, and this time I believed her. I should have the first time."

"She's going to stay now?"

"I think so. I don't suppose she's certain. This is no time to make a decision, and I wouldn't press her. All I know is that now I have my two daughters and I'm that proud of the two of them I could shout it from the rooftop."

474

"I'm glad. You look done in. Have you had any sleep?"

"Well . . . not exactly. . . ."

He seized my hand. "Come along. We'll both get some rest. If they let us."

SEVENTEEN

For another ten days the plague swept through the country and through our town. If fifty were ill, thirty became well, ten or so recovered, but not completely and remained very ill, the others died—often so quickly we were at a total loss to do anything to help. There wasn't much to be done, anyway. We struggled, sometimes thought we might have pulled someone through—and that person would be dead an hour later. It was discouraging and frightful to a point where we finally became immune to sorrow and pity.

Then Evelyn died. Helen had come rushing to town for help. Nobody could find Glen, and Patty refused to abandon the makeshift hospital where she was so vitally needed.

"I'll go," I told Helen. "Nora is not to know about it until later."

"You have deprived us of the comfort she could have given her grandmother," Helen said angrily. "And of the help we all could have used. Her place is with us, not with these . . . these . . . people. . . ."

"I'll be at the house as soon as possible," I said. "If you find Nora and prevail upon her to go with you, I'll see to it that whatever happens on the Hill, you will have to handle yourself. And that means digging graves, if necessary."

She paled at the thought and stopped arguing. When I reached the mansion, I found that Helen was right. Evelyn had died sometime during the night. I looked in on Gabriel, who was barely conscious. There was nothing I could do for him. I returned to the room where they'd taken Evelyn after she'd grown so ill. There I prepared her body as I had that of Martha, the housekeeper.

I went downstairs to find Loran slumped in one of the big chairs. The drawing room was dusty, the furniture disarrayed, and the whole house needed an airing.

"She died about three this morning," Loran said without looking up. "She just . . . closed her eyes and died."

"Gabriel may die tonight," I told him. "He has no stamina left, and the disease had made him terribly weak."

"Sending your husband to see him won't do any good, will it?"

"No. I don't believe he'd come. He must devote himself to those he can save."

"There's no improvement in town?"

"No, not that we can determine. I might say you could have been of some help."

"Down there with all those sick people? Oh, no! There's enough sickness here. I'm not going down. I'm not raising a finger to help anybody. I think they'll all die anyhow."

"There's one thing you'll have to do," I told him. "Dig Evelyn's grave—and perhaps Gabriel's later. It's impossible to send anyone here to do that."

"They came to bury Martha."

"The epidemic wasn't as bad then. There are no men to spare."

He arose, a trifle unsteadily, I thought. "What have

476

you done about the papers giving us full control of the mill?"

"Nothing. Not one thing."

"You promised to deliver them to the bank. . . ."

"There is no bank. It hasn't been open for days. I'll look in on Gabriel again before I leave, and I likely won't be back. Take care of your own, Loran."

Gabriel was unconscious, muttering feebly and out of his head. Helen had remained in the room, seated close by a wide-open window as far from the bed as she could get. I walked over and closed the window.

"It's almost November, and cold," I reminded her. "What the patient does not need is to be chilled."

"They said those not sick should breathe fresh air. . . ."

"Then go outside—or to another room."

"You delight in giving orders, don't you? You hate all of us."

"Helen," I said patiently, "I'm tired. I've been tired for nearly three weeks. All I've seen is sickness and death. I don't want to argue with you."

"My mother would be alive if you hadn't prevented your husband from coming up here to care for her. He should be here now, to help my father."

"In town there are nearly two hundred sick people. Here there are two—and you and Loran both quite capable of caring for them. Helen, the family doesn't dominate the town any more. The Spanish influenza does. And believe me, it's far more powerful than any combination of Camerons."

"You won't get Deborah," she said.

"Helen, this is nonsense now. In that bed your father lies dying, and all you can think of is yourself. I don't know what will happen after this is all over. Maybe we'll all be dead. The way it's going . . ." I closed my eyes and turned away. "I didn't mean that. But whatever differences there are between you and me—or Nora and me, if there are any, can wait. Everything can wait, because, you silly, selfish woman, death doesn't wait."

I walked out of the room angrily and didn't stop to tell Loran I was leaving. I went out to the car and drove back to town. On my way down the hill I remembered the time when I'd intercepted Helen so that I could lift Nora from her carriage and hold my baby in my arms. I remembered how Helen had berated me, threatened me. It all seemed so long ago. I drove to the mill and the temporary hospital Glen had set up there.

Patty, in a soiled uniform, had just made her rounds and entered the last temperature reading on the chart suspended from the foot of the last bed. She tried to smile, but it was too much of an effort. I took her arm and led her to the mill office, where I made her lie down on the big leather sofa Loran was accustomed to use.

"Why didn't you tell me this sofa was here?" she complained. "I could have used it. . . . Oh, Mother, forgive me. I'm so tired. . . ."

"Where's Nora?"

"Washing my uniforms and ironing them. Can you imagine her doing that? I didn't have to tell her—she just gathered them up and went to work. She's as tired as I. Have you seen Papa?"

"No," I said in sudden alarm. "Is he all right?"

"He must be made of iron. He hasn't stopped in hours."

"Is there any improvement here?"

"Papa thinks some. We had two empty beds for a couple of hours this morning, and that hasn't happened before. Oh, Mama, it has to stop soon. We can't stand much more of this."

"I know. Evelyn is dead, and Gabriel won't last the night. I'll tell Nora when I see her."

"If you don't . . . I'll try. . . ." Patty closed her eyes and fell asleep in a matter of seconds. I closed the office door and pulled down the window shades. There were no blankets, nothing with which to cover her. I left her there and tiptoed out of the room.

I asked for Nora, and someone said she'd gone home. That information startled me until I discovered it was my home and not the Hill where she'd gone. I drove there at once.

Nora was in the kitchen ironing uniforms. Her face dripped with perspiration, and her hair was clinging moistly to her head.

"I'm not very good at this," she confessed, "but I'm doing my best."

"It's fine," I said. "Let me finish."

"No—please. I have to do this. I must, Mother."

"Very well." I sat down at the kitchen table. "These are times when you need courage, my dear. I don't have good news."

"The Hill?" she asked, without pausing in her work.

"Your grandmother died last night. Your grandfather is terribly ill."

"Yes, I expected they'd not come through." She closed her eyes for a moment. "They were old and not in very good health." She was holding back her sorrow only with great effort.

"Helen and Loran seem to be all right."

"Yes—I'm glad of that." She seemed to shake herself back to reality.

"Patty just told me the epidemic might be letting up a little."

"I haven't been able to see any improvement. Don't you wear your mask any more, Mother?"

"It became a nuisance, and people wearing masks were getting sick every hour."

"I discarded mine, too—for the same reason. I saw Glen about an hour ago. He looked awful."

I arose hastily. "Where did you see him last?"

"Walking down Main Street, going from house to house as always."

"Thank you. I'll try to find him."

I drove slowly along the street. Glen wasn't using the car these days; he claimed it was easier simply to walk from patient to patient, there were so many of them. Finally I had to pull to the curb and simply keep watch until he emerged from one of the houses. Then I shouted and caught up with him.

He was unshaven again, this time with at least a two-day growth of beard. His face was pale and drawn and his eyes bloodshot, with the lids so heavy he could barely hold them up.

"Get in," I said. "I'm going to take you home."

"Can't . . . too many sick people. . . ."

"You're as sick as your patients. Or you will be, if you don't stop. Glen, please . . . get in the car. At least come back and have something to eat."

He pulled himself onto the running board and finally tumbled onto the seat beside me. "I am tired," he admitted. "You're right. I'd better rest. I just needed someone to tell me so."

I brought him home to find Nora ready to drive down to the mill with Patty's uniforms. She looked at Glen and shook her head in sympathy, but she didn't comment, for which I was grateful. I fed Glen, though he didn't eat very much. Then I made him go upstairs, undress, and go to bed. He was asleep before I left the room.

I went to the kitchen to have a cup of coffee and sit alone to think about this tragedy and to wonder what it meant. There were going to be great changes in Cameron after this. With Evelyn and Gabriel gone, Helen and I would own the mill, sharing equally. Unless I went through with my original plan and sold out. At this moment, I didn't know what I'd do. I was half tempted to slip into the bedroom while Glen slept and consult the mirror, but I decided the time didn't seem quite right for that. Besides, I was afraid

480

of the thing. All it seemed to predict any more were catastrophes.

I was very tired, though I was able to think lucidly. Glen would have his chance to take over a large, new hospital. I knew he'd dreamed of that for years. So long as I retained an interest in the mill, I doubted he'd leave Cameron, so it would be best if I did dispose of the stock. That would make Helen the sole owner. But—what if anything happened to her? Nora would inherit, no doubt. There was always Loran waiting in the background, and I knew very well that if Loran saw the slightest opportunity of gaining control of the mill, he'd take it, no matter what he would be compelled to do. I didn't think he'd find Helen hard to handle. She hated the mill, anyway, and longed to go abroad again, once the war was over. It came to me then that Loran was eventually going to own the mill. It was possible he'd schemed and waited for this chance, ready to take advantage of anything that would weaken the hold his brother and his niece had on it.

The coffee cup clattered against the saucer as I let go of it with nervous fingers. Perhaps—and the thought did stagger my imagination—even to the point where Loran would resort to any means, including the death of his nephew, as well. Setting the stage twenty years ago for what was happening now. In all that time, the thought had never occurred to me, but it did now, because Loran was suddenly in a position to achieve his life-long ambition. Getting rid of Helen would be non-violent and easy. Send her away, with Nora preferably. There'd be no one else to oppose him then. Except me!

If I refused to sell my shares. Then I'd become his target. Perhaps I always had been.

Glen didn't awaken until seven that evening. Neither Patty nor Nora had come home, so while Glen shaved and cleaned up, I prepared his supper.

When he did come down, I was so shocked by his appearance that I couldn't hide it. Without the growth of beard, he looked terribly pale and worn. His eyes, especially, were sunken and listless. He wasn't even angry that I'd allowed him to sleep away all that precious time he could have been with his patients. But he'd had some news.

"Last night I talked to Dr. Burnette in Boston. He's with the Massachusetts Health Department. He thinks the epidemic is waning."

"Oh, Glen, if only that's true."

"It doesn't hurt to hope, anyway. Up here we've not had a real good idea of what this sickness has done. Dick Burnette told me last night. Up to this date, forty-five thousand people died in New York State alone. Hundreds died each day in New York City. In Philadelphia the death rate was seven hundred times normal. Reporting facilities from all over the world are not too good, but it's estimated that maybe twenty million died of it."

"Twenty million!" I exclaimed.

"In three or four months that hellish germ killed as many people as the war killed in four years. Oh, Germany has the plague, too. Nobody escaped. Whole armies were destroyed by it. Shiploads of troops sent to France arrived with half the men sick and many dead. We've been through one of the great catastrophes of history."

I shook my head in dismay. "I was taught nothing had ever been, or would be, worse than the potato famine in Ireland. But this. . . ."

"Let's hope it's coming to an end. Because I'm almost there, darling, and I'm forced to admit it."

I looked at him keenly. "Glen, if you do not make your rounds tonight, will more people die than if you made them?"

"I don't know. They seem to die no matter what I do."

482

"Then you're not going out again this evening. If there are any calls, I'll simply say I can't find you. Glen, I insist on this."

He nodded slowly. "You don't have to insist. I feel terrible, to be truthful about it."

"The flu?" I asked anxiously.

"Must be. Throat's sore, I get dizzy, and I'm growing weaker. I knew it the moment I woke up."

"You've done all they could expect of any man. Patty and Nora will handle everything, and I'll help. I want you to go back to bed. Please, Glen, don't fight me now."

"I couldn't fight a gnat," he confessed. "Bring up some of the yellow gargle, will you, please? And my instrument bag. I'll want you to take my temperature."

I got him into bed without an argument, proof of how ill he must have been. His temperature reading was a hundred and two. It could have been worse. I set about bringing it down.

Nora arrived about an hour afterwards and promptly took my place at Glen's bedside. She'd learned a great deal quickly from Patty, and she was already a good nurse. When Patty came home, I was downstairs and she saw at once the tear stains on my cheeks.

"Papa?" she asked in alarm.

"He's come down with it," I said. "I'm afraid it's going to be bad. The man's worn out. There's nothing left with which to fight the illness. Nora's with him now, so there's no need for you to go there immediately. You've not been eating regularly, or well, and I want you to eat a decent supper first. I insist, Patty. What will I do if I have two—or even three—sick people on my hands?"

Patty ate—without appetite, but she ate—while I advised her of the facts and the statistics Glen had told me. She was as shocked as I'd been to learn of the real damage this illness had caused.

"Nora's grandmother and grandfather are dead," I

told her. "I'm not sure if I told you that. It's getting so I'm constantly confused. Anyway, I told Loran he would have to bury them. I also had a dreadful row with Helen."

"I wonder why those two ungrateful people didn't get sick," Patty grumbled.

"Everything is going to change with the Camerons gone," I said. "This won't be the same town or the same mill any more."

"I'm going up to relieve Nora," Patty said. "She's all in, too, though she won't admit it. Remember how I used to say she was stuck-up? Mama, I was never so wrong about a person in my life. If only we could have grown up together."

"Your father and I wanted it that way, but . . . those people on the Hill. . . ."

"I know, Mama. I don't blame you, and neither does Nora. When things settle down again, there's going to be so much for all of us to talk about. Nora's full of questions I can't answer, and I've got a few myself."

"We'll explain everything in due time," I said. "You run along now."

"I'll send Nora down. . . ."

"No. I'm going out. To see Glen's patients. When he wakes up, he'll be anxious to get out of bed and make his rounds—until I tell him I've made them. Don't worry about me. I've been able to catch catnaps all along. I'm fine."

I had Glen's record book, which enabled me to schedule proper visits and to inform me of each patient's condition the last time Glen saw that sick person. Glen's notes were skimpy because he was always rushed, but there was enough to route me and to give me a good picture of what to expect.

Within the next three hours I knew the agony and the work Glen had gone through. There did seem to be some hope, however, because I didn't encounter

484

a single death, and only two new patients were brought to my attention. I did my best to bring down fevers, instruct relatives how to care for their ill, and how to maintain cleanliness, for it did seem that carelessness did help spread the ailment.

I returned home to find both Patty and Nora at Glen's bedside. They were extremely worried by his condition, and after a quick examination my worries exceeded theirs. Still, I had to retain my sanity and try to be as practical as I could.

"Both you girls go down to the mill. Conditions must be getting bad with nobody in charge. I'll take care of Glen. No one is more suited for that than me. Run along now and, mind you, rest as soon as you feel tired. I think the trouble is letting up, but one can never be sure of that."

Nora went to change into fresh clothes. Patty, already wearing a newly washed and ironed uniform, had time to motion me into the corridor where Glen couldn't hear her.

"Mama, I'm frightened by his condition. The fever doesn't go down, and he seems to be getting weaker. He's been doing a lot of coughing, too, though that has subsided."

"We can be thankful for something, then," I said.

"There's a time when they get too weak to cough, and that's the most dangerous of all. If his fever goes up one degree, please send for me."

"My dear, what can you do that I can't?"

"I can be with him," she said.

I drew her to me and held her in a tight embrace. "I'm sorry, darling. Of course you want to be with him. I'm proud of you."

"He—may die, Mama. I've seen so many of them go. I hate to say it, but you must be warned and ready. . . ."

"Yes, Patty, I know. I think I've known since he came home and went back to bed without a struggle."

485

"Have you looked in the mirror?" she asked.

"No. I've not had the courage."

"I thought about it, but I didn't, either." Nora came out of the room she'd chosen as her own. "I'd better go along with her."

"Be careful of yourselves, both of you," I said.

Then I entered the room Glen and I shared, and I sat down beside the bed to do what little I could to help him endure the torture he must be going through with every gasping breath. Later I prepared a steam kettle with a thymol and eucalyptus jelly that vaporized. By dawn he was breathing a little easier, but he'd not awakened, and I was afraid he'd slipped from normal sleep into the deeper world of unconsciousness.

His pulse was weaker and at times quite thready, which alarmed me and set me to wondering what else I could do, only to find myself barren of a single idea. I'd done all that was possible. It was now up to Glen—if he had the strength.

Nora came back at seven in the morning, sent by Patty to relieve me.

"While you rest," she said, "I'll sit with Glen. Then I'll rest a spell, and after that, Patty will come to relieve you again. We can keep going that way."

"He's not good, Nora. I think he's weaker."

"I'm always optimistic. I've seen them worse than this and come back. Please get some rest now."

I didn't bother with breakfast, but tumbled into bed still dressed. I managed to dislodge my shoes and let them thump to the floor. Seconds after that, I was asleep.

I awakened at noontime. Patty sat by Glen's bedside, dozing, but coming fully awake when I opened the door. She motioned me to go back into the hall, and she followed me there.

"He stirred a few times, as if he was waking up, and I don't want to disturb him. His temperature

486

went up one and a half degrees but went down half a degree an hour ago. I've kept cold towels on his forehead, and I've kept sponging his wrists."

"He didn't awaken?" I asked.

"No—not once. He never opened his eyes."

"Can you stay with him another few minutes?"

"Of course. As long as you like."

I managed a weak smile. "You can barely stand on your feet. I'll make breakfast, have mine as quickly as I can, and leave yours on the table. After you finish, go to bed. I'll wake you in time to go back to the mill and give Patty a chance to rest."

"Two hours," Nora said. "No more, please. Patty's exhausted."

"Two hours," I agreed, and hurried downstairs.

I sent her off at her designated time, after sitting by Glen and wondering if he had even a slight chance. Patty came home, and when she left the sickroom I heard her burst into tears before she could make the privacy of her own room. She did fall asleep, and I had to awaken her three hours later. After she freshened up, I made her something to eat and sent her off. Then I resumed my vigil. A frustrating, sorry vigil it was, because I could do nothing for this courageous and wonderful man who had given so much of himself for others that he was now in danger of dying. I prayed for him, and I cursed the illness that seemed to have done its best to destroy the world.

Glen lasted for thirty-six more hours, and then, as the epidemic took a definite turn for the better, he quietly died without ever having regained consciousness.

Had the epidemic kept on or even grown worse, it would have been without me. I was finished, in a numbed state of shock. We buried Glen two hours after he died, in a simple casket. We didn't have to beg or bribe grave diggers. There were a score of volunteers. There was no church service, in accordance with Glen's own rules, though the funeral procession stopped in front of the church long enough for the priest to administer his blessing, and then it continued on to the cemetery, where there were so many fresh graves.

Patty and Nora were my strength all through the ordeal of the formal service there. I was too tired and stunned to think. When it was over, Patty gave me a strong sleeping powder and put me to bed, where I slept for eighteen hours. It was a deep, dreamless sleep from which I awakened feeling better—until I recalled what had happened. Now the flood of tears finally came, until sheer exhaustion from weeping, and the commonsense thought that this was doing no good, prevailed over my sorrow.

I took a long, hot bath. The sound of water through the pipes brought Nora hurrying to my bedroom. By then I had toweled myself dry and was partially dressed.

"I just got in," Nora explained. "You've slept the clock around, almost."

"Thank you for not awakening me," I said. "I feel better. Is Patty all right?"

"Oh, yes. Tired, but things are beginning to ease up. There's been but one new case, and that not very severe. No more deaths, and Patty sent a number of people home from the hospital. If that's what you call what we have at the mill."

"I'm glad," I said. "You look tired."

"I'm fine. Both Patty and I are getting more sleep. She did some telephoning and learned the epidemic is on the wane all over."

"Yes," I said. I turned away from her, thinking of Glen, and then I turned back and held out my arms to her. "Forgive me, Nora. I'm selfish in my sorrow, and I've no right to be. We all risked our lives these last weeks. Glen sacrificed his, and that makes me proud of him. Just as I'm proud of my two daughters."

She wept briefly on my shoulder, as if she, too, had been holding back her tears, but I spoke softly to her, and she dried her tears finally and helped me finish dressing. We had something to eat, my breakfast, and what was actually her late supper, I'd slept so late.

"We've a great deal to discuss," I told her. "Much to decide. Everything has changed now."

"Will you sell your share of the mill?" she asked.

"I see little point in continuing with it. If you'd like, I'll be glad to sign over everything connected with the business to you. That will place you on an even footing with Helen, and I'm sure you'll get along with her better than I could."

"Mother, I can't just let the mill go."

"I realize that. Your father wouldn't have wanted it to happen."

"I have to stay. Loran will run the place, but I'm going to insist on changes. I won't accept your stock, Mother, but I will carry out the plans you've outlined. Helen may do her best to stop me, and so will Loran. Especially Loran, but I think I can handle them."

"You and Helen should work together well. She did bring you up. You spent most of your life with her."

"I've been thinking about her. Isn't it possible that they made her do what she did? To pretend she was my mother? Let me believe it?"

"No, dear, it was wrong even if she was forced to do that. Even threatened if she failed or refused. I cannot forgive her, but I can see how you can."

"She wanted only the very best for me."

"That's to her credit, of course. Oh, what are we talking about? We don't have to make up our minds now."

"Would you object if I went back to the Hill to see how things are there? So I can try to determine what they intend to do."

"Someone must, that's certain. I won't object. They are your people, too—and there are so few of them left."

"Then I'll go when Patty and I have everything taken care of and we're sure the epidemic is entirely over. Now I'd better run—and send her home.

"I'll keep her supper warm. We'll talk further about all this later on."

Patty drove Nora's red car back. Patty had deep circles under her eyes, and exhaustion showed in every move she made.

"How much more can you stand?" I asked her.

"There won't be much more, Mama. It's just about over."

"Nora thinks so, too. I've not had the time to consider what's going on."

"In this little town," Patty said, "three hundred and sixty-two people got sick out of less than six hundred. A hundred and twenty died. In this little town! All over the country—the whole world—millions died."

"Your father talked about that, too, some days ago."

"He wore himself out. He couldn't stop. He knew he was coming down with it, but as long as he could stand up, he insisted on trying to help others. Oh, Mama, I saw him getting sicker and sicker, but he ordered me never to mention it to you."

"That was his way. We can remember he was as courageous a man as any man could be. He saved many lives, I'm sure, and that was what he wanted to do. My father was the same way. He was a doctor, too, if you recall what I told you. He gave up his life to save another's, and he did so as willingly as your father did."

"What's going to happen now?" she asked. "I never thought about him not being here."

"Nor I. I just don't know, Patty. I don't have any

490

plans. Nora was talking about it. She wants to remain in Cameron."

"I know she does. She feels an obligation to the mill and the people who work there. She's going back to the Hill to find out what Helen and Loran intend to do."

"Yes, she told me. It will be a good thing. We can't very well make any plans of our own until we know what theirs are."

"We won't have to wait long. I think we can have the mill cleared of beds and sick people in about three or four more days."

"I'm glad to hear that. Really, I don't even know the date, that's how confused I've been."

"It's November 9th, Mama."

"I haven't read a newspaper, talked to anyone . . . I've got to bring myself back to earth. There's so much has to be done."

"I'm going back to the mill for a little while," Patty said. "Just an hour or so. Nora will stay all night, so I'll get a good sleep for once. She's been a wonder, Mama."

"I know. I'm so proud of you. Both of you. Because of everything. The way you held up . . . everything."

She just smiled, but I knew she was pleased. She bustled about clearing the table and then she wrapped herself in a greatcoat, for it was cold, and I heard her turn the red car around and drive back to the mill.

I went about my housework, with an ache every time I came across something of Glen's. There was so much of him remaining in this house, so much of him still in my heart. What I had to do was try to think as he might and get matters in order.

The first thing would be to find a new doctor. Loran wasn't going to like what we'd have to pay him, but Loran no longer worried me.

EIGHTEEN

Two days later the Armistice was proclaimed and the guns grew silent in Europe. Our little town managed a weak celebration. Someone blew the factory whistle at eleven o'clock when the papers were signed somewhere in France. The church bell was rung—and Patty came down with Spanish influenza.

She was the very last person in Cameron to contract the disease. Like Glen, she was overtired, and an easy prey to the germs. Nora and I put her to bed, and once more we began a vigil that alternately resulted in scaring us and then giving us hope, as this ghastly sickness had a habit of doing.

Three days later, Patty was able to take nourishment and her fever had broken. The build-up of my anxiety had left me a wreck, and Nora wasn't much better.

"Do you think I can go back to the Hill now?" Nora asked me that night when Patty passed the crisis. "If you need me you've only to send me word. But I'm concerned about the mill. It has to reopen, and up there they don't seem to be doing much about it."

"The same thought came to me. If they wish to know how I feel about the matter, tell them to get the mill going again and we'll discuss our differences and problems as soon as Patty is well."

"I'll go in the morning. I'm sure Patty is out of it now."

"She's young and strong. Yes, she'll be all right

492

now. Nora, don't let them intimidate you. Loran has made that a fine art."

"They won't. I have to respect Helen. I do trust her, but I saw through Loran long ago. I'll stay a day or two. By then perhaps Patty will feel up to this conference we've been wanting to hold."

"The sooner we make our decisions, the better all around," I said.

Nora sat with Patty the first part of the night, and then I took over so Nora could rest for the ordeal of going back to the Hill in the morning. By the time she was ready, Patty seemed better and was sleeping quietly. I kissed Nora and watched her drive away. I stood there in the doorway watching the red car disappear down the street. How many things had happened these last months! I half turned about to say so—to a man who would never be there again—and I sighed and gathered my wits and returned to my sick daughter.

By late afternoon Patty's condition grew somewhat worse. Her fever went up, and I couldn't bring it down. She had some trouble breathing, too, and she wasn't aware of what went on about her. There was no doctor, nobody I could turn to. Calling Nora back would be of little help. All I could do was pray and hope.

When I grew so desperate I had to do something definite, I went after the mirror. I would know what to expect, good or bad.

I unwrapped the piece of metal and I pressed it hard against my breast and I spoke, like a prayer, to the memory of Queen Maeve.

"You have shown me—and my daughter, the last time—only death and misery. My youngest child now lies ill. I would know if she will live. I beg of you, if there is any power in this world which you may control, give her back to me."

I slowly moved the mirror away from my body and upwards that I might look into the part which still reflected. I saw there Patty, smiling and happy and more beautiful than I'd ever seen her before.

"Thank you," I whispered. "Soon now I will pass the mirror to her and to my older daughter. May you give them only favorable prophecies and may you guide them well, for it is they who will carry on your name and your memory."

I put the mirror away and resumed my chair at the bedside. By morning I was beginning to doubt the power of the mirror, for Patty seemed no better. People came to ask if there was anything they could do. I sent them away, but they did manage to cheer me and to lend me some of their strength and hope.

That evening Patty opened her eyes. "How long have I been here?" she asked. "I have to get back to the mill. . . ."

"My dear, the epidemic is over, don't you remember? The mill has been cleared of beds and sick people. The war is over, too, in case you've forgotten that, as well."

"That's good," she said. "Everything seems to be good. I think I'll sleep some more."

In twenty-four hours she was sitting up and eating heartily. I was happy about that, for she'd lost a great deal of weight. She was bright-eyed and alert now. My worry was over.

"Have you heard from Nora?" she asked.

"Not a word."

"It's been several days now, hasn't it?"

"Four days. She expected she'd be up there for some time. With her grandfather dead, there's the estate to be settled and the books gone over. Loran's not very good at that, and I doubt Helen is, so the burden of it has likely fallen on Nora's shoulders."

"I hope she doesn't let them talk her into going back there to live."

"It isn't likely. She told me she saw through Loran sometime back, but she admitted that she trusts and

494

loves Helen. Who can fault her because of that? For Helen did bring her up well and provide for her generously."

"I wouldn't trust Helen any more than I'd trust Loran," Patty said, with a rare display of animosity for her. "Any woman who'd be part of a conspiracy to deprive you of your own daughter doesn't stand very high with me."

"Nora said she'd come back when she had things settled up there. It does take time. Besides, she was worried about the mill getting back into business, and I understand they're putting it in order now so work can resume on Monday. That shows Nora's been busy and getting results."

"I guess so," Patty conceded. "Have you made any decision as to what we'll do?"

"Not yet. Do you want to stay here?"

"I want to do whatever you want to do, Mama. The way I feel, Papa gave his life for the people in this town, and we'd surely not be acting in the same spirit he showed if we walked away from it now."

"That's quite true," I said. "However, if we bring in a new doctor, if I sell my interest in the mill, and Nora remains to supervise the factory and see that Loran doesn't overstep, I think we can safely leave. You're young, and there's a great deal more out there in the world than the town of Cameron can provide."

"I've given that a great deal of thought, too," Patty admitted.

"We'll just let it lie. Before long we'll see which way the town is going—and the mill. We can decide then. Nora, I'm quite sure, has already made up her mind to stay."

"She has something to stay for. Well, I'll be up and around in another day or two. There's no hurry, as you said."

Two days later Patty was visiting all of her former patients, making certain they were still improving and that there were no more cases of the flu. I still hadn't heard from Nora, so I decided I'd go to the Hill myself and find out what was going on. Loran and Helen would want to see me, anyway—for I had not yet signed the papers turning the stock over to Helen and I had not delivered them to the bank or claimed the money that was supposed to be there for me.

I drove down Main Street slowly, and I could see the difference in activity since the epidemic had ended. During the wave of sickness the streets were empty for the most part, but now they seemed busier than ever. It was a crisp November day, and I decided to visit Glen's grave. As always, I found it heaped with field flowers, the tribute of the respect and love his former patients held for him.

I knelt and prayed and then arranged the flowers before I drove away slowly, filled with a combination of sadness and pride. I turned the car up the hill toward the mansion.

There was no Martha to admit me, dourly and silently. It was Loran who came to the door.

"It's about time you showed up," he welcomed me. "I'm getting the mill into production on Monday."

I walked with him into the drawing room where Helen was seated, as primly as her Aunt Marcy used to sit. She said nothing when I spoke to her. I sat down with a feeling of foreboding. Something had happened here.

"Where is Nora?" I asked.

"Never mind her for the moment." Loran stood before me in his old belligerent attitude. Legs apart, glaring down at me while he applied a match flame to one of his cigars.

"Well, I do mind her!" I exclaimed. "I want an answer."

"Why haven't you signed the agreement we drew up weeks ago?" he demanded. "Our money is at the bank. We've kept our part of the bargain."

496

"I will not comment on anything until I talk to Nora."

"That's quite impossible," Helen finally spoke up.

"What makes you say that? If you've done anything to that girl—"

"She's gone. She went off somewhere. She didn't tell us where."

"She—just left? I don't believe it," I said. "She'd have come to tell me why."

"You tell her why, Helen," Loran suggested behind a cloud of cigar smoke.

"I showed her the deposition we obtained from Ireland," Helen said.

I brought up both hands to cover my face and rocked from side to side for a moment, realizing as I did so that this was what old Grania used to do when she was troubled. I raised my head.

"Do you mean to tell me she believed that document?"

"She read it, she went up to her room, packed two bags, came down, and drove to the railroad station. She bought a ticket for New York. We found her red car at the depot."

"She gave no hint where she was going?"

"She didn't have to. Anywhere to get away from you."

"Now perhaps we can talk about the papers you didn't sign—" Loran began.

"Helen, of all the despicable things you ever did, this is the worst. That document is a lie, and you know it. You've held it over my head for years and years, and I bowed to your will and that of your father and . . . this man. . . ."

I motioned toward Loran in a gesture of disgust.

"Nora came back to me. I told her everything you held against me was a lie, and she believed me. She and Patty worked together, as sisters should, and they did more to help the sick people in this town than you would even dream of, if you were the sort of person who might help someone in distress. What else did you tell her—besides insisting the deposition was the truth?"

"I told her she belonged with me, not with you. Nothing else was necessary."

"So now she belongs with neither of us. Is that what happened?"

"She'll come back to me," Helen declared complacently. "I know she will. She won't go back to you. She may have believed you, but when she saw the sworn document, when she listened to me tell her you hadn't dared refute it over these many years, then she knew you'd lied to her."

I arose slowly, restraining my temper but settling my fresh determination into a solid decision I would never change.

"You did this because you hate me," I said to Helen. "Well, now I'm going to give you reason to hate me. I have not signed the documents of transfer and I will not. I will retain my fifty percent control of the mill, and I will use that control to be rid of Loran as quickly as I can find the means to do so. And I shall insist upon such liberal terms for the workers that you will never again grow rich through their sweat. You can't buy me out, and you can't scare me out. Furthermore, I intend to have the truth known about a number of things that have happened over the years. I'm sure both of you know exactly what I mean."

I walked out quickly, and I wondered how many times I'd left this house in anger. I drove home and waited there until Patty returned. I brought her into the drawing room, where we sat down and I told her about Nora.

"Helen believes that Nora became so angry, or disgusted, that she went off to get away from all of us. Do you think that, Patty?"

498

"Nora is not like that, Mama. I don't know where she went, or why, but she wasn't running away."

"She never came near me. If she believed that filth, she should have come here and told me so. At least I deserved that from her."

"Why would she have gone to New York?" Patty asked.

"It would be a good place if she was trying to break away from us and make it difficult for us to find her. I don't know why she did what she did, but I do know that if she ever comes back . . . I'll change that. When she comes back she will never again have cause to doubt me or my word."

"Mama, she doesn't now. . . ."

"She went off, didn't she? We're going away, too—as quickly as I can make the arrangements. We're going to Ireland, and I'll find this Cathal Dolan and make him tell the truth."

"If he's alive. If he will admit he lied."

"He was a broth of a man, strong as the stones in his fields. He lied, and I'll make him recant. He will not deny me. And there's another reason why I want to go back. I haven't heard from my brother Jimmy since I learned he was wounded. He was supposed to look up Cathal and get him to tell the truth, but not one word has he sent me. He never was much of a letter writer, but he knew this matter of Cathal Dolan was important to me. I must find out what happened to him."

"Mama, I can be ready by morning. I'm well and strong again. I want to go with you."

"Aye," I said, "it does my heart good to hear you say that. But there are passports to arrange, passages to get, and mind you, the war is barely over, so I don't know how we will fare as to ships."

"They will be bringing the boys home from the war," Patty said, "and going back for more with ships mostly empty. We should have no trouble."

As usual, Patty was right. We obtained our passports on an emergency basis, using as a reason my brother's strange disappearance after being wounded. Passages were very easy to come by, and within four days Patty and I boarded a liner, not given to luxury because it was still a troop ship, but it was clean and it was fast—and there was no longer any danger from lurking U-boats.

It was a lovely voyage and, under normal circumstances, we would have thoroughly enjoyed it. As it was, Patty found it difficult to resist dinner and dancing with a young man attached to the United States Embassy in Belgium. He was still in uniform and cut a dashing figure in his Sam Browne belt and his captain's bars.

The days and nights gave me time to think and to adjust to my new situation in life. I had lost so much in losing Glen. And now worry for Nora filled my heart as I sat on the deck and stared at the water. But besides the grief and the pain, there was a sweet longing in my heart for Ireland, the village I'd known and loved—and once again to be close to my father and to Joel. Gentle, kind Joel whom I had never ceased to adore.

NINETEEN

War conditions were not yet completely relaxed, and our ship docked at Liverpool. From there we crossed the Irish Sea to Dublin.

"Clear across the continent from county Mayo," I

told Patty. "But there are rail connections. Nora's father made the journey twenty-odd years ago about once a month, so I have no doubt we can make it, too."

We reached Galway finally, where we were able to rent a car for the remainder of the journey. Not that we suffered from boredom during the days spent on the trip, for to me it was going home again and to Patty it was a revelation of beauty and simplicity—and the greenness unknown elsewhere in the world. The motor trip through Connemara was especially beautiful, although the road was somewhat treacherous in places. We stopped at country inns, and it was my warm pleasure to once again hear the accents of my youth and to bring them back to my own tongue and indulge myself in their soft rhythm.

Then we reached the village, and my heart ached with the longing I'd always held for it. There wasn't an iota of change. In another hundred years there likely wouldn't be. The same cobbled street, the uneven sidewalks, the cottages, the green hills in the distance, and the old, familiar slope which led down to Clew Bay and the sea.

Patty regarded it somewhat grimly. "It's not much like Cameron, that's certain. And Cameron's not very much as towns go."

"This is where I was born and raised," I declared stoutly. "I love it. You will, too, if we stay long enough. Oh, it's not the same kind of life you know, and I have come to know, but enjoyable for all of that, my girl. Don't you go running down this beautiful, lovely little village."

"What in the world did you do here?" Patty asked.

"Exactly what you did as a little girl. We walked, we swam in the sea, we had picnics, we worked—hard, I will admit—and we had friends. Only friends, Patty. No one had an enemy."

"Not even Cathal Dolan?" she reminded me with a smile.

501

"Even Cathal, the black-hearted scoundrel. Now it's come to my mind that it was more than twenty years ago that I left this village and the house where I was born, and which became mine when my dear father died. We have not yet come into view of that house, but I will say now that when we reach it, and enter it, nothing will have changed during all those years. It will be exactly as I left it."

"After more than twenty years? It couldn't possibly be the same."

"You will see what I mean. Not a stick will have been moved. Oh, the place will be clean as when I left. The dusting done, the polishing, too, and if age brought on any cracks or trouble, they will have been repaired. Still, the house will be the same as if I'd never left it. That's the way we lived here, Patty dear."

I turned the wheel over to her as we began to enter the village street to bounce and be jolted over the roughness of it, but free of driving I could see more and I could easily direct Patty.

"First," I said, "we will visit the cemetery. You will continue on down this street and at the end of it turn onto the old dirt road to your right. It will take you halfway up the slope overlooking the sea. That's where all of us wanted to lie for the last time. There's a kind of peace at that spot I've never seen before or since."

We had to walk a fair distance, for the car couldn't travel over the narrow road leading directly to the cemetery. It was the custom, as I explained to Patty, that the coffin was carried on the shoulders of the village men for the rest of the way.

"In fact," I said, "it used to be the coffin was carried all the way from the church, with the bearers changing from time to time."

We knelt, finally, at the foot of the three graves where my mother, my father, and my dear husband lay. There we prayed, and there I told Patty about

502

the kind of man Joel had been and how I loved him.

"Someone else did, too—loved all three of them—for there are so many fresh flowers," Patty said.

"Aye, I'm aware of that. It's the custom. The villagers never forget."

"Mama, the other graves have no flowers. Not many, at least."

"Aye, but Joel and my father were special people to the village. Father because he ministered to their ills so conscientiously. Joel because of his generosity and his love for the place. Aye, they'd not forget those two. Nor my dear mother, as well."

It did seem to me that there were a great many flowers on the graves. A bouquet or two after all these years—yes, but the graves were literally covered with them, and there was still dew on some.

"We'll go back to the house now," I said. "I want to prove how well it has been cared for."

"If the flowers on these graves are an indication, the house must be in fine condition," Patty said. "It's remarkable, just the same."

We drove along the street. Our presence was known here now, and people stood outside their cottages. I recognized a few—a very few—and I had been saddened at my first look at the cemetery, for it had grown twice as big as it had been when I left. I should have expected that, but somehow it hadn't entered my head that people died here, too, and things changed, even if it didn't show on the surface.

A middle-aged woman waved and called my name. I peered at her and shouted back my greeting, too, when I recognized her. So it went all the way to my house. Patty and I went inside. She stood in the small parlor and turned around slowly.

"It's just as you said it would be," she marveled.

"I knew it. That's the way people are here. The rest of the house will be just the same. Tonight we'll sleep in my old bed, and I warrant the sheets will be spotless and well-ironed."

Patty had moved toward the fireplace. "Mama, the bricks are warm. There was a fire here last night. Did your old friends expect you?"

"Someone's been here . . . living here," I said slowly. "I feel it now."

Patty's face lit up with hope. "Mama . . . could it be Nora? Do you think it's possible?"

"I don't know. If anyone is in the house, they'd be down from upstairs by now."

"Where can we look? Ask the people outside."

"Come on," I said, and seized her hand. "Never mind the car or asking questions."

I led her down the old route to the bay and the bright sands of the beach, and as we came into sight of it I saw a man, head bent, walking slowly with his shoes tied around his neck and his feet wading in the cold waters of the bay.

"I hoped we'd find Nora," Patty said.

"That man is Jimmy, my brother. Even from here I recognize the size of his body and the brawn of his shoulders." I raised my free arm and shouted Jimmy's name.

He stopped short, looked in our direction, and shaded his eyes. I began running toward him, and then I saw, with shock and pity, that he had only one arm. His left was gone, and the sleeve of his coat was pinned down. But he held out his one arm, and when I reached him he held me with the strength of two.

His hair was white, but there wasn't a line on his face and, curiously enough, his eyebrows were as red as his hair used to be. He was, all in all, a handsome and outstanding man. I held him for a long time, in sheer joy of seeing him again.

He eyed Patty with a bold appraisal. "Aye, lass, you're as comely as your mother."

504

"If you say how I used to look, I'll throw you into the bay," I said happily.

"You'd attack a one-armed man?" he asked lightly. "Aye, Maeve, I couldn't bring myself to write you about it."

"Oh, Jimmy," I cried out, "and you a surgeon."

"Well, now, what's the matter with a one-armed surgeon, may I ask? Especially if he spends his time teaching youngsters how to cut up a person. Don't worry your grand head about me, Maeve. I'm fine and doing the work I'm cut out to do. You're looking well, indeed."

"My husband died," I said. "The in-laws I inherited by my marriage to Joel have increased their burden upon me until recently—"

"I've heard," Jimmy said.

"And I've come to face Cathal Dolan and make him testify that he lied."

"Well, now," Jimmy said, "you'll find what's left of him at the shack he still occupies, bachelor that he is, for none would have the man. I got to him first, and he has already given me sworn statements that he lied and that a man who called himself Edward Lorraine paid him to give false testimony."

"Edward Lorraine?" I asked.

"Aye, you'd know him better by his real name of Loran Cameron."

"So it was he all this time," I said softly. "I'd known it in my bones. Thank you, Jimmy . . . now I have what I wanted."

"This man also came here before he paid Cathal, the bloody fool, to make this false testimony. He was here at the time someone took a shot at you and Joel, remember? And Loran brought with him a new and modern rifle—to do some hunting, he said. He didn't tell anyone he was hunting a pair of humans. He wanted to be rid of both of you."

I said, "Jimmy, you're a wonder. Patty, did you

hear that?" I glanced to my left, but Patty wasn't there.

"She's gone up the hill," Jimmy said. "To meet her sister coming down. A likely pair you have there, Maeve. A proud woman you can be."

Patty and Nora were walking slowly toward us, their arms around one another while they chattered at a marvelous rate.

"She came to me in Edinburgh and begged my help," Jimmy said. "I was about to take leave of my teaching to come here and confront Cathal, anyway. Until now I'd not been well enough, and I wanted all my strength because I intended to beat the man up good and proper. Which I did, using but one arm on the big slob. We've been here a few days, waiting for you. We knew you'd come."

"One way or another," I said through my tears of happiness, "I'll get back at you, Jimmy. To hold out on me like this when you could have cabled."

"Ah, Maeve, don't you find it better this way? To suddenly know all your troubles are over and your family is together again. Aye—that's the truth. We four are all the family left. But the girls will soon take care of that."

I left him to meet Nora and take her in my arms. We didn't speak. That came later, after we returned to the house to find supper ready for the table and a comely lass to wait on us—a privilege vied for by every girl in the village, I learned later on.

"When Helen showed me that awful legal paper she'd been holding over your head all those years," Nora said, "I made up my mind to find this thick-headed Irishman who'd signed it and make him tell the truth."

"Thank you," I said, "for believing in me."

"Mother," Nora chided me, "anyone in her right mind would know it was a lie. Oh, yes, Helen also told me about this man Arthur Standish who, Helen

506

said, you invited out of the house for some romance in the dark. I found him, too, a sorry old man who went before a notary and made a sworn statement it was all a lie and that Helen's husband had enlisted him to forcibly compel you to leave the ballroom. I gave him twenty dollars. The truth came cheap from him."

Patty said, "I can't wait to go back and present the truth to Loran. I wonder what he'll do about that."

"From what I understand of this situation," Jimmy said, "he's guilty of murder and several attempts at murder. I'd nail his hide to a wall if I were you."

"I don't know what I'll do," I said. "Quite likely nothing, beyond dispensing with Loran's services at the mill. I think even Helen will go along with that when she learns the truth."

"Mother," Nora said softly, "Helen was as much dominated by him as I was. I think she believed him because she had to—though I'm not forgiving what she did to you. I only think she deserves more sympathy than punishment."

"Yes," I said, "I agree with you. So it's over. Done with! We'll be going back now to arrange our lives in the proper order they should have been in from the first. We have a factory to run. We have a great responsibility to several hundred people who will depend on us. And a responsibility to the memory of two fine men. Your father, Nora, and your father, Patty. What they are not here to do, we shall do. Jimmy, it would do my heart good to have you come back with us."

"Not me," Jimmy said promptly. "Ah, no, Maeve, not me. With such men as Loran there, I'd likely lose my other arm to them. No, I'll stay and keep teaching the lunkheads in my classes how to sew up a man after they get through with the cutting. That's what I was meant for."

"Of course you're right, Jimmy," I said. "You've

507

never had any doubts about that. Oh, there have been times when I've wondered what I was meant for. Many, many times it's been."

Jimmy regarded me somewhat solemnly, I thought. "Look to the left of you, darling, and then to the right of you, at a pair of beauties that are a credit to Ireland and to you. That's what you were meant for, among a thousand other things. And now we'll speak no more of that. Why don't you two girls run along somewhere and let a man talk to his sister? Get on with you, the pair of you."

They promptly and gaily fled, and Jimmy and I settled down to talk of old times and of the interim when we'd lost track of one another. Our plans for the future were already made, so we wasted no time on them.

We did spend a week in our village. Not once did I encounter Cathal, but then, Jimmy was with me most of the time, and from what I had heard said about his encounter with my brother, Cathal would not care much for another.

We cabled Helen before we left to keep her from worrying unnecessarily over Nora's absence, but we didn't mention how our misson had turned out. We reached home a month later, after stops in London and Paris.

It turned out that our weeks of pleasure-seeking had been at the expense of the people of our town, for the mill had opened and then abruptly closed two weeks later because there was no one in authority to operate the factory.

"Loran's body was found in the millpond," Helen told us. "We talk of an accident of some kind, but everybody knows he killed himself. Now that you have explained to me what he must have guessed from the cable Deborah—excuse me—Nora, sent me, of course I realize he took his own life."

"Then you and I and Nora will run the mill," I said. "Patty's ambitions run to other channels."

"She will no doubt be one of the first lady doctors," Nora said with a touch of pride.

Helen refused to live alone in the mansion on the hill. She turned it over to the new doctor—young and handsome—who came to practice here, so that he might convert it to the town's first hospital. With all those rooms and all that space, it proved to be ideal.

I settled down to run the factory, and a grand time I've been having, working alongside my Nora. And one of these days, but no need to hurry, for when the Lord made time He made plenty of it, I'm going to consult the mirror again. I had a dream about it. And in the dream the mirror showed me a stranger's face, a man's face, distinguished and strong, energetic and wonderfully vital. I think perhaps I'll see that face again. I'd like to.